Jorge Sanz Moraleda is passionate about artificial intelligence, machine learning, analytics, and data governance/management. He has lived and worked internationally for several decades in countries including Spain, England, Australia, and the United Arab Emirates.

With *hAInds and the Quantum Mind,* his debut novel, Jorge has fulfilled his lifelong dream of writing a science fiction novel motivated by his vivid imagination.

Now, Jorge wants readers to immerse themselves in the world of hAInds and explore the depths of their own imagination.

To Macarena Sanz Lozano, David Sanz Lozano, and Lydia Sanz Lozano, who adapted, enriched, and translated the original Spanish version to the English version.

To Nuria, who has supported the team during their journey.

Jorge Sanz Moraleda

HAINDS AND THE QUANTUM MIND

AUSTIN MACAULEY PUBLISHERS™
LONDON • CAMBRIDGE • NEW YORK • SHARJAH

Copyright © Jorge Sanz Moraleda 2024

The right of Jorge Sanz Moraleda to be identified as author of this work has been asserted by the author in accordance with Federal Law No. (7) of UAE, Year 2002, Concerning Copyrights and Neighboring Rights.

All rights reserved. No part of this publication may be reproduced, stored in a retrieval system, or transmitted in any form or by any means, electronic, mechanical, photocopying, recording, or otherwise, without the prior permission of the publishers.

Any person who commits any unauthorized act in relation to this publication may be liable to legal prosecution and civil claims for damages.

This is a work of fiction. Names, characters, businesses, places, events, locales, and incidents are either the products of the author's imagination or used in a fictitious manner. Any resemblance to actual persons, living or dead, or actual events is purely coincidental.

The age group that matches the content of the books has been classified according to the age classification system issued by the Ministry of Culture and Youth.

ISBN – 9789948768463 – (Paperback)
ISBN – 9789948768456 – (E-Book)

Application Number: MC-10-01-8561030
Age Classification: E

Printer Name: iPrint Global Ltd
Printer Address: Witchford, England

First Published 2024
AUSTIN MACAULEY PUBLISHERS FZE
Sharjah Publishing City
P.O Box [519201]
Sharjah, UAE
www.austinmacauley.ae
+971 655 95 202

Prologue

6 July 2001, 12:06

A family Ford Focus drives along one of California's coastal country roads, picking up speed as it cruises by the never ending and ever peaceful trail. Inside the car, a small bright-eyed boy gazes out the window, looking up at the warm natural landscape bathed in the sunshine of a hot summer's day, just before sundown. His innocent smile washes over his complexion as it reflects in the backseat mirror, contemplating the beaming sun. That child is me, and my name is Henry Silverstone.

"We're going to California!" I shriek loudly, throwing my arms into the air with a contagious enthusiasm, barely being able to contain my excitement.

"We're going to California!" both my parents chorus, as they look at me through the rear-view mirror, their faces beaming with joy as their smiles widen.

I never thought this day would come, but here it is, and I couldn't be happier. Today was the day that my father would finally act upon his promise. Months ago, my dad had sworn that one day, we would visit California and do nothing but surf. My uncontrollable curiosity had counted down the days with eagerness. And now here we are: driving to California to make my dream come true.

In his youth, my dad had been the best surfer in the world, a champion of the coast. He assured me that with nothing but a few days of learning, practice and the help of his friends, I would be able to ride the waves effortlessly, taking up all the beauty that comes with surfing. Soon enough I will be gliding through the soft clouds of the sea at the speed of light.

A few weeks ago, the school year had finished, which meant that now, for a few days, I would finally be able to spend some time with my parents on vacation. There's nothing better I could have asked for. My parents are extremely proud of me: not only did I manage to get the highest grades in my class, but my school's headmaster had called them to personally congratulate them on what an intelligent, hardworking and special boy I am. He wasn't wrong, that's for sure, because when it comes to the things that I am passionate about, I can watch the hours pass by timelessly, as I am consumed by the possibility of learning the ins and outs of just about anything.

I'm a thirteen-year-old boy, whose main passion is what I call the holy trinity: science, math, and technology. It may be a bit of a stretch for a name, but for now, I'll leave it at that, since it has a nice ring to it. These will someday be the empowering stepping stones that will help me create something innovative, something out of this world, something that would enable my parents to finally be able to retire and live the rest of their days on the sunny coast of California, bathing in the golden rays of never ending sunlight.

I love to explore the world that surrounds me, finding the answers to the problems that keep me up at night, as once I do, I ravish with the taste of what true success tastes like. I guess it's a hobby I picked up from my mother, who also happens to be a scientist, and has never spent a day in her life bored about the world she lives in. That explains why she's always darting in and out of our house, taking week-long trips (sometimes with my dad), and brings home colleagues of her own as they discuss what I could only imagine is some advanced science. I will one day hope to understand myself. But I don't mind, sometimes these scientists are nice and let me play with their miniature models of their brain as they swarm me with explanations of what their research aims to uncover: battling memory loss, preventing old age, and some more advanced topics I have trouble understanding.

My bedroom is my own kind of laboratory, a large and spacious room that allows me to set up my scientific equipment and follow my intrinsic intuitions as I delve into my profound questions that I come up with on a daily basis. I have always been told that investing in knowledge is necessary for my future, so I have no shortage of books or computers, not to mention all the scientific equipment that crowds my room. I have to say, I am very lucky, I have everything I could ever ask for; beakers, textbooks, boiling tubes, monitors, tongs, tablets, microscopes (my own personal access to the world's best scientists who happen to be my mother's best friends). The list goes on and on, and so does the extent as to which these can be found lying in all four corners of my bedroom, hoping that I will one day use them for something greater. I also have a small operating table, in the center where its surgical lamp brings to light all my newest discoveries. It is on this table that I can be found heavily at work, removing animal brains, as I aim to study them and their neural functions. Sometimes, as my mother tidies up my room, she can be seen taking some of the animals' remains from the fridge, and examining them herself with extreme curiosity. I guess that the scientist within her never fails to pursue her boundless curiosity.

At school, I'm referred to as the resident 'nerd', the one whose nose is always in the books. Although they're not wrong, their attitudes towards me being different never fail to be anything but antagonistic and hostile: jealousy is what my parents describe it as, but I know it's something else too. Whilst many see my differences as a sign of distrust, my best friend, Hugo, 'The Giant', would obviously disagree, he thinks that it is my differences that make me unique. I don't think there's ever been a day where he hasn't reminded me of that. I wouldn't know what to do without him. He's built like a monster truck, with a sturdy build, a strong jawline which extends from cheek to cheek, muscles which intensify his menacing stance and hands like frying pans; large, round and sturdy. If anyone dares to insult me or lay their hands on me, he never fails to defend me. Not once. My father says he is very noble, an unconditional loyalty and an unbreakable bond which can only be described as that between brothers. We spend countless hours together, and we support each other through our toughest struggles. He helps me with the school bullies and I aid him with his academic studies. It's a win-win situation, really.

My favorite film is *2001: A Space Odyssey*. A movie in which a computer can think for itself and makes its own decisions, as if it had a mind of its own. It wouldn't surprise me if in the future, technology will be able to decide our fates for us: Robots controlling the destiny of mankind. What could go wrong, right? A lot, actually, but with every great potential that technology presents, there is always an equal and opposite reaction.

My parents are singing in the car, loudly belting out throwback songs from their youth, their smiles broadening. They're super-cheerful. My whole life, my parents have always been in a good mood; happy, positive, enthusiastic; honestly, they're amazing. I don't know what I would do in this world without them.

But, suddenly, the fun ends. And it ends right in front of my eyes.

I turn in my seat as a large, dark, menacing, shadow passes by us, at an accelerating speed . My dad is tense and nervous, shouting, trying to control the chaotically changing situation. I can see his concentration furrowed between his eyebrows, beads of sweat dripping down his neck. I see the problem. Next to us a big red truck is coming straight at us … It's in our lane … I hear a scream as my father turns the wheel, but it's too late.

I feel the weight of the car being lifted as the world slows all around me. In mid-air, we float, tumbling with an unnerving and stressful sense of nothingness, with no control over the chaos inflicted upon us. As the car drops back down on the ground, shattered glass rains down. There is a strong and poignant smell of smoke that makes me choke. Something is burning.

I close my eyes … my mind involuntarily shuts down. For an instant, I'm frozen, paralyzed.

Screams envelop the darkening atmosphere, I hear the chaos unfold. People screaming, car tires shrieking to a stop, my ragged breathing slowing down. But I am blinded by the nothingness around me. I struggle, yet I force myself to wake up and manage to open my eyes. My head feels like it has a memory of elephants parading on it and a sharp pain stabs me at the back of my neck. The pain is paralyzing.

"Where am I?" I whisper to myself.

I move my arm and see a piece of glass sticking out of it, a stream of blood rains down my arm and onto my fingers. These parts of the accident will forever be tattooed into my memory never allowing me to forget what has transpired here. The pain in my neck becomes unbearable and I notice that the seatbelt is constricting and holding onto me, for which I try to push it away from me with every single bit of strength left within me.

I'm trapped.

I'm locked inside the overturned car; ensnared within the debris of the crash. Breathing heavily, I manage to free myself from the seatbelt that has saved my life, but was constraining to trap me nonetheless. I climb through the window and begin to look for the door, hoping to find an escape from all the destruction that surrounds me. The door is smashed, dented, but thankfully for me, still intact, so that I can go through it. I crawl slowly to the front of the vehicle, dragging my body across the floor with the little force that I have left in me. Up ahead I can see my father, still in the car, asleep. Looking up at the rear-view mirror, I glance up to see my reflection. I'm a mess. My hair is hanging loose at the back of my head, tussled and rattled, my lips and eyes are swollen, darkening in blood and bruises. I scan my surroundings, hoping to find my mother, praying that she is also in the car, sleeping.

She isn't there.

Where could she be?

The red truck belches smoke from the engine, the head of the vanished driver presses against the glass and blood flows over a circular metal object with the zodiac sign, a libra, and the inscription: 'The Court of Pi'.

Suddenly, I hear my mum's voice, her screams echoing and slicing through the silence of the aftermath of the accident. Scanning my surroundings, I look beyond the proximity of the wreck, but I still can't see her. I move towards the source of the cries, towards the edge of the side of the road. I get as close as I can; it's a cliff, so I have to be careful and stay on balance. My legs push me forward, but the pain is so unbearable that I am unable to run forward. I move carefully, slowly placing one foot in front of the other. As I reach the edge of the road, the side of the cliff, I look down, and see the waves break violently against the rocks. And in the midst of it all is my mother, clinging on to a branch, her only life support.

I know that if my mum falls, she will not survive.

"Mum, Mum, hold on! Please! Please, hold on! I'm going to get something to save you!" I plead, tears streaking down my face, with a tone of urgency and fear in my cracking voice.

I drag my injured leg behind me and with my open arm I reach out for her. Drops of blood leak from my arm and fall meaninglessly to the dark oblivion below.

"I can't, honey! I can't take it anymore! I can't hold on any longer! I don't have the strength left in my hands!"

I see her face consumed in terror, her eyes wide open, fear consumed within her dilated pupils. I know that she has accepted her fate, but I cannot.

"Please, Mom! Hold on, I hear sirens! Okay? You're going to be rescued! Mum, please! Please! Hold on!" I cry, scream, shout, overwhelmed with emotions.

I look around helplessly trying to find something, anything that I can use to help her, to reach out to her, something for her hands to hold. But I find nothing. I look down once more at the cliff, at my mother's face.

She can't take it anymore; I look at her bloody hands which are trembling at the same pace of my own beating pulse. One hand comes loose, it opens up, it lets go of the branch, then the other hand follows. I see both her palms. She looks up towards me and smiles; her calm eyes reflect a deep brightness contrasting the darkness surrounding the oblivion.

She whispers one final sentence: "I love you" and falls helpless into the void below.

I scream, I cry, I shout. I am consumed with anger, frustration, and grief. What I feel is crushing and leaves me with no strength. All I see is darkness, emptiness, death. All I see are my mother's open, bloody palms with her two bright blue eyes staring at me.

I wake up suddenly, grasping for breath.

Where am I?

I'm in a bed, my wrists tied to the rails. A small tube is coming out of my arm, extending itself right into a bottle labelled 'saline solution'.

What day is it?

I look around, up at the bright blinding LED lights above me, then to the sides where I see medical equipment enveloping me, as I lay on this bed. I'm in a hospital room, but I'm all alone. The room looks familiar, just like the hospital room of my Uncle Hill had, just before he died. He died of a strange brain disease, a tumor, they called it.

My whole-body aches, throbbing impulses of discomfort, a constant reminder of my fragile hurting body.

What happened?

And then, in that moment I remember. I remember the crash: the instantaneous chaos that catalyzed the catastrophe. The truck: its blazing uncontrollable speed, that blinded all other sense of being. The truck's symbol that morphed from the ashes. My mother's eyes: burning with pain and pleading for dear life. My mother's bloody palms: outstretched, begging for help as she falls into oblivion beneath. All I can think about is the crimson red drops that plagued the darkness around her .

"Mom! Dad! Where are you? Help me!" I cry out desperately across the room.

Two policemen enter and make their way across me with an imposing stance enhanced by their well-built composure. Their faces are grim, eyes blank, and their non-existent smiles lack any sort of emotion. They tell me to calm down and try to reassure me that I'm safe, despite my initial apprehensions. One of the police officers offers me some chocolate bars, but the truth is that I don't feel like eating anything, I'm exhausted and confused. The only thing I want to know is where my family is, because that is the only thing that matters to me right now.

One of the police officers takes me by the arm and tries to get me to eat but I pull away vigorously.

"I don't want to eat anything" I tell him, with an agitated and forceful tone, as tears of frustration stream down my face, my eyes red in anger.

He looks at me. His eyes, although serious, radiate a hint of sadness, his smile although unmoved, implies affection. Slowly and carefully, he places one of his hands on my shoulder.

"I'm sorry, boy, but your mother is dead. She didn't survive the fall," he says in a monotonous tone.

Unable to control the cascading emotions that overcome once more, I break down again, in tears and sobs, as I did on the day of the accident. Only this time, I don't move, I sit there, paralyzed, shocked and frozen by the overwhelming sense of grief, and guilt. The police officers stand there, looking at one another in dismay, and try their best to comfort me, but their efforts go in vain. One of them touches my arm again, another tries to shake me, he lifts my chin. I struggle to make out their words, all but one of their sentences.

"Your father lives. You have been unconscious for five days," he says, failing to project a cheerful smile, and instead produces one of sadness.

"I want to see him!" I cry out.

"Do not worry, boy; he has already been informed that you have regained consciousness and will come to see you soon."

I sulk in tears, pondering over the pressure of the emotions. Time passes; seconds, minutes, I lose track. But then the door opens, and my father appears, stepping through the frame rushing to get by my side.

"Dad, Dad! Where's Mum? She can't be dead. I saw her, I saw her hands, holding on to life. Please, Dad, tell me she's not dead," I plead, hoping that his voice will wake me from the nightmare that is consuming me, an escape from the pain and the darkness that has been created.

"Henry, my son, I'm sorry, it's true, Mum has passed away. I'm so sorry, but you have to be strong now, okay, you have to be brave," says my father, stumbling for words as he tries to contain his own tears.

My father fumbles to embrace me and as he tries, I realize something that will change my life forever. His touch feels different. Disconnected, foreign and new. As I hold on tight to him, I look over my shoulder and I see what has bothered me: he no longer has any hands. I look at his arms; they are sticks covered with white bandages at the ends, the hands missing, detached from the arms, no longer there. I cry, I cry and I cry. I feel my tears fall and wet his hospital pajamas; my crying hurts him, it weakens him. His face is unbearably sad: nothing like I had ever seen before.

"What happened, Dad? Where are your hands?" I ask.

"Henry, the car spun around several times, tumbled out of control. As the roof hit the cliff's rocks at high speed, it produced an infinite number of red sparks which turned the sheet metal into a sharp knife, slicing through the flesh of my arms. It was sheer luck that I didn't bleed to death," he fumbles to say, as he spits out words in between tears.

"The doctors have been able to recover the hands, which are locked away and frozen with the hope that one day they will be able to re-implant them. But this hospital is so advanced. I know that they'll be able to in a couple of years," he replies, his voice soft, hopeful somewhat, but I manage to hear the sadness that creeps between words.

I think about the scene my father has described; I imagine it: I see how the sparks and the red-hot metal produced a quick amputation and prevented bleeding, preserving his hands in all their perfection. It was very much like a laser dissection, similar to those I had studied and carried out in my own lab back home. It was possible, because at the end of the day it was science that saved my father, and it would be science that would keep him alive. But this time I wouldn't leave anything up to chance. It would be my science.

That day, I made a promise to my father.

"Dad, I'm going to study to give you back your hands, I swear."

I hug him tightly as tears stream down my face, holding onto him, a reminder of life, of what is left of our family. He begins to cry too; he loved her so much, we both did.

We stay like that, hugging each other and sobbing in rhythm, taking in the emotion of grief. My father's arms dive deeper into my sides, and I am reminded forever that his hands are gone. Accepting it, coming to terms with fate, with the reality of the accident and with the death of my mother, will not be easy. But I sense that something deep inside me will keep me going. And that will be the memory of what has happened today.

I make a promise to myself that this will be the last time I ever shed a tear in my entire life.

Chapter 1

John – An eventful morning

What I hate most in life is being woken up by the same phone's stupid ringtone in the early hours of dawn, as I am removed unwillingly from my placid dreams. What I hate even more, is when I am called on my day off, especially after I've just spent the whole night playing poker with my friends. But what I hate most of all is the caller responsible for this disruption. And I think I know exactly who it might be: my dear loving boss, Stephan. If I'm being honest, I could think of some particularly unpleasant words to describe him right now, but I don't think I'll enjoy the mental effort it will take me just when my brain is waking up, not to mention the likely consequences that I will face …

They say I'm the harshest guy in the NYPD Crime Bureau, but how can I not be when I have to chase criminals on a daily basis, risk my life to catch them, and then deal with the scumbag politicians who run this corrupt system? If my stupid, useless, lame excuse-of-a-boss contacts me at this hour, I'll be forced to answer, because at the end of the day, he's my boss and I'm nothing but his loyal servant; or so he thinks. I've got a couple of things up my sleeve. All he has to do is wait. I'll have my revenge, I always do.

"What do you want?" I snap curtly, as I try to rub the sleep from my eyes, and bring myself to life.

But I fail.

"John, come to Chinatown, number eighty-nine Canal Street. See you in fifteen minutes," a snide voice replies, hissing through the speaker.

And just as promptly, the echoing silence returns. The phone beeps as the call is disconnected, and I am left talking to myself.

"The guy just hung up the phone!" I shout angrily as I toss the phone across the room in distress.

My dear boss, Stephan is the main character of a novel, who everyone is in love with and everyone wants to read. But here's the thing: he's also the novel's author, despite not even writing a single word nor coming up with the ideas in the first place. Basically, he's a fraud, a prick. He has no manners or appreciation for the people who work with him. All he does is suck up to all his supervisors and eat up their praise as it is handed to him. Just look at the number of plaques he has in his office and the pictures of him smoking cigars and playing golf with VIPs. It's nothing but meaningless symbols of his power and disregard for those around him. Says a lot about who he is, but very few people pay enough attention to break away the enveloped mask that clouds everyone's image of him. Well except for me, and my team. We were uncharmed a long time ago, and we're better off for it, really.

Time is of the essence on days like these. I put on a pair of normal denim jeans and my yellow T-shirt that illustrates one of Picasso's greatest works. I bought it on my trip to Spain last year. I had the best time of my life, with the most amazing people and the most spectacular of views. Not to mention the extraordinary food I devoured on a day-to-day basis. For example, I ate the best lamb in one of Segovia's treasured villages; Riaza, I think it was called. This T-shirt reminds me of this feast as I devoured a mixture of flavors intertwined in my stomach. One can only describe it as the raw beauty of Spain's diverse gastronomy. This was the same week I spent with Marga and her boyfriend Tito; a very kind and generous couple with whom I often hung out with during my Spanish travels. Anyway, let's leave the memories behind and get on with the day.

After minutes of frantic, stressful preparations, I go down to the street and signal for a taxi to take me where my boss instructed me to go. 20 minutes later, in between slight snoozes of going back to sleep in the taxi, I arrive at the apartment, and tell the driver to park just outside the police cordoned area. Making my way through the piles of trash bags that have been left on the street, I rush to the apartment.

It's a rundown building, with peeling walls and broken cement that bears the age of another era. As I get closer, I see my admired supervisor, surrounded by both the special analysis and sample collection teams. In these groups are my friends Michael and Jennifer, two great guys and even better professionals, who love their jobs and would do anything to serve this community. But because of our selfless nature, we are always the ones tasked with dealing with the dirty work of the police force, all while our superiors are buttered up and made to look glamorous with our successes. Just the usual share of unfairness relay, nothing too out of the ordinary in a police department of the amazing United States of America. Luckily my team is something out of the ordinary. The best precinct in New York's suburbs, if I'm honest, and totally unbiased.

Jennifer Jameson. One of NYPD's youngest female lieutenants, and a force to be reckoned with. With a flawless photographic memory, and the stamina of a professional triathlete there's nothing she can't do. Her brown eyes are hypnotizing, as is her straight medium length brown locks which highlight her perfect complexion. But don't let her charming beauty fool you, because if you happen to get on her bad side, her snorting laughs will become commanding retorts, and you will be wishing you had never confronted her in the first place.

Next we have Michael Smith. A leading police scientist, who can decipher just about any clue left behind to chase down the most skilled of criminals. But under this nerdy personality, his sporty demeanor shines through, as he never denies the opportunity to work out. This is all while wearing the best of Italian brands, and perfectly combed-back blonde locks.

I say hello to everyone except my boss who is pretending to listen to Jennifer, when in reality he is constantly checking the time, waiting for the right moment to get up and leave. The right time for people to suspect that he's probably been called to a more important case, but the ones that know him better know that it's really all a setup, leaving just enough time to remove all suspicions and leave him being the hero he wishes to be, just as he returns back to bed. Stephan Wilson's classic move.

So predictable.

If I didn't know Captain Stephan as well as I do, I too would be under his charm. His walk inspires the confidence of royalty, and his golden Egyptian hieroglyphic ring of Maat's feather portrays his undefinable wealth. His addiction to cigars produces a rough and deep tone of his voice, which he uses to impose respect, but really just shows how time is slowly consuming him. His long black hair, his darkened black eyes and his hairy eyebrows only mark the surface of his devil-like appearance.

Michael and Jennifer nod, wave back at me as they wish me a good morning. Meanwhile, my dear supervisor doesn't even look at me. He ignores my mere presence and even has the indecency to interrupt Jennifer halfway through her question, even though he hasn't been paying attention. Looking sharply in her direction, Stephan gives out instructions to the team in a commanding and direct tone.

"Get on with the sampling and analysis, I'm going back to bed … I mean I'm going to investigate some things. Oh, and by the way, I'll be late tomorrow."

Stephan turns around and starts to leave the flat in a hast, only half looking where he is going and so, as a result, slams into the wall.

"Serves him right," I mutter to my team.

Stephan glares in our direction but just stalks away without another word. Once he's gone, we look at each other and start laughing uncontrollably. This guy will never change in his life. That's how he is, careless in nature and a complete klutz. He's over fifty, yet manages to look forty.

But what does he do? Nothing at all. This is not leadership! It's a crude and harsh dictatorship of which we are forced to succumb to. The day Stephan leaves the precinct, I'll be personally responsible for paying for everyone's drinks. I'll even throw a celebratory dinner and decorate the place with a large hanging banner. And who knows what else I'll come up with. But there's one thing I know for sure: I will make it a day to remember for the ages.

Michael and Jennifer think I'm a good guy and I think it's because of the friends I surround myself with. I think it's better to have just a couple of people to share my experiences and thoughts as opposed to lots of people, who in reality care very little about you as a person, and what makes you "you".

That's what I learned living in the orphanage where I grew up: place your trust in a few people. That's how I kept myself alive. And that's the motto I live with now. I never knew my father, barely even knew anything about him. My mother disappeared when I was young, so I can only remember sparks of what she was like. Memories of her are scarce and blurry, unlike my still childlike curiosity to know what she was like. She was a busy woman, and so she was rarely at home. She was always working and traveling, just like any other executive of a shipping company. But to make up for lost time, whenever she got back from her travels, she would always reward me with small red toy trucks that bore the company's logo. I used to play with them all the time, whenever my mum had other people over and they brought their kids along to keep me company. But once she vanished, I never heard from her again.

I wasn't an only child though; I also had a younger sister. Oh how I remember how much my sister cried, the first day we entered the orphanage. She would bundle herself up and scream for our mum, for hours on end.

But the hardest thing was losing her too. I could not bear to be more alone. No father, a missing mother and a long-lost sister. After she was adopted, I lost track of her, I didn't know where she was. That's the reason why I wanted to become a policeman in the first place. I had to find my family, and this was the only way I could do so. After some years in the force and some investigating by myself, I managed to find my sister. It was wonderful. At last, seeing her, all grown up, happy with the life she created. I could not be any prouder.

But I never managed to find my mother. Not her. I still have no idea what happened to her, and the possibilities are endless. They torment me and are a reoccurring worry aching me in the back of my mind. I spend hours and hours of my free time on this case, hoping that something will come up. This is the only one of my cases that I haven't been able to close. And if it wasn't for my colleagues, my friends, who continue to help me, it would have been closed long ago, burrowed deep into the shadows of the past and the guilt of my failure.

I would give my life for them; they are like the family I never had and always wanted. All of them still remember every single one of my mischievous shenanigans. Especially the time when I hired a dozen chimpanzees, disguised them as thieves wearing balaclavas, handcuffed them, and brought them to the police station. Once in position, I began shouting that I had caught the most anticipated and chased notorious criminal gang of all times. Yes you guessed it: 'The Gorillas'. So I called Stephan and told him they were in his office under surveillance, and as you can imagine he didn't waste any time rushing to the office, to show off the arrest of the century that he had made all by himself.

That day, our dear Stephan had the extreme luck of having met with the head of the NYPD, and so as soon as he heard about our work (all because of his own merits), he immediately told him about what he had accomplished, and quickly made plans to show him that same afternoon. Throughout the meal and the trip to the police station, I can only imagine what he must have been saying. He probably gave himself all the credit by talking about how he 'told me' what I needed to do and how he 'taught me' exactly how to catch the criminals. Showing off and taking all the credit, as per usual.

The department spent hours laughing at the look on Stephan's fuming face, enraged with shame and fury when he discovered that the criminals were actual chimpanzees. Not to mention his disgust at the sight of his vandalized office: peeling walls, broken chairs and desks being thrown around aimlessly.

This little 'shenanigan' cost me three months off work and payroll: one can only consider it as my consequence for standing up to Stephan and uncovering his falseness. A decent punishment in my opinion.

It was definitely worth it. I took the opportunity to travel to Spain, a dream destination of mine.

Stephan was not pleased, unlike everyone else in the department that admired my glorious work of art. Well except his loyal lieutenant, Jim, an emigrant from Europe. A very clever guy, who has an insane police vision. But he has one flaw: he's lazy as hell. Reminds me of someone we all know and definitely don't love.

"John, go into the bedroom and examine the body." Michael instructs me, as he inspects the ground for clues, hoping to find any missing key. He bends, on his hands and knees, looking around for anything that seems 'out of place'.

The flat is very small, it only has a kitchen, a living room, and a bedroom; but all appears to be perfectly in place. Inside the bedroom, the layout is simple and orderly, but the chaos of death sweeps in as I realize that there is a dead person lying on the bed. Strangely, though, it looks as if he has not suffered; he lies in a placid position on the sheets with a calm expression on his face and no visible marks of violence or force. He is a large man, limbs outstretched on the bed which he lies upon. From the photos on the bedside tables, it looks as if he worked as a truck driver.

The peculiar thing is … there is no blood.

The bedsheets are stainless. The walls are clean. The floor, the chair, the desk, all of it, is spotless. There is not a single drop of blood nor any sign of a struggle. I stroke my chin in thought, as I try to make sense of this very strange situation.

I look at the walls of the room carefully, but I still don't see any markings that catch my attention. My eyes trace a fair line around the room, scanning every corner and wall until they land on a detail that catches my notice. There, on the far-left wall, there is a painting which hangs loosely. This painting shows a red hand wide open, palms facing me, the darkness defined by the black background surrounding it. In the painting, I can make out the shape of some wide, emerald, green eyes, and a face, partially hidden by the blood red fingers obscuring it. It is a dark painting which appears to suck out all life around it. I can't imagine owning something like that. I will have to talk to Michael so that he can analyze it in more detail and therefore study the psychological profile of the victim.

"Jenny, do you have any theories as to how he could have been killed?" I ask while turning away from the painting, forcing my eyes to leave the hypnotizing dark artwork. "It seems that not a drop of blood was spilled."

"Look, John, there's a small hole above each wrist, maybe he was injected with a serum or had some kind of extraction. I don't know. That's our only lead so far," she replies, pointing at each of the victim's wrists and biting her lip as she often did when she thought things through. "There's also one in the neck, in the skull and elsewhere. Michael will have to examine the body in more detail in the forensic lab back at the research center. I'm inclined to think that the killer must have a medical or pharmaceutical background, the marks are too clean. The killer definitely knew what he was doing."

She looks at me, her eyes inviting as if asking for my thoughts on all this, but I have none. For once I'm lost for words. Instead, I turn to Michael, who is still on the floor, now looking under the bed where the victim lies.

"Michael, any clues?"

"I don't know, there are fingerprints all over the floor, but it's very strange. There are so many. Too many. It looks like I'm going to have to work on this for a while. I need to collect all the evidence and take photos of everything; I don't want to miss anything. It's going to be a long day, guys," he replies, still not looking up, his eyes peeled on the crime scene, as if he does not want to waste a single second of the investigation.

"Michael? How exactly did you find him? Who called us?" I ask, hoping his answer can bring to light something we missed. At this point, anything is helpful.

"The door was left open and a neighbor who knew him thought it was strange and so he decided to go in. He is now in hospital with a panic attack, the vomit on the stairs is his." Michael reports.

I wince internally, feeling bad about the neighbor and also feeling incredibly inclined to look at my shoes to see if I had stepped on the disgusting vomit from the first-floor stairs. I'll have to check that later, there are more important things to deal with first, I'm afraid.

"Do you know if anyone has seen anything?" I wonder aloud to my companions.

I trust them completely and really value their thoughts and ideas; three brains are better than one after all.

"No; the street was empty," Jenny says then ponders on it. "Except for a beggar who was sleeping off the side of the sidewalk; we didn't ask him, but we don't suppose he saw anything,"

"He won't contribute much, so it's best that we let him continue as he is, he's got enough on his plate," I say still exploring the house for clues.

There's bound to be something we've missed and my questions are not leading me anywhere right now.

My boss had left as abruptly as ever and here we were, helplessly looking for clues, collecting evidence, taking photos, and making assumptions about what could have happened. But all we could do now is rely on assumptions and wild theories. Nothing is locked in as certain.

Making my way across the bedroom, I peek at the furniture the room contained. I open the drawer and see the victim's wallet; it has everything you can imagine: a credit card, a debit card and a family photo. The photo shows a man, a woman and a boy between them. They are all smiling. I look at the photo, but I realize that it's not of the victim. It must be of a friend or relative. It's hard to say since they're all strangers to me.

Nonetheless, it crushes my heart, filling me up with sadness and an overwhelming sense of loss. I get in a very bad mood. Whenever I'm up close with the victims, it's frustrating to see what happened to them, especially given the drastic turn of events. But that's exactly what motivates me as I must remember that we can find the culprit. That we can help this man and his family and erode some of this never-ending suffering.

Chapter 2

John – The morning worsens

After a few long hours of tedious and meticulous work, I invite the team to breakfast in the cafeteria downstairs for a much deserved break. It's only six o'clock in the morning, but it appears as if we've been working for an eternity, consumed deep within the investigation, scouring for clues here and there. I must say that despite the chaos of a crime scene. The one thing that I can always count on to relax is sharing a meal with my colleagues: it's amazing what sitting next to each other can do to bring us all together.

During the time I was in the orphanage we used to fight constantly, huddling over our plates protectively so that no one could take our much desired food away from us. The table was a place of anarchy, it comprised survival of the fittest, and it was every man for themselves: no one could be trusted. Our hands would wrap themselves tightly around our food to protect it from the merciless glances and snatches of the other hungry children. Those were difficult times; I was constantly in pain, as I was beat up every day, my head bashed against the foreboding walls and punches thrown to my jaw at every possible opportunity.

But I learned to endure it. I learned to defend myself, summoning up the courage to stand up to the bullies.

And that's another reason why I wanted to become a cop: I wanted to help the little guy, who like me was against the big bad world and its ruthless bullies. I wanted to become the person I wish I had had growing up to watch over me and protect me from a world that had given up on me.

The weight of the memory gives me an uncontrollable appetite, and although the taste is sour, I get a sense of relief and satisfaction that my past is well behind me. Unlike the future and the impending pressure to solve this crime scene, but that can also wait, as I now want to take a moment to relax.

My colleagues and I have one rule and one rule only: we don't talk about work when we eat. And there are no exceptions to this rule.

In between small talks and the flashback of memory, I manage to tell the waiter my order: a burger with bacon and fries and a couple of fried eggs, because I won't have anything to eat until tonight. I also order myself a nice cup of coffee to keep me up during the long hours ahead, because at this point caffeine is the only thing that will keep me going after being woken up so early. The only remedy to Stephan's unsympathetic actions. After I finish eating and recharging my batteries, I'll have to go downtown once more to work on the case. But, right now, I have to say something to Jenny, otherwise I'll burst with an uncontrollable excitement.

"I'm telling you, Jennifer, you get prettier by the day. Franky is the luckiest guy in the world. He has everything, I tell you: a good sense of humor, kindness, compassion, not to mention, you, most importantly. I curse the moment I introduced you to him. I should have kept you two very far apart!" I say, pretending to be wounded (when in reality, it's true, I'm a little hurt).

"John, you're my brother, man," says Jennifer, giving me a kiss on the cheek, in a sisterly way, as she takes both my hands. "I love you, but in a brotherly kind of way. I can't imagine you any other way, and you, Michael, I say the same thing; you're both my family. Never forget that."

Jennifer's words are always full of character, even when she turns me down for the millionth time that month, despite my arsenal of compliments that she always manages to dodge. She has a competitive nature that has no limits, but our weekly poker game wouldn't be the same without her. She's like a second sister I always wanted but never had, so in some ways she is like the missing puzzle from my life that was taken away from me.

Sitting beside her, working tirelessly, as he sends text messages to coordinate his next steps is Michael. His concentrated complexion defines his toned physique, and it is still a mystery as to why he has yet to settle down and find the perfect woman. Like Jenny and I, Michael loves what he does, it is what gets him out of bed every morning. We are proud to have him on our team; he's a guy who likes to have fun and never misses an opportunity to enjoy the excitement of life. That is except at work, because just like us, that's the one time where you'll find us in complete concertation; that and our weekly poker nights, we take them very seriously.

"John, how was your Friday?" Michael asks jokingly.

"Yeah, yeah, whatever, it could've been better, if it wasn't for your constant complaints about what I was cooking. Jenny, answer this truthfully, isn't a good slow-cooked, marinated Christmas turkey better than twenty chicken burgers?" I reply pointing my fork at him while still shoveling my food into my mouth with no regret.

Suddenly my mobile phone rings, and I snap back into reality as the pleasure of the food stops abruptly. It's the 'Useless one'. Of course it is, who else could it be? What does he want this time?

"What do you want this time, Your Majesty?" I say formally, rolling my eyes as my tone betrays me with a subtle yet present sprinkle of sarcasm.

Jennifer and Michael crack up, and struggle to contain their laughter. It happens every time I speak to him in this 'friendly' and 'charismatic' tone.

If Stephan noticed my mocking tone, (which I doubt he did because it was very believable) he doesn't say anything. He cuts me off before I can start ranting and his direct tone pierces my ears.

"John, come to a flat in the East Village, 12th Street and First Avenue, northwest corner. See you in fifteen minutes," he says in a monotonous voice which briefly paralyzes me.

"What are you talking about? A flat? What flat? No, we're having breakfast. Screw you, we're not going!" I start shouting as I lose control of myself.

"Damn it, he hung up on me! Again!" I tell Jenny and Michael as I realize that my protests have once again gone in vain. "No, screw him!" I shout angrily to nobody in particular, as I stuff another mouthful of food in my mouth.

I turn to face Jennifer and Michael who are trying very hard to keep a straight face. But it's not working.

"We'll go as soon as we're done," I say politely as I take a deep breath to calm myself.

We continue eating and laughing as if nothing has happened. New rule: if he calls us while we're eating, we let him wait …

Half an hour later we leave the café and get into Jenny's pink SUV to make our way to the famous and mysterious 'flat' our boss has told us to go to. Jenny loves the color pink, there's no doubt about it. I'm not exaggerating when I say that just about everything she owns is pink: the walls of her house, her furniture, her devices. It's all pink. But the best thing is that her husband hates pink, oh the irony. But, as Franky says, he gives her everything she could want, and never complains, even if it means living in a house which envelops him in his least favorite color.

Franky is a great guy, it really is a shame he took Jenny away from me, before I had a chance to seduce her with my flawless humorous charm. Everything about him screams greatness. I'll admit, I'm a bit jealous. His job is to test cars, how cool is that? When a manufacturer is about to bring out a new model, they call him up at once and ask him to try them out. He goes all over America just testing cars. The truth is that the guy is a really good driver. Okay, fine, a great driver I'll admit. He's amazing and, of course, he doesn't test just any car: only Corvette, Lamborghini, Ferrari … only the best of the best.

Jenny double parks the car on the side of the street. The area is coned off, taped and restricted for the public. No one can get in or out unless you are meant to be there. As we make our way towards the epicenter of the crime scene we are enveloped by a rush of people, who overwhelm us with questions about what's going on. Now this is true police work.

"John! John! This is Priscilla from 9 News, can you tell me why there is so much commotion and the area is closed off?" a familiar voice asks me with the determination of a journalist and a smile of a friend.

I could recognize that voice anywhere.

Priscilla Lopez. Leading journalist in the field of police work and criminology, who never fails to follow a lead and discover the truth. 'Pris' (a nickname I came up for her, as her name was too hard to pronounce for a 10 year old kid) is what one would call hyperactive, she is always on the move to get the scoop first. She is an avid kickboxer, whom I have come to fear, so I tend to always stay on her good side. So don't let her beauty fool you: because behind those bright green eyes, freckles and straight, ginger hair is a feisty individual who is not afraid of anything.

"Pris! How are you? Good to see you. How's your dog? How was the operation?" I ask, turning towards the sound of her strong voice and hugging her in a tight embrace.

"Tim's all right thanks. If you'd like to come by the house one day, you're more than welcome to. I know my dog would be so excited to nibble on one of those bones, you usually bring him," she replies with a smile so big; her dimples show and light up her face as she grins from cheek to cheek, making her freckles light up.

"If you like, I'll come over on Saturday, okay? Now I have to see what's happened; it's been somewhat of a night," I say as I move towards the building, carefully avoiding all the news reporters and motioning for my team to follow my lead.

"Tell me, John, do you have any idea what happened?" Pris asks, rushing up behind me, as she has transformed into a journalist once again. "By the way, what can you tell me about the Canal Street murder, is it true that the guy had marks like he was injected with something to end his life?"

"Wow, I'm amazed, Pris. How did you find out? We haven't said a word or anything to anyone. It was meant to be classified until further notice."

"I have my ways." She waves off the question, continuing to encourage me to spill the latest investigation details, her eyes sparkling with curiosity and interest. "What can you tell me?"

"Sorry, Pris, I'll talk to you later; I have to find out why this useless guy called us again. By the way, you look beautiful." I add as I make my way into the building.

Pris is a lovely person, a journalist at 9 News in New York. But I've known her for years. The truth is that we met at the orphanage. We joined at around the same time, so we've always had each other's backs. We were family at first sight. Pris, like me, was an orphan. But unlike my mother who disappeared, her parents died in a plane crash on their way back from a neurology conference in California. For her, I was the only family she had, because I still had some hope to find mine. We spent many years together growing up, and I guess we never lost touch. This means that she knows the lives and gossip of all of us, inside and out. No wonder she's a journalist, she sure does know how to do her work.

She is one of a kind, I have to say, no one I've met is quite like Pris. We both have a great professional relationship and strong friendship; we share information and help each other every chance we get. Sometimes I ask too much of her. But what else can I do when certain people step on my toes and do nothing but nag us for results and put up barriers in the process. Pris is always willing to help, and I would give up anything for her; she is a great friend. She became the sister I lost. I got a lot of support from her when I needed it most, and that's why we love each other so much, it was under traumatic conditions that fate brought us together and what also stopped us from tearing apart. For as long as I have known Pris, her dream was to be a journalist. She would tell me over and over again that she wanted to help me find my mother, and she never gave up on that promise. And now, even in the midst of the chaotic world that is journalism, she is adamant about writing a book about the life of her parents: two famous neurosurgeons fighting against Alzheimer's.

As I leave Pris behind, the team and I have made our way towards the crime scene by entering the building. We go directly up the stairs, and we see the 'Useless one' berating us for how long it took. Jenny comments that there was traffic and asks him if the department will pay to clean up the mustard spilled on her car for speeding. He looks annoyed even though he doesn't even care to look at her. He ignores her, leaves her without an answer as he looks unamused, and instead turns towards me.

"John, I'm leaving; I have to report this to my superiors, so I'll talk to you later. I want a report by 5 pm. See you later!"

This guy makes me sick; he picks up his briefcase and leaves again, darting right across the door without even glancing back to look at us or ask us how we're doing.

"What the hell! We're stuck in this mess, puzzled out of our minds, looking everywhere for clues and he doesn't even say thank you or how are you? Only thing he wants to know is the conclusion to this morning's murder, which we obviously don't have yet …" I ramble on for a while until I notice my team's disappointment.

"Bah, let's just leave it, John!" Jenny says as she taps me on my shoulder for comfort.

We enter the flat in a rush. It's modern, functional, and quite spacious. It has a kitchenette and a seventy-inch TV in the living room. He must be a New York Knicks fan because there are pictures of them everywhere.

We go into the bedroom and look at each other back and forth when we see that there is, once again, a corpse on the bed. A corpse with similar marks to this morning's murdered victim. We are flooded with the memories of this morning's flashback.

It has happened again …

Chapter 3

Henry – My new friends

Today has been a very complicated day. It was the first time I had ever done this. I thought it would be more difficult. That I wouldn't be able to do it. That the fear of the unknown and the pressure of the task would make me succumb and fail. But I did it nonetheless.

I believe it's the right thing to do, once you look at the bigger aspect of the phenomena I am trying to achieve. It's the long term versus the short term. It's about the preservation of knowledge versus mere meaningless information. It is simply intelligence versus mediocrity.

When I tell you that I didn't want to do it, I'm telling you nothing but the truth. But I was given no choice, it had to be done. And it had to be done by me.

I am going to die.

What I have is incurable, and there is no going around it. I am dying, and I cannot be saved. But I don't deserve it. Not me. Not after all I've had to sacrifice and give up just so that I could belong on this planet. I am not done here, and there is nothing that will stop me from living, not even death.

My life revolves around sick people. Day in and day out, I am submerged in the pain and suffering of others, looking desperately to find a cure. A cure which for me, does not seem to exist. But I have to find another way; I will find another way. Because I cannot imagine my life ending, I don't want it to end. What good is all this money and fame if I'm not going to be able to use it to help others? No, I have to live. To save them, I must first save myself.

Pulling up to the front gate, I can finally end the long journey that I have been on. Slowing down, I approach the residence which I now reside in, a private estate on the outskirts of New York. It is bordered by a large stone wall and patches of evergreen grass, which sway in the evening breeze. As my Lamborghini nears the gate, it subtly slides open with a soft 'ding!', allowing me to pass through and down the smooth ramp into the garage underneath the house. It sure feels good to be back.

My mother died in a car accident when I was little. I can only describe it as a fatal inopportune death, which haunts me even today, as her screams echo deep within my thoughts. My father, also present in the accident, was not quite so lucky to have been gifted with death. Instead, he lost both of his hands; they had to be amputated with a swift cut of the blade. I worked incredibly hard so that one day he could have them back, but I failed, I was too late. I didn't make it in time. That was the only time I failed, and I was sure to make it my last. Because even though I couldn't save my father from the doors of death, I would still save mine.

My father loved my mother endlessly and a day didn't go past where he wouldn't be reminded of her disappearance. The grief consumed him until it was too much for even him to bear. If you ask me, that is a worse fate than death. My parents dated for ten years, they were married for fifteen. It was love at first sight.

I was thirteen when the accident happened. I still remember it vividly, shockingly, and painfully. Every day I am reminded of the chaos that consumed the echoing silence in the apocalypse of crash: the screams, the terror, death itself. Damn the stupid truck …

Today I'm thirty-three and I don't think I'll live for much longer. That is, unless the miracle I long for comes true.

I get out of the car drowsily, and head towards the rearend to open the boot. As I lift it open, I reach inside and grab a small electric fridge, holding it tightly with both my hands as I press it towards me. Balancing the weight of the fridge in between my palms, I walk over the blooming garden of flowers and into the house, as I open the front door with one hand and balance the fridge under my chin.

I start to leisurely make my way into the living room after closing the door behind me with the top of my foot. Still with the fridge in my hands, I stroll over to the bookshelf at the back wall of the living room. The walnut bookcase contains my large and precious collection which covers my wide range of interests: medicine, aeronautical engineering but most importantly artificial intelligence. Because with that, anything is possible.

From the vast array of options of books presented in front of me, I instantly select Hybrid Artificial Intelligence Neurons: Deep Science, and press the spine towards the back of the bookshelf, gently pushing it away from me. A loud

'Bang!' echoes through the room and suddenly a ramp in the floor opens beneath me. Lights flicker below me and the steps ahead of me lead me down to the chamber beneath me: the basement.

I've done a lot of work in this place, this is where I have spent countless hours pacing around impatiently, going through thoughts no one would have ever dared to think of. It is the basement's complex structure that gives life to my inner self. It's a mixture of a machine shop, an operations room, a telecommunications center, and a computer lab. Wires, cables, and computers populate the room, occupying every space available from each corner of the room. I must say that it's a vast space and expertly designed to give life and intelligence to my little friends, the birthing place of my companions whom I deeply depend on during this moment of crisis.

After the accident, my father lost his job as an engineer in a well-known car company. Without his hands there was little that he could do besides being the company's legal burden where thousands of dollars would be dumped into paying for his medical expenses. However, because of his life insurance, he received a monthly amount that allowed us to just barely get by. We were forced to live very humbly. It helped us cover our daily necessities, and nothing more. We were forced to sell our home, my childhood home that I had shared all of my memories growing up with my parents. My lost home was only one of the things I lost the day of the accident. But I didn't lose it forever, I managed to get it back later, when I was older. The first second that I was able to afford it, I jumped at the chance to regain the property that was so valuable to my family.

But it was too late, my father had already passed away. I was too late.

The day of the accident flipped our worlds upside down. We went from being a family admired by everyone, to one disowned and ignored by most. We were at the bottom of the pile, discarded, left to fend for themselves and looked down upon with nothing but pity and disgust. That's the price to pay when you run out of money. People start to see you as a problem to avoid. When life is going well, everyone surrounds you, they come over to your house, you go out to places and eat out at restaurants together. But when you can't keep up with them or they can't get anything out of you, they forget you, and you start finding yourself alone. All of the time.

But I couldn't ask for anything better. Removing myself from the eyeline of people, helped me to solely concentrate on what was important to me. I was able to delve into my passions and dedicate time to achieve everything that I put my mind to. Back then, time was limitless.

I had one obsession: my father's hands.

I wanted him to get them back one day, after all the suffering and pain he had to endure. The poor guy would spend hours and hours in front of the TV, watching videos of his life before: my birthdays, his wedding, and the moments he spent with my mother. He was like a statue: broken and frozen in time, unable to move, paralyzed by the memory of the past. His brain had shut down. He had lost all will to live. He had no reason to fight. He couldn't do anything; even the simplest things were now an impossibility. He needed help with everything: he was even fed through a tube.

His life was a series of cyclical, never-ending events: bed, couch, couch, bed. Sleep, TV, TV, sleep. Over and over and over again.

When I was 23, I had degrees in medicine, aeronautical engineering, computer science and mathematics. It was exactly this academic knowledge that I needed to research and finally be able to start creating my new best friends. I was almost there. The pulsing adrenaline of the possibility of life, was now more real than ever.

I had all the time for myself. My sick father was the perfect excuse to avoid any and all distractions. This meant that I could finally use all my energy on what I really wanted to do.

My father was my one true driving force.

Going down the steps, I go into the basement and place the fridge on top of my operating table. A couple of months ago, I had simply borrowed it from the hospital I work in. It was easy, nothing too strenuous or difficult; I put on a balaclava mask and took advantage of the darkness of a moonless night to blend in, go in unnoticed and steal my prized possession. I simply left the van in the car park and picked it up the next day. To cover up my tracks, I spray-painted graffiti on the door demanding the US president for public health care for all and that was it. I went unnoticed, because socialist scandals like these usually do not bring much attention.

I switch on a lamp placed by one of the hundreds of desks. I bring the operating table to life and open the fridge to find tonight's trophy.

Everything leading up to this moment, has been worth it. Two hands covered in freezing blocks of ice can be seen, with their palms and fingers outstretched, screaming with the infinite possibility of life. They are ready to be worked on …

I take one of the hands aside and place it inside a cold storage room which I bought from a bankrupt restaurant. It's perfect; it keeps the meat at the ideal cooling point for maximum preservation, so that its one lively state can never be eroded. The other hand, I keep in the small fridge for safekeeping.

This hand in particular belongs to someone very special to me. It belongs to a lorry driver, who I remember quite well. This massive, strong and 'apologetic' hand will be very faithful to me and my work. But that will all be discovered in due time.

The best thing about a hand, the vital part of a human body, is that it needs very little training. Since it has been used to perform the same monotonous daily tasks for countless years, it needs very little training. Therefore, it learns quickly.

I am passionate about the human brain, robotics, and data, just about everything that ranges from reality to the impossible. I am interested in just about everything related to artificial intelligence. and the use of these practical elements of this science of creation.

One day, whilst I was looking at a family photo, I zoomed in closely at my father, paying close attention to the wide smile spanning across his face and brightening up his appearance. His joy reminded me of the promise I made in the hospital, all those years ago; that I would give him back his hands. It was the same promise that I kept repeating to him during his final days, for which I hoped would give him the last bit of hope to keep on fighting. At the time, I had one year left to finish my medical degree. I had already completed all my other degrees. Whilst I flew to California, to visit the hospital that stored my father's hands, I left my father in the care of a nurse I was able to hire with the money I earned from tutoring children and adults in mathematics.

Once I arrived at the medical center, I asked for my father's hands to be retrieved and handed over to me, so that I could once and for all have in my possession what I had been fighting for all these years. As I was of legal age and my father was ill, unable to move, they didn't even hesitate to give them to me. All I had to do was reminisce about the symbolic importance of my father's hands and how I wanted to accompany him on the day of his death. Simple manipulation of emotions, for a good cause of course. Their saddening and softening eyes betrayed them, words of grief and pats on the back for encouragement was all that was needed to convince them. They gave me a certificate from the hospital, wishing me a safe, restful flight, as well as something about wishing my father all the best in his recovery, but at that time,

I had stopped paying attention, I had bigger things to focus on. I finally had my life's greatest prize in my hands. And no one was going to take it away from me. Not again, not ever.

As soon as I was able to exit the hospital, I went straight to the airport to board my plane back to New York. The only thing I could do during the flight was reflect on how close I was getting. I was almost there. I didn't let his hands leave my side for even a second; it was proof of the promise I intended to keep. I had to give my father some joy in his life. I owed him at least that.

I had specialized in neurosurgery, with a particular passion for the brain, the universe and I often dreamt of the possibility of creating one, a fully functional brain from scratch. After five years of constant work, constant step backs and little successes I was able to invent something of a small watch that could serve this exact purpose. It contained a camera wired to manually created pieces of hardware, software, an artificial respirator, and a micro-heart that would pump human blood back and forth. My first trail experiment was getting me close to replicating life itself.

This was the initial first step, as it allowed me to succeed in creating two fundamental building blocks for life, a half-human, half-machine hybrid brain and heart. Two organs, that once in dual power could mimic life itself, and would be essential in my future creations. The stem cells were a crucial part of the process. The human part of the brain will contain some of its memories and information, but not all of it. Some things are lost in this process, and I am yet to uncover why. This is something I need to improve so that my creations can rely on the completeness of their memories. So that my creations, my hands can truly utilize their past experience. This worry of mine was also my university mentor's own obsession as he too would often worry about the loss of knowledge after one's death.

At this point in the process, I am about to insert the watch into the truck driver's hand. The watch contains a large number of micro-valves that fit into each of the veins perfectly. This is why the cauterization process I perform when sectioning the veins is so important, and I have to be extremely precise with my movements, so as not to leave anything up to chance.

When I attach the watch to the amputated part of the hand, carefully making sure it is perfectly in place, the microvalves penetrate the skin and connect to the veins. Depending on the size of the hand, the process can take about two hours.

But this time is nothing compared to all the years I've had to wait to get to this point in time. I am here now, and nothing and no one can stop me.

The mask I am wearing now, is merely one of the many designs I have come up with. It completely conceals my face, with its white as the snow background and pair of black hands curling in around the bloodshot eyes. With it on, I seem quite intimidating. It is connected to each of my creations to monitor them and allows me to control their functions and command the hands that I create.

I start the pumping process with the heart, and the beats start thumping by every microsecond. After more than half an hour, a small red light lights up and I know that the time has come upon us.

It is time to start the heart, the organ of life. The miracle of birth is upon us.

"Assign the name, Driver, to the new hand. Activate the heart," I say solemnly, through the mask, as my voice radiates through the opening and fills the silent void of the room.

The mask picks up my voice and the command I have given, as a result of the voice recognition mechanism I had installed, some time ago. The mask is at the mercy of my command because of the beauty of technological algorithms. The red light inside the mask switches to a bright shade of green, and the hand begins to take life.

The hand starts to move and awaken itself, as it becomes aware of its surroundings for the first time. It reminds me of when a foal is born, fumblingly feeble in its first seconds of life, but in no time at all it starts to get up, by shifting its weight onto each of his legs, as it begins to experience the phenomenon of walking. I feel the same raw emotion a mother has when her child is born. I look at it; slowly, the fingers start to move, they rise upwards and stretch in all directions. The back of the hand remains rigid, resting on its fingertips. During the first few hours, my newly created hand will start to move and walk, as it starts to learn from the software installed in the watch, by copying some of the more than ten thousand hand movements. The basics, as I say. The thumb, index finger, ring finger, little finger and middle finger touch each other, and the hand jumps up and down multiple times, as its fingers start bending and extending as a repeated action.

All of my personalized watches have built-in artificial intelligence in order to allow them to learn more movements simply by observing other hands: whether it's in real life or through a computer screen.

Driver begins to execute each of the programmed moves, signaling the start of his life as a new hand of mine. This process will take several hours to complete, but this is a necessary step. If any of them fail this initial part, the hand will have to be destroyed and another one found. I'll wait, because after all, I've waited enough, and what is a couple hours in the grand scheme of time …

But while doing so, I'll keep myself busy. I've got other things to do. I have to bring to life the other victim's hand: one which I will call Trigger. It's not the simplest nor fastest of jobs, but I have to say that as the minute hand ticks by it becomes one of the most satisfying ones I have the great honor to undertake.

Time is a precious and scarce commodity; once it is gone, it never comes back …

That is, unless you live forever.

Chapter 4

John – Detective work at its finest!

Jenny slowly looks at the photos and objects in the house searching for some kind of link to the previous victim: places, hobbies, acquaintances, friends and similar tastes, anything is helpful in this initial point of the investigation. Because even if we find something, we can hope that it'll lead us in the right direction. Meanwhile, I chat with agents who had arrived before us, to get caught up with the basic facts and timeline of events. In the early hours past the murder it's important to visualize what happened. And right now it's all dark and we have nothing. But hopefully that will change soon.

There is one thing that we know. This murder feels familiar. It looks identical to the one from this morning. Everything points to it. The way it's set up, the way the victim was murdered, and just something about the eerie atmosphere that looms over us has the same unsettling characteristic. For all we know we might be dealing with a serial killer who has just taken its first victims. But for now it's still too early to tell.

Turning my head around, I can see that Michael is carefully observing the scene, kneeling down here and there, for which I can only assume is him documenting possible clues, and making a mental log of just about anything that seems out of place. As he makes his way across the room, finally makes it to the bed, standing next to me, both us in silence as we fixate our vision on the corpse below, the one that lies there motionless and lifeless. Just like the one from this morning.

"Look, there aren't any blood stains here either. The marks are also in the same places: behind the head, on the stomach, on the hands ... It kind of looks like a pattern, don't you think?" Michael asks, as he explains that all the marks we see in front of us were imprinted in our morning victim as well.

"Maybe, that is strange," I say, puzzled by the sheer similarity that these two victims appear to have, and I am transported to relive this morning's event. An inescapable grasp of the clock ticking and our failure of being unable to solve the puzzle that is currently laughing in our faces.

Michael looks just as stunned, as he runs a hand through his wild blond hair, a gesture he does in times of confused concentration. He begins walking out of the room with his inspection equipment in his hand, mumbling under his breath, something I can only guess is his gears trying desperately to click into place.

"Jenny, can you confirm that the patterns here are the same?" I ask her once Michael has left the room, and motion for her to join me by the bed where the corpse lies.

I take a closer look at the scene, while Jenny leans over the bed, searching for tracks or clues that we might have missed on a first glance, but for now nothing seems more out of place than what it did just a couple of minutes ago. Yet there has to be something that we've missed. A clue, a thread to pull tightly on and get somewhere. This can't be the end.

One of the windows is open, the curtains flapping uncontrollably with the wind, as the wind gushes inside.

"Man, how could this guy have slept with the window open when it's freezing cold?" I ask Jenny, as I pull my coat on tighter.

Right now, the only thing that I can think of is leaving the crime scene and regaining the necessary human body temperature that has been so unfairly snatched away from me. It's insane that someone could sleep like this. That is unless … he didn't actually sleep with the window open … because that would mean …

BINGO!

"Michael, I need you to take a closer look at the window here." I call out, getting Michael's attention from outside the room and hail him over. "See if maybe it was forced open from the inside. I have a feeling, this might have been the magical entrance the killer made last night," I continue to cry out to make sure Michael can hear me from wherever it is that he may be hiding, and looking over the clues we've found.

"As soon as I'm done with the fingerprints, I'll get right on it, John," he shouts back from behind the wall, vibrating through the walls of the apartment.

"Alright, Jenny, check the body for marks of violence, just like we did this morning. I need to know if there is anything at all, no matter how small. We can leave no stone unturned!" I say as she nods, moving her eyes from the bed over to the victim, examining every inch, lifting the arms, legs for any signs which seemed out of the ordinary.

Meanwhile, I turn, look around the room and notice a painting with a familiar hand drawn on it, a red palm surrounded by a blacking void of darkness. I gasp and drop the pen I was subconsciously fidgeting with. This cannot be happening.

"Michael, come, look!" I exclaim anxiously, while a thousand thoughts swivel around in my brain.

Michael rushes in, looking anxious and I point at the wall on my right.

"It's a painting. No, it's the painting! It's just like the one in the other house!" At this point I'm shouting, unable to control my excitement which flushes over me and almost knocks me into an inescapable route of could haves.

"Michael, I need you to send it to the lab right now! Jenny, call someone and make sure they collect the painting from the other apartment." I instruct, as I pace back and forth, unable to calm my racing thoughts that have just about hundreds of possible conclusions that they are reaching to reach.

"The killer is sending us a message, and we're going to figure out exactly what he is trying to tell us." I add, moving my vision back to the victim, staring deep into his undying eyes that have no more life yet to give.

This cannot end here.

"OK, John, no problem," Michael replies, "but I figure I'll be here for at least a couple of hours, before I can get started on the painting. I see that there are a lot of fingerprints on the ground, so it's going to take me a while to go through it all."

"That's fine, Michael, just try to get started on it as soon as I can," I say, as I place a reassuring hand on his shoulder, as I make my way to where he is kneeling down and inspecting the masked clues that crowd the floor, waiting impatiently hoping to never be discovered, not knowing that with Michael nothing can be missed. He has the eyes of a hawk and cannot be easily fooled, no matter how hard the killer appears to try.

"Thanks, John. Oh and one more thing. I've noticed something weird ... I've been looking at these footprints, or maybe should I say fingerprints. There are about a thousand of those lying around the floor, but ..."

"That doesn't make any sense ..." I finish him off.

"Yeah, I know," Michael continues, "what's even weirder, John, is that I can only see one set of footprints. And those belong to our victim." Michael begins to ramble. "What I'm trying to say is that the only remains we currently have of our culprit are his fingerprints, how is that even possible?" Michael asks, leaving me once more at a loss of words.

This case is becoming more and more confusing by the minute. Things are not adding up, and what's worse is that I don't know why. We're doing everything right, we're looking at everything that we can find. But right now it looks like we're a step behind our killer, and he's not slowing down.

As I am left alone with my thoughts of inevitable conclusions and potential deductions, I continue to peak around the bedroom. Putting on a pair of gloves, I open the cupboards and look inside to find anything that can tell us about our victim. Inside I find nothing out of the ordinary: multiple waiter 'spotless' uniforms (from The Carlyle hotel, one of the best in New York), shoes, more clothes, a wallet (containing cash, debit and credit cards) … But just like before nothing seems out of place.

"Nothing has been taken. Absolutely nothing." I tell the team as I make my way to them, who are huddled deep into conversation in the room next door. "The mobile phone I found on his bedside table is not cheap, believe me it's one of the most technologically advanced models in today's market. And I would know, I do whatever I can to avoid them." I add, hoping to lighten up the mood, but either they found it unassuming or are too into their own thoughts that they simply didn't hear me. I would say it's most probably the latter.

"And as far as I know," I continue, drawing back more attention from the team, "to work in this hotel, you have to be one of the best in the field: the difficult entry tests are just one of the requirements to ensure those employed make the cut. And your reward for working there, yep you guessed it, just about the highest salaries in the industry." I add hoping to create a better profile of who are victim is, and to get to the bottom of how he met his untimely death.

"Maybe this could have just easily been the crime scene of a break-in robbery gone wrong?" Jenny asks, but her bulging eyes tell me something else, she is not certain.

Because if that was the case, what does that mean about this morning's murder, and the two paintings. They have to be connected. They have to be the plantings of the killer. It would be too big of a coincidence for both victims to have the same art taste and be faced with the same end through the same means. And that would be too many coincidences. That can't be right. This is bigger than a simple robbery, and Jenny knows that even if she secretly wishes it would be as simple as that.

I pick up the phone; which looks very advanced. I don't like it. Until a couple of days ago I used a mobile that was more than ten years old, a shoe phone, as I say. With my old 'grandpa' phone, no one could access the device to steal my data and they were unable to locate me: in other words, I was untraceable. I am what some people call the enemy of social media, I work as a police officer and I know that with one of those things just about anyone can know everything about you, without ever having to meet you. The fact that they have so much information about me bothers me, because that means that I never know who might be watching my every move. And today that can also mean that the killer is watching me, hoping that I mess up soon. And that is a risk I would rather not ever have to ever take.

A phone rings. And it just so happens to be mine. I grumble about my 'so perfect' boss, fully expecting him to be the caller, only to get the pleasant surprise of it being a good friend of mine: Dilya Ramirez.

"Hi, John, how are you?" Dilya asks me.

She is a true computer geek, and if I could see her right now, I would guess that she would be showing off a new colorful and flowery shirt, to complement her bright light blue glasses that balance on her nose. Her appearance could not fit her bubbly and charismatic personality any better.

"Hello, Dilya." I greet her across the phone. "I'm going at 100 miles an hour, because you'll never guess what happened this morning. Our 'best friend' called me at three o'clock in the morning and I haven't stopped since then; it's all adrenaline and stress that's keeping me going at this point. Moving on, we've had two murders today and we're certain they're by the same killer. I want you to get me all the information you can about the deceased. Anything and everything, I want to know both of them inside and out. As if I had known them all my life. We can't leave any stone unturned."

She knows me very well and knows exactly what I want. Dilya is a very kind person, with a great sense of humor, always ready to help. She says she gets her spirit from her neighborhood in Brooklyn, where she grew up, and I couldn't agree more. She is diabetic and has to take insulin injections, but other than that nothing can stop her. Well that and her other weakness: chocolate cream-filled cakes. We've had to take her to the emergency room on more than one occasion, as a result of episodes of low blood sugar.

"No worries, John, I'll get right on that," Dilya replies, as she hangs up the phone, and I left once more looking at the place where someone said their last words pleading for mercy and took their last unnerving breaths. The darkness of murder settles in once more.

Two innocent people have been killed. One person is responsible. A hypothetical heavy truck driver and an employee of one of the best hotels in New York. People with normal, humble jobs, with nothing seeming out of the ordinary on a first glance. No family. Two murders on the same day, perhaps at different times, but nevertheless, connected. Because that which ties it all together is the merciless culprit who stopped at nothing to end their lives and leave clues to misdirect our search. But don't worry, we're more concentrated than ever and we will find him. It's only a matter of time.

Chapter 5

Henry – In control and in the shadows

I like to know exactly what is going on, all of the time. I may not have eyes and ears everywhere, but I stop at nothing. Nothing gets past me. And that, today, means knowing at every second of every minute of every hour what is happening with the police's 'little' investigation. And for me that means getting to know the people working on the case inside and out: who they are, why they do what they do, why they are good at their work but most importantly why they sometimes mess up. That leverage gives me the advantage I need to succeed in the miracle I have to make come true.

By knowing everything about them, I can anticipate any potential moves they may make against me in the near future, that is if my enemies ever get close to me, because from what I hear they've got a lot on their hands at the moment. For me, this is like playing a never ending game of chess. But like any traditional game of chess, I am the white pieces, I go first and they react to my every move. I am fully in control.

Turning what information I know about them into a pre-meditated and purposeful action against them gives me the edge as I move the pieces of my masterplan into place. I am always one step ahead, while they are always two steps behind. Why? Because I have something that they don't know about. I have eyes and ears in the places that matter. Well maybe not literally. Let me rephrase, I have hands everywhere. My dear hands connect me to the scene of the crime in real time; but that is just one of the many functions I need them to perform.

Three years ago, I met Cameron, a private detective, who had just retired from the police force. He came to my office one day and in the time span of an hour, his whole life got turned upside down. I discovered a brain tumor. It was feeding off and compromising Cameron's survival. He was deemed a life expectancy of about four or five months, although treatment could prolong his life and subdue the effects of the illness; but even that would do very little to keep him alive. He was only fifty-seven years old, and in his time, he had solved numerous influential cases, which brought him all the fame and wealth he could ever wish for. So, when I told him the news, he said,

"I always thought I'd die at any moment, but not like this. I always thought that it would be in action, a quick, painless death, I never could have guessed that it would be like this. I'll be able to enjoy a few months, that's at least something to be grateful for." He spoke with a happy voice but his eyes told a different story, truly saddened by the news I'd given him, tears waiting to escape from his eyelids.

Then, a few days later, he told me that, as there was no solution, he didn't want to undergo any sort of treatment.

The world of detectives has fascinated me ever since I was a child. Because of this, I would constantly ask Cameron to recall the many adventures that he had taken part in. He became the father figure I had lost and longed for. I established a wonderful relationship with him, a blossoming friendship, and fatherhood. He would tell me about his cases; how he analyzed the details at the crime scene, how he sometimes detected false leads and went on stakeout missions in his car, on the street, underground, wherever it was necessary. He would also talk about how he used to gain access to homes, evidence analysis laboratories, forensic centers and many more, without having the necessary identification in the first place. He had done it all. For me, it was both exciting and exhilarating to hear about his greatest adventures, but for Cameron retelling his old memories: it brought him the joy that his rapidly ending life was missing.

Sometimes, we would stay up until the wee hours of the morning, as Cameron would not be able to stop himself and I could not draw my attention away. He would describe chases, escapes, fights and even standoffs, all of them in great detail. However, the parts I enjoyed the most were the interrogations; Cameron's methods of collaborating with the police whilst also using his informants to dig deeper into the social profiles of the possible suspects, almost as if he was becoming one with the case. Leaving no small detail out, he also taught me, unintentionally of course, how to get into police databases and access any kind of information one would require. Individuals, police documents, dossiers … I guess that's another secret weapon of mine. The intelligence of one of their best recruits.

All those long days I spent with Cameron are going to help me now. They are vital to helping me uncover priceless information, mislead key individuals and most importantly save time. Because, unfortunately, I myself have very little time indeed.

Shortly after, Cameron died as a result of the tumor, nothing short of the expected. There was nothing that I could have done to help him at the time of his death. On the day of the funeral, I went to The Calvary Cemetery, to pay my respects, but most importantly to welcome my friend back into the realm of the living, that we had always fantasized about during our long conversations revolving around the world beyond.

I desecrated his grave and amputated his hand, a final sacrifice and a gesture to honor our friendship. The hand told Cameron's story. The wrinkles snaked through the edges, the coursed veins bloomed of the life that they had once bore, the finger extended depicting the exhilarated the adrenaline of the chase, the short broken finger nails told of the stress of the uncertainty of an investigation, and the dirt underneath, act as remainders of each and every crime scene ever solved by the great Detective. Never to be forgotten.

I knew what I was going to call the hand, I was going to name him Cameron. Because it would be Cameron after all, just in a different form, but with the same motivations as before, to help others. He's strong, fast, skilled and more importantly very, very sneaky. And today, he's doing exactly that.

Through my connected lenses, I can see the hand which remains hidden at the crime scene, shadowed by darkness and enveloped deep within. My hands are all perfectly coordinated by the micro-brain of the watch and the micro-cameras, give me their vision to observe, through my own eyes, as they are connected to my personalized lenses. Each and every one of the hands I create has these same features. As I've said, I have eyes and ears everywhere, kind of.

"Cameron, can we talk?" I ask through my mask, my deepening voice going directly to the hand Cameron.

"Hello, sir, I'm stuck to the outside wall, under the windowsill, I'm barely hanging on." Cameron adds as laughter fills the earpiece that I use to communicate with him.

"Alright, Cameron, hold steady," I reply.

"Sure thing, sir, but you could always make a better suit, it's freezing cold here, sir. Anyways, I've deployed the microtubule from my watch camera to the crime scene. All we have to do now, is wait for it to perform image recognition for each officer assigned to the investigation, then we'll know exactly who we're up against." Cameron's shivering voice replies through the speaker installed in my mask.

"Do you have your drone ready, just in case of an emergency?" I ask anxiously, nervously fidgeting with the keys of the van in which I sat, waiting for the plan to be executed.

"Yes, sir, it's on the roof. I've instructed William to monitor it from base. Don't worry everything in under control." Cameron adds, his deep voice ricketing through.

William is another one of my little creations. The hand of a stunt pilot who died in a horrible accident. It didn't take me long to get hold of it and now it will be very useful, due to its agility and flexibility that will once more allow us to remain deeply hidden within the wisps of the shadows.

"Sir, there are three people at the crime scene: two men and a woman. I've just captured their faces and I'm about to run the facial recognition algorithm from our database." Cameron stops talking, allowing only a beeping sound to echo from his earpiece. He then continues, as Frank has fed him through the information that also appears on my screen. "Sir, the people analyzed are Michael Smith, from the scientific division, Lieutenants Jennifer Taylor and John Duffy. They are under the command of Police Captain Stephan Wilson."

"Well, if it isn't just who we asked for. A fair match: the best in New York City. This will make it all the more interesting won't it, boys," I add, giggling under my breadth as the adrenaline flows through my veins.

The good thing about receiving data is that our central computer cross-checks information with the messages on these people's mobile phones and discovers patterns of reference about the relationships and communications between them. I know them as if I was their long-life best friend who had never once met them. Genius, isn't it?

It seems that not everyone likes their captain. They see him as an ungrateful suck up, who couldn't care less about the people who make up his team. Michael, Jennifer, and John are all close friends and loyal professionals who have each other's backs. At least that's what we can infer from their supportive texts and memes that flood their 'Poker Night' group chat. According to what Frank was able to find, John has had some serious run-ins with Stephan (one of which was labelled as 'a humiliating monkey swap' whatever that means).

Now that we have both of their mobile numbers it's about time to track all of their movements and monitor their conversations closely. As I've said, eyes and ears everywhere.

The reason why I'm able to do this, is because a couple years ago I bought a telephone network here in New York, thanks to the money I received from my Chinese patents. Thanks to them, I'm invisible …

"Sir, Michael is taking fingerprint samples from the floor. What a surprise he'll get when he finds out who they actually belong to. Heh, heh." Uncontrollable laughter escapes through the watch on the hand until I finally tell him to calm down, as he waits impatiently for his grand reveal.

"Yes, Cameron. It's going to be a surprise for them, which will help us buy time. That is what's most important right now."

"Sir, Jennifer is looking at the painting and talking to John. They said they are going to go to the other house to see the other one. What a great idea about the canvases with the hand! Good job, boss!" Cameron says in a childlike humorous tone of excitement and content.

"That was smart, wasn't it? It'll keep them busy for a few days at least. Analysis of the frame, the paint, see what shops sell the materials. They're going to go from one end of New York to the other, and back again. And for what? For nothing …" My train of thoughts comes to a sudden stop, and I shout, "Watch out, Cameron! I sense Jennifer approaching the window."

Cameron retracts the cameras and hides under the mantelpiece. His fingers stick to the walls and the ceiling, he is positioned as a spider.

Jennifer looks out of the window, but the look on her face indicates that she hasn't found anything.

"Cameron, go to the roof and come back. I think we've had enough fun for one day."

The hand slides down the wall and climbs into the waiting drone with the engine running. The drone takes off and, in complete silence, disappears over the rooftops of the buildings of New York City, never to be seen again. Because we are invisible in the eyes of those that are so desperately looking for us …

Chapter 6

John – New clues, New knowledge … New Leads?

Just as I'm looking around the crime scene for what is probably the millionth time, I get the call that I've been impatiently waiting for. Time has been ticking by agonizingly slowly, but my mind hasn't stopped running around in circles, lost in the chaos of today's events.

The caller is Michael. He's cracked the codes of the fingerprints. I know exactly what I have to do.

In that instant, I put my rampaging thoughts on silent, and grab Jenny's hand pulling her into the car.

"John, what the hell? What's going on?" Jenny demands, struggling to fasten her seatbelt, as I start zooming out of the parking lot.

"Sorry, Jenny." I apologize. "It's Michael, he's finally figured out who the mysterious fingerprints found in the scene belong to." I explain, as I start up the engine and drive off to the police precinct. The hope of good news was the adrenaline we were all relying upon now, and it is every bit of hope that we must now hold on to tightly if we want a shot at beating the killer at his own game. We are going to find him.

It's only a couple of minutes pass before we pull up to the police station, and as soon as we make our way through the door down to Michael's office (aka the laboratory), we see none other than New York's best forensic scientist hard at work. Michael has been working endlessly for several days, and I can only imagine that he's taken just about the necessary hours of sleep to hang on to his human self.

"Looks like you've been busy," I say bluntly pointing out the obvious. "You turned nocturnal yet?" I ask, smiling at Michael, who looks like he hasn't slept or washed in days.

He has ridiculous bed hair, and all his clothes are wrinkled, untucked and scruffy.

"Very funny. Unfortunately not, although that would make things easier. I'm exhausted," he replies with a good-natured laugh, as he turns his head away from me. "By the way, Jenny, you're looking very pretty today."

He beats me to it and leaves me with my jaw dropped and mouth hanging open. Even with limited sleep he manages to beat me. But don't worry, Michael, I'll get you next time.

Jennifer blushes, and her eyes wander to the floor, a clear and rapid instinct of her embarrassment. It happens every time someone compliments her. But I think it's adorable.

Clearing her throat and tucking a loose strand of hair behind her ear, she speaks up from behind her hair.

"Here, I brought you a cappuccino with soy milk," Jennifer says, as she stretches out the cup she's been holding towards Michael. "I thought you might like it after all the work you've had to do. After all, you are not nocturnal. Yet." Jennifer adds jokingly, turning slightly towards me, where her eyes meet me with a small yet noticeable wink. I knew that she had found my humor irresistible.

"Thanks, Jenny; I really needed it," says Michael with a tone of relief, as he takes the small cup from her hand, carefully sipping the coffee, a calm look washing over his face as if the coffee had some sort of magical powers, that at least for an instant, washed away the worry that had been eating Michael up for the last couple of days.

He sighs, breathes in deeply and draws himself in. "Well, let's get down to business. We have no time to waste."

"The first thing I did was to analyze the fingerprints I was able to collect from the crime scene. And by that I mean all of them. There were an unusually large number of them this time, scattered all around the crime scene." Michael begins in between sips of his cappuccino coffee. "But get this guys, there weren't any footprints. It looks like whoever did this tried to cover the shoes so as not to leave a trace, yet took no precautions to hide these fingerprints, which makes no sense at all. Isn't it easier to identify someone from their fingerprints than the sole of their feet," he asks us, although Jenny and I look every bit as confused, for which we simply shrug implying for Michael to go on.

"What I mean is that when we arrive at crime scenes we expect to find the typical clues: footprints, hair strands, some DNA samples. But here I didn't find anything besides some fingerprints and fingernail scrapings to extract DNA from, which doesn't make any sense."

"But how is that even possible?" I ask Michael, interrupting his never ending train of thought.

"I don't know, John, none of this makes any sense." Michael answers, shaking his head in confusion. "But here's the best part. After I ran the first set of fingerprints through the database, I was able to find who they belonged to …"

"Who?" Jenny and I exclaim in perfect union, as eyes brighten up from childlike curiosity.

"Someone who has been dead for a while." Michael concludes, pausing and letting us process the information that has just been dumped on us. "And get this, the other two sets of fingerprints also belonged to two other individuals who are no longer among the living."

"But how can that be?" Jenny asks, running a strand of loose hair behind her ear, as she continues to fidget with her ponytail.

"Michael, are you sure? Maybe there's been a mistake in the system?" I try.

"No, John, it's not an error. I ran them through three times each, and I still got the same thing. Three sets of fingerprints, belonging to three dead people. Three corpses, who cannot move and certainly cannot kill someone in their sleep!" Michael exclaims, pacing back and forth in anticipating, shouting in frustration.

"Ok, let's think about this logically." I try, hoping to calm down the stressful Michael rampaging around the lab and the paralyzed Jenny that has been lost in her own mind and is staring helplessly into the white wall in front of her. "First, Michael, tell us who each of the fingerprints belong to."

Michael walks over to his desk, where he has his laptop connected to a monitor. He scrolls down with his mouse, and scans the screen for the information he had previously gathered.

"Right, so as you both know now I found three different fingerprints," he says motioning us to come closer to the laptop and we all lean over his shoulder. He points at a brown smudge on the top of the screen "The first one belongs to Cameron Parker …"

Cameron Parker: one of New York City's most renowned detectives, known for solving the hardest of crimes, even when the odds were against him. The best in his field bringing a much needed change of the times, revolutionizing what detectives could do and who they could be. One of my idols, whom I looked up to as a child, and acted as my inspiration to join the police force to bring justice to the injustices that I had seen in my own life.

"I knew Cameron." I speak up. "We actually worked on several cases together, when I first joined the force. I didn't know he passed away." I add as a wave of guilt washes over me, as I remember the times that we spent scouring cases and the celebratory calls he made with his brother, Anthony, once we solved a case. I always wanted that same sibling relationship.

"It was two years ago, from a brain tumor." Michael explains, pulling up his file on the screen and motioning for us to look.

"Maybe the killer is someone Cameron sent to prison, and this is a way to get revenge and justice once and for all, by framing him for a crime he couldn't have committed. I'm sure he must have accumulated a list of enemies throughout his life." Jenny wonders, voicing theories that have been speeding through my brain ever since Michael mentioned his name.

"I'm going to look for a list of all his cases in the archives," Jennifer reports, a grim expression on her face as she hates the idea she has just come up with, as a long road ahead of her awaits.

"Great idea; let's start there." I reply. "And who do the other fingerprints belong to, Michael?" I look at him but he is too busy pacing to look my way, running a hand through his messy hair.

"The second set of fingerprints belong to a woman called Mayka Swim. A nurse specializing in anesthesia, and from the search I've done, she was one of the best. She was in her sixties when she died a year ago in a car accident." He stops, letting the information sink into our minds, before continuing, and adding the finality of the dreaded information we are not wanting to uncover.

"The third set of fingerprints belong to Joseph Calbani, a former military special operations expert, who was highly commended as a skilled sniper during his time in the American military. He died at the age of fifty as he was shot in the head during an offshore military operation, around the same time as Mayka."

I look out of the window with my eyes lost, trying to fit the pieces of this puzzle together. Fingerprints of a detective, a nurse and a military soldier. But how since they have all been dead for a while? Why is there a dead person walking around on their hands in the crime scene? Had the killer used their fingerprints to send us an encoded message?

"As crazy as it sounds, the killer must have frozen the hands and passed them around the room as if they were a paintbrush, painting an incomprehensible picture to get us off track." Michael adds, discontented from the scene as a million more questions form in his racing mind. "I don't know, guys, I'm stumped for now."

"Alright, Michael, that's fine. Here's what we're going to do next." I begin "We are going to find out everything we can about these three people: Who were they? Do they have families? When did they die? Why did they die? And why are they important to the crimes committed?" My eyes widen but I shake my head to clear my shocked face as I finish listing the questions that have been bugging me the whole time, hoping that the answers can bring to light the truth.

"I agree, John, that's the right way to start. And then we should contact their relatives," says Jennifer, as her stone called expression darts direct focus towards me.

"I haven't finished yet," interrupts Michael, with a look of grimace, and raises his eyebrows in deep concern.

"What else could there be?" I ask, as Michael shakes his head as if to signal that he thought otherwise.

"Then there is the matter of the paintings."

"What about them?"

"They both have miniscule hands and eyes that you can only see when you enlarge the painting. Both hands appear to be of a female owner, considering the details of the fingers and the shape of the hands overall." Michael explains.

"Well if there's something we've learned from our mystery killer, it's that he sure loves to challenge us with unsolvable riddles, doesn't he?" Jenny asks, puzzled as ever.

"Okay. Let's think about this carefully. Everything within the painting is a clue, taunting us as we struggle to find its hidden answers. We need to look at the frame, the glass, the material, everything." I begin.

"Alright, I'll take photos of everything and send them directly to Dilya to see if she can find something else by running the image recognition software," says Michael.

"Hopefully then we'll know exactly where our killer bought these paintings from. If it was an online purchase we can track the bank account. And if we have a bit of luck with it being a face-to-face sale, we can have a look at the shop's security cameras. And then ladies, and gentlemen we would find our murder," I add.

"I don't think the murderer would be that naïve, though," adds Jennifer, quietly under her breath.

"I also want a report from the telecommunication companies, to provide us with the phone numbers and the people who were at the murder site at those specific times. Use their exact geolocation to see who we can narrow down as potential suspects." I continue to give more instructions to my team, with the hope that we can discover more about this crime.

Michael writes everything in his notebook in such a schematic way that only he understands it. He closes it and nods firmly. We are ready to go.

"One last thing." I add, before we all dart into different directions. "Where does Anthony, Cameron's brother, live?"

"20 minutes away from here," Michael replies after doing a quick search. "What do you have planned?"

"I think it's time we pay him a visit and ask him about some things that have been throwing me off."

Chapter 7

John – The Parker brothers

"Alright. Michael, keep looking. Jenny and I are going to pay Cameron's brother and Mayka's husband a visit," I say, as I update him on the rest of today's agenda. "I'm hoping they can shed some light on this investigation."

"Michael, do me a favor. Ask Dilya for all the financial and transactional information she has on these three people, as well," says Jenny with a friendly smile as she radiates a pulsing hope to motivate us forward.

After all the instructions, we make our way out of the police station and we get into my car where the silence is deafening and consuming …

Jenny doesn't talk, that's her thing. When we have a case, she usually spends a couple of hours thinking and visualizing the scene. She uses silence as a way to let us know that she is in deep concentration and must not be disturbed. Her staring into a random space tells us that she is centering herself in the middle of the crime as if she had been there all along, trying to piece all the clues together. But mostly, I think that the silence is really just a way to tell us to shut up, and stop joking around.

The first item on today's agenda is to visit Cameron's brother.

I like to drive. Taking control of the steering wheel, I turn on the radio and eighties music plays. Thankfully music does not seem to bother Jenny today.

After forty minutes, we arrive at Cameron's brother's house: 54 Delancy Street. It is a detached house with a garden, fostering blooming flowers of different species. We walk down a slate path to the front door, and I ring the bell anxiously waiting for it to open. Footsteps are heard approaching the front door and the sound inside is muffled. The door opens, and a person appears behind it. A man in his sixties looks at us with excessive seriousness, as his eyes move slowly up and down. He has short hair, bushy eyebrows, a white moustache curling above his mouth, round glasses encircling his eyes, and he wears a crumpled floral shirt with spotted shorts and flip-flops, as if he had just been on vacation.

"Are you Anthony Parker, Cameron's brother?" I ask, before he has a chance to ask us anything nor slam the door in our faces.

"Yes, that's me. Is something wrong? Who are you?" he replies anxiously, shaking his head in confusion.

"We're police lieutenants, Jennifer Taylor and John Duffy. We're here to ask you some questions about your brother. I was lucky enough to have worked with him in the past and I am proud that I was able to work with such an incredible professional and an amiable human being," I say.

"The truth is that it was a huge loss, we were very close. Since he died, I feel a great emptiness deep within me." Anthony gets a faraway look in his eyes as he reminisces about his moments with his brother. However, his head snaps up as he realizes that he is not alone. Hurriedly he steps to the side, waving his arms in a welcoming manner. "But please, come in, let's talk more inside."

As Anthony invites us in, the first thing we find is a glazed porch, with a table and chairs in the center. Photographs of different cities around the world hang on the walls, bringing to life the atmosphere of the interior. He motions for us to sit down and offers us a cup of coffee and some sweets to indulge in while we talk.

"Please sit down and try some tea pastries." Anthony offers as he outstretches the box in front of us.

"I have travelled all over the world and I have become very fond of having coffee and pastries for breakfast wherever it is that I go. A habit I got from my European travels in Spain, Italy and France, I must say, although it may not be the healthiest one," Anthony says as he giggles slightly, rocking his head back in his chair.

"I used to work as a photojournalist, covering news around the world and writing articles about all the wonders of the world. That's why I have all these pictures that you see hanging up on the walls around us." Anthony mentions as he serves us some coffee and directs our attention to the masterpieces that encircle us.

"Last time I visited Europe was when I visited Spain. Such a wonderful country with open and welcoming people everywhere you turn." I add, with a smile spreading across my face, hoping to be able to connect with him.

As we talk about Anthony's experiences, he appears more relaxed and comfortable with us. Jenny listens to every detail, as her eyes bright up with curiosity. I know for a fact that she is recording everything he says in her fabulous (incomprehensibly human) memory: every photo, every story, every detail and every gesture that our host makes as he retells his greatest adventures. Jenny is compiling a preserved freeze frame of our visit, which I know she'll be able to recite by heart at any moment.

We are all amazed at Anthony's life, and once I realize that he is comfortable around us, I take my chance and change the course of the conversation. It's time to ask him about his brother. I know this could be the perfect timing to get the answers we have been waiting anxiously for.

"Did you ever travel with Cameron to Europe?" I interrupt him, before he has the chance to tell us about another one of his travels.

"Yes, we went to England and Ireland one time." Anthony starts, as his expression changes to a more reflective and saddening depiction, as he reminiscences about the past.

"We had such a great time touring the famous landmarks and enjoying the nature that surrounded it all." Anthony stars

"Not to mention …" Anthony begins to laugh as he is filled with the joy of the past. "All the food and drinks that we had at the pubs in the evening. The pints of beer were definitely a highlight of ours." Anthony continues, rocking back and forth in happiness and laughter.

They were very close indeed, that is something that I've been able to deduce just from this simple and short conversation. It's something that stands out as he looks back at the memory he shares of his brother. Anthony's so fortunate to have been able to form such a close friendship with someone, it reminds me of the past that was robbed from me and my sister. Luckily my sister now has a seven-year-old son, which I can share some of the memories that I never got to build for myself. It's a long-lost sibling relationship, finally mending itself after years of distance and struggle.

"Would you mind giving me details of your brother's last days?" I ask, as the conversation changes tone to a more interrogative approach, as the air of death settles in.

"The truth is …" Anthony starts, puzzled in thought, as his face changes from the happiness of the past to the harsh reality of the present, "is that I can't, because he didn't talk to anyone about his illness, no one knew what he was suffering from, exactly."

"During that time, I was abroad, in Africa actually, taking photos for a report on the black market for elephant tusks and smuggled ivory pieces." He begins. "It was a shock, I didn't know anything, until it was too late, and there was nothing I could do. He kept it to himself and kept it quiet until the last minute so as not to hurt anyone, but that also meant that we weren't prepared for what was coming. Cameron was the type of person who didn't think about himself for even a fraction of a second, he always put others first. He believed that he would die at any moment, whether it would be as the victim of a shooting, a stray bullet or an assassination. I'm sure he never thought he would die of cancer." Anthony tells us, as his expression saddens with longing for his brother.

Nothing of this makes sense. An unseeable and unpredictable death, an illness that no one knew about until it was too late? There's definitely something that doesn't add up here.

"Excuse me for asking this question, but do you think he could be alive? I know this may sound crazy, but what if there was even a possibility that your brother didn't die? Do you think this may be plausible Mr Parker?"

"What's going on? Why are you asking?" Anthony adds forcefully, agitated and confused by my questions, as he starts to move in his chair with the force of the confusion that settles over him, dropping the cup of coffee forcefully on the table.

Anthony is sweating and shaking his shirt collar to air himself out as he talks. He is in shock.

"This is confidential, so I trust your full cooperation and transparency. Anthony, Cameron's fingerprints were found in two crime scenes yesterday. This is nothing to be alarmed by, but at this initial stage, we just have to tie up as many loose ends as possible, you know, discard potential theories one by one until we find out the truth once and for all."

Anthony looks at me, as the white of his eyes magnify in dimension.

"Would it be possible to have your permission to check that the corpse has not been removed or replaced. May we carry out some DNA checks?" I ask politely and softly, to calm down Anthony.

Anthony rests his head in his hands and meditates, as he considers the proposal at hand. He looks up and watches us, looking at Jenny and then finally his eyes dart back to mine, and fixes his gaze directly towards me.

I know he is as good a person, just like his brother was. I know he's going to help us; I can feel it. He looks at us; and begins to speak, as he's made up his mind about the difficult decision at hand.

"I think, if Cameron were alive and in the same situation, he would want the coffin opened." Anthony admits. "He would want to rule out any possibility that he was still alive. He was an impeccable, truth-loving detective. So, now that I'm in this scenario I'm gonna have to agree with what Cameron would have decided. John, please open it and do the necessary tests," he says shrugging his shoulders and rubbing his eyes dry. "It's what needs to be done, John. I trust you."

"Thank you very much, Anthony. I know how difficult this is for you, but I know that this is the right thing to do," I say, placing my arm on his shoulder.

"Jenny, would you mind going to the car and getting the release forms for him to sign? I'll give them to the judge to authorize Cameron's exhumation," I say as Jenny stands up and leaves for the car. "I'm very sorry to put you through all this and I assure you, we'll see it through to the end. I promise Anthony." I conclude, as we wait for Jenny to come back with the forms.

Anthony and I sit in silence, until Jenny returns from the car. She shuffles forward, digging into her pocket and fishing out a blue pen, which she hands over to him to use. Anthony puts on his glasses, grabbing the files from Jenny who explains where he should sign and he completes the necessary paperwork. Once we have all that is needed, we get up and walk towards the door, as Anthony motions us outside. Before we leave, we both hug him goodbye, and wish him the best.

We have been talking for not much more than an hour, and although it's been only for a short time, I can see that Anthony is a true reflection of his brother. An exemplary family culture that, unfortunately, is not abundant in our own modern society. Corruption replaces familial values, as money, position, power and image come first, and family, affection, values, education and many other things come last.

Jenny and I make our way out of the house, waving goodbye to Anthony one last time. Jenny starts the car, and as we put on our seatbelts, Jenny finally speaks up.

"John, I think we should go to the judge now, to get the order approved as soon as possible and open the coffin today, if possible," she says, with a firm and confident tone.

"I agree. Let's go. Let's leave the visit to Mayka's husband for tomorrow, then," I reply, and we make our way to the courthouse in silence save for the clicking of my finger against the screen of my phone while I text Michael. I think today's visit has taken a toll on both of us.

Judge Jessica Walsh is a sweetheart. And she is exactly who we need today, because if you ask me, she's definitely one of the best in her field, (although I may be somewhat biased in that decision). She is meticulous, and she knows we work our asses off on every case, so she always manages to help us out one way or another. We are completely different when it comes to tidiness though. Her desk has only the documents she is working on and is always clean, unlike mine, where coffee stains invade the randomly constructed paper towers and make my fingers stick to the letters on the keyboard. She doesn't like my boss either, which makes her a very smart woman.

As we arrive at the courthouse, we make our way towards Jessica's office as Dilya has arranged for our meeting to be held at 17:45.

The door to Jessica's office opens, and a tall slender woman makes her way towards us, as we are sitting down in the chairs opposite her. Her blond locks perfectly coincide with the brown sparkle in her eyes, and the red in her cheeks, and her rose colored lips. She is wearing a lightly colored suit with high heels, and her hair is pulled back in a slick bun. Jenny is the first person to speak, as I am still in awe of the woman's presence.

"Hi, Jessica, how are you?" asks Jenny, as she taps my hand lightly to get my attention, and I stop daydreaming.

"How are my favorite lieutenants doing?" she asks, beaming with joy. "What important case do you have on your hands this time?" She has a soft voice that I know can grow menacing and authoritative when in court.

For the next thirty minutes, we give Jessica a rundown of the details: two murders, fingerprints of deceased individuals found in both crime scenes, (one of which belongs to a dead man whom his brother could not say goodbye to), two paintings with bloody hands, all in the spam of just a couple of days. We ask her to authorize the exhumation of the body. Jessica agrees without objection. I knew that I had placed my trust in the right woman.

"Thank you very much, Jessica. You are as kind and understanding as ever," I reply, as my eyes dwindle in a childish reflection of awe.

"You're most welcome, John; it's a pleasure to work with you. If your boss, or should I say the 'Ape' ..." She does sarcastic air quotes in the air and continues, "… had asked me, I would have given it to him too, but it would have been accompanied by suffering and a whole lot of begging." She winks at me, and her mouth curls up into a smile. "He came here today just to be in the photo of a trial in which the chimpanzee gang was convicted. Does that ring a bell, John?"

"It might do, Jessica," I reply, as I giggle under my breadth.

"That was a good one; I wish I could have been there."

"I'm glad you enjoyed yourself, at least. Although, I was suspended, but I really didn't mind it. I would've given anything to see Stephan's priceless face and enraged fury. He got what he deserved, and I'm glad I was the person able to put him in place at least for once in his life." I boast proudly, for which Jenny rolls her eyes, but Jessica looks at me admiringly so I continue. "Luckily, I was able to take a much-deserved holiday, which I used to travel to Spain. I would highly recommend it, Jessica, I could even show you around next time. By the way, let me know if you want to have dinner with me one of these nights, it's on me."

Jessica blushes. "Thank you, John; I would love to. I'll call you. I'm looking forward to it," she says kissing me goodbye, on the cheek, and shaking Jenny's hand before we leave.

"Come on, John, that's enough! Flirting in front of me, gross!" Jenny says as she punches me lightly in my arm. "Grow up!"

"You're just jealous, that you're not her" I add jokingly, and Jenny smirks in disagreement with yet another roll of her eyes.

"You know, Jenny," I continue. "I love that woman: she's smart, she's hard-working, and I find her very attractive. We are the perfect dream couple. Don't you think so?" I say, as my eyes dazzle with joy.

"Yes, yes, perfect!" she says hurriedly in a somewhat sarcastic tone. "Come on!" Jennifer smiles and pats me on the back, like I'm her little brother.

Jenny takes a moment to call her husband, and I guess now I'm the third wheel. Well played Jenny, well played indeed.

"Hi, honey, hope you've been having a great day. I miss you. Please don't wait up for me, I have to do something urgent for work, I'll be there around one o'clock," Jennifer speaks into the phone softly, as she gets out her car keys.

"Tell him you're going to party with me, that we're going to be dancing all night! Tell him not to get too jealous!" I say out loud, hoping I'm loud enough so that the phone's speaker can pick it up.

"Hey, John insists me to tell you that we're going to a party and that we're going to dance all night long." Jenny repeats on the phone, turning back to me. "I'm sorry, John, he's not buying it," she says between laughs. "If it was Michael, maybe …"

"You break my heart, my life will never be the same after this," I reply with one hand on my heart and the other outstretched to the sky, in a dramatic way, which makes her smile.

The paperwork has taken some time, but at least that gave Jenny and I some time to grab something to eat while we waited. With the permit in hand, I call Dilya to organize everything and off we go to the cemetery to collect the cadaveric samples. I call Michael and tell him to meet us there.

In front of the tomb: Michael, Jennifer, the workers who will remove the top of the casket and I, circle around it. We've set up some very powerful spotlights and the workers have started digging. It's cold and windy; ropes wrap around the wood and lift the coffin up. They carefully place it on the ground, and we ask them to leave. Now it's time for the forensic police to kick in. We are all wearing our special suits so as not to compromise nor contaminate the collected evidence. Gloves envelope our hands and we set to work looking at the coffin.

They insert a lever to open the coffin, move the lid and we approach to see a skeleton. There is no indication that the body has been replaced.

"Quickly, Michael, take the body and the coffin to the lab for DNA analysis. See if there is anything unusual. Work on the hypothesis that the body is not his and that he may still be alive." I order him.

"Michael, take as much time as you need, I'm going to memorize and analyze the situation," says Jennifer looking around with wide eyes as if enlarging her vision.

We stay for more than two hours at the grave site. At eleven o'clock we decide to go home. The day was hard and with many surprises, we have to digest everything and think. The coffin and the corpse have now been taken to the laboratory, where Michael will spend the next few days doing tests and studying the details. Today there is nothing more to do.

Chapter 8

Henry – Shifting Gears

With time running out, I desperately need new members for my team.

They need to be hands with very specific traits, which will support their certain objective. Every hand must carry out its specific task without complications.

But this won't be easy. The mental and physical toll it is taking on me is immense, but I can't give up. I won't give up. This is my life now and I can't turn back.

"Frank, I need you to locate possible candidates for hands. They must have transplant experience." I tell Frank via my glasses. "You know what I'm looking for."

Frank will need a couple of hours to process the information, but once he does, he'll be able to compile a list of names for the potential candidates. At the end of the day, I'll know everything about them: it will be as if I'd known them my whole life, and from there I'll be able to make the decision as to whether they are right for my team.

The team that I create has to be so carefully planned that everything must be taken into account including their personality. My plans need hardworking, selfless and loyal workers.

That's why Frank follows the criteria I set him, word by word. We can leave no stone unturned. And we cannot take any chances in selecting the wrong person. Nothing can mess up the plan that I've been pursuing so long. Everything has to be perfect. But this also means that the 'perfect' candidates are not always easy to find. And I do not have much time. Sometimes I have to cross from one corner of the country to another just to locate the perfect candidate and be able to make them a part of our team. It's a difficult, yet very much-needed process. Because after everything, it'll all be worth it. Because my plan will be a success.

As Frank begins to search, I take the opportunity to go and see Driver for the first time. Right about now, he should be all ready and trained after being brought back to life earlier today. And I for one can't wait to see my creation in action for the first time.

I walk into the training room and watch as Driver goes through several Formula 1 racing videos up on the screen in front of him. Driver, being a literal 'driver', needs to immerse himself in the world of professional racing in order to get the feel of his upcoming role.

For each hand, I set up a personalized plan, looking at their unique skills and the role that I need them to play. I am careful and think through this process, step by step, careful to look at every option. Because just like any human, every hand is different, and I need to be able to tailor it to their needs. Because after all I'm their creator, and that is part of my role.

This is the same process any Human Resources department would do for a new employee, so after all I'm not that different when creating my own 'empire' even if it's built around hands and not assets. The difference with my vision is that this particular process (and anything I do for my hands) is that I do it with compassion and care, as I focus on how to best benefit them. I consider them my children. They are what I now call my hainders.

I am not looking to profit from them, but rather support them in their development journey after the life they knew and loved ended, because of something they could have never prevented.

After all, I am their creator, the one who gave them life, after death. My main aim is that we have fun, as I give them the chance to live the life that was so unjustly taken away from them. In exchange, I only require one thing: that they fulfil their predetermined function so that I can achieve my ultimate purpose. Because when I do, they will be free just like me.

"Hello, Driver, how are you?" I ask as I make my way down to him, from the place where I was watching him from above.

"Are you okay?" I ask in a comforting tone, for which Driver jumps up and down in response. I continue talking, "You can call me anything you like: sir, boss, dad, mister, anything but my real name of course. We wouldn't want anyone to know who we are, of course."

The truth is that I put a restriction on all my hands to prevent them from calling me by my real name, to avoid being discovered, so even if they tried, they wouldn't be able to. I have full control now.

"I feel great, boss! I can't wait to start driving at full speed, doing some drifts, spins, left and right. You're going to freak out; you've never driven with someone like me in your life. It's going to be great." Driver responds with a childlike excitement.

"One thing, how the hell am I going to get to the pedals? I don't know if you've forgotten but I can't reach, I don't have legs or feet for that matter," says Driver, wiggling and jumping around, climbing on top of everything in his reach.

I've worked incredibly hard to masterfully design Driver's language to align it with his unique personality, so every word he mutters, is one that brings the hands alive and reflects the persona they once were when alive. The owner of these hands was a very cheerful person who loved his job. He was extremely careful at the wheel, although he had some accidents in his career. A day didn't pass where he wasn't haunted by the overwhelming regret of the consequences that these accidents had for others.

But he was loved. His friends adored him and would hang out every weekend laughing for hours on end. Driver's person never married, nor had any children, yet he never missed the opportunity to volunteer, by getting involved in soup kitchens in his local community. I wanted to add a language to remind me of what he was like, and how he expressed himself. I wanted his hands to mirror every single aspect that we had observed and studied during the selection period which went on for several months. Cameron and Frank are phenomenal at this, they are able to find and monitor the best candidates, which is why I now delegate more and more tasks and responsibilities to them, as I have full trust in their abilities.

"Driver, come with me to the Alpha basement! I want you to see something!"

My estate is huge, and that is even an understatement. When I bought it, I took advantage of everything it offered. It had a very big basement built. I'm not exaggerating when I say that it measures about twice the size of a football stadium. Inside the basement, Driver's surprise awaits him. I take Driver with my own hands, pick him up and place a towel over him, so as not to ruin the surprise.

"Close your eyes," I tell him, with a fatherly tone of affection.

Driver doesn't have eyes of course. But the hands' watch allows them to see 180°, like the eyes of a fly. The dial glass is oval shaped, allowing a single eye to capture everything in their surroundings, and place particular detail to it all, thanks to the zoom and night vision mechanisms installed.

Going down to the basement, I hold Driver in one hand, and with the other open the door. It is a large space with various types of terrain: asphalt, dirt and mountain to drive all kinds of vehicles. On the roof there are devices that allow you to simulate different training environments: rain, snow, storm, fog … At the back there are several vehicles: A truck, some motorbikes, a limousine … just about every single vehicle possible.

"You can open your eyes now, Driver." I whisper, as I remove the towel away from his eyes to show him the basement and all its wonders.

"This is wonderful, this is amazing, boss!" Driver responds in joy as his fingers join up and tickle the insides of my palms. "Can I – can I pick one up and drive it?"

"Yes, of course, but I'd better explain the details before you go overboard," I say quickly, with a voice of hesitancy as I need to calm down Driver's excitement, before he starts doing flips all around the basement.

I spend a couple of minutes explaining the ins and outs of how the basement works due to the complexity and history behind it, taking special care to include everything. I slowly explain how each of the vehicles is driven, placing particular emphasis on how they have been adapted to be driven by only one hand. All the functions, apart from the accelerator, brake, and gear shift, are either on the steering wheel or the dashboard. The whole set-up is designed so that the car can be driven by the hand. Some things can also be activated by Driver's voice.

"Driver, I'll leave you here. Get a feel for the vehicles and I'll come check on you later. You know the artificial intelligence system will incorporate different tracks for you to race on. All your progress will be evaluated." I stop as I hear a faint: "Geez no pressure," and smile. "Please let me know how you get on. I'm excited to hear how you find it."

I turn towards the door, calling out to him before I leave. "By the way, dinner is at eight o'clock. We all have dinner together. We chat about our day, but above all we have fun together."

"Okay, boss, don't worry, you're going to love my training and my conversations." His watch forms a winking eye image.

"I'm looking forward to it. See you in a few hours."

I leave Driver to use to race track and a faint buzz goes off in my ear followed by Frank's voice.

"Boss, Cameron and I have selected two candidates. I'll pass you the files." Frank tells me through my earpiece attached to my glasses, and it wakes me up to the reality of my mission once again.

"Great, send the files to my desk. The three of us can meet in my office in twenty minutes," I reply, excited to know more about the potential candidates.

I call Cameron and tell him to come to my office as per the arranged meeting time. It's a very large room, with a fragile glass desk and a bookshelf behind the chair. There are several computer screens flashing with updates and information. On the bookshelf, you can find almost any book you need: there are books on engineering, technology, mathematics, and medicine. The office is also a meeting room with a large wooden table whose legs are roots growing out of a log. One of my many other passions is interior design, but unfortunately, I don't have enough time to curate it. I ordered it from a carpenter who specifically used the roots from my desired forest. An unscrupulous lumberjack had cut the marvelous tree down, after reigning the forest for thousands of years old. In its place, I planted one of the same species. I hope that it will grow to be as magnificent as the one that now takes form as my meeting table.

The twenty minutes are up, and I join Cameron and Frank.

"I've seen the reports, good work, guys." I praise them and Cameron bounces around Frank in a cheerful way. "The assessment is excellent and you're going to be great partners," I say positively. "The surgeon has extensive experience in organ and bone transplantation, but he will need to be given a lot more training, I'm afraid." I continue running a hand through my hair, slowly. "Frank, I want him to be educated in all sorts of known transplants, don't miss any of them out in his personalized training. He needs to be informed of all future options, and be able to calculate for all sorts of outcomes, successes, failures, etc. After that we'll give him some real tests to practice and innovate to uncertainty so that he can be ready for anything."

"It is going to be a critical piece for both my future and humanity's. The world is going to change," I say, with building joy and uncontrollable excitement as I am getting close to completing my mission.

"As for the nurse." I continue, reading from the screen for the information on her. "I love her. I truly do. She has a lot of experience, and has very high ratings from her bosses, her colleagues, and, most importantly, her patients. She has years of practice in healing patients who have had car accidents, amputations, and transplants. Our particular area of interest. She has collaborated in the rehabilitation of people who were first identified as handicapped. She appears to be a loving, caring, and an active professional.

"Her children are older and live far away from her. Her husband died shortly after they had their second child, and she was the one who pulled the family along. She comes from a large family and has thus had to take care of her siblings and parents all her life."

I look up from the screen and smile at my two superstars.

"Great work, guys. I am very happy with your research. I can see that we will have to spend a week traveling, to get our team up to speed, but it will be worth it." My hand begins to twitch the way it always does before an important mission.

"Frank, get everything ready. We'll be leaving in a couple of days." I pause, letting him absorb the information as I make my way out of the room, my head held high.

"It's time for step 2."

Chapter 9

Henry – New plans and ideas

It is now the 20th of October and it had been a year since it had happened. One year since the unforgettable 6th of June, where I had stood in Dr Samantha Evans' office for the very first time. I had been suffering through the most terrible headaches and dizziness for months. As a world renowned neurosurgeon, I knew something was wrong right away. But I never would have predicted how wrong things were about to get. After some thought, I was lucky enough to be able to come up with a plan that would save me.

I have cured more than ten thousand patients in my lifetime. Yet there were some that were impossible to save. The brain is a very difficult organ, because we know very little about it. Nonetheless, I am passionate about the wonders and mysteries it possesses, because once you learn all its secrets you can begin to dominate it. And that is where the true power of immortality lies.

Cameron is with me today; I carry him in my briefcase, so no one can see him. Cameron has a brother; Anthony; and sometimes I go and talk to him. Cameron always accompanies me and without being seen he moves around the house and we communicate through the earpiece. I ask Anthony all the questions Cameron tells me. He loves him very much and so did Anthony. So I'm glad that at least my presence can do some good for both of them. Even if it doesn't replicate the past exactly as it was once before.

One time we were discovered by the dog, and he is now able to identify Cameron and lets him be petted. It was a close call, but I think we've managed to keep it all under wraps for now. Although we risk being spotted when we go, the therapeutic experience of these conversations helps Cameron and I stay sane and connected to our mission. It shows us why we are right in pursuing this crazy twisted path to what appears most impossible.

I'm anxious, my hands are shaking with nerves, my forehead is drowning in sweat. I think that whatever is wrong with me cannot be cured. I know there is. Worst outcome is undergoing surgery and the best is taking medication.

"Mr Henry Silverstone?" calls the nurse.

"Yes, that's me," I answer as I order my shaky hand up to signal where I am.

"Please come in. Dr Samantha is waiting for you."

I get up from the sofa in the waiting room. It's a small cozy room, with a lot of modern up to date magazines of all kinds. I wonder if travel magazines are the most popular in places like this. Maybe they serve as a luxurious escape for the patients before hearing more terrible news. We enter the doctor's office and Samantha is there, spectacular and friendly as always. We've known each other since our university days, and we've gone out as a group on several occasions. She's a very good professional and the only one I'd let perform this kind of medical test. When she sees me, she smiles, stands up and we hug.

"It's good to see you again, Henry, how are you feeling? Have you had any problems again?" asks Samantha.

"Hi, Samantha, not really. I feel great and with the medication you sent me, I haven't had to take a single day of work from the hospital. Tell me, how are the tests going?"

"That's what I wanted to talk to you about, please take a seat and look at the report."

We sit down, she takes a seat in her chair opposite me and hands me a folder with the results of the scan and tests.

I read them carefully and coldly, frowning and shaking my head as if that could change what lay in front of my eyes.

"It doesn't look good, does it?" I whisper, wringing my hands with a whole lot of stress. "I was expecting something, but not this."

"No, I'm sorry. In these cases, as you know, it's best to treat conservatively to prevent further progression," Samantha replies, reaching for my hand.

I can see her sadness in her eyes and in the trembling movement of her lips. She gets up, comes towards me and we embrace.

"I know you're sorry but don't worry about me. I'll figure something out," I say to encourage Samantha. She pats me comfortingly on the back.

"I'm sure you are capable of anything. With your knowledge and your international network, you will find a cure. For the time being, let's delay the breakthrough."

I give her a kiss on the cheek and say goodbye. It's worse than I expected, but we'll have to find a solution. Unfortunately, we're running out of time.

Once in the car park, I start the car and leave the building. I don't feel anything, yet somehow I also feel a lot as the overwhelming emotions swirl inside of me. The news has been very hard for me, harder than anything I could have ever imagined. I didn't expect it.

Driving aimlessly through the city, thinking about how to save myself, I realize that I haven't seen my mentor and beloved university professor, Julian Forty, for a long time. I remember the hours when he would point out to me his fear of dying and losing all the knowledge he had accumulated. In the last days of my PhD, he told me that he had found a way to prevent the information in our brains from being lost. I will go and visit him; at least, if I die, my knowledge might survive and be used for science. At this point, I'm willing to try anything.

I'm looking forward to seeing him again. I'm sure he must have invented something new; he was always coming up with new ideas. He's brilliant. At university they said he was a bit crazy. In my personal opinion he's nothing short of a genius.

I cross the city and arrive at his house. I love where he lives, it's a Victorian house in Manhattan. The entrance has the same doormat as always with a drawing of a scale and several words that have lost their color around it. I knock on the door.

Julian opens the door, he is a person with a thin and fragile complexion though very intelligent. He's always accompanied by his old black leather briefcase where he keeps his inseparable notebooks and notes. His long black hair, his rectangular glasses, and the scar formed by small warts aligned on the right side of his face make him look like a mobster instead of a famous teacher. His interest in the brain began at an early age when he watched his mother cook tortillas with lamb brains. More than once he took them without being discovered and studied them until they rotted over time. His mother believed that the stink in the room was caused by a fungal disease of the feet and took Julian to the doctor to be examined and prescribed some type of antibiotic. More than once, students have called the university medical service when observing that Julian remains stopped in the middle of the explanations for spaces of more than ten minutes as if his mind left his body.

"My dear Henry, long time no see! What a joy to have you here! Please come in," he says as he welcomes me inside and gives me a warm embrace.

I enter the house and cross the hallway to the living room, where there is a person dressed in military uniform that surprises me. I thought we were alone. That's what it was meant to be like.

"Henry, this is General Adam Brown, a very good friend of mine."

At first glance he seems to be 1.90 m tall, I can see that he has a strong and muscular build. He must be close to 50 years old. His hair is brown, short to blonde and brown eyes. His eyebrows are bushy and his wide and fleshy nose stands out, a long scar crosses his face and he lacks the lobe of his right ear where he wears an audio phone. I've been watching it for several seconds, it makes me nervous the constant noise produced by the pen that presses rapidly by pulling out and inserting the tip.

"Pleased to meet you, General Brown," I reply, shaking his hand firmly.

"It's a pleasure to meet you, Henry. Julian has told me a lot about you. I hope we can meet soon and perhaps collaborate on something together. Now, if you'll excuse me, I have to go to the car for a moment."

Adam leaves the house.

"It's been such a long time? So, what brings you here, my dear friend?" Julian asks, surprised by the visit and the suddenness of my arrival, almost shocked by my intrusion.

"I wanted to know if you had made progress on what you told me before you finished. You said you had discovered something so that the knowledge would not be lost. I would be very interested to know more about your developments."

Julian switches on the stereo, selects a Beethoven symphony and turns up the volume.

"My dear friend, I have made great progress in this area, if I do say so myself. I invented a way of transmitting all the information in brains to a computer, it's genius. But so far I am unable to read it. I have tried it with apes and it works, the problem is when I do it with mice. Strange, really. In a few months I hope to have solved it and then I will try it myself. Maybe in the future we will need your help."

There's a knock at the door, which interrupts our conversation. It's General Brown.

"Julian, we have to go, the plane is waiting for us at the airport."

Julian gives me a hug, strongly holding on to me, with the warmth of our friendship.

"You must go, my friend, I'm sorry, but I must catch a plane and continue my experiments. There's something I must do. I'll keep you up-to-date the moment I have it figured out. I'm sure you'll be able to help me, I always knew there was great potential in you."

I say goodbye to both of them, leave the house, get into the car and open my briefcase.

"Sir, how are you? I'm stunned; you seem quite worried. I overheard your conversation. Can you give me more details? I'd love to help you in some way."

Cameron's watch flashes a smile and he stands with his thumb up, but his tone mirrors a hint of worry and compassion.

At that moment, listening to Cameron, I notice his hand, the life it has; an intelligent hand, with its own thoughts, personality, feelings.

"What is it, sir? Did I say something to upset you?" Cameron asks, confused and puzzled by my expression.

"On the contrary, Cameron, you have just shown me the way, and saved my life!" I exclaim with joy, picking him up and giving him a hug, which almost chokes him.

Cameron looks at me and smiles. The hands have a functionality in the crystal to express emotions. Learning algorithms are also geared towards developing feelings, raw human emotions. This is something I discovered and have never shared with society, but I know how to evolve artificial intelligence towards artificial emotion. This is one of the fields I am most passionate about and it carries a lot of risks, because not only can they reproduce feelings of joy and compassion but also hate, fear and schizophrenia. And those can have severe implications. So far, I have only added the positive ones and I don't want to incorporate the negative ones, but all the algorithms are ready and in good hands.

Seeing Cameron, listening to him, has given me a rush of emotions and ideas, ideas that will allow me to live and defeat any threat that might harm me. I look at his fingers, his eyes, and he smiles at me. He was always a good guy and he still is. Now I'll have to make more hands like Cameron.

That is the only way to save myself.

Chapter 10

John – Working around the clock

It's been a tough couple of days ever since we started investigating these strange murders; we haven't even had the chance to rest. We're working around the clock, and struggling under the pressure from our bosses, who to no one's surprise, are of zero help. Our countries' politicians and the media add constant stress as they too push us for answers that we do not have. Everyone wants to know everything but the thing is that we don't know everything. Right now, we know absolutely nothing. Nothing at all.

We'd gone to talk to Mayka Swim's husband today. He told us that the body was burned in the crematorium and that the ashes were scattered at sea according to Mayka's wishes. Once again we were faced with a dead end. No surprise there.

In addition, Michael confirmed that the DNA from the skeleton we found in Cameron's grave was that of the victim. Which once again led us to yet another dead end.

So, in conclusion, we have nothing, absolutely nothing, to go on. Just a couple of pictures and lost trails. But it's no help. We're right back where we started: confused, annoyed and getting nowhere.

Still, I hold on to foolish hope that Dilya's investigation will lead us to crucial information and steer us in the right direction. But every passing day makes me open my eyes to the harsh reality that we don't know what we're doing. We are trapped. Caged in by the cunning murderer whilst being forced to play his games.

It's eleven o'clock at night and that's enough for today; I'm going to sleep, however futile it is. I can already see the night ahead: constant twisting and turning as these thoughts chase me all through my nightmares.

Tomorrow's my day off. A much needed one at that and I'm going to invite Pris out for lunch to enjoy her company. Maybe I can talk to her about the case, share the information I have and desperately ask her to shed some light on the murder. Because if there's one thing Pris is known for, it's for her intuition and ability to see clues where others wouldn't even think to look.

I take a shower, put on my pajamas, and go straight to bed. The simplicity of a drained routine, at its fullest.

But just when I am able to forget about the chaos that has been pursuing me, the sound of my mobile wakes me up. I must confess that I am, sadly, quite used to the disturbing sound and really should've seen it coming. But I am still shocked whilst my brain screams: Not again!

"What time is it?" I ask the empty room, as I groggily get up from my bed, turning towards the alarm clock on my bedside table and frowning. "Damn it! It's three o'clock in the morning!" I pick up the phone, suppressing a yawn that was about to escape my lips and answer the call.

"Who is it?" I ask into the phone, stumbling for the right words as sleep tries to take over once more.

I look at my mobile phone and my frown deepens to its fullest. Surprise, surprise, it's my dear boss, Stephan. Again!

"John, I need you to take your team to 18th St. NW, Washington, District of Columbia. Estimated time of arrival should be four to five hours. Take the department's car. Once you get there, analyze everything you find. It's the same killer. I've already taken care of the jurisdictional paperwork myself, so don't worry about that," says Stephan, and that's all I hear from him.

The guy hangs up the phone, and leaves me in the dark. As per usual, he instructs and passes the duty of organizing everything else to me. This means it's my turn to call everyone, and break his bad news to them. With one last groan, I pick up the phone again and start doing my 'duty'.

And whilst, I'm not going to detail their responses, believe me, they were not happy at all.

Six hours later we are at the place indicated by my wonderful boss. During the trip, the only thing I was able to think about was how to annoy Stephan. Honestly, it was all I could think about, so as not to fall back asleep.

I need another holiday and who knows, maybe even a transfer. At this point, I can't take it anymore and neither can anyone else. The team is very upset with him. Especially Jenny, who starts suggesting possible punishments for our 'so sweet' boss and I note down a reminder to never to get on her bad side.

We get it, we are professionals, but first and foremost we are people, and we deserve the respect of a leader, not that of a commanding boss who doesn't care about anything besides himself. I've had enough!

The best thing about the journey is that we get to stop a few times to replenish our growling stomachs, who are clearly not happy about the early wake up.

The crime scene is located in a small house, cordoned off and surrounded by police cars and the press. Great. More people are involved and wanting answers to questions that we don't even know how to start talking about. What a great way to start the day!

We put on our special, professional suits in a hurry. Jenny re-ties her ponytail and we go inside. We climb the stairs to the master bedroom and are gratefully greeted by the Captain of the Washington homicide headquarters. He is a very friendly, well-built man, who fashions a special suit under his toned muscles and rustled, yet perfectly styled hair.

"We have been waiting for you," he says straightening his suit and shaking each of our hands in turn. "I thank you very much for being able to come here so quickly, and on such short notice. I'm Captain Jack Davis, I spoke to Stephan, and he said he'd send his best men right away. He's a real pro, that man. Moves everything so quickly. I hear he's very well positioned for promotion," he says as he outstretches his hand to shake ours.

"Thank you, Captain, for your kind words. That's what we all hope for, that he will be promoted very quickly," I reply wryly, with a hint of subtle sarcasm snaking its way through the words.

Nobody notices it, of course.

This is unbelievable, the guy looks great in front of everyone. Everyone sees him as the 'hero', the 'professional who works tirelessly on troubling cases', 'the man who doesn't stop until all the work is done'. Everyone sees him as a good person, while he's nothing but a jerk. And here we are, with the early start on our day off, whilst he is nowhere to be seen, probably bathing in his eternal glory.

"We were alerted by a friend of the victim's who had been invited to dinner at her house. When she knocked on the door and saw that the light in the victims bedroom was on and no one was answering, she thought her friend had fallen, but it never crossed her mind that she could've died." The captain explains, raising his eyebrow in thought.

"Can you give us some information about the victim? Anything that you think could help with the case?" Jennifer asks, biting her lip, thoughtfully and tucking a loose strand of hair behind her ponytail.

"Yes, of course. Her name is Margaret Brown. She used to work as a nurse at the paraplegic hospital. All the reports and references only speak of greatness. Patients comment on her effective work and her superiors say only inspiring words about her work," says the captain, reading directly off a small tablet in his hands. Once he is done with the update, he hands the device to Jennifer for her to have a closer look for herself.

I listen to what he says, and my eyes begin to analyze the scene, as I drift my focus away from him.

"John, look at the painting. It's the same one!" Jennifer exclaims eagerly, pointing directly at the all too familiar painting. "Again, the one with the red hand and the black background with a face."

"Damn it, again! Michael, check for fingerprints that match the previous ones. Enter them on the laptop," I say eagerly, although I'm not sure how much closer we'll get this time.

Michael moves us away from the scene and starts looking for fingerprints everywhere, searching high and low. On the ceiling, the floor, under the bed. Everywhere.

In the next room we discuss what we know with the captain and our progress in the investigation. Twenty minutes later, Michael calls us and motions us to follow him.

"Captain, John, Jenny, come here; I've found some relevant information about the footprints," he says excitedly.

We enter the room hurriedly but in a professional way, and he shows us the exact spot where he found them. Again, footprints of the same foot, a size forty-two and a lot of handprints. In the other scenarios there were three types, those of Cameron, Mayka and Joseph. Now there is a different one as well. Michael has labelled them on the ground and is taking photographs.

"I had the third one analyzed and you'll never guess who it's from. It's from the driver. The one who was killed the other day. How on earth is that possible?" He looks around at each of us, his eyes landing on me the longest, but I can't offer a single plausible explanation. Once again, the killer has managed to catch us off guard. Damn it!"

The four of us look at each other and shake our heads in frustration. This doesn't make any sense. The killer is leaving us clues for a reason. But why? Why does he want us to know now that the driver was also at the scene of the crime? Even though the driver is dead, so he couldn't have made those fingerprints could he?

We are dealing with a psychopath. That has been clear from the moment we started investigating. And this criminal keeps leaving us paintings. It seems like they are part of a puzzle. But what puzzle is it? And what is the key?

Is he trying to get in our heads? What does he want with the dead?

"I want the cameras in the area to be analyzed," I say furiously, with a tone of seriousness as I dictate the following instructions. "I want to know every single vehicle that was on this road before and after the time of the crime. I want data from mobile operators and phone numbers of people who were in the house or in the vicinity. I want all kinds of information. Anything you can get." I order impatiently, as I run my hand through my hair back and forth.

We stayed at the scene of the crime until 10 pm, looking for more evidence and questioning neighbors.

But no one saw anything. How surprising!

Disheartened, we collect everything we found, and say goodbye to the Captain as we go to a nearby hotel.

We're so tired that we eat dinner in our rooms and go to bed as soon as we've showered.

I lie down, and my eyelids can't stay open; I pull them together and my vision disappears pitch black darkness enveloping it instead as sleep finally captures me.

Chapter 11

John – New leads

I'm once again in the peaceful oblivion that is sleep when a very familiar ringtone startles me and forces my eyes to snap open.

"Don't bother me, not again! Go away!" I rage kicking my bedsheets off and punching the bed in anger.

I am tempted to ignore it but I know that I can't and so reluctantly I accept Stephan's phone call and his screechy voice fills my ears.

"John, I need you to go with your team to the Pennsylvanian Apartments in Pennsylvania. Estimate another five hours. It's the same killer. Don't worry about jurisdiction either, I've already got that covered," says Stephan.

The guy hangs up the phone. Again! Once more leaving me without a chance to reply. Now, to wake up the team. Again!

"Hello, beautiful. Good morning, it's me, the prince of your dreams," I say to Jennifer, dreamily batting my eyelashes, as if she could see me through the speaker of her phone.

"The demon of my nightmares, you mean." A calm voice corrects from the other side of the phone. "What's up, did your best friend call you?" Jennifer asks with a laugh.

"You nailed it," I say sarcastically. "We have to go to Pennsylvania."

"Okay. I'll shower and meet you in the lobby in thirty minutes," Jennifer replies, with a sigh and then hangs up.

I plug in the next phone number smirking as I think of something hilarious to say. Nothing comes to mind.

"Hello, Michael, surprise! Guess who told me we have to go to Pennsylvania?" I ask, trying to conceal my frustrated sarcasm.

"To Pennsylvania? Quit messing around and don't call me at this hour to play jokes on me. What's the matter, you can't sleep because you left your stuffed animals at home?" Michael says with a tone of frustration.

"Orders from our dear boss, I'm afraid," I reply, choosing to ignore the stuffed animal comment.

A harsh sigh sounds from the end of the phone. "All right. Give me thirty minutes and I'll meet you downstairs," Michael replies with a chuckle.

Michael and Jenny are lovely people, goody-two-shoes one might say; they rarely say anything bad, whereas I'm more irritable and have a short fuse. But I guess someone has to say something and be the voice of everyone's thoughts.

We meet in the lobby, after 30 minutes. I have already paid with the police card to cover the expenses of our short stay. Luke from accounting will be here to ask for receipts and details. What a guy, he doesn't laugh at anything. I bet he goes out to dinner with his calculator and his mobile phone to make sure all the receipts add up and there's not a single unjustified expense.

We leave the hotel, get into the lab van and head off to see our next victim. And no one says anything through it all.

The truth is that we are puzzled: how can the driver's fingerprints be found if he was recently killed and buried? I can't think of asking Jessica for a new exhumation, she'll think I'm losing my mind. I can't do anything to compromise our dinner and remove me from her list of acquaintances. Maybe I'll suggest it to her during the evening if she brings up the conversation. Just a subtle comment, nothing too elaborate.

The journey comes to an end, we leave the vehicle in the underground car park so as not to alert the neighborhood nor the press. If they were to find out about another murder, it would generate more pressure than we have now, and that's the last thing we need. At the reception of the flats, we are met by the captain of the Pennsylvanian homicide headquarters.

"Thank you for coming so quickly; we're sorry we had to get you up so early," a young woman of mid-twenties says. She strides towards us, her short, lightly dyed pink hair bouncing with each step. A gold badge over her navy uniform catches my eye as she continues speaking. "I'm Rose White, the city's homicide captain. Please come with me. You must be John, Jennifer and Michael. I've been informed of your experience in similar cases," Rose says as she introduces herself and shakes our hands. Her eyes lock with mine as we meet and I am surprised by the intense greyness to them as well as the great confidence and knowledge that swirl inside them.

"By the way, I take it your boss is a special guy. I graduated with a degree in psychology so I greatly enjoy psychoanalyzing people." She continues.

"Oh no, here we go again." I whisper softly to Jenny who is standing by my side.

"I get the impression that he doesn't have many friends and that he likes to show off in order to be promoted. Am I right?" she asks, and she smiles at the sight of our dropped jaws. "As you can see, I truly am a psychologist." She shrugs and smiles sympathetically, and I, for one, am glad someone finally managed to unmask the façade our dear Stephan puts on.

"Let's just say he's a very special kind of guy," Michael replies as he agrees with her, nodding his head in response.

"Thank you, Michael, for confirming that." Rose laughs, fixing a strand of her wavy pink hair behind her ear with a smile that told me that she had suspected this to be the case from the moment she had met our boss. I smile at her and instantly reach the conclusion that I like her.

"The crime scene is on the 24th floor. Let's go upstairs, then shall we?" Rose says as she motions us to follow her upstairs.

"The victim is a renowned transplant surgeon," she says, her heels clicking on the glass floor as we walk. "His specialty is the heart, but he also has extensive experience in other organs: liver, hands, corneas … The list goes on. He was very well known in both the scientific and the university world. He was dedicated to the collection of donations in the area of organ transplants. A person loved and adored by all, so his death will be a tremendous loss, felt by all. A real tragedy, which we hope you can get to the bottom of." She informs us, nodding towards the lift, as we all huddle in and take ourselves to the 24th floor.

We exit the lift, one by one, and walk down the corridor to the front door of the victim's apartment. Rose knocks it gently with a very specific set of taps and a policeman in a special suit like ours opens it for us. As we enter through the doorway we begin to analyze the scene and take samples.

We enter the same scene as before. As if the nightmare is on infinite repeat. The victim lies on the bed, hands turned over, palms facing us, eyes wide open but unseeing. The punctures are identical to the previous ones. I draw the conclusion that one puncture must be to administer the drug that kills the victim while the others are to draw blood. As usual we look at the wall and once again there it is, another painting with the little hand showing us the palm and the face in the background. Everything is a true copy of what we have been seeing and if it weren't for the two different bodies I would have assumed it was the same crime. I feel a sweat break and fidget nervously. I now see the danger even more clearly than before and I'm worried. I don't know what we're going to do now.

Jennifer looks at everything, examining every detail, as perhaps today we may find something that we missed before. Michael very kindly sends us out of the room. And by that I mean, that he cornered off the area with police tape and made sure that we stayed on our side. He needs to analyze the footprints, the body. Just the normal procedure that awaits him every single time. Jenny takes photographs and I tell Rose the details we know.

"You're right, John. This is strange, it seems that the murderer is playing with you, that he wants to confuse you. Why does he kill them and then extract blood from different points? He must be someone with medical knowledge, no one would be able to do such a crime without a medical background. Especially in a manner that is so clean and precise." Rose begins to think out loud, tapping a finger to her lip in thought.

"I agree, Rose." I begin, looking at her. "But why does he choose these victims in particular? They're in different cities and states, they couldn't be less related to one another. Why does he go through all that trouble."

"Good point, John, and I honestly have no idea." Rose adds. "We should look at the video cameras in the building as well as the ones on the roads, highways, and streets. Anything can be useful." Rose taps the edge of her nose pensively as she gives out instructions to people around the room. She digs out a mobile from her pocket and starts tapping on it continuously as she informs certain specialists.

"John, Rose, I've found something." Michael reports from the inside of the room, shouting for us to come over. Rose pushes her mobile into her pocket and we both rush towards Michael.

We duck under the police tape and enter the room. Michael turns off the light, and before any of us can object he shines a green torch on the floor.

We look at the floor, and at first we don't see anything. But then Rose gasps and we notice what Michael was beckoning for us to look at. There are small finger-like footprints moving across the floor of the room, along the walls and the ceiling. And they all lead to the air-conditioning vent.

Rose quietly places a finger over her lip, indicating us to stay quiet and goes to the laundry room in the kitchen. Michael and I look at each other with wide eyes until Rose returns with a ladder, which she places under the vent. She motions me forward and I climb the ladder, reaching for my flashlight. With another flashlight, we shine a white light, and look around the vent to discover that something isn't right. I can't quite put my finger on what until Rose points at a corner, her forehead wrinkling with surprise.

That's when I see it.

One of the screws is … missing.

"Look, here it is," whispers Jennifer as to not make a sound and she almost gives me a heart attack with her sudden appearance. She holds her hand out, showing us the metal piece in her grasp. "I found it on the floor."

Quickly, Jenny grabs a screwdriver from one of the tool boxes we always carry. She moves me off the ladder and climbs it herself, using the tool to unscrew the three remaining screws on the vent, pulls it away from her and places it on the table as quietly as she can but not quite managing it as a soft noise echoes and she flinches.

Suddenly, we hear a noise coming from inside the vent. Something is moving along the metal panels of the AC vent.

"Quickly. Someone's here. Let me get in, Jenny. Your husband would never forgive me if anything happened to you," I say, smiling, while she playfully glares at me, and I beckon her to move faster.

I take Jenny by the hand and gently lower her down the ladder. I climb up, holding the ladder with one hand and the flashlight with the other. Once I'm at the top of the steps I peek inside and as I shine the light inside I see something small moving at high speed.

"It must be a rat; from the size and the way it moves. We need to bring the robot to explore further. Let's go and get it from the van. Quickly," I say as adrenaline curls in my veins.

The robot is a small mobile object with wheels, a television camera and deployable arms which allows it to deploy a multitude of cameras – both color and infrared. It can reach a speed of about 60 km/h, whilst also autonomously collecting samples and taking videos in the dark for several hours.

We put the robot through the air hatch and Jenny rushes over to me, grabbing the small color camera and connecting it to the computer monitor, so we can start to see what is going on inside. I rush to turn on the lights as Jenny sets up the screens in the living room to let Michael make progress on the investigation. The robot allows us to see the fingerprints and transmits them back to the computer so we can see who they belong to. The image shows hand marks on the ducts and everyone is quick to lean forward and stare at the screen as the monitor identifies the handprints and displays the faces of their owners. Jenny gives me a confused look, which I'm sure is reflected on my own face. How can it be?

They belong to the driver and Cameron.

We increase the speed of the robot, but we have to be careful, we can't go too fast, as the turns are ninety degrees, and hard to control.

Jenny is the one who controls it. She spent three months in the Army, taking courses that trained her for this specific operation. Her hands move swiftly as she eyes the screen with the pure determination of catching a glimpse of whatever is in there.

"Look! There's something there but I can't see what it is!" says Jenny, her eyebrows pressed close together in concentration, as she shows us what she means on the monitor.

"Come on, Jenny! Accelerate!" I urge her, placing a reassuring hand on her shoulder. "That rat must be what's leaving the trail. Look at the monitor."

It is very dark with a million clouds of dust obscuring our vision so that we can't see properly. So much for a luxury flat when the AC doesn't work properly.

Suddenly, the barrel holes of an automatic pistol appear, pointing at the screen, and it fires several shots, destroying the robot and the cameras. I squint at the monitor, trying to understand what is happening.

"What happened?" I ask.

"The robot has been shot; the killer must be in the ducts." Jenny exclaims in excitement.

"Call reception downstairs and have them locate the maintenance staff. We must find out where this AC vent ends!" I smile and tilt my head back as I laugh. "We can take him! We can finally catch this psychopath once and for all!"

Rose radios the police officers she has in the building to be positioned at all entrances and exits. She then calls headquarters for backups, and instructs vehicles and personnel to block off the streets, to corner the killer.

"We've got him surrounded; he's not going to get away from here. Not this time," I say cheerfully, clearly jinxing the whole thing.

Suddenly, the power cuts off.

"What's going on?" Jennifer says, as we are left in complete darkness.

I make my way towards the sound of her voice, shielding my head as I wait for something worse to happen. After a few minutes I sigh with relief, jinking the whole thing once again as a loud BANG sounds from nearby.

"Take cover!" Jenny orders, and we all dive towards the ground as the gunshot echoes all around us.

Chapter 12

Henry – Stuck in the tunnel of cold

"Sir, we have a problem!" a nervous voice comes in through my earpiece, and I am snapped back into reality. I quickly put the glasses back on, that I have taken off momentarily to rub my eyes from the lack of sleep that has been depriving me these past couple of days. As soon as I do, I get a more precise shocking view of what my hands are seeing. But everything looks dark.

"We've been spotted, and frankly things are getting complicated." Driver begins, as I see Cameron scrambling ahead from him. "Fortunately, we haven't been seen yet, but if we don't get out soon, our whole plan is going to go down the drain." Driver continues, his voice hasty and worried, mirroring my own discomfort. My plan cannot fail. We have come so far already. And I'm only just getting started.

"Boss, we need you to give us a hand to get out of here. Ha, ha, ha, ha. Get it, I said hand?" says Cameron in between giggles.

"Don't worry, boys, I'm on it," I say as I step on the van's accelerator as hard as I can.

"Frank, Cameron and Driver are inside the building, find their exact location and find the shortest exit," I say to Frank. "Put this on a 3D hologram and send it to their watches. Monitor the security forces through their radios and mobile signals, and alert me of any sudden changes."

I think for a second, trying to think of a way to delay the security forces in the building and come up with an idea. "Turn off the lights in the building." It is a pretty simple trick but it will have to do. "Tell me you have an exit route, mark it on a hologram image of the building, and send it to my glasses so I can direct them where to go exactly." I tell Frank, who takes less than a minute to send everything my way.

Frank sends everything my way and I smile. "Fantastic, Frank; good work, I can see it." I thank him.

"Cameron, Driver, I know where you have to go." I tell them, as I give them further instructions of how to help them escape, as they begin to interpret the 3D hologram that I've had Frank send to them directly.

"Frank, activate the drone on the roof to pick them up and bring them back to the van." I order.

And just like that, as if everything starts falling into place. My rescue plan is put into action. The lights of the building turn off and the police find themselves in the dark.

"That should keep them busy for a little while longer." I tell my hands, as I see them scurrying through the vent, hastily moving to escape from the peril we are in.

With my glasses on I can see exactly what is going on inside the vent: it is as if I was there. I live through my hands. And right now I have control of where they are and where they will be going. I will not let them down.

Cameron and Driver head for the exit; the clock gives them the hologram and the path to follow, following from the directions that I gave them previously. The tunnel takes them to a downward-facing conduit, which is more than 20 meters high. They jump into the void and, when they have traveled some distance, they press a button on their glove that opens a parachute. Once they have reached the ground, they press the button again and the parachute retracts automatically. The hologram shows them a grate, which can be opened from inside and outside. It is the access way to a maintenance room with various machines.

Cameron and Driver have night-vision functionality, so they can easily move around without being seen, at least that is what I hope. The hologram shows them a window as the only way out, and that is where they go. The two hands approach the window and with the laser built into the watch, make a hole in the rectangular-shaped glass. As the laser cuts through the glass, a hole is revealed and both hands squeeze their way out to exit the flat. The hands move towards the drone that is waiting for them on the roof. The device contains a small container with a lifting door that opens, and they climb inside. The drone takes off and disappears into the darkness.

Suddenly, on the ascent, it encounters the helicopter that the police have sent to cover the area. The pilot does not notice the drone (thankfully!) and it disappears between the buildings, as if we were never there.

"We were lucky, man, we almost got caught," says Driver with great relief but also laughing at the fun of being chased.

"Yes, we came very close, but the boss solved the problem very quickly," says Cameron.

"Guys, good work. That was close, huh? Did you get the blood and the necessary material for all the organs?" I ask from the radio on the watch.

"Yes. Mission accomplished. See you in 376," says Driver.

"No problem; I'll drive that section, but then you go on. Okay?" I respond.

"OK, done, man. Today was a blast," says Driver, putting a 'thumbs up' gesture which is mirrored in my own glasses …

"Frank, switch on the apartment lights. Let's give our police friends a break," I say. "I think we've left them in the dark for long enough."

But this is only the beginning. We have a long road ahead of us. And if we want to get there, we're going to have to throw the police off our scent in the near future. They need to be behind me. They must not get in our way. Because if they keep searching for too long, they'll jeopardize everything I've been working so hard to achieve my whole life. And I can't let anyone stop me. I need to do this. I must do this. There is no other way. It has to be done. One way or another.

Chapter 13

John – An unexplained escape

The light comes on in the apartment block and all of our agents appear to be hidden behind the room's furniture. As the lights come on and my eyes adjust to the brightness, I'm able to see the whole scene. I see Michael, Rose and Jenny huddled behind the sofa. I signal Rose to go to the door carefully while I cover her. Rose looks and sees that there is no one in the room. Jenny covers her too and makes sure there is no one in the corners of the room. Once the whole house has been explored, we check that there are no intruders and enter the hallway where we check that everything looks normal.

"What happened? It looked like we had seen someone and then the lights just suddenly went off. What happened?" asks Jenny, shaking her head and letting her hair loose, attempting to retie it once more in frustration.

"That was crazy. The murderer must have had people on the inside, otherwise how else would he have been able to turn off all the lights in the apartment," I add.

"Go to the light control room and investigate exactly what happened. Ask the maintenance crew if they know anything and ask whether anyone saw someone missing or if there had been a change of shifts. See if you can find anything out of the ordinary." Rose orders her colleagues, with a strict, imposing voice. I stare at her.

"Wait. My colleagues tell me that the power cut was building-wide." I motion to Rose, who then modifies her instructions to the team.

"They must have someone else working for them, they can't possibly be working alone. We were about to find him, we were so close." Jenny starts and her frown deepens. "Plus, he seems very athletic, after all how else would he fit through the vents? I don't like it. This criminal we're dealing with is extremely dangerous." I place a comforting hand on her shoulder and turn to Rose, who is staring at the vent, deep in thought, twirling a strand of her hair absentmindedly.

"Rose, would you mind giving the order of securing the area and confining all employees and residents to the flat." She snaps to attention, her eyes steely with determination. "No one is allowed to enter nor leave the building until we have questioned absolutely everyone." I instruct and she nods, leaving with long strides.

"It's going to be a long day," I mumble, rubbing my aching head and sighing loudly.

At that moment my mobile phone rings.

"Oh, no, if it isn't the one who's never here," I protest.

We all look at each other and shake our heads in dismay.

"John, how can you be so useless?" Our boss's heated voice sounds from the other end of the line. "I'm seeing on the news that the killer is back in Pennsylvania. You're incapable of keeping it a secret. You're useless! I want this case solved in 48 hours!" Stephan screams more and hangs up on me, leaving me unable to reply and therefore angering me even more.

"And the guy hangs up on me again!" I say not even managing a shout as I am truly exhausted. "Looks like we have a very long day ahead of us. Let's get to work. Someone order food and coffee."

"Lots of coffee." Michael agrees, smirking at me.

We look at each other, instantly agreeing that, yes, a lot of coffee would be needed for we have very long, stressful, frustrating hours ahead of us as we try to advance in this impossibly complicated case and try to comprehend the criminal behind it, who might very likely be messing around with us.

Chapter 14

John – A lunch with my best friend

Many hours have passed since the team and I have had a rest but Jenny finally speaks up, saying what we have all been dying to say: it is time for a break. I must admit that we have gotten nowhere in the past three hours and are absolutely exhausted. I wouldn't be surprised if I were to fall asleep right now, as I wave goodbye to Michael and exit the workspace we have been in all morning. I feel myself slipping but I remember my plans for lunch and are instantly wide awake. I open the car door and get inside quick as a flash, stepping on the gas and speeding away, afraid of arriving late.

 I enter the La Pierna restaurant on Seventh Avenue, one of the best in New York. It's Spanish and my friends recommended it to me when we were in Segovia. Bernardino, Marta's cousin, is the owner and chef, and he decided to open it after emigrating to the United States years ago. Having previously owned a famous restaurant in Sigüenza, a Segovian province, he took the chance to bring Spanish culture and taste by creating a new restaurant which would be highly valued by the specialized press and its loyal customers. The menu includes roast lamb, suckling pig, torreznos and other local delicacies. The waiting list is so long, it's almost impossible to get a table. But my friendship with Bernardino allows me to always have a table available. As a thank you, I protect him from mafia gangs that may want to extort money from him, as it is common knowledge among the gang leaders that I often come here. So one could say that I scare them off.

 Manuel, the maître d', is Bernardino's cousin and Marta's husband's brother. He is a professional like no other. When he recommends a dish, you order it without question. When the dish is served, you close your eyes in pleasure as you take small bites, wishing for the rush of flavor to never end. A normal Spanish meal consists of a first course, a second course, dessert, coffee and a glass of liquor at the end. It is a time when people, families and friends enjoy a nice conversation and an amazing meal together.

"Hi, John, how are you? We've missed you; you haven't been here for over three weeks. We thought you'd become a fast-food junkie." Manuel laughs.

Manuel is a short person, barely a meter and a half tall. He has a growing moustache, and is one of those guys who has just four lone hairs and always combs his hair in a straight line. He makes a lot of jokes about his baldness; he is very funny and always in a good mood.

"Can I get you a beer, some olives and some torreznos? They're as good as always," says Manuel, putting the ends of his five fingers together and kissing them in a way famous Italian chefs do when describing something delicious.

"Not at the moment, no, I have to wait and be polite. I'll have company today," I reply with a rueful face.

"Whoa, stop right there. Don't tell me that Master Don Juan has finally met a beautiful lady?" Manuel laughs as I become embarrassed and start fidgeting with my tie. "Who is it? Don't worry, don't worry. For dessert we have dulce de leche and some torrijas that will make her fall in love with you. We'll make sure she remembers this day for the rest of her life." Manuel laughs as he heads towards the lobby, after telling me my table. He leaves stating that there is someone there waiting for him.

"Can I help you, Miss? My name is Manuel, and I am the maître d' at La Pierna."

The receptionist gently removes her coat and hands her a token.

"There is a reservation under the name of John, my name is Pris," a cheerful voice says.

"Oh, you're the guest?" says Manuel with a cheeky smile and a raised eyebrow. "Don't worry, we'll treat you like a queen,"

Suddenly he comes up to her ear and says loud enough for me to hear: "You must be a very important person to John, because he's been able to wait for you without an appetizer, and believe me when I say I've never seen him do that with anyone. Between you and me, he's a hungry eater. Waiting for a good snack and a beer is torture for him." Manuel laughs.

Pris also laughs and asks him with suspicious eyes: "Does he come here a lot with other women?"

"Señorita, señorita, you want John to take the floor from me." Manuel laughs again.

They arrive at my table and I pretend I haven't been listening to their conversation, acting surprised when I feel a light tap on my shoulder. Pris comes over and kisses me on the cheek, surprising me so much that I jump a little in my seat.

"Hello, handsome, long time no see. We have a lot to tell each other," she whispers in my ear. I turn towards the sound and smirk. There in front of me is my guest, looking as beautiful as ever.

I smile and stand up.

"Nice dress, Pris." I tell her and her cheeks turn a faint shade of pink, the same color as her open necked dress. "Sit down, please. I hope you like the place, the food and the company. Of course."

"Thank you very much, John. I'm sure it will be unforgettable," says Pris with a kind smile.

Manuel comes over and brings us some torreznos, some very large olives accompanied by a beer and a dry vermouth, one of Pris's favorite drinks. After a few minutes of lively conversation, Manuel leaves us the menu and we choose a salad of piquillo peppers with ventresca, Jabugo ham, Manchego cheese and two legs of suckling lamb.

Pris and I talk, we laugh and we talk some more, but at one point Pris grabs my hand, looks me straight in the eye and says: "I know you well, and when your eyelid twitches, it's because a case is stressing you out. You know we share information and work together where we can. Let me know what's bothering you," she says with a calming voice, eyeing me cautiously. She bites her lip. "Is it the case of the serial killer?"

"Yes." I admit. "We have nothing. We were close in Pennsylvania, but he got away. It's very strange. We found the fingerprints of three deceased people, the last one being those of the murdered driver. We also keep finding them at each crime scene, but not in the last one. The dead were loved by their colleagues and families. They did not lead dark lives, nor did we find any abnormal transactions or debts. From what we know, no one would've wanted them dead. We are very clueless at the moment. And then there is the issue of the paintings and the modus operandi by which he kills the victims. Things can't get more complicated." I explain then continue.

"We don't understand why he is taking blood from them. We exhumed one of the graves and the DNA was that of the victim. We thought he wasn't dead. We all thought so, but that would have been too easy."

"Maybe he made a copy of the fingerprints and left the trail to throw me off the scent and buy him some time. I'm investigating the possible links between the victims, I don't think he selected them at random. I think I found a sequence pattern: male, female, male, so the next victim should be female," I continue to tell Pris, who is listening intently to what I say. "I don't know, it may be a criteria. Normally, a killer of this type looks for victims with a common trait. But why the pictures? What does it mean?"

"Tell me about them, John. Do you have any photos?"

"Yes." I scroll down my billions of photos on my phone until I find one. "Look at this one. The painting depicts a red palm and a face behind it in black. The features of the face are not well defined, but from the eyes I'd say it's a woman. If in one murder we find the right hand, in the next we find the left."

Suddenly there's a phone call; it's Michael.

"Hello, John, can you talk?"

"Yes, of course; I'm with Pris. No problem. Tell me."

"The autopsy reports have been sent to us. All the victims have been injected with pentobarbital to cause an uncomplicated and nonviolent death. None of them were victims of violence. There are no marks indicating that they were forced, there are no signs of beatings and it seems that the perpetrator does not make his victims suffer. There are no traces of drugs or chloroform, no gaseous substances to induce sleep in the victims. This is where it gets interesting. I believe that the victims were awake when the injection was given. The surgeon wore a wristwatch and we have accessed his records.

"In his sleeping hours, they decreased; the data indicates that they went down to zero. If we subtract the average time it takes to take effect from the time the clock shows the last pulse, we can deduce that the victim died at 22:30." Michael reports by phone.

I hang up the phone and tell Pris about the conversation with Michael.

"Pentobarbital? I wrote an article about it quite recently actually. Here it is only supplied in hospitals and under strict restrictions. Not just anyone can access it. Perhaps you can investigate if there's been some kind of theft of it recently in nearby hospitals. If there is no theft, the person must be someone with access to a hospital, either as a patient or employee. Most probably the latter," says Pris, passing a hand through her hair in concentration, as she gets into the details of how to proceed.

"I'm going to send a message to Dilya and have her put out a request to all the hospitals in the state to see if there have been any pentobarbital thefts or inventory errors recently," I say, with a tone of hope, wishing that Pris' intellect is getting us closer to the truth.

"Good idea, John. But how is it possible that there was no evidence of violence? Maybe the victim gave it to him, maybe he wanted to euthanize himself for some reason, maybe our killer was contacted and helped him die, or maybe he put him to sleep with something we don't know about and then took his life. What is clear is that he doesn't want to cause any suffering, that's why he uses pentobarbital. This is my theory, what do you think?"

A hand touches my shoulder and I turn around.

"A little dessert, partner?" asks Manuel.

"Yes, I think you've come at the right time. Let me choose for you, Pris. I want to set a high standard. We'll have a dulce de leche and some torrijas." I indicate to Manuel with a smile and wink my right eye.

We thoroughly enjoy the dessert, the coffee and the pacharán. We keep talking about the case, and the more we discuss, the more theories Pris uncovers. Pris is an excellent woman and a great professional. She always helps me toss ideas around. Tomorrow she will go to Pennsylvania to investigate on her own. A journalist is often able to go lengths unreachable by the police. It's great for me that we're friends, she'll be able to keep me updated.

We finish eating and I take her outside to call a taxi. Before saying goodbye, she kisses me on the cheek and says: "Thank you very much for the food, it was delicious."

"I wanted to ask you a question, Pris. How is the reporting on your parents going? Have you found out anything else?"

"Yes, John, I was at the university where they worked." Her eyes twinkle as she speaks and a smile is plastered on her lips. "Several of their colleagues told me that they were collaborating on an experiment with other scientists to find a cure for memory loss. The project was funded by a major company. They will give me more details, but with all this business I don't have much time to continue with my own family stuff at the moment. Moving on, what are you having for dinner tonight with the judge?"

"It's impossible to hide anything from you. How did you find out?" I ask with a roguish grin.

"One that has eyes and ears everywhere knows things." She smirks, proudly. "I think she's counting the hours. I think she likes you. Next time we'll meet for dinner, and I'll pay the bill, okay?" Pris suggests.

"It will be a pleasure, my dear friend. By the way, as soon as this is over and I have a little time, I'll give you a hand with your parents' report. I promise."

After carefully watching Pris enter the taxi, I decide to go back to the office so that I can complete the paperwork piled on my desk. But as I leave I get the nagging feeling as if someone is watching me …

Chapter 15

Henry – First-hand information

Meanwhile, as John was having fun in his little lunch in la Pierna restaurant, I had plans of my own. In between tables and right above John were my secret agents that I had sent to watch over him. I was leaving no corner unturned. There was no way that I would leave John out of my sight. He was getting too close.

"Sir, I have two of them in sight. I've found a seat in the VIP box." Cameron tells me from somewhere above.

Cameron is hidden in the air-conditioning vent once more, and with his camera he records and transmits the scene to my glasses for me to see.

"Be careful, Cameron, don't get caught." I warn with a serious voice.

"Can you believe it? John found a sequence pattern: male, female, male, so the next victim should be female, eh, Henry? Ha, ha; for gender. Man, Henry, look on the bright side: they're not going to accuse you of not complying with the 50/50 rule. You're not sexist!" Cameron tells me laughing his head off.

"I hadn't really thought about it, but I can follow that pattern in the next search, if they really want me to!" I laugh. I can't believe that this was what they had pieced together maybe just to spite them I'd make my next victim a male.

I continue listening to the conversation between the lieutenant and the reporter for some time though I get bored quickly until they mention a watch.

"Chief, did you hear that about the watch? It seems I underestimate their intelligence. We didn't realize to take his watch with us. The truth is, we were a little short for time last time. I think the guy had an alarm mechanism; maybe if his watch stopped registering his heart rate, he'd call 911 to come and check on him. He must have been a little bit paranoid," says Cameron quietly from where he is still hidden in the ceiling.

"You're right, next time we'll ask them to take off their watch and give it to us. We were a bit too reckless last time. We acted like amateurs. This can't happen again, Cameron, we made a big mistake if they piece together what happened out plan will be ruined ..." I shake my head in disgust as I rethink all of our planning sessions and preparations. I rub my face with my hands in frustration as I start to think ahead of what we should do next.

"Amateurs, yes," says Cameron, still recording and listening to the scene below him. His eyes scan the vent and he adjusts himself to listen to the conversation better.

"Yuck, boss, this vent is super dirty. Why can't we eavesdrop somewhere nicer next time like in a perfume shop or at a hairdresser. Or even better: a nail salon! I could get my nails done red! Wait no! Blue! No! YELLOW! Yes, yes! What do you say, boss?" Cameron asks me. I laugh and shake my head, amused by his sense of humor and I can only imagine the putrid smell inside the vent.

"Funny. Now stop talking!" I order. "You're interrupting everything John is saying!"

"Sorry, boss," Cameron whispers, then speaks loudly again. "Speaking about interrupting, you know one time I was listening in on some of the other hand's conversations and I heard the most interesting gossip." He stops abruptly, probably realizing that he should be quiet. "Sorry, boss."

"Cameron you can't disobey me, start talking about gossip and not tell me what it is," I say, fully intrigued, but just as I was about to hear the news, I look into my glasses and see John and the reporter get up and exit. I frown, saddened by their departure and the end of my present fun.

"Send the footage to me, Cameron."

"Sure thing, boss!" He declares and a second later, I get the full video of the police officer's lunch. I replay the full length of it and watch it with interest, especially at the theories sprung by the reporter. What was her name? Pris? Her theories are truly fascinating.

As I see that John is clearly never going to leave the case, an idea starts to form. It is time to speak with him myself. But not as Henry Silverstone.

As HAInds.

Chapter 16

John – A special dinner

Before I know it, it's time to go to La Gamba y el Pulpo, another Spanish restaurant, specializing in seafood and fish. In the evening, something light is best, seafood with white or rosé wine. I really like the judge, she is friendly, funny, and has a very strong yet flirtatious character.

The first time I saw her in court, my stomach tingled, and did a thousand flips of pure nerves. When I went to testify, the smell of her perfume drove me crazy. I couldn't speak. For once in my life, I was speechless. I remember she was laughing, and I was as red as a tomato. After a few minutes and a drink of water, I was able to say something. I think she liked me from that moment on. She had been told about my strong character: indomitable, tough, determined. But she immediately discovered the lamb deep within me.

This time I meet her in the foyer of the restaurant. It has a bar where people drink wines from Spain. I love them; they are excellent. After many years, I appreciate the taste of Ribeiro, Albariño, wines from Rioja, Ribera del Duero and other areas. With each drink of the wine or beer they serve you a tapa. My favorite is definitely either the boiled potatoes with octopus on top, a piece of Galician empanada or some almejitas (small clams). I'll wait for Jessica at the bar with an Albariño and a portion of cockle empanada.

We had arranged to meet at 20:30. It's 21:15 and I smell a familiar scent of perfume, I turn around and see Jessica. She is radiant, gorgeous. Her hair is loose, shiny, and golden, and she wears a short cobalt blue dress that matches the blue eyeshadow on her eyelids. I hope my voice isn't shaking as she looks at me, smiles and kisses me on the cheek.

"I'm sorry I'm late, I got caught up with a case, but I managed to get away in the end." Jessica smiles as she talks to me.

"The important thing is that you're here. By the way, I love how beautiful you look and how well the dress suits you. Would you like a glass of wine?"

"I am thirsty; yes, please." She responds as she smooths out the tiny wrinkles on her dress.

I order an Albariño and the maître d' accompanies us to a reserved table. The view is spectacular, the night makes the city glow and lowers our defenses.

"I love this place; the wine is very good. I see it's a Spanish restaurant, isn't it?" Jessica asks inquisitively.

"Yes, the food is from north of Galicia, where the variation in seafood, meat and fish is plentiful. It rains a lot in that area, it's very green and beautiful. I've never been, but my friends in Spain recommended it to me and they've sent me YouTube links to see what it's like and, believe me, it's incredibly beautiful. Just like you," I say, whilst I blush with shyness, realizing how desperate that last sentence sounded.

"I agree," says Jessica, with a slight blush in her cheek as she glows with radiant beauty.

We start to have dinner and the evening passes quickly. She loves the food and we discuss the case several times. I let it slip that I want to return to exhume the graves for further analysis but Jessica is sorry that she cannot be of more help. On this occasion, there are no solid grounds for a new request, especially given the aggravating factor that the relatives could claim damages.

At that moment my mobile phone rings and I instantly ignore it for a while as I know that it has to be my dear boss calling once at the number is that of the hain. When I finally can't take it anymore and Jessica nods at me to pick it up, I do and am surprised to find out that it is not Stephan who calls. It is the head office.

"Yes, John speaking."

"Hello, John. Don't waste your time. You'll never find out why I did it. But I will tell you something. I'm having a lot of fun. You're going to have a hard time catching me. I'll leave you some clues to follow though, just to help you get started; don't worry I'm not becoming careless. There's a reason for everything. Especially for important people like me, who are irreplaceable, who do great things for our society," says a mysterious voice in a loud, distorted, menacing voice as if they are using a device that distorts their original tone.

"Who are you? What is your name? What are you looking for?" I ask, shouting into my phone and surprising Jessica, who gives me a worried look.

"You're right. What bad manners. I haven't introduced myself. This is hAInds," the voice replies and the line cuts abruptly, before I have the chance to respond.

I'm shocked, paralyzed in a strange combination of fear and adrenaline. That was him. The killer. The nightmare that has been laughing at us these past weeks. He was there. I had him. And I can't lose him again.

I frantically get up and look around the restaurant, pacing around my chair impatiently. Jessica looks at me with a troubled expression, not knowing what is going on. I get a nervous feeling in my stomach.

"It was the psycho; he has my number. He called from the office, from my number; he must be there. I've got to go. I'm so sorry, Jessica, we'll have to meet another time." I apologize, and fumble around, unsure as to what to do next.

"Don't worry, I understand. See if you can catch that killer." She clenches her fists, obviously mad at the interruption but showing me a determined look. "As for a new date, how about Saturday night?"

"Perfect, I'll keep you posted."

We stop two taxis, we kiss each other on the cheeks and we say our goodbyes. What a pity, the dinner was going great …

Fifteen minutes later I'm in the office searching, but I find nothing. The systems guy tells us that they haven't used the phone, no one has been there. He deducts that the killer is probably able to manipulate the mobile screen to simulate a number that isn't there.

I think it's about time to upgrade my phone to a more modern one and catch this killer once and for all.

Chapter 17

Henry – My laboratory

I am an extremely lucky person. I know most people repeat this to themselves as a daily mantra, to protect them from the negativity and unfairness of fate, and although to me this is true to some extent, for the most part I am being totally genuine. I have seen nothing but death and grief as a child, a nightmare of the past which never ceases to abandon me as it holds on tightly as a memoir of the guilt and pain of powerlessness. But in all that darkness and chaos, I have been gifted with something that has guided me into the light: my brain.

My brain holds the intellectual capacity capable of supporting my ambition to complete the range of proposed undergraduate degrees I intended on pursuing. This not only helped me to catch up on the promise I kept for my father but also distract me from the burden of the past. After immersing myself in these fields, I finally found that this was what I was most passionate about. And surprisingly, that was the brain. So I became a neurosurgeon. As I say, I fix neuron engines. Working in this particular field excites me, as it gives me the opportunity to combine research with practical change whilst exploiting my childlike curiosity for the brain.

I started working at the Mount Sinai Hospital, 1468 Madison Avenue, during my residency, post medical school. There I began to collaborate with the best neurosurgeons in the country, hoping to learn from their techniques as I observed their every move. In my spare time, I worked for foreign governments. This was something which brought me a substantially large amount of money, very quickly. At the age of 23, I had a large fortune and a large salary at the hospital. I was becoming a millionaire. I had everything that I ever could have wanted.

But I didn't. I didn't have everything that I deserved. And I would stop at nothing to get what had been waiting for me my whole life.

Once I had the chance, I bought my parents' house and renovated it, although nobody lives there now. I sometimes stay there to sleep over and reminisce about the good old times. Being inside allows me to reconnect with my parents, and feel the warmth of their love even if they are no longer among the living. It's a way to keep them alive, when everything else feels like it's plummeting in a never ending chaos of darkness.

After that, I bought an old estate in Lake Placid. It was large, spacious and covered infinite acres of land. I began to devise the infrastructure I would need to carry out the other promise I made to my father before he passed: to feel useful in society again and to be happy again.

I have always considered myself as a hardworking individual. Every day, I aim to utilize my time most efficiently and make the most of every moment. This is why, for example, I don't watch TV, not even the news. I like to insulate myself and focus on what matters most to me, cutting off all external distractions. My ambition is to learn as much as possible in as little time as possible. I want to save and recover lost lives. The brain is the most complicated organ, but it is also the most important for survival. This is why it interests me. When I hit the right key, the patient is cured. If I succeed, I am immersed in an elixir of infinite happiness, which erodes the feeling of loss and guilt which haunts me from my childhood nightmares.

I only need three to four hours of sleep a day to be rested and perform at my best. For me that is sufficient. I am lucky to live in the era I live in. Technology and mathematics give me something indispensable: artificial intelligence.

I have one fear, and one fear only. And that is the fear of death. Leaving this world, and being consumed by the darkness of death would mean that my brain would be lost, for all of humanity. Finding and cultivating a talent so immaculate and perfect as mine would not only be difficult for someone else to mimic, and dare I say impossible. I have saved millions of lives over the years. People who have come to me in times of distress looking for salvation, and I have been able to help. This is a journey I have to continue. I must prevent many, many more from dying.

This is no longer a passion of mine. It is a duty; an obligation.

The patients I have performed such countless operations on have brought so much joy, and I must keep fighting to rescue those from the closing doors of death. Because sometimes I have not been able to. The one thing that keeps me up at night, is my failure and inability of saving those from the finality and closure of life. If only I could bring back good people who died from terminal illnesses. If only, I could stop those destined to suffer from the unpreventable death of terminal conditions from meeting their ends. This is something I would be intrigued and anxious to conquer.

We constantly capture data through our senses: sight, hearing, smell, taste and touch. We classify that data as secret, restricted, public or even something else. We define data; we know what a first name, a surname, a profession is. It is imprinted in our brains and it evolve over time. We have a dictionaries and glossaries which allow us to classify and store the data that constantly circles around us. We have good, average and bad quality data. And we have the tool to distinguish this: good from bad, truth from false. Our neurons move the information between them, travelling back and forth, connecting pieces of the puzzle together to string along the story of reality. We create data, we distribute it, we share it, we store it and we destroy it. But sometimes we cannot destroy bad data.

The most important thing is that our brain converts data into positive, negative or neutral information. Our brain can associate emotions with what we input, acting as a reminder of the memory of the first encounter. For example, if we touch fire and get burned, the data we receive from the fire is transformed into negative information. This means we will never voluntarily want to get burned again. On the other hand, if we are cold and we make fire and it warms us up, the information becomes positive. My goal is to go even deeper into this phenomenon. This is called deep learning and reinforced learning. What I want is to not only combine but to also align data governance and data management.

So if I create something, it must be internal and confidential. I can't make the codes roam around networks I don't control, even if they are encrypted. I have to prevent the programming language from being analyzed, interpreted and copied. In other words, I have to keep this data restricted. I have been researching technologies, processes and human beings for many years. Even before I started my degree, I knew that I wanted to create everything from scratch.

First, I needed to define the inputted data and its source. I wanted to preserve people's knowledge, feelings, memories and way of being. I didn't want these to be lost. I wanted these to remain even when the host dies.

Then I worked out my strategy. It couldn't be broadcasted for everyone to see; it had to be secret, with cutting-edge technology. I could only rely on people who trusted me and believed in the project. This was the most difficult part. Human greed knows no bounds and I can't trust anyone. I had to create a hybrid of what had already been created and what modifications I could impose. These new inventions had to be a mixture of supervised and unsupervised learning. The underlying foundation of machine learning algorithms.

In my personal strategy I would manufacture new languages, to allow for undetectable communication. I would incorporate modern technology, to support the sophisticated model. I would have my own telecommunications operator as well private power generators to support my process. But, I also had to create something that would automate the processes. Robots. The word 'robots' popped into my mind, as a solution to the problems that had begun to entangle me. I have to surround myself with robots. But my first step was to build a laboratory and a central computer to center the creation of what I had envisioned.

The idea filled me with illusion, with hope, an encapsulating sense of relief and affirmation that I was advancing. I had intertwined periods of frustration, joy, failure and success, which tumble-turned my emotions. That was until I heard Frank, my great central computer, speak for the first time. I saw that he was capable of programming, searching for information, interpreting situations, warning me and designing improvements in the system. All on his own.

While creating Frank, I made myself a mask with which I would communicate with him. There are multiple masks designed and created by me, my favorite is a tight-fitting black helmet, the size of my head and shaped with hands around the eyes. It is imposing, its darkness restricting and it inspires respect. I thought it was fun and I might have to wear it outdoors sometime, just to see the reactions of the general public. Through the mask, I can communicate easily with Frank in the lab, and create a permanent channel of communication between all of us. But once I'm in public, I settle for the earpiece, contact lenses and glasses combo as a substitute. If anyone asks, I just make up an excuse, saying that I can't hear very well in my right ear. When in reality, it really is to allow me to wear it all day and stay connected to Frank.

Frank keeps me company and is a great help in the development of my project. Once he was set up, I began to rely on him. Together we designed everything we could ever need, the laboratory, my office, the meeting room, the operations room, the vehicle shed. We also defined the system for the operation of orders, purchases, payment of taxes, bank transactions and many other issues that had to be taken into account so that the State would not suspect me or open an investigation into what I was actually doing. I needed to remain invisible, alone so that I could proceed unsuspected.

Frank has everything installed: image and voice recognition, natural language programming, neural networks, deep reinforced learning, as well as other technological and mathematical advances that we discovered through our research. I really hope he doesn't become like the computer in my favorite movie. I would hate for him to build up a desire to kill his creator. There is one final functionality that I implemented into Frank: artificial sentience. He only has good feelings; he is programmed to never hurt me. That avoids the whole repeat of the movie plausible scenario.

It took us a year to get the lab and facilities the way I wanted them. The mobile 3D printers were very helpful and efficient. They reduced costs by more than 70%.

The laboratory has several floors and one of them is totally confidential. In fact, only Frank knows of its existence and it must be kept that way. All of my secrets are hidden behind the wall. And if I want my plan to work, there's only a couple of things that need to be kept in the dark for now. But all will be revealed when the time is right.

If, and only if, the time is right …

Chapter 18

John – One hundred doses of pentobarbital

It is half past ten in the morning, we have been going over everything we have on the case and trying to make connections for more than two hours. I hate to admit it, but we are stuck in an endless cycle of chaos and uncertainty. I look across the room assigned to the case. It's funny, the name of the room is The Handcuffs. My boss took it upon himself to name all the investigation and meeting rooms: The Handcuffs, Stop or Shoot, You Have the Right to Remain Silent, The Slammer, Good Cop, Bad Cop and many others. The fool had nothing else better to do.

Speak of the devil.

The door opens and Stephan enters, his face flushed from a few too many drinks, and he stumbles inside.

"You are incompetent, you have no idea how to solve a case! You're going to force me to ask for help from the FBI, who will be happy to solve it in a couple of days. Newbies, what's wrong with you? You better not tell me anything, I'll get pissed off. I'm out of here! I want an update by the end of the day, I have a meeting with my superiors tomorrow," says Stephan, slamming the door, muttering sentences without letting us interrupt him.

We look around the room, at each other, with the same face of dismay.

"I can't stand this guy. One day we'll have to do one of those monkey things to him again. He's going to give me the next suspension, I'll tell you that!" Michael laughs, with a tone of frustration as his humor masks his anger.

"He'd better give it to all of us and then we can all go somewhere together to relax. I've got some savings." Jenny laughs, determined to do something to rally our spirits after Stephan plummeted them in the span of 30 seconds.

"I'm in too. We're going to tour Spain with my friends." I smile and wink at the team, already in a better mood.

There's a knock on the door, it's Dilya. Dilya is a technology freak. She loves technology. But I must warn you, don't give her your phone number or email address because she hacks everything. In my case, I gave it to her for security; she knows everything about me, but she keeps a close eye on me and protects me in case someone accesses my mobile, laptop or other device for criminal purposes. She is the human symbol of my personal firewall, as she has, on countless occasions, stopped criminals from being able to access my personal information: usernames, passwords or even managing my applications. Without her, I would be hopelessly lost and in big trouble.

"Hello, guys, can I come in?" asks Dilya with a smile that lights up the room.

"Of course, Dilya, please come in and join us. Please take a seat." Michael pulls up a chair and offers it to Dilya.

"Thank you, Michael, always so kind. By the way, you have 200 new likes on the dating app. Congratulations."

Dilya winks at him as she pats him on the back. They all look at Michael, who blushes.

"He must not be as good as a flirt, if he has to go out and advertise himself," I say, laughing and pointing my finger at him.

The group laughs in unison, connected by a spirit of comradery. Michael always claimed to be a success with women, but we just didn't know how he managed to do it so effortlessly. This explains everything.

"Man, the tough guy isn't so tough anymore." I squeal in delight. "Dating portals. Of course! The myth of your success has been solved."

Jenny approaches Michael and strokes his chin, where he has his famous dimple of good luck and triumph.

"There's news, I think we've got something. At Queens Hospital Cancer Center there's an inventory shortage of a hundred doses of pentobarbital. I accessed the systems and found manipulations in the reports and aggregate data," says Dilya, bringing our taunting of Michael to an end, and leading the conversation onto more pressing matters.

"However, the hospital is unaware that it has a supply shortage. Someone with access to the financial and logistical information systems must have manipulated the data reports to hide any trace of a fraud. I've arranged for John, Jenny and I to meet urgently with the CEO, the CFO and the logistics director. As soon as you arrive at the hospital, they will meet with you," adds Dilya, as she details how to proceed.

I take my laptop while Jenny gets both her coat and Dilya's jacket in a hurry. We are eager to sink our teeth into this new possible lead. As we leave the room we pass our boss, whom we ignore, to avoid any more humiliation:

"Sorry, we have an important meeting to attend." We add unapologetically, as we turn our backs away from him quickly. I can tell he is annoyed and I grin to myself.

The hospital is an hour away from the office, but as always the drive passes in silence, as we begin to think of questions that we are likely to address in our meeting.

My train of thoughts come to a stop as Jenny decelerates and before we know it, an hour has passed, and we make our way directly to the visitors' car park. We race out the car, hastily grab our equipment and dart to the nearest elevator which takes us up to the 24th floor.

Once the doors open up, we are greeted by the assistant director: a woman in her fifties, with gray hair which marks her age. But nonetheless she wears an elegant and friendly smile which brightens up the room. Her name is Rita. She keeps talking and asks us if we are married, if we have children, if we are a couple, and finally what films we like. A whole interrogation into our personal lives really. She talks to us about her passion: art. She is very knowledgeable about art and gives us her phone number in case we want to go with her to an art center, a museum or even a bookshop during the weekend. I must say her charm is infectious. I love this type of person who knows what to say to brighten up your day: cheerful, talkative, funny. It's been a very entertaining five minutes and I'm sure I'll call her to have a good time and go and get some sort of a cultural education (which I am in dire need of). We go into the meeting room and as we introduce ourselves one by one, we are offered tea and coffee for refreshments. I choose black coffee and Jenny asks for ginger tea. After a round of introductions, Jenny takes the floor.

"We have information about a discrepancy in the number of units of pentobarbital in your stock. Our data indicates that 100 doses of this drug are missing from the warehouse. There is a computer entry in the accounting system, but there is a mismatch with the warehouse system." Jenny starts with a pursuit of clarity as always.

"Would you mind checking the inventory just to make sure that everything is in its place?" Jenny asks with a purse of her lips.

The CEO orders others to go out and verify the figures we asked for. Jenny gives me a worried look then turns back towards the other people in the room with us.

"We're really sorry, but at this time, we can't give you any more information about the case," says Jenny to the CEO. "But if there is a discrepancy, we would have to find out when it happened. We would need to access the data and ask the employees for any leads."

"Of course, we will give you all the help you need. If the mismatch is confirmed, only a madman would want to take pentobarbital. Especially in such large doses," says the hospital director, who appears to be in shock by the discovery that has just been dropped upon him.

"Maybe it could be someone from here, who wants to spare suffering to sick people who have no chance of being cured," says Rita mostly to herself but I hear her and something about her theory pleases me. Her boss on the other hand thinks she is quite mad.

"Rita, you're always fantasizing about your fictional novels. You should have been a police officer," replies the director as he laughs and rocks back and forth in his chair.

"Yes, I should have been a police officer. With the lamp focused on the suspect in a dark, dank, musty interrogation room with mold creeping up its slippery walls. Oh, no, better to beat the suspect until he breaks and tells the truth. I should've been an officer. Yes, sir, and you should have been a commissioner!" says Rita sarcastically, picking up the cups. She frowns, annoyed that no one takes her seriously.

At that moment, the financial director, the logistics director, the systems manager and Dilya re-enter the meeting room.

"Indeed, there is a mismatch. The warehouse inventory does not match with the data in the ERP system. There are no outgoing orders recorded in the system related to those 100 doses. The entry in the system was made six months ago and the change occurred at three o'clock in the morning. We have the username and the name of the employee, we have checked them, but Human Resources has confirmed that the employee died that same day in the morning in a traffic accident.

"He was always on a motorbike; he loved two wheels. He was a very good driver, and had the terrible fate of stepping on an oil slick and crashing into a nearby truck. He died on the spot. His identity has been kept confidential." The director adds.

"They must have hacked into his account, then. He wouldn't have been able to commit the crime." The CIO observes. "We have found out that the access to the systems was carried out from outside."

"Yes, but the doses were obtained from inside. Someone had to get into the warehouse." I reason, as I scour my brain for possible steps of how such a task could have been undertaken.

"That's the most surprising thing. In the access logs to the site, that employee is listed at the same time as the accounting adjustments are made and in the warehouse system," says the CIO.

"I don't understand this anymore. For once in my life, I'm lost," I whisper to Jenny and Dilya, as my eyes dazzle in confusion. They look just as confused, which reassures me a little.

I pick up the phone and call Michael to come with his team to see if they can find any clues. Within an hour, Michael scans all the fingerprints he can find and checks them against his computer. After three hours of field work, he calls me. I'm with Dilya trying to fit the pieces together, but until now we had had no success.

"John, come to the warehouse, we've found out who stole them."

We go to the warehouse smiling that we now finally have a suspect we can investigate and link to the crimes.

Michael stands at the laptop with his face unhinged, his hand on his chin and his head turning from side to side in disbelief.

"Look at the fingerprints," Michael says, tearing his hands through his hair and ducking his head in a gesture of helplessness.

"It was Cameron …"

Chapter 19

John – Two months of madness

More than 60 days have passed since we discovered that Cameron or 'whoever it was' stole the hundred doses of pentobarbital. Worst of all, there have been more than ninety murders in the subsequent days that followed. All the victims were given pentobarbital before they died. Every murder the same as the one that preceded it. A never-ending cycle of death.

There is national alarm in response to high death rates rising at the hands of the so-called Dream Killer. It is becoming increasingly difficult to do our job. As soon as a death is reported to us, the press is already there by helicopter, even before we have the chance to investigate ourselves. We don't know who leaks the news, but someone does.

We work under enormous pressure, and we are reaching the limit of what we can physically handle. Jenny has already started to have problems with her husband. She now lives with Dilya and works nonstop. Things are getting very bad, very quickly. Things are escalating beyond control, and if we don't catch the killer soon, we are in deep trouble.

And unfortunately, there is no good news. Because at the end of the day, we are still clueless, completely left in the dark by it all. Perhaps the only hope we have is that the killer will stop killing as soon as he runs out of pentobarbital.

Our boss is hysterical, he's never been more lost in his life. All he does is ask for more and more and more. But as always he doesn't help.

The team's morale has hit rock bottom. And to be honest we don't know how much longer we can keep this up.

But as a policeman, there is never an end until the freak is put behind bars. And that means persevering, even when all the odds appear to be against you.

Maybe it's time for us to look at the case from a different angle. Perhaps we need to look for the link between the victims chosen, rather than looking at each murder as an individual case. Because after all, it's not like these victims were chosen at random. Right?

"What do they have in common?" I wonder quietly, as a million other questions flood my curiosity.

The team is gathered at Sole Mio, our favorite coffee shop at 385 Broome Street, it's a place where we can get some much needed downtime. It's crucial for us to now support one another, we rely on each other to release this burdening stress that is suffocating us at an alarmingly fatal rate.

We need to get back to square one, we need to travel to where it all began. Only then, can we retrace our steps, and hope to find the path that will lead us directly to the culprit.

On the table, a feast surmounts and draws our attention. We have ordered just about everything to refuel our energy stores: burgers, hot dogs, soft drinks, fries and coffees. The cafeteria has a booth upstairs where we usually discuss difficult cases. It's separated from the rest of the customers, so it gives us some distance and room to breathe. We need that room today more than ever.

"Let's go over the suspect's psychological profile. Why would someone who kills, bother to supply something that makes death manageable? Isn't that counterintuitive for someone with a blood lust as potent as his?" I ask, hoping that the eyes that surround me can invite some hope of a resolve.

"Maybe he's a sadist who just simply likes to kill for the thrill of it, but prefers to do so in a rather elegant, classy way," replies Jenny, shaking her head, as she knows that her conclusion does little to solve our greatest worries.

"Maybe he's not a sadist, maybe he's sick and doesn't want the victims to suffer like him, since he knows what pain is like. What if he's not a murderer? What if he's just sick?" says Dilya. We all stare at her. Michael shakes his head first.

"Maybe he's not a sadist, maybe he's not sick, maybe he's normal," he says, with a tone of pity.

I had been quietly thinking for quite some time, when an idea suddenly comes to me and the strange feeling that had bothered me from the warehouse starts to make sense.

I smile, snap my fingers and exclaim: "Rita! Rita was right! He's probably a sick man! But not the murderer!" I shout as I look at them.

"Who knows, maybe, just maybe …" I begin, as I stand up and pace around the booth.

My team gives me looks of confusion as well as pitying glances, possibly thinking that I have gone insane. I grin at them.

"Maybe the victims were sick! Maybe they were going to die, and wanted someone to help them to do it!" I say confidently.

"If this is true, we have to be very careful, because people might see him as a hero," Jenny suggests, sparking the group's interest.

"Dilya, since you haven't found a pattern in bank transactions, phone conversations, text messages, emails … look for patterns in visits to doctors, hospitals and website access history." I order, hoping that this can be the link we were so desperately looking for.

Dilya, who had already finished her double grilled burger and chocolate chip pancakes, goes to her office, a computer lab to which only she has access. I have been there several times so I can say that it is geek heaven. She has more than fifty screens on which she displays all kinds of reports and alerts she has prepared, to support the group's investigations. So I know she'll definitely be able to find something that can help us.

"But there are a lot of things that don't add up." Jenny begins. "For example, why does he decide to leave fingerprints of dead people? That's the work of someone who is mentally unwell, if you ask me."

"He's probably trying to make us think he's sick or sadistic to throw us off the scent," Michael replies who appears to be deep in thought as his pupils fixate on something in the distance. I stare at the same greased spot on the wall, hoping for a spark of thought.

"It is possible. Well, at least today we have opened our spectrum to other alternatives and a new research focus," I say, then I lower my voice so as to not attract attention, even though we are alone. "We have to be cautious and keep this to ourselves, because who knows who else he might have on the inside."

"I totally agree. Our boss can't know anything either. We don't want him getting the praise for something he didn't do. Again," Jenny says with a tone of frustration.

My mobile rings, disrupting our motorized flow of thought. It's the office number, Dilya's landline.

"Man, Dilya, that was fast! Tell me you found something. Please let it be good news!" I plead as I answer the phone with a tone of joyful excitement.

"Don't run so fast. Or you might just crash," replies a loud threatening and paralyzing voice which resonates through the speaker.

I freeze in fear. Jenny and Michael look at each other, they've rarely seen me like this. My face must be encapsulated in a tightening depiction of raw terror.

"You are good, I didn't think you would discover the theft of the doses so quickly, but you still have a long way to go, if you want even a small chance to catch up. I suggest you step away from the investigation. Let other, clumsier people do the job," the voice continues and hangs up suddenly.

"It was him again." I start, my voice shaking, as I struggle to find the right words.

"He … he … he called from Dilya's phone," I say perplexed while I dial his number once more, as my mind focuses on nothing but catching up to him.

"Who ARE YOU?" I scream into the phone, awaiting the cold voice to snap back.

" John?" a familiar voice replies instead.

"Dilya? Are you alright? I got a call from hAInds on your landline," I tell her anxiously, as my voice shakes with apprehension.

"What?" she asks aghast. "I'm fine. I'm working in my office and I assure you no one has used my number, unless it's a spirit or a ghost. No one has accessed my phone physically." Dilya reassures me.

"We're going to the office right now. See if you can find out if someone has accessed the landline and would be able to make a call from there." I instruct.

I pay the bill and we make our way to the police station immediately. Once we arrive, we go into Dilya's office and Michael examines the phone and the room for any clues. He checks that Dilya is okay. Jenny and I sit down at our desks, tossing our heads back in frustration.

"Jenny, how is it possible that this guy knows how to make phone calls from the inside and knows all of our phone numbers?" I ask, with a debilitating tone of worry.

"That question can only be answered by our expert, and she is currently busy seeking medical quotes from each of the affected victims," says Jenny, looking at me carefully. I see something that makes me change the subject.

"Jenny, did your husband call you?" I ask, looking directly into her eyes and noticing tears forming around the edges, as my change in tone throws her off balance.

"No, he's gone. You know, it's not the first time this has happened between us. It's not easy for me to get sucked into a case, and forget about everything else but this one's a real handful, and I've been having a hard time handling it all.

He'll get over it, and if he doesn't, it's the streets and a blanket for him." Jenny assures with an affirming tone, as she wipes away her tears.

I've never seen Jenny speak so bluntly in my life. The argument must have been so intense for her to have gotten so worked up. Jenny always puts her family life before her professional life, but there is something else that bothers her. I can tell it's something big but I don't ask, I merely put an arm around her. Knowing her, she'll tell me about it when the time comes. But right now, what she needs is time for herself to reflect and make her own decisions. She needs good friends to stand by her and that's what I'm here for.

We sit silently for a few seconds, then I change the subject back to crime.

"What does Mr Injections mean by 'I suggest you stay away from the investigation' and 'Let other, clumsier people do this work'? Is he threatening me? Why is he calling me? Is he nervous that we are going to find out something? But how does he find out about our progress?" I progress my thoughts out loud, in a way that Jenny probably thinks I've completely lost it. Chances are that she might be right. I sigh.

It's clear that he's spying on us. But how is it possible that he knew about our conversation in the cafeteria? Either they have microphones, or they use a vehicle to hear us from a distance, because in the bar's booth we were completely alone, I am sure of it. I checked!

I stand up and tell Michael to drop everything he's doing in Dilya's office and come with me. It's urgent, I think I'm finally onto something. And that is a first in this investigation.

We leave the police station and go to the bar once more, there's something we've missed, I'm sure of it. I've told Michael to bring everything this time: the bugging equipment, the fingerprint scanning technology, all of it.

We get to the bar, making our way up to the booth and Michael starts scanning for bugs left and right. Initially, there's nothing. He puts on his suit and scans the area. The device he has is amazing. It consists of a camera that photographs the whole area and, through artificial intelligence it's able to identify fingerprints and send them to the primary database to find similarities. Once, Dilya explained to me that they use some networks and algorithms. It was all too complex for me, so the details are very vague.

Before entering the bar, we agreed to write messages to each other on paper notes. We promised to avoid talking and refrain from using our phones. After several minutes, I get a note from Michael.

I found footprints of Cameron and the driver on the upper ramp of the restaurant's floor.

I look up and I see what Michael was referring to. We grab a ladder to access the roof and we climb up the steps. Michael is still tracking the trail left by the footprints downstairs. What's strange is that we only find fingerprints.

How can he be able to do that? From the roof, I can see that the fingerprints head towards one of the side walls. Michael comes up and he looks at what I have just found. Holding Michael by the feet, I lift him up and he indicates with his hands that the trail of footprints goes down the wall of the house to the pavement in the street below.

We run back to the ramp, descend from the restaurant's booth, and find Jenny, looking angry with us having left her back at the office. Together, we go out into the street.

We head towards the wall leading from the roof and Michael traces his fingers until they reach a black van with the logo 'hAInds' drawn on it, parked on the side of the pavement. It has tinted windows, so we can't see anything inside. Jenny nods in my direction and the three of us draw our guns and slowly approach the vehicle.

Suddenly, one of the windows opens, a hand appears and shoots directly at us. We drop to the ground and take cover. The van starts up and speeds away from us at an alarming speed.

We shoot at the tires, hoping to stop its movement. The bullets hit the tires, but fail to puncture them, so the car keeps distancing itself from us, as are our hopes of catching him. We notice that the car has no number plate and, on the back, the same logo: 'hAInds' appears.

The killer was in that vehicle, and we just lost him.

"Damn it!" I shout into the distance, as I throw my fists up in the air in frustration.

We return to the bar to thoroughly analyze the scene, as disappointment burdens us, but we have a tiny bit of hope to propel us forward. Therefore, we call for reinforcements and the area is cordoned off. Several police helicopters patrol the area in an attempt to locate the van.

How could a person leave fingerprints all over the scene? On the floor, on the walls, on the roof, on the pavement. It doesn't make sense. I can't help thinking we're missing something over and over again. How can we not detect footprints? How does he know our every move?

"Lieutenant John, excuse me, can you tell us what happened? We have been informed that there has been a shooting in the area and that you have had to respond. Is it something to do with the Dream Killer?"

I can recognize that voice anywhere. It's Pris. Seeing her should make me happy, but at this moment my heart is racing too fast because I know the press is here, and we have once again failed. I struggle to breathe but manage to reply.

"We are investigating what has happened as we speak; we do believe it is related, but we can't give any more information at this time." I answer with a stern face of concentration.

"Can you tell us if there have been any new murders, have you found any bodies in the cafeteria?" asks Pris, determined to get anything from me.

"Fortunately, there are no new victims. I think we got ahead of ourselves and came close to catching him, but unfortunately, we weren't able to apprehend him." I answer to the press that has now ensnared me, and I am now once again finding it difficult to continue to breathe.

"Do you think the killer was here to increase the number of victims?" asks another journalist, as he directs a microphone in my direction, and cameras blind my vision.

My face shows how surprised and irritated I am, because despite my mind racing for answers, it hasn't found any. If I say that the killer was here to kill, the alarm will go off and panic will prevail. But if I say no, they might ask if the killer is watching us.

"At this stage, we can't say anything else. We ask you, please, to let us work. We have another long day ahead of us, I'm afraid." I conclude, grasping my chest, hoping to slow down my heart's racing palpitations.

I leave the journalists, pushing my way through the crowd and I walk around the place imagining what happened exactly. We go back up to the roof once more and trace the route.

"John, come here; look what I've found," says Michael as he picks up a piece of paper, writes on it and shows it to Jenny and me.

All of the footprints belong to Cameron and the driver.

Chapter 20

Henry – In the Hospital

Cameron's smile lights on his watch glass as he jumps up and down with joy.

"Chief, this time we've really gone for it! A little longer and we would have been caught. They'll be looking for the van and trying to trace it through the cameras in the area." Cameron tells me in the living room of the residence, beaming with excitement.

"I agree, boss, it was very fun but we took an immense risk. The good thing is that the camouflage function is incredible. We've got to hand it to your boss, you're a genius," Driver says, perching himself on my head and climbing down the side to my right shoulder.

I smile and as I stand up, I walk towards the large windows of the mansion. The view of the trees and the lake helps me to meditate and think carefully about my next moves.

"Guys, I'm going to need time until I force them to stop the investigation. John and his team are very good and it won't take them long to find the link between the victims. Besides, I have to go to work at the hospital this week; I've run out of holiday time. Continue training and get some rest, we have some difficult days ahead. You're going to have a lot of brothers and sisters in a very short time."

Cameron and Driver look at each other, jump up and down and clap their palms in the air, screaming.

"Finally there are going to be more of us, the fun has only just begun!" Driver screams in happiness, beaming with joy.

I leave the mansion and I head straight to the hospital. I drive my 1969 Ford Mustang, a classic that I have upgraded with new safety features, a modern engine and a range of accessories to meet my needs.

It's eight o'clock in the morning and I'm getting ready to visit my patients and check on their progress. I wear the glasses that allow me to communicate with Frank. These glasses also have a built-in camera and microphone to record the conversations I have without anyone noticing. Then, quietly after work, I analyze the details so that I can improve the treatment and shorten their recovery. It also means that I can quickly switch views with my contact lenses to see what my hands are getting up to, back home.

I love all my patients dearly and I do my best for them, to help them recover. I have often slept in the chair next to the patient after an operation, unable to leave their side as I pray for them to recover. The hospital is very fond of me, even though I declined to be the director of the center on many occasions. I want to be with my people and save many lives. And this is how I can do that.

Among my patients are two seven-year-old twins who I had to operate on and remove a malignant tumor in a very delicate area. I spent more than twenty hours with each of them individually in the operating room. They were then in the ICU for several weeks without knowing how their condition would develop.

I didn't go home a single day during those two weeks: I stayed with them all the time. The nurses brought me broths, soups and purées to eat. I kept an eye on the equipment.

One day the twins woke up at the same time and started calling for their mother. I was asleep, and their joyful screams woke me up. I immediately welcomed them into my arms, beaming the same childlike enthusiasm.

The worst was over, and I had saved their lives. That day I was hugged and congratulated by everyone in the hospital team: nurses, fellow doctors, cleaners and their managers.

It was a pioneering operation in the world and I was able to carry it out and make the parents and children laugh again. Then I realized that I had a gift, the gift of healing, and that this gift belonged to the world.

"Hi, guys, how are you today?" I ask the twins.

"We're fine, Henry, did you bring us any presents?" asks Peter, eyes beaming with curiosity and affection.

"I've found a little something over here. Here you go," I reply, holding up two large packages and placing them in the twins' laps.

The children open them, ripping apart the wrapping paper. As they tear the paper, the twins uncover two digital music keyboards with built-in learning courses and headphones.

"How cool! I love it!" they shout in unison, beaming with joy as they hug each other, and I wrap my arms around them.

The nurses help them set up the instrument, and they start playing immediately, as music fills the silent and empty hospital corridors.

The twins' mother enters the room, she makes her way towards me and as she takes me by the arm she whispers: "Thank you very much, doctor. We are eternally grateful to you. Not only did you bring them back to life, but you have also managed to make them laugh again as you bore gifts to give them back their infancy. We don't even know how to thank you. Paying the hospital bills doesn't seem like enough. You are their guardian angel, and we will always be forever grateful to you."

"For me, it is a pleasure to stop people from suffering and help them to recover. That is my greatest happiness. Believe me, your smile, your children's smile, your husband's smile, the children's grandparents smile …" I go on. "That is the only gift I could ever want."

Many people are obsessed with money and work. They worry about being more than others by stepping on other people's toes by embarrassing them and making them feel inferior. But what they don't realize is that at the end of the day health is the most important thing. Health is happiness, especially mental health. How many people are there that have no legs, but continue to immerse themselves in a normal life and smile, because even through their ups and downs, they are happy nonetheless. And that is because they are mentally healthy. Their mindset is what is most important.

At the other extreme, we have the billionaires, who do nothing for anyone. They have everything because they can buy it, it is as simple as that. They are bitter, unhappy and dissatisfied with all that they have. And that is because they have a poor corruptive mindset. Believe it or not, I am also interested to see what causes unhappiness and how to stimulate happiness. Much has been written and researched but to no avail.

We give each other a hug and I say goodbye to the little ones. I have checked that they are well and I have filmed their movements and coordination progress, so that I can later check up on them once I come back home. The keyboards are fundamental in their recovery process of rehabilitation and will help me to evaluate their progress, even without them realizing that I am watching their every move.

They have been out of the ICU for a few weeks and their movements are still limited. The boys are still weak, and I am worried that any bacteria could affect them. A simple cold could mean we lose everything we have been fighting for.

I leave the room and go into room 27, as I wave goodbye to a family that means so much to me. I feel a great affection for Patrick. He is seventy-two years old with long grey hair, a skinny demeanor of a sun-kissed tan complexion and light blue eyes that brighten up the room as he beams a smile in my direction. I still remember the first time I diagnosed his illness and told him. I'll never forget the exact words that he said to me.

"Doctor, don't waste your time nor the insurance's money on me. I have lived long enough; devote your efforts to the younger ones." He pleaded.

His words gave me strength, because I knew that I could do something, that this wasn't the end for him; unlike for so many patients I had met over the years. He could still live among us, wholeheartedly, with his body in one healthy piece.

Patrick lives alone and is a grandfather to more than twenty grandchildren. He is busy every day of the week. During the parents' working day, the two assistants who live with him look after many of his grandchildren. The children are dropped off at seven in the morning and are picked up in the evening. They often stay at his house for dinner, and so one could say that he gives his life for them.

Patrick was a successful entrepreneur back in the day. His factory produced radiographic plates which later evolved into digital diagnostics. He made many donations to hospitals over the years, although some political parties were critical of his decisions and scrutinized him, often accusing him of wanting to profit from his benevolence.

Patrick suffers from Alzheimer's. That was the diagnosis I made a couple of months ago. But I knew that even if there was a small chance that I could stop him from forgetting, I would never forgive myself for not trying.

So I did. With the hospital team by my side, he underwent an operation which allowed me to insert stem cells to stop the disease from progressing. And we succeeded.

"Hello, Patrick, how are you today?"

"I feel like a kid, and I'm getting my memories back thanks to the videos you asked my daughters to bring me. God bless my family," says Patrick, giving me a hug, as tears start to form in his eyes.

"I have good news for you. Tomorrow you'll be out of my sight and back home," I say joyfully as I pat him on the back. "However, we're going to miss you here at the hospital wing, especially at dominoes and darts competitions. You've become quite the champion."

"What joy you give me, Henry! At last I will be able to see my little ones, my children, my caregivers, my daughters-in-law and sons-in-law. Oh! What a joy! I can't wait! You are a great man. The door of my house will always be open to you. Remember that."

Patrick's face is bathed in tears now. He is a big, burly, good-natured man and a great help to science worldwide. It would have been a shame to lose someone so valuable.

"I'll take your word for it. When you get settled in your house and a few days have passed, invite me over for the barbecue you never seem to shut up about," I say jokingly, as I tilt my head back in laughter.

I get emotional too, as my laughs are replaced by small sobs. Children and elderly people touch my heart because they always need someone to be with them. Patrick has two people at home who helped and cared for him during his illness. Now he will be able to enjoy his grandchildren.

Maybe one day Patrick will become part of my little group; he has that human element that I admire so much.

After reviewing each and every one of my patients, I sit in my office to check the list of people I will see today. They come from all over the states because they trust me to find out what is wrong with them and cure them.

I look at my computer and tablet; a soft voice calls for my attention, following a gentle knock as my door creeps open.

"Mr Handsome, can I come in?"

A very beautiful woman in a doctor's coat smiles at me and enters the office. Her dark brown eyes beam through her round glasses, with her black hair strands curling around her cheeks. She comes up to me and places her lips on mine, placing both her soft and gentle hands around my face.

This is Ann, a world-renowned neurosurgery specialist, who is the best in her field, because she's not only intelligent but also driven in what she loves. A true natural.

And my girlfriend. We have been dating for years. Ann is five years older, but it was love at first sight once she saw the way I operated and treated patients. Ann is part of the hospital team and we often operate together and spend long days here at the workplace. I love having her by my side in everything that I do. Well, almost everything.

"My door is always open for you even if it's broken down, darling," I say, building up a tone of confidence, but I know that she's giggling underneath her large beaming smile.

"Shall we have dinner tonight? I've heard about a very good Spanish restaurant for dinner. Say yes and I'll make a reservation right now," I say, taking her hands and looking her straight into her captivating light brown eyes.

"I'm off work early today, so of course, I'd love to go out for dinner." Ann smiles, as her affectionate grin rises from each of the corners of her cheek.

"It's done then; I'll pick you up at your place at 19:30, okay?" I ask excitedly as if it was my first date with her.

"Okay, handsome, can't wait!" she replies bubbling with joy.

"So, how's your day going?" She continues as she changes the conversation.

"Splendid, everyone is doing very well and Patrick will be discharged tomorrow. In a couple of weeks, I'll meet him for dinner and you're coming too." I smile in relief as I beam with pride.

"I'm looking forward to it, he's a wonderful person. Whenever I've had a conversation with him, he's been nothing but kind and understanding. He seems to have responded very well to the operation and treatment you provided. We'll have to write the article to get it published."

Ann strokes my hair with affection, as she runs her hands through my small tight curls. She turns and speaks with a smile.

"Well, I'll leave you to it. I have some questions, but I'll talk to you later, when I call you. Is that okay? You're going to be in your office all day, aren't you?" Ann asks.

"Yes, I'll be here all day since I have no operations today. I just have a couple of patients coming for visits and check-ups, but that's all."

Ann leaves the room and goes to close the door gently behind her. I smile as she disappears from the room, after blowing her a kiss with my open hand and winking my right eye.

Then, I take the time to read the reports that Amanda, the department secretary, left on my desk. I usually set aside an hour or so to examine each medical file and their corresponding tests. I like to be thoroughly prepared for each visiting patient.

After sixty minutes, the phone on my desk starts ringing.

"Tell me, Amanda."

"Hello, Henry. You've got five patients today; fully booked. I'll tell the first one to come in and I'll escort him personally to your office," Amanda replies in her sweet voice, which resonates through the phone as does her brightening personality.

Her bright colored red glasses, and blonde curled locks reflect her bubbly personality, as does her choice of brightly colored outfits that she changes every day. I think her fashion sense alleviates some of the initial tension of the patients, and her warm and concerned tone calms them down before our consultation. I couldn't have asked for a better assistant.

I like that Amanda takes care of my patients from the start, as she accompanies them from the waiting room to my office. It's a way to take the edge off during the first part of the visit.

"Henry, can we come in? asks Amanda, as she knocks on the door and slightly opens the door to peek inside.

"Yes, of course, Amanda. Mr Baker, don't tell me you haven't been offered something to drink yet. I'll call the hospital director and have him bring something to you immediately," I say to Mr Baker, who smiles at my offer.

"No need to worry, doctor, they offered me a cappuccino before and I took it," replies Mr Baker, who had come in very tense, but after the joke he seems more relaxed.

His muscles slacken.

"Call me, Henry, please. There's no need to use the formality of doctor, it's too serious." I laugh.

"Tell me, how are you feeling? How's the movement in your arm? Is it still stiff? I've seen you've been to the emergency room several times and I've read all the reports extensively."

Mr Baker is amazed, he just called to make an appointment and filled out a digital form. He never thought I would read all the reports beforehand. He's used to the kind of doctor who needs to be explained what's wrong with the patients even after more than five visits, even though he has all his records.

"I've already been told that you are a great person. Many say you are the best," says Mr Baker, sighing in relief. I smile and he continues.

"It's stiff now, doctor. I can't move it. It's very strange, mobility comes and goes. I thought it might be due to a sporting injury or a pulled muscle. So I stopped, and for the past three months I've been doing nothing. But as you can see from the reports, the muscle is stiffening more often and for more prolonged periods of time."

Mr Baker points to his arm. It's stiff as if it's in a sling. I tell him to sit on the stretcher to examine him. As he takes his place, I carefully check that he can't move whilst I feel his arm and muscles.

"We're going to do a general MRI, a scan and an EKG." I tell Mr Baker, to keep him in the loop of what we're going to do next.

I call Amanda, who takes control over organizing everything. Once it's all in place, she comes in once more with an assistant nurse to accompany Mr Baker and help to administer the tests.

After several hours, I welcome Mr Baker back into my office, once all the results have come back. The hospital is one of the best in the world, so it's able to perform the medical tests and acquire the results in record time.

"Well, Mr Baker, we have all your results. I have studied them carefully and you needn't worry too much. You have a small spot in your brain, which is pressing on the area responsible for sending orders to the limbs of your body to direct movements. Don't worry; we've caught it in time. We're going to have to open you up a bit, clean the spot and that's it. I do this operation about thirty times a year, so there's really nothing to worry about. "

"I have a '69 Mustang, a one-off, and everyone I operate on gets a day to enjoy the car. You will be no exception. Besides, a little birdie told me that cars are one of your passions." I tell him, hoping to calm the atmosphere.

Mr Baker looks at me, smiling and beaming with joy, as tears start to form in the corner of his eyes and run down his cheeks. A normal reaction, many of my patients have. He wipes them off with a handkerchief, and as he stands up, he wraps his arms tightly around me, and hugs me with gratitude.

"Thank you, Henry, I knew you would cure me. I come from Florida, as you know. But, I was very worried, given that during my last visit to the emergency room they told me they couldn't see anything. I was worried that I had come all this way for nothing. They asked me to consider going to different specialists, such as orthopedic surgeons, internal medicine and neurosurgeons, but I knew there was only one person who could help me at that point: you. I would like to ask for you to give me some time before the operation as I have to prepare the logistics of work, travel and everything else."

"It's not urgent, so we can schedule it in a week's time. Would this be convenient for you?" I ask, and he nods his head in agreement.

"Make an appointment with Amanda and don't worry about anything. It's a simple procedure, so all we'll really do is cut your hair and give you a dashing new look." I continue, laughing at my joke.

Mr Baker smiles, and as he gets up to leave, he shakes my hand before waving goodbye.

Later today, I'll ask Frank to give me a report on his personality and background, so I can learn more about him.

As I progress through my day, I have a short lunch break, which I use to sit with Ann and the rest of my co-workers in the hospital's cafeteria. We have a good time joking and laughing, releasing all the tense stress of dealing with the bag prognostics we have to confront every day.

Then it's back to work until the end of the day. I get back into the routine of reading the files and welcoming patients into my office. But on the back of my mind, and Ann's as well, is our upcoming dinner at one of the best Spanish restaurants in New York later that night.

Chapter 21

Henry – The appointment

Ann is wearing a beautiful blue dress with a tight-fitting neckline which intensifies her hypnotizing eyes. She wears a shimmering pearl necklace around her slender neck and matching earrings to compliment her regal look. Her red lips, the soft make-up on her face and her warm tone of voice make me feel like the luckiest man in the world and, for the moment, I temporarily forget about my greatest worry: my illness.

"I didn't know about La Gamba y el Pulpo, I had never even heard of it," says Ann, taking my arm as we walk into the restaurant. "I've never eaten anything typical of Spain and I've never even visited the country. But we should definitely go on holiday to Spain this summer if you like. I hear it's spectacular."

"Yes, I've heard that it's wonderful and that in Segovia you can taste unforgettable suckling lamb. I think that in each region you can find gastronomy that is different yet nonetheless incredible. We'll go on holiday this year." I respond to Ann, as we take our seats and look at the menu, to decide what to order.

After much deliberation, we decide what to order and we are rapidly served our appetizers. We quickly devour what is put in front of us: octopus with cachelos, grilled langoustines and some barnacles accompanied by an excellent Albariño.

"If this is the appetizer, I can't wait to see what the rest of the menu has to offer!" Ann exclaims, as she daps her mouth with her handkerchief after making sure her plate was spotless.

"We are working on a new hypothesis. We think it could be a sick person, a macabre murderer or someone who has been hired to kill sick people." A distant voice echoes through the restaurant and grabs my attention firmly.

The voice sounds familiar, I've heard it somewhere before. I turn my head discreetly, to avoid being seen, and I identify the source of my worry. It's John.

The voice belongs to John. I see him with Jessica, talking to each other as they are suddenly seated at the table next to us. My memories, my fears and my goals rush involuntarily to the front of my mind, and I am woken up to reality.

'What on earth is John doing with the judge here? Why are they here? What are they planning? And how did I not know they were meeting?' A million thoughts form in my head, and throw me off balance.

I continue to listen to Ann, although my attention has been captivated elsewhere. Not only do I want to know what they are talking about, I need to know. So nodding occasionally, to avoid throwing suspicion at Ann, I excuse myself by telling her I need to use the bathroom. I use it as an opportunity to call Cameron. It's urgent.

"Cameron, come to the restaurant immediately, it's an emergency! John and Jessica are here; I need you to fill me in on what they talk about, I can't do it myself without being seen. Whatever you do, don't use the van." I tell him quickly, as my palms sweat in anxiety.

"Ask Driver to come with you. Use the logistics transfer drones instead. Come prepared with spying equipment to listen to their conversation through short and long-range microphones." I continue to instruct Cameron through the microphone in my glasses.

"Right away, boss, we'll be there in ten minutes," says Cameron, understanding the severity of the task at hand.

Although I am somewhat calmer, I can't seem to shake this feeling of uneasiness. I return to the table, keeping a stern expression under the masked smile I use to look at Ann. Quickly, I glance slyly at John and Jessica, trying to read their lips, but I can't seem to make out their words. As I sit down, I order rice with lobster as we continue to enjoy more of the appetizers that have been served, and I mask my worry with laughs here and there.

After twenty minutes they serve us the rice stew. We taste it, and as we take the first bite, we instantly look at each other and comment on how good it tastes. Ann acknowledges the restaurant's success and the dishes chosen. We continue laughing and chatting.

Suddenly, I look up and see Cameron gliding across the ceiling unseen. He makes his way to one of the walls near my table, down to the floor and moves between our feet to where John and the judge are standing.

My heart is racing.

Cameron gives me a thumbs up indicating that everything is under control. You can tell he's been through similar adventures and knows how to temper his nerves and handle himself. His hand indicates that everything is ready. With gestures he reveals that he has placed a microphone under the table. I have no way of communicating with Cameron, but at least with my contact lenses I'll be able to keep one eye on him and the other in my conversation with Ann. I'll just have to be careful not to make it too obvious that I'm not giving Ann all of my attention. But it shouldn't be that difficult.

Ann keeps talking, but soon enough I realize how difficult this is getting, as I become just a bit too interested in Cameron's position, and I ignore her completely.

"So what do you think, Henry?" asks Ann.

"I completely agree. You are absolutely right. There is no room for doubt. You've stumped me."

I don't know if I've come out of it well, we'll see how she reacts. For the moment, her face has changed, she's serious. She comes up to me, grabs my shirt and ... kisses me.

Well I guess I said the right thing.

"I knew you would agree that we could get to know each other better if we moved in together for a while," says Ann.

My hands start to shake, a cold sweat runs down my neck and down my back, paralyzing me with fear. My God, what a mess I've got myself into.

"But, don't worry, there's no hurry, we'll find a date to live together for a while. There's no need to rush, I want to get to know you a little better. If all goes well, we could do it in ... six months?" Ann calculates.

At that moment my heart relaxes and I notice that my heartbeat slows down, and my palms stop sweating uncontrollably.

"Of course, there's no rush no rush. One step at a time." I reply, wiping the sweat from my hands on my napkin.

I feel relieved, not because I don't want to, but because it's not the right time. Ann is extraordinary and I can't see myself with anyone else. But with everything that I have going on right now, I don't want to get her involved, and moving in together would complicate things.

Suddenly I look under the table and see the two hands, Cameron's and Driver's, making the shape of a heart. It really doesn't help that Cameron was funny before becoming a hand. That pre-possessed humor is now also running through his veins and in that half-electric, half- hybrid brain of his. Driver has formed a strong connection with Cameron, so the two hands are now inseparable.

I move my eyes to the left and tell them to get inside, but before they leave, their hands are positioned in front of them with their fingers together, joining and separating as if they were a couple kissing each other. Once they're done having their fun, and messing around they listen to me and hide under the table.

It's time for dessert. We order some caramelized filloas filled with cream and a piece of Santiago cake. And we are definitely blown away.

A real delicacy. One of the best dinners I've had in a long time, firstly for the company and secondly for the food, which was like nothing I had ever experienced.

"Thank you very much for the evening, Henry," Ann says, looking me in the eye, as she takes my hand and smiles.

Suddenly I feel something caress my leg. But it can't be, they wouldn't be so reckless as to do it again. Both hands are in Ann's direct eyeline. I lean back and peek slyly under the table. Cameron's hand is tickling me. I slap it to the floor, signaling for him to disappear to avoid being seen.

I'm done with him today. He deserves to be locked in the darkroom with no music for a week. My hands are like my children, and sometimes I joke about setting them punishments. Because how else can I control them?

Cameron smiles and walks over to John.

A hand touches my shoulder and I turn around with a start; I'm sure it's Cameron. This is it, we're about to be discovered.

"Sorry to bother you, sir," a familiar voice begins.

Fortunately, it's not Cameron, but rather John instead. Oh no, what is happening? We are so close to getting caught now. But soon I realize that we are not in danger but rather are rather in a marvelous situation. We have an opportunity.

"Would you mind taking a picture of us on my phone? I need to remember this moment with my friend." John continues.

"Well, of course!" I agree, jumping internally with joy as I know exactly how to turn this encounter into an opportunity for us to get even closer to him.

So, unnoticed, I instruct Cameron to put a mic on his mobile. As John hands me the phone; I clumsily drop it on the floor in such a way that it looks like an accident, and it falls under the table.

"Excuse me, I'm so sorry I dropped it, but here, let me get it for you."

I reach down and grab the phone, which has fallen just under the table. In that short time span Cameron has managed to attach a mini device to it. Now I'll be able to listen to all his conversations and everything that goes on.

I focus on them with the device's camera and press the shutter button several times to take the picture. Once I'm finished, I look at the final product. I have to say, they've turned out really nice.

"Thank you very much. My name is John and this is my friend Jessica."

"Pleased to meet you. I'm Henry, and this fantastic woman is Ann, my girlfriend. Pleasure. How was your dinner? Ours was unforgettable; this place is unique and it's the first time we've been here. I've heard so much about the exquisite quality and the view."

 "I come here a lot, Jessica less often. Although we haven't been coming much lately," says John, as he shakes my hand.

"Yes, very little. We're very busy with our jobs, I'm afraid," says Jessica, shaking her head.

"It's the same for us, we get too absorbed in it. But today we have to enjoy some time away from it and forget about it, even if it's for only a while," Ann replies with a smile.

"I agree, let's enjoy this wonderful company."

I invite Ann to sit down, and John does the same with Jessica, on the table next to us.

As I sit, I look down at the floor in the direction of John's table and see Cameron clapping soundlessly. The scene brings a smile to my face.

"What are you laughing at," asks Ann, with a puzzled expression forming on her face.

"Nothing, just the fact that I'm clumsy. He hands me his mobile and the next second I drop it. It's a good thing it didn't break, otherwise he'd shoot me on sight." I crack up.

"What are you saying? Is the albariño kicking in already?" Ann questions with a look of confusion.

"John is armed, I saw the gun under his arm. Maybe he's someone from the mob, he might be a bodyguard, or perhaps he works for the police. I bet it's the latter. He's got the face for it, you know," Henry whispers in Ann's ear.

And suddenly, just like that, our conversation is cut short, as the room echoes with the sound of gunfire rocketing from the corners of the restaurant.

"What was that? Gunshots? It's coming from the street," Ann says, shaken with fear.

We hear police car sirens and the loud crash of an accident. In a flash we see the people who were at the bar enter the dining room and an individual in his forties holds a girl by the neck and points a gun at her head.

The girl screams in panic and he threatens her: either she shuts up or he kills her.

That's all I need I think to myself. My hands under John's table and us in the middle of a scene. Just our luck.

John stands up, pulls out his gun and points it in the man's face.

"Don't do anything, man, I'm a cop, drop the gun," John orders menacingly.

"No way, you put it down first. You're the one who's going to drop the gun, or I'll kill her. It's your choice, but if you pull the trigger, so will I," he replies, as his eyes enrage with anger. He squeezes the girl's neck more and she squirms.

"Excuse me, my friend, don't be nervous, I'm sure we can come to an agreement without you killing anyone," I say, standing up with the bottle of Albariño and a glass in my hands, as I approach the attacker, acting as if I've drank a little bit too much.

"I'll make you a deal then: let everyone out except the cop and me; I'll trade myself for the girl. I'll pour you a little drink and you can drink it while you point your gun at me. Do we have a deal?" I continue.

I look sideways at Cameron. He's on the ground with a gun pointed to the attacker's head. I stand close to John, who is still in the same position, with the gun pointed straight at his target. At that moment I pretend to stumble and hit John's head with the wine bottle. He misses the shot.

In front of me, the hostage falls to the ground and the kidnapper is shot in the forehead by Cameron's tranquilizer gun. He falls from the shock and Cameron and Driver hide under the tablecloth once more, quickly rushing to hide amongst the shadows.

Thankfully, Ann and Jessica seem fine. Although I can't say the same about John; it appears that he's lost consciousness.

We quickly gather around John, and Jessica swells up in panic.

"Jessica, don't worry, we're doctors." Ann reassures her, as she gets ready to inspect John.

"Clumsy Henry fell and broke the bottle over his head, knocking him out. Let me take a look." She continues, carefully checking up on him.

Ann takes his pulse; it's normal. Thankfully, all he's left with is a bump on his head to remind him of my clumsiness.

"Don't worry, Ann; I'm a criminal judge. I'm familiar with this kind of situation," says Jessica as she calms down.

Cameron and Driver climb onto the roof and leave unseen, obeying my silent, gestured orders, that I manage to send through my contact lenses.

Through my double vision I can quickly see them as they climb onto the roof and head off in the drones to the residence.

John has a headache. Luckily, I know exactly where in his skull to break a bottle without there being any consequences.

"What happened?" asks John, a little dizzy, as he pronounces his words.

"You shot the kidnapper." Jessica informs him as she puts ice on his head, and strokes the little hairs that populate his forehead.

"Next time we'll keep our mouths shut about having quiet evenings," Ann says and everyone laughs.

Two hours later, as soon as the police take statements from everyone present, John and Jessica tell us that we can leave the premises. After saying our goodbyes and thanking them for their service, we make our way out and drive to Ann's apartment.

"Do you want me to stay with you tonight?" I ask Ann in the doorway of flat 15A at 300 Mercer Street in the Hillary Gardens building.

"Another day. Tonight's events have shaken me up so I think I might take something to help me sleep," says Ann, rubbing her eyes as she struggles to keep herself awake.

"I think I'll do the same. It's been a long day. I'll never forget tonight though," I say with a smile appearing on my face, as I wink at her direction.

"Neither will I, take care of yourself," Ann asks me as she waves and kisses me goodbye.

As soon as I say goodbye to Ann, I get into my car and drive back home. The night isn't over. There is one more thing left for me to do. And thanks to the phone mishap I know exactly where we have to go. I get my friends in place, and I run them down what's going to happen next.

"I hope this works, guys and it scares the living out of him once and for all. If it doesn't, I'll be forced to do what I don't want to do," I tell my friends, as I start to put my mask on.

"Knowing him, you're going to get the opposite reaction you're expecting. We'll just have to wait and see what happens next," says Cameron.

"Ah, Cameron, I have to say though, I didn't like your little jokes tonight. I may be forced to pull the plug on you."

I look at Cameron with a menacing but sarcastic expression, which bleeds through the darkness of my mask.

"Boss, I had to do it. You were so funny being all flirty with Ann. Might I even go as far as saying a bit too much of a try hard?" Cameron laughs.

"But don't worry we had it all under control." Cameron adds, before I can tell him off again.

"Well for the record, just so you know, I, unlike you, am the best ladies' man in NYC, at least back in my time. All the women's hands are going to be begging to have a piece of me, you'll see." Cameron laughs and Driver seconds him.

"I'll show you my skills when you make new hands. I've had my eye on a few. Heh, heh." Cameron giggles.

And as soon as we're done messing about, we start to get ready.
Afterall, we have a very important job to do.

Chapter 22

John – Threats and Tactics

At the restaurant, Jessica and I order the establishment to be sealed for further tests and photographs to be taken tomorrow. It's a good thing we were here to get the job done, otherwise it would have taken a lot longer to clean up this mess, and the last thing I need right now is another long, endless night.

I do feel bad that I dragged Jessica into this. I was hoping for a calm, relaxing evening, but as per usual, the crime followed me and ruined our plans. But at least I can say that we had fun overall, or perhaps maybe that's the bump on my head going.

Point is: I really need some sleep.

The restaurant owner thanks us both as soon as we're about to leave.

"Thank you, John, and congratulations on diffusing the scene. We were lucky to have you today, and of course you're welcome back anytime. Our treat." He adds, as he shakes both our hands in service.

As we make our way out of the restaurant, Jessica offers to drive me home, but before I can even manage to protest, she's got a billion arguments up her sleeve, ready to be used in her defense.

"No, John, please, I insist, with that accident, we're not going to take any more risks. I'm taking you home, and that's final," Jessica says firmly.

And I, like the coward that I am inside, hypnotized by her charm, cannot refuse.

During the drive we can do nothing but talk about what a disaster our dinner turned out to be, laughing about Henry's fall and my injury.

"I have to say, John, I had a great time tonight, even if there were some unexpected turn of events." Jessica laughs, as she continues to drive us back to my place.

"I agree." I respond. "But hey, at least we met a nice couple, I'm sure we could meet up with them sometime."

"Of course, be sure to call them." Jessica agrees in joy.

"But maybe we'll have Henry sitting at a different table. Don't you think, Jessica?" I joke, for which Jessica responds in laughter.

The rest of the drive, we laugh about anything, and just like that we arrive at my apartment in Soho Square.

I get out of the car and as we say our goodbyes. I thank Jessica and promise to take her out next week.

I'm exhausted. Today has been one of the busiest days yet, and I don't have any more energy left in me, and so I get ready for bed.

After brushing my teeth, I collapse on bed, and quickly fall asleep. In between dreams, I start to move my head from side to side, yet my legs appear to be stuck as I cannot move them around in my mattress. I feel tied down. I can't move. And suddenly something punches me in the face, and I am shaken awake.

There is someone in front of me.

Wearing a black mask, shaped with hands, and dressed entirely in black with a leather trench coat. The dark figure begins to speak to me in a distorted voice.

"At last we meet in person." He begins as his menacing voice appears once more to be distorted, as if fake. "I am hAInds, the person behind the deaths. Don't try anything, you're tied tightly to the bed by straps that will loosen in about four hours."

"By the way, you can take the gag off later." He laughs sarcastically.

"You're wondering what I'm doing here." He continues, as I begin to shake my head in frustration.

"You're good, you're very good, and so is your team. Therefore, I need you to step away from the investigation. Otherwise I'll be forced to intervene. Believe me, I know how to hit you where it hurts. I think you have a family with a wonderful nephew, and I don't think you would want anything to happen to him, would you?" He snickers.

"You must let me finish what I have started." He concludes.
And just as quickly as he entered my apartment in the first place, the hooded figure makes its way to the open window, and throws himself out, into the darkness of the night. And for one second, I think that he may be flying, out and away, to seek what I must presume is his next victim.

Chapter 23

Henry – My new colleagues

It's five o'clock in the morning on a Saturday and I'm meeting Ann for dinner and a drink later on. But for now, it's going to be more than thirty hours of work, more than what I have available until I meet her. So I'll have to work fast.

I'm going to turn the dead hands of more than ninety people into intelligent hands, with a life of their own. They're going to have their own memories, thoughts and feelings. They will be alive once more.

Today is a special day. It is the birth of my children. Not to mention the annual dinner of the NY City Neurology Professionals, that I'll be taking Ann to later this evening.

Frank took it upon himself to select the right people with experience in different areas to add to our team. We have a wide range of professionals: air military soldiers, police special forces, pilots, surgeons and more. We have just about anyone I could ever need.

My friends Driver, Cameron, Mayka, Joseph and the others sleep in special beds, but they'll be awake soon enough to help me out. At night they also rest, just like any other human. I connect them to a machine that allows them to learn while they sleep. This machine inputs more information, re-running their learning models and producing software updates.

Meanwhile, the other part of the brain (the one created from their stem cells and crafted onto the watch) sleeps like a person's. It can also generate dreams, which they sometimes tell me about.

This was why it was so essential for me to select good people with good feelings. Who knows what they could have learned otherwise, and what threat they could pose to me in the future.

If this experiment falls into the wrong hands – politicians, military, thieves – you name it ... I rather not think of the consequences. Global chaos just about touches the surface of what could go wrong. A madman could rule the world, and everyone else would be under his control, all because of my creations, that were brought to life with the sole purpose of doing good.

Even holding the hands of the wrong people can carry a great risk to humanity. Once I finish my plan, I'll have to think very carefully about what I do next. And how I can help more people.

"Good morning, friends, it's time to get up. Breakfast is on the table." I shout across the estate, and my contact lenses pick this up to alert my hands.

But the fun part is that I always play the same joke on them; they can't eat.

"At your service, sir! We are ready to embark on the mission. Come on, I want everyone in position," says Joseph with a military salute which imposes order and compliance.

The others obey; they know he is in charge and they respect him. They get up and accompany me to the room where I will make it possible for the others to come back to life.

The hands split into two groups: Joseph with Mayka and Cameron with Driver. They go to the cold storage room containing all the hands. They select ten and place them on the operating table near the wall. It's time to get started.

I put on the mask, and now it is all or nothing. As the hands are carried to me, dead and motionless, I start to carefully install a watch on each hand one by one. The microvalves are then fitted to the veins.

I repeat this meticulous operation until all ninety hands are completed.

It was quick, faster than I thought. I guess my medical experience did set me up well for this after all. It took me just three hours to finish the operation.

After waiting two hours, a necessary time for the veins to attach themselves to the watch, I activate the pumping and assisted respiration.

Once the red light comes on, I instruct Frank to name each one and activate the organs. It is at this point that the heart will begin to beat. Previously, its mission was to pump blood, but now it also oxygenates the blood simultaneously. The clock allows air to flow in and out. It is wonderful to see that when the light turns green the hand starts to move as it did with Driver and the rest.

That's when life begins.

I look at each one of them. They start jumping up and down with joy and the training of their artificial and natural intelligence takes place. They will spend several hours connected and my friends will watch over the process.

I think Cameron, with Frank's help, would be able to repeat this and bring more hainds, as I call them, to life. They are as excited as I am. We now have about fourteen hours ahead of us, until we complete their teaching and run the algorithms.

It's half past six in the evening, so I take that as my time to start getting ready to meet Ann for dinner.

As soon as I've showered and put on my black tuxedo with a bow tie, I make my way to the car to meet Ann at her place. I can't wait to see her.

When I arrive I knock on her door.

"It's open, come in," says Ann from inside, welcoming me in.

I walk into the living room and I see Ann, looking gorgeous as ever in a tight, silver dress, matching earrings, and a sparkling necklace. Once again I am blown away.

"You look beautiful."

I go over and kiss her. I want to marry her and be happy for the rest of my life, but first I have to figure out how to deal with my situation and make sure I can live that long.

"You too, gorgeous."

I giggle, as she holds my hand and we make our way out to the car.

It's a starry night and the moon illuminates the darkness. Ann is wonderful, she is everything I could ever wish for. We get in the car, I start the engine and we listen to *My song* by Elton John: her favorite.

We laugh a lot during the drive and we talk about our dreams. I have always wanted to retire in a place close to a Mediterranean beach. Listening to John, I think Spain could be a good place, but first I would have to find someone who could take my place and save so many lives. For now, that seems like an impossible plan.

I stop the car at the red traffic light, which I use to stare deep into Ann's eyes. Finally, it turns green and invites me to pull into the tunnel in front. I turn up the music a little when all of a sudden I notice a big flash of white light coming towards us. It all happens so quickly, that I begin to lose control of the car, as I'm blinded.

Stumbling for control, we inevitably crash into the side of the car and it rolls over several times. The airbag activates, protecting our bodies, but my memory is hurt with the agonizing stimulus of the past. The horrendous sound of metal dragging on the hard asphalt screeches and blocks out all other noise.

Not again! I think desperately but it is no use. I lose consciousness and everything turns dark.

Chapter 24

John – An unexpected accident

It's eleven o'clock at night, and I'm sitting in front of the TV, eating a slice of pizza and watching *It's a Wonderful Life*: One of my all-time favorite films. George and his wife are my role models, especially George, who helps everyone without asking for anything in return. I love both their generosities. But I often debate with my friends whether it's because he doesn't know how to say no or whether the character can stop himself from thinking only about his personal gains. I love convincing everyone that it's to do with virtue because it's not about not knowing how to say no, but rather knowing how to help others.

The mobile rings, it's Jessica.

"Hi, Jessica, what a wonderful surprise. I was thinking of taking you out for lunch tomorrow if you'd like," I reply.

"I'd love to, John, but I've just been called away on a case. As I'm on duty as judge tonight, I'd like you to come with me, I think you'd be interested. Shall I send you the address?" Jessica asks with a concentrated tone.

"Yes, of course, I'll see you soon," I say, already focusing my mind on the task at hand.

I take the gun and my jacket before closing the flat door.

Twenty minutes later, I'm at the entrance of a tunnel, where the supposed crime scene has taken place. I show my badge to the policemen who have cordoned off the area, and step inside. Jessica approaches me as soon as she sees that I have arrived.

"Thank you, John, for coming so quickly. I've called your boss and he's agreed that you should take on this case as well. We don't know if there might be any connection to your killer, but just in case we want you to handle it." She begins.

"It's about Ann and Henry, the couple we met at the Spanish restaurant. They had an accident and Henry's body is missing. It may have nothing to do with your case, but we want to be sure." Jessica informs.

"I'll call the team and we'll get to work." I say, my mind already racing with possible explanations for tonight's turn of events.

As if in no time at all, I start to call the team one by one to get them here immediately. I start off with Michael.

"Tell me, John, where is the emergency?" Michael replies hastily.

"I need you to come to the address I'm going to send you." I order quickly.

"Don't worry about it. I'll be there as soon as I can, after picking up the car and the stuff I'll need from the office," says Michael.

"Take as much time as you need," I reply.

After talking to Michael I decide to call Jenny as well so she can provide us with her intelligent mind as we try to solve tonight's midnight case. She'll be here in ten minutes.

Meanwhile, Ann is unconscious and has been taken by ambulance to the hospital. After we look for clues, I'll make sure to go and visit her in the hospital myself to make sure she's okay.

While I wait for my colleagues to arrive, I start to instantly analyze the scene for clues and immerse myself into my surroundings. The good thing is that when I arrived, Ann had not yet been taken out of the car and I was able to record the scene and take some pictures on my phone for future reference.

The first thing that I notice is the car. Henry must have spent a fortune on it, as it was reinforced and accident prone, which thankfully spared Ann's life. The driver's door is detached from the car, which means it must have been hit so hard that it flew off. The wheels are turned all the way to the right, as if something had come from the front and forced him to swerve. The intricate details are only the initial pieces to a larger puzzle we must solve.

As thoughts race through my mind, I alert Dilya to access the cameras, so that we can see exactly what happened in the tunnel.

Jenny and Michael, who were able to make their way to the scene quickly, turn to face me once they see me deep in thought, and I smile back, mouthing: "I'm sorry."

Jessica thanks me for my time today, and begins to address my team of detectives. She tells them that she called us to rule out the possibility that the accident was related to the Dream Killer; the operation is known as Operation Insomnia. Jessica explains to the team how we met Ann and Henry, days before.

"John, Jenny, look at this!" shouts Michael excitedly.

The lieutenants hear the voice and race to the car. Michael has found some fingerprints which he has analyzed.

"There are prints all over the car and they belong to Cameron and Joseph. Clearly, Henry has been captured by our suspect."

Jessica and I look at each other. This case is now personal, since we knew two of the victims, and I can't help but feel a sense of guilt that maybe it was my fault the killer came for them.

Maybe we can connect the pieces if we rescue Henry soon, and find out once and for all if this was always part of his plan or simply another distraction of his to keep us in the dark for a little while longer. Either way we're not going to let him get away. Not this time.

The image of hAInds from the other day comes to my mind, but what's the point of hurting Henry. He's not someone he's close to, so I don't think that's the point. I'll have to talk to Ann later, as she's now a part of the investigation, and the sole victim who has managed to survive the Dream Killer's attacks.

"Thank goodness, I called you. The case is yours," Jessica tells me.

"You're right, they would have assigned it to us in the end when we matched the fingerprints, but it would have been too late. I'm going to the hospital; I want to be the first one to see Ann." I tell Jessica, as I turn my head away darting to my car.

"I'll tell Dilya to place police officers at the door. I don't want to rule out that they wanted to abduct her too, because maybe they did and they just simply ran out of time. Jenny, are you staying or do you want to come?" I say.

"I'm staying, I have to memorize the scene and analyze it," she Jenny.

And with that I am gone.
To chase up the Dream Killer's first weak link.

Chapter 25

John – Visiting a victim

I stand outside the hospital room where Ann is, anxiously waiting for a green light so that I can check up on my new friend. It's been a couple hours since the accident, so if everything goes well she should be waking up soon.

The green light turns on and I cross the road at a run, only to arrive and be told to wait as there is no one there. Pacing up and down the hallway, I suddenly spot one of the nurses and explain to her my situation, hoping that she'll be able to let me in.

"Hi, this is John, from the Police Department. Your patient, Ann, I know her personally, and I was wondering if I could go in and check up on her if that's okay?" I ask.

"Sure, she's just woken up." She responds in a soothing tone. "Just sign this consent form, and I'll let you in to see her."

And with that, I do as she says, and the door is opened to reveal a lying figure on the bed, tumbling from side to side as it wakes itself up.

"Where am I?" Ann asks groggily, rubbing her eyes as if she can't see anything yet. "What are you doing next to me? Wait, who are you? I can't see." She fumbles away as if frightened of me and tries rubbing her eyes.

"Hi, Ann, don't worry, It's me, John, the lieutenant you met in the Spanish restaurant this week. Remember? You're in a hospital," I tell her with a calm and soothing tone to ease her worries.

"Oh, I know, the policeman we found in the restaurant! The one who Henry accidentally hit with the bottle. The one who shot the kidnapper that broke into the restaurant. Yeah, I remember the whole thing, the man ended up shot and you ended up with a big bump," Ann says quizzically, as she begins to gain consciousness.

"Yes, that all ended well, Ann. You're here because you were in a car accident yesterday with Henry, no longer than a couple of hours ago."

"Henry? Yes, I remember, we were going to the annual NY City neurosurgeon's convention." She begins. "We were listening to music, and when we went into a tunnel a big light hit us and we lost control." She continues as she begins to remember.

She sits up with a start. "Where's Henry? I want to see him, how is he? Take me to his room!" Ann says nervously, grabbing onto the sides of the bed for support as she tries to stand up.

"Ann, please, don't move!" I plead and reach forward to restrain her. "I'm sorry to have to give you this news, but we haven't found his body. He has disappeared. We think someone may have kidnapped him."

I take Ann by the hand and I tell her how sorry I am. Between Ann's sobs, I make a promise to her that I will do everything I can to find him.

Once Ann appears to have calmed down, I call the nurse so that the doctor can further analyze her, now that she's obtained consciousness, and gained back her vision. Hopefully, a similar fate awaits Henry, wherever he may be.
Though I wouldn't be so sure.

Chapter 26

John – A new case for the FBI

Several days have passed since Henry's disappearance. The news was picked up by the press and so now New York and the international neurosurgical community are in a state of shock. Henry is a much-loved and appreciated professional, and everyone believes that his kidnapper is the Dream Killer, who is seeking the limelight.

Pris takes the story to her TV station; we talk every day to exchange information, but we don't come up with any key leads to investigate. Her journalists are working day in and day out; we have about a hundred people involved.

Our dear boss has called us in for an urgent meeting at eleven o'clock this morning. I can only imagine that he'll have nothing to tell us but how badly we are working. He'll shout at us to work harder (as if that was humanly possible). Honestly, we're doing everything we can, and sometimes the cost is just too high (it has already cost someone their relationship).

It's eleven o'clock and our team is waiting for the boss in the meeting room. Knowing him, he has chosen the name on purpose, so don't expect anything good from him.

We see through the open door that he is laughing with four other people. He sees us looking outside and glares at all of us, especially me. Stephan enters the room, his hair styled to perfection as always, and gestures with his hands for us to sit down; he stands in front of us and next to him are his guests, two on each side. They wear dark suits and sunglasses.

"John, I have called the team together to tell you that you will not be continuing with the investigation. It will now be handed over to our dear colleagues in the FBI." He starts, his eyes looking at me directly, as if placing the blame with his gaze.

"You have shown that you are incapable of solving it. Not only are you totally lost, but you are so incompetent that you're not even close. From now on, the real professionals will take over." He mentions, and I can sense my team being riled up in frustration.

"Your heads are in the clouds! You just happened to get lucky with the previous cases you managed to solve. In the end, time has proved me right and, as soon as we got a somewhat complicated case, it took you no time to fail; yes, fa-il-ed." He pronounces the last word very slowly as if he is speaking with two-year-olds.

"Now get out of here and give all the information to the FBI! If you have any questions, direct them to your new boss, whom you will meet tomorrow. I'll leave you to enjoy my new promotion as they transfer me to the Washington DC city department." He waits for some praise, frowning when he receives none.

I have a terrible urge to punch him, but now is not the time. With Henry missing and the killer on the loose, I can't lose my temper.

"Stephan, on behalf of the team, we would like to tell you that we wanted this promotion with all our hearts and that we are very happy for you." I place my hands over my heart dramatically as I speak with sarcastic passion. "You don't know how happy we are that you will be assigned to another precinct. This means that we can enjoy our own careers and successes from now on without you."

Irony is the best remedy against morons. At last, we are rid of this obnoxious self-interested villain. But at what cost have we been forced to pay.

Without giving him a chance to reply, we get up and go to our desks, from which we remove all the folders and reports related to the case. We put them in boxes and mark them with a marker: 'Operation Insomnia'. We pack up our only hope of ever being able to solve this case. Having given up, I make a phone call and ask Dilya to text Stephan that all the investigation materials are packed up on our desks to be removed by the FBI.

The team's dissatisfaction is enormous, we know each other well enough to know exactly what we are thinking. And today it's nothing but discontent and surrender. We get up and go to the cafeteria for lunch together. Today we will take the rest of the day off. We need time to process the outcomes of the day and come to terms with the fact that the case has just been taken from our hands.

Besides, we don't deserve to hear Stefan tell us such insulting and demotivating words. But, if I've learned anything in life, it's that I believe in karma. We must act responsibly in each of our actions and then we might get rewarded. Stephan will also have his own karma for all that he has said and thought about on a daily basis. Though his will be negative.

We go into the cafeteria. Today, Renata, the owner, is there. Daughter of Italian parents, her great-great-grandparents emigrated many years ago to New York and established this business, which has been passed down from generation to generation. They offer typical Italian and American food on the menu. Their espresso and cappuccino are the best I've ever had. Renata has known us for many years and brings us our food as she sees the look on our faces when we arrive. Today we are going to stay for a long time. We need to let off steam and release all the negativity which entraps us. Dilya also accompanies us today.

It has been more than twenty minutes, and yet no one has spoken a single word. My team is on the verge of tears, their eyes wet and red. Our gazes are lost, and our faces hide the pain with expressions devoid of feeling. We are sunk, we have failed. Stephan's words have fallen on us like unexpected stabs. Our hearts are shattered with unfixable pain.

We feel like we will never again have a chance like this to prove our worth. We have never failed at anything before, we have always tasted success, and all we can sense now is the bittersweet taste of failure.

Operation Insomnia won't let us sleep for a long time. We will be haunted by its memory until we solve a case worthy of challenging its magnitude.

What can I even say to my team, how can I cheer them up? They are people who are used to winning, they don't know what it's like to lose. And today we lost, hAInds won. Big time.

I don't want to be pessimistic nor self-involved, but I don't think the FBI will be able to solve it either. It's a case that would need the collaboration of both institutions. It's going to be very complicated for a single entity to solve as it's a case that blinds anyone and leaves them lost in the dark.

I look at Jenny; she's completely devastated. She has sacrificed so much. Her relationship was torn apart. It's true that we were all disappointed in him, we didn't think he would even dare to cheat on her. But we were wrong, so wrong. We thought it was because Jenny was so involved with the investigation. But it wasn't. Her now ex-husband had been in another relationship for years, and neither of us had any idea. What great detectives we are.

The food has been brought to us, and there it stays, isolated and out of reach. Nobody tastes it. It's going to get cold. But we don't care anymore. My mother hated it when I ate my food cold, it was the only time she got angry, and I jokingly called her 'stress lady'. It's about one of the only memories I have of her now.

I stand up and lift one of the beers they have brought for us. Everyone looks up and stares sadly into my eyes, hoping to find their sense of location.

"I know what you guys are going through. Believe me. We've worked so hard and we've been taken off the case. It's not fair and we know it." I start, struggling to get the right words out.

"The worst thing is that we have never lost before and today we have. The only thing I can say is that we must continue to strive past our struggles and continue to put the same dedication as before. May our failures help us to rise up stronger than ever before. May we never give up. We must toast, because, as my father used to say, every cloud has a silver lining. Let us toast." I never knew my father, but it fit well, so I let it slide. Jenny looks at me and giggles slightly, because she picked up on that.

Everyone looks at me, bow their heads and rest them on their hands. It's the first time a speech I believe in doesn't work.

Minutes go by and no one says anything. We are left in endless silence, and just when I don't think anything will get us out of it, I'm brought back to reality.

Suddenly, a post man asks for permission to enter and asks for me. He hands me an envelope, which I quickly sign. I look down to see who sent me the package. The sender signs as hAInds.

I get the group's attention, interrupting their fixed gazes and silent whispers.

"Guys," I say as blood starts to pump in my veins once more. "It's from hAinds."

Everyone gasps. Only they know of the existence of that name. It has never been reflected in any document or recording. So that's when we know it's a direct message from him: from the Dream Killer, from HAINDS.

I frantically tear open the package and read a handwritten note.

Yes, I was there all right, but I wasn't the one who kidnaped him. Look at these photos and comments carefully.

We impatiently take out the photos from the envelope, as we struggle to contain the excitement that propels us forward. The photos appear to have been taken from special infrared cameras.

There are four snapshots. The first shows footprints that look like hiking boots, the second shows boot marks, the third shows tire marks with footnotes that read: 'Project Plasma', and the last one shows burn marks on the bonnet of the Ford Mustang.

We look at each other; nobody has these documents and we didn't discover this evidence in the investigation. So who did? And why would they send it to us?

But what are we seeing exactly?

"Tonight, we will have to go and check everything for ourselves." I tell the team.

"We will split up, Michael and Jenny, you'll go to the tunnel and Dilya and I will go to the garage where the Mustang is." I instruct, as I feel the excitement of the case return to my body. And I feel once again what it means to have a purpose.

We all bade farewell to ourselves, and despite not saying anything to each other, I know that we are all asking ourselves the same thing: why was hAInds there?

I have a theory that I follow in all my research: chance never produces consequences; chance does not exist. Everything that happens, happens because of something that is not by chance. Everything happens for a reason. And so did this. Although I don't know why exactly.

Dilya pulls out her laptop, and I know that she's onto something.

"I think I've got something John," she tells me, as she finishes her frantic typing and motions the team to look at the screen.

It appears that Dilya searched up the name of the brand that makes those boots. They are made by a company in Greenland that sells them exclusively to the army, through one classified organization in particular. They are special snow boots, used by elite cops.

Not just anyone can have access to them.

Right there and now, it's as if these four photos have shown us once again why we still need to fight. We have worked up an appetite with the desire to continue the investigation on our own. Our spirits have been restored. A simple glance at Jenny's determined look, Michael's subtle nod and Dilya's smile is enough to say that we are all in. We return to the restaurant and start eating the hamburgers, hot dogs and pizzas. Now we are back. And we are never giving up. Even if they force us off this case again.

Dilya, in between bites of her burger, continues to search for the other clues. And she tells us about the Plasma Project.

"It is a prototype that was started some years ago. It contains a laser powerful enough to destroy all types of army weapons and vehicles. It is currently still in the experimental phase" she reads "and it seems that they stopped investing when they realized that the results were not what they expected."

"Look at the pictures of the prototype and especially the wheels, they seem to match the dimensions and shape of the picture on a first glance. I will check if I can find the year of manufacture of the wheels and which company produced them." She then laughs happily, as she gets her character back.

"Bingo, I've got the name of the company! We're in luck, I'll phone up and pretend to be a secretary in the Army's Purchasing Department and see if it works. Guys, we're getting some answers!" She continues.

At last, the food is where it should be: resting deep inside of our happy lively stomachs.

We continue our research to see if we can find the answer to all this mess. But this time, we have the driving passion behind us to propel us forward.

Once we'd finished eating, Dilya and I don't hesitate to do what we had set out to do. We go directly to the garage to look at the car.

"Good afternoon, I'm Lieutenant John Duffy and this is Officer Dilya. We'd like to take another look at the Ford Mustang you brought in today," I say to the guard at the police garage, as we enter through the doors.

"Yes, of course, follow me." He motions us inside.

In this garage they keep most of the cars that are involved in cases: from robberies, chases, kidnapping, you can find just about any vehicle that was used during crime scenes. In front of us we see Henry's Mustang. Bingo. In the daylight we can check the details better. I pull out the photos and sure enough, there are burn marks; they're circular like tree rings, but they're barely visible to the naked eye. How convenient.

It's time to investigate the Project Plasma prototype in detail, find out who might be using it and why.

As Dilya and I make our way out the garage and get into the car, I call Jenny and put her on speaker.

"Hey, Jenny, it's John, how are things going there?"

Jenny and Michael are in the tunnel, investigating the crime scene. As they are policemen, they have full access to the area with no disruptions. I made sure to set up access for them before they left.

"Hi, John, we've got nothing so far, but we're looking. Michael's running some footprint scans, and just like before we're finding fingerprints of Cameron and Joseph all around. It's looking like a distraction, I'm afraid."

"Hey, Jenny, can you come over here?" I can hear Michael shouting across the phone.

"Yeah, I'm on my way, just talking to John," she replies. "Give me a second, John, I'll be right with you." She mentions to me.

As we wait for Jenny to update us on the situation Dilya's running some scans on her computer. A couple minutes pass and Jenny's back on the phone.

"John you there?" she asks.

"Yeah, tell me," I reply.

"Okay, great. So we followed up the trail of footprints, and it looks like they go to some sort of rooftop area, and suddenly disappear as if they've come and gone from thin air." She tells me.

"This is really strange, we don't know what we're looking at I'm afraid." She continues.

"Don't worry about it, Jenny." I reply. "Just go home, and we'll talk about it tomorrow. Good job today."

It's been tough, but they'll keep going until they find something that can bring them back on the case and restore their lost prestige. It's a team with such high ambitions and great achievements that they will never give up.

In the evening I get an email; we have another meeting with our boss tomorrow at ten o'clock: Introduction of new boss. I try to see who it might be, but there are no names to label our new secret captain.

I can only hope they'll be better than our last one.

Chapter 27

Henry – Where am I?

My head hurts so much. It's as if I've been taken back forcefully, and the effects of the shock have penetrated deep inside, my headache being the remainder of the pain inflicted. The darkness prevents me from seeing where I am, I can't move, I'm tied up. I'm lying on what I think is a bed. In front of me there is a door, the light outside forms the silhouette of the frame's edges, although I struggle to see very far due to the suffocating darkness closing in around me.

My hands. Where are they? I frantically try to force my concentration to focus and connect with them through my lenses but without my glasses it's a futile effort at most. Without my glasses I can't communicate with them, and the emergency feature I set on the lenses to at least see where they are doesn't seem to be working. I only get flashes of what Cameron's seeing, slight movements back and forth of some of the other hands I struggle to make out.

But I can't seem to remember. What happened? As I scour my brain for answers, I get glimpses of what happened although I fail to put it in order. I was driving my Mustang, when all of a sudden, I was blinded by a powerful light in front of me. I lost control of the car. I hit the wall and flipped over several times.

I was in a car accident.

That's why I can't find my glasses anywhere, they must have been left behind in the wreckage. I assume that my concussion is the reason behind the lens not working and I struggle in my chair.

"Nurse, nurse!" I shout.

As if right on cue, the door opens, and two men come in. But even in the darkness I can see that they are not the nurses I was expecting. Instead, they are two heavy built men in military uniform. They are armed.

They turn on the light and I lift myself out of the darkness once and for all. Now that I can see further, I realize the additional details of the room that I'm in: a bed, a bedside table, a table and a chair, all simple furniture. Two doors are aligned on the room's walls: in one I see the shower and toilet. The other door leads to a corridor. An exit, a way out.

"Don't worry, Henry;" one of the men's voices whispers, "you had an accident. Your fiancé, Ann, is all right, she has recovered, and you will too. Get dressed in the clothes we left on the chair. When you have finished, ring the bell on the bedside table and we'll come back to talk."

I'm so confused that I don't even bother to confront them, and I do as I'm told. As soon as I'm dressed, I press the doorbell beside me and the two men re-enter the room.

"Follow us please, Henry," they ask, as they open the door for me to follow.

They put handcuffs on my hands, and I am led down several corridors, with only a few spotlights overhead here and there to guide me. I am unaware of my surroundings, but what I do know is that I'm someplace cold.

As we traverse what appears to be a never ending set of halls and locked doors, we finally arrive at one that catches their attention and we stop in front of it suddenly. They place their hands on a device that reads their fingerprints, right by the side of the handle, and just like that it opens.

As we make our way through the doorway we are invited to a large room, full of computer monitors that scour the scene. In the middle of all the technology that surrounds us, is a large black metal cabinet, with a single blue light which emits a blinking light.

But what is most intriguing is not the high tech that covers this room from one corner to the end but rather a large anagram that is centered in the middle of the room. It looks vaguely familiar to me, but I can't remember where I've seen it before. This anagram depicts a weighted scale, as if rocking back and forth with an unbalanced weight, and the pi symbol as a foreground holding it all in place. Encompassing it all is a semicircle which reads: 'The Court of Pi'.

I am shaken from my thoughts as a hand grabs my shoulder, and a soft menacing voice begins to say: "All you have to do is cooperate and nothing will happen to you." The voice hisses behind me.

I direct my attention to the overbearing voice and can see that it belongs to a giant. He stands towering over me, his dark beard dangling inches from my face. I turn to face him and notice his arms dipping my shoulders, and I can make out the thousands of intricate tattoo designs weaved deep within the surface of his skin.

His face rings a bell. I see the name on his badge: Adam Brown.

"We are delighted to have you with us, Mr Silverstone. My name is Adam Brown, we met at Professor Julian Forty's house." He begins.

"Henry, we've brought you here because you are the only person in the entire world that can help us. I don't want to threaten you, but I will if I have to. I need your cooperation and I'm not asking for it."

"The project we are working on revolves around something that we call 'The Quantum Mind'. I know it's a lot to take in but everything will start to make sense soon."

"You see the big black cabinet with the blue light on the side?" He points directly to draw my attention.

"See that, Henry? That is the most powerful computer in the world, a quantum machine. As you know, it is capable of processing information much faster than the best non-quantum computer." He goes on.

"The Quantum Mind Project started more than fifteen years ago right here, deep within this secret base, built right into the mountains of Greenland."

"The goal is to extract all the data, information and knowledge from a human brain, pass it to this machine and then be able to read it. We want to be able to access a person's wisdom, knowledge and memories. We want to hack a person's mind."

"With all this, we will be able to achieve our ambitious plans. The project is at a very advanced stage, but unfortunately its predecessor died during one of the tests. We tried to get the government involved in the programme, but they did not believe in the idea. They were too focused on the morality of our actions rather than the potential it brought to mankind. But they will believe in it soon, once they realize the power within."

"Our research is now at the stage where we can extract a person's information from their brain. We can even transfer it to a computer. But our work is not done; it's just beginning. We need you, Henry, because only then will we be truly able to read the transferred information and pass it into our own minds." Adam Brown finishes.

"What are you asking of me?" I mumble.

Adam grins maliciously. "It's simple really. We believe that only you can achieve what our researchers have yet to accomplish. With your brain and our plans, nothing can stand in our way. All that we ask is that you collaborate, and you and the rest of humanity will be rewarded." He answers as his eyes narrow in my direction.

"And if I don't?" I reply.

Adam's smile broadens. "Well, then I'm sure we can think of something to get you on board, my friend ... I'd hate for something terrible to happen to your dear Ann ..." he says, with a pitiful look in his eyes.

If only I had my team here. This group of lowlifes would not last 10 seconds, and soon enough their smirks would be replaced with a worrying look of fear.

In that instant, I get a flash, something breaks my concentration and I'm transported somewhere else. I think the lenses are working, and for one instant I see them. My hands, my creations. Through Cameron's view, I see a couple of my hands scouring away, in what seems to be a darkened ally. I am back where it all went wrong. Where they captured me and forced me to collaborate on a project that will dictate the course of all of humanity.

Is the idea of a Quantum Mind ground-breaking? Well, yes, of course, I can't argue with that. The simple act of reading one's brain and then transferring this elsewhere poses significant opportunities. Just think of what one could do: the options are endless. We would have a digital storage: zeros and ones, zeros and ones, a repeating sequence that could be decoded at the snap of one's fingers ... Maybe this will give me an alternative to my plan. The hands will be able to retrieve all their memories and knowledge. I would have thousands of hands, all those people who want to, will still be alive. I could help people with Alzheimer's and other mental problems. The idea is brilliant, liberating, the solution would allow you to be able to pass on everything you know to other people. That would take a lot of pressure off my life, because it would be possible to transfer my professional wisdom to other doctors depending on their learning and brain capacity. It's a very interesting use case. I will accept it. I will collaborate to apply it and see if it can be successful in my ambitions and goals.

I look at Adam, my pupils fixating and glaring down at him. I know what I need to do.

"All right, fine, I accept. Just tell me what I need to do." I yield, never looking away.

"Perfect, it's settled then, let us show you where you will be working from," Adam replies.

And with that he leads us away through the never-ending corridors where everything blends in and appears to be an inescapable maze full of surprises. By looking up and down my surroundings it wouldn't surprise me if there were more than 20 floors here. Even though I'm yet to figure out where I am, every couple of minutes, we pass a new hangar and I can't help but think that maybe soon I'll be able to escape from here. But for now that is nothing but wishful thinking.

Adam Brown walks us in complete silence, and I am left to wander about this place and the project. I know that I'll have to start by mapping the regions of the brain and being able to identify an individual's maximum capacity, and how they are likely to respond when new information is received.

After what feels like an eternity, we finally approach a door for which Adam opens by scanning his eye and motions us to follow him inside.

"Henry, this will be your primary office from now on. I'll leave you to get started. Please make a note of any new materials you wish to acquire, and we'll be sure these get delivered to you as soon as possible. Your bedroom is connected at the back of this room, and you can easily access it," he says as he makes his way out the door, and gives a subtle wink as if masking his traitorous expression.

I may have been left behind alone, who knows how many miles away from my little creations. But I will escape, I just have to figure out what's next, what they're planning, and how to destroy them. I need to finish my plan, and for that I need to get out alive, even if it is without the help of my hands.

Chapter 28

JOHN – New boss

It is ten o'clock in the morning, and while we're waiting around we take the chance to talk amongst ourselves and ease a bit of the pressure that we've been carrying for the past couple of months. And just like that, the calmness is disrupted when our cherished boss walks in through the doors, and soon enough chaos will erupt from the room. Yet, what surprises us all, is that behind him is a woman that follows closely. We've never seen her before.

I can only assume that she must be in her early fifties, and through her demeanor and stance, I can tell that she keeps herself active.

As she walks over to take a seat at the table, I get a closer look at her face, which radiates confidence yet in an approachable manner. The brightness of her blue eyes radiate her toned facial features, which I can only assume have hard work done, as not a single wrinkle can be seen. She smiles, as she begins to scan the room and look at us directly.

Our dear former-boss on the other hand, is serious, his face lacks any sort of emotion. Stephan closes the door with a BANG and sits down in one of the chairs at the head of the table, next to the woman.

"I just wanted to say two things: one, this is Captain Ballantine, and two, goodbye."

Stephan stands up and leaves in a hast, leaving us speechless. And just like that he leaves just as suddenly as he arrived. I get excited thinking that this may just be the day where we finally get rid of him. I make sure to control my composure, I don't want to get overly excited and jinx the good news.

As if on cue, the woman gets up and closes the door softly, as if shutting us off from a world where Stephan exists. She walks to the front of the room, where the space is open and signals for us to stand in a circle at the front. She then drags a chair from the table and motions us to do the same. Once we form the circle, her expression changes and she wears a big smile once again.

"Hello everyone, allow me to introduce myself. My name is Zara Ballantine, my grandparents were Scottish, hence my first and last names; I'm single because frankly no one can stand me. I am short as you can probably tell …" She gestures down, and we let out a short laugh along with her. "… and my good friends call me 'Cockroach'. As you can see, I already have a nickname, and I invite you to use it as you wish." She starts and her perfume of wood and a hint of vanilla, drifts through the air.

Zara laughs, as her smile fills up her brightening rosy cheeks, and I can feel from the room that my teammates are already liking her better than Stephan. "From now on I'll be your supervisor. I hope I can do better than my predecessor, whom I can see that you were all very anxious to get rid of." She winks, and we all let out a sigh of relief as if right on cue.

"She is one of us," I whisper to Jenny, who's sitting next to me.

"Everyone in the police department knows who you are as a team. They know how hard you work, the commitment you give to your job and the leadership you demonstrate daily." She continues, praising us dearly.

"That is why I have fought hard to be your new commanding officer, I wanted to be the leader you always lacked. I hope that we can become a team that involves everyone. I want to be by your side and be involved as much as possible. I want us to cover for one another, no matter what. I know what type of professionals you are." She continues, her voice powerfully charged with emotion and confidence.

"And that is why I want Operation Insomnia to be rightfully handed back to us. I've read every last detail and it annoys me that the FBI could just come in and take over the investigation. In principle, it's not in their jurisdiction." She stops and takes a calming breath, smiling once more, as she recollects her growing frustration.

"I'm sure there's something fishy about how the case managed to end up in the FBI's hands but since I have friends in the FBI we're going to work with them internally to clear it up. I've been on the case since day one, even from the background, but my hands are tied. I've had a look at the reports and all your notes and I think we need to start by looking at the angle of health problems." She continues.

"Dilya, I need you to record all medicine card payments to clinics and hospitals by the people killed. Call all the centers and ask them to verify the presence of our victims. I know it will take several days, but as soon as you receive any news, let us know." She orders. Dilya gives her a worried look and Zara reassures her.

"Don't worry, I have the support of the FBI to run the investigation in parallel, but we must be careful that the agents who were here don't find out just yet. We'll continue talking about everything during the day at your favorite coffee shop; I've booked the upstairs area and today the 'Cockroach' is paying." She finishes her speech and takes a deep breath, as if satisfied with her delivery. I know that I've surely been convinced.

Zara smiles and laughs again.

Just by looking around the circle, and looking at each member of the team, I know that they are just as surprised as I am. A boss who not only wants to be involved and is interested in the case, but also cares about each one of us as human beings. I don't really think the day would come, where we would get rid of Stephan and have the boss we truly deserve.

Unable to contain our growing excitement, we stride out of the meeting room and make our way directly to the cafeteria and sit down in the booth. Zara gives us each a notebook and writes something in hers: 'Put all mobile phones on the table and stand up.'

We listen to her and look at each other in amazement. She takes a device out of her backpack: it looks like a metal detector and brings it close to us. She checks every part of our bodies for anything.

Now she turns to the mobile phones, but doesn't seem to find what she's looking for. Suddenly, as the metal detector scans the last phone, my own, the detector emits a red light. Zara frowns and writes in her notebook hastily. She shows the note to me: 'You have a suspicious device in your phone, tell the café's owner to put it in a cupboard and then after we finish we'll take it. Forward calls from that number to this new phone I give you. We'll use it when it suits us.'

I take the phone, give it to the owner and she puts it away, just as Zara instructed.

Zara is good, it never occurred to me that I was being spied on. And for her it's taken her less than an hour to work it out. I take it back. She's really good.

'Who's behind it, the FBI, hAInds?' I think to myself. And just like that some things start to make sense, the calls, the information, the misleading. Although I can't seem to connect all the dots yet, a picture is forming in my brain and I'll be able to decipher it soon enough. I'll have to tell Michael to run it for fingerprints. If I'm correct that device must have been on my phone ever since

HAINDS scared me that night. And if that's the case, that means that he's been watching our every move for a lot longer than any of us would have guessed.

"Now that there are no bugs." Zara begins.

"Fill me in on all the details, including the latest visits to the garage and the tunnel. I don't want you to think I'm spying on you, but I've been keeping track of your movements to protect you. You are all in great danger, I'm afraid," says Zara very seriously as she conveys concern.

For several hours we explain everything in detail and show her all the evidence we have. The footprints, the names, the chases, the Plasma prototype, the boots, the burn marks on the plate, what happened to us here, the shooting and what we saw on the roof. We are careful not to leave any detail too small out. Because if there's one thing that we have learned about this case is that everything is important.

Zara instructs Dilya to investigate Cameron's past; she wants to know absolutely everything: payments, income, phone records, where he used to go. She wants to find out all about his past, especially during the last three years, she believes that could be a critical period of great importance. And once again I'm kicking myself that I didn't think to do that before.

"Jenny, John, I've set up an appointment with the Pentagon for tomorrow. I have very good connections with the Army, so I'm sure that their help will be invaluable. I'll be sure to tell them about the Plasma and the boots; because from what I've already noticed, is that with this new information, they will be more interested than ever to collaborate with us," she says, as she talks to Jenny and I directly.

"Thank you, Zara, this is definitely the right direction to move forward." Jenny adds, and I know that from her tone, she's desperately trying to control her childish excitement.

And it's as if she can feel my eyes fixating upon her. She turns slightly and mouths to tell me to stop as she blushes. I've caught her, and she's embarrassed by her reaction.

"We'll have a meeting with a general, a friend of mine and people from his trusted team. Regarding the FBI, they are going to pass me internal information on the agents assigned to the case, their history and their command structure in the organization." Zara continues to inform us of the proceedings of the investigation.

"Dilya, whilst we deal with this, I want you to carry out a thorough investigation of these agents. I have sent you an email with their names." Zara informs her, and now proceeds to look at each of us directly, her eyes beaming with pride and concentration.

I know that this is going to be a productive day. I can feel it. Watch out hAInds, wherever you are out there, listening to us, watching over us, we're coming for you.

Chapter 29

John – Technological advances

It is now four o'clock in the afternoon, and after a morning of traveling, we have finally arrived at The Pentagon in Washington DC. The team was anxious the whole ride here, as perhaps today we might just get the answers to some of the questions that have bugged us for so long. We are now at the Pentagon waiting impatiently in the reception, my foot tapping loudly with impatience. The room is large and spacious, the entrance brightened by the lights overhead and the classic furniture surrounds the room. Plaques crowd the walls, and my vision wanders around.

It is not long until a man approaches us, his steps marching along the marble floor. His boots march in unison, as he places one foot in front of the other. He wears a uniform, and as he comes nearer, I can just make out some of the many recognitions that he wears proudly on his chest.

"Welcome, my name is Gerald. Please let me show you to the meeting room." He introduces himself, as he motions us to follow him.

It's the first time I've ever been inside the actual building, and I for once am amazed with the building that we're in. I thought the lobby was impressive, this cannot compare even in the slightest.

We walk down several corridors and enter a large office with an oval meeting table, and a large monitor at the front of the room. It's a room like no other, one that asks for power and respect, and just like that I notice just how deep we are getting ourselves into. This is not just a typical neighborhood murder anymore, it's a national emergency. Our worst nightmare.

We are asked to sit down and are offered something to drink and eat, by the staff that guard each of the entrances to the room.

As we all take our seats, Gerald confirms that we are ready and asks for the officers to make their way to the meeting room. In a couple of minutes, the door opens, and four officers enter: two of them female, and the others male, all of them radiating energy of confidence and superiority. We are now in the big leagues.

As soon as they make their way through the doorway, Zara stands up and hugs two of them fiercely. She introduces us to them: General Arthur Williams and Sergeant Sarah Miller , who give us the names of the other members of the meeting, and as such get us up to speed with everyone that is here today.

"Thank you for coming, I am, as you know, General Williams. I'm in command of the special forces and I'm in charge of many secret projects here, but hopefully, I'll be able to help you all today with uncovering some of these." He begins, clearing his throat for attention and looking around the room with a calm and poised expression.

"Please, before we start, I would like you to brief us on everything that you've discovered. Particularly with the boots and the Plasma prototype. We want to help you as much as we can, and for that we need to be perfectly transparent with each other if we really are going to get to the bottom of this." He continues, motioning for me to explain.

"Thank you, General Williams, I'm sure that you'll be of great service to us today. So, let's begin," I say, as I turn on the monitor and walk them through everything that we've managed to uncover.

But for now, it's nothing but a hunch and a few hypothetical guesses at best, that are surely miles away from the truth. So, the presentation ends rather quickly as I go over what Dilya has found out.

"Thank you, John, for the information. I'll take it from here, and let you know what we've managed to investigate from our side ever since we agreed to set up this meeting," General Williams says as I finish going over everything that we've uncovered.

He takes to the floor by placing himself in front of the presentation screen.

"What you are about to see is top secret, but it's important that you are made aware of this nonetheless, and so we value your discretion at all times," he says, and we all nod in response.

"A few years ago, we started investing in building a vehicle with a weapon we call 'Plasma'. The basis of this weapon, and why it was so important that we researched it, is that it emits a large laser-like light with the power to destroy any type of weapon, any type of vehicle, anything that is placed in its path."

"So, I guess you can understand why it was important for us to find out how to use it first and keep it off the wrong people's hands." General Miller adds from the back of the room, as she's been paying close attention to everything that has so far been discussed.

General Williams, once again takes to the floor as he continues showing us images of the technology, and with every next picture that is shown, the more and more that I start to worry about the true parameters of the mess we've (involuntarily) gotten ourselves into. As if things couldn't get any worse.

"What is interesting about this technology is that at its lowest level, it emits a light that blurs a person's vision and thus blinds them for several hours. That's what we assume happened to Henry and Ann on the night of the accident, causing them to lose control of the car." He explains as everything starts to fall into place, although the motive is still up for grabs. Why would anyone do this?

"The beam also leaves a trail of burns in the area where it is applied. These would be identical to the ones found in Henry's Mustang." General Williams concludes, as he motions for Sergeant Miller to lead the discussion from this point.

"The prototype …" she begins, "was evolving quickly, faster than any of us would have predicted. A couple of months ago we started testing it but shortly after the Pentagon decided to stop the funding and pump the money into other more valued projects. There has only ever been one model produced." She continues.

"So naturally, when we received the call from Zara, we investigated internally to see where it was. We were shocked to discover that the weapon was in fact stolen," says Sergeant Miller as she shakes her head in frustration.

"We are investigating who it could be. We are in the process of viewing tapes, analyzing access, and activating multiple investigation protocols, but for now, there is nothing conclusive, simply leads to follow. On the monitor, you can see the three suspects, all of whom no longer work here. They are the ones who were seen at the crime scene under the possible timestamps for the day Henry was abducted, thanks to our image recognition algorithms. Andrew Stones, Susan Allister and Peter Cook," says General Williams, pointing to the photos behind him.

"Our main theory right now is that there must have been someone on the inside to help them gain access through the security clearance. And based on previous incidents we think that it was most likely General Adam Brown, as we have footage of him meeting them that day and later inside an armored transport truck leaving the compound, as we picked up from the nearby traffic cameras." He continues.

"What we know, is that they all have a reputation that precedes them." The general explains. "For example, they were all mercenaries who worked for different governments in their lifetime, and often collaborated with companies who dealt with weapons and highly advanced technology. None of the suspects have families, they are very dangerous and elusive: a threat to us and most possibly Henry if they have managed to abduct him," Sergeant Miller says.

"From what I've gathered from all my years working here, in particular when collaborating with General Brown in several projects …" General Williams takes over, "… is that General Brown's ambitions have often got the better of him, he's been disciplined on more than one occasion. He is the type of person that fails to empathize with others, and his dictatorial-like principles stop at nothing to get what he wants. God only knows how he treats his enemies in missions overseas. But stealing from the Pentagon itself, that is another matter altogether." General Williams concludes.

"These are only some key details to keep in mind, but hopefully you'll have a better understanding of the type of person he was. No one can explain how he was promoted so quickly. We are investigating his promotions, emails, documents and associated justifications to learn more." Adds another military officer, who has been actively taking notes the whole meeting.

"The other point is the boots. These boots were also bought by the Pentagon and are used in cold places, primarily in snowy and mountainous regions. We have since then discovered that the whole batch, about two thousand of them, were stolen days before Henry's abduction. The information we have leads us to believe that General Brown and his followers have moved to a remote region," Sergeant Sarah Miller says.

"We are thinking of areas near Canada or in Greenland, as the transport truck where we believe the prototype was being transported has been found abandoned just over the border. The problem now is that they are in another country and the search is more complicated, not to mention our jurisdiction that may be compromised should we need to make an arrest. We have asked for cooperation with the military in both countries because of the risk of the prototype being out of our control, but that also means that our classified information is no longer a secret. The more people we involve, the more we risk being exposed. Who knows who else Adam has working for him." General William adds, with an ashamed shake of his head, as he realizes that the situation is getting rapidly out of hand, despite them not noticing anything strange just a couple of days ago.

Zara turns to her bag to pull out her notepad. But she notices that the bag is open. Zara frowns.

"That's odd, I could have sworn I had my bag closed. I must have left it open when I gave the IDs at the entrance and forgotten to close it. Thank goodness this place is secure." She mentions.

I can see Zara writing down the key points in her notebook, and from her face I know she's got a couple of ideas up her sleeve. She puts the pencil down on the table and inadvertently moves her hand and the pad falls to the floor. I quickly bend down and pick it up for her, when my vision blurs, and I see something moving away into the darkness of the shadows. But just like that, it's gone. I can't understand it. I shake my head confused and find no trace of anything. It must be just the light and lack of sleep playing tricks on me.

Chapter 30

Henry – Old friends, new enemies

Flashes of light push through my mind, I can see my hands. They're somewhere, again. I can see them again. But this time the image feels more centered and clear. Like I'm able to be in contact with them again. Cameron, I call out frantically, but I know that without my glasses, it won't do any good. I can see them, but I can't talk to them, I can't even hear them.

This time it seems as if they are in a coveted room hiding underneath a table within the shadows. A pen drops and someone picks it up, but I can't make out who it is. The hands jump out and move away. Within seconds I get a glimpse of Joseph climbing up the wall, and Cameron following close behind, as I know that what I'm seeing is through him.

They climb up to the roof and slide down until they find a trap door to squeeze through and move through the air vents. They move at top speed, their fingers moving quickly across the metal.

The tops of the watches open up and each expels a tight black suit, which covers their hands in whole. It is a suit that I designed to help insulate them from the cold and protect them from the heat; it was designed to be able to move through the vents as it provides great mobility. I can't exactly figure out what they're up to but I'm guessing that they're in the air ducts making their way to somewhere I now realize is a server room due the computers that lurk beneath. They open the grate and jump into the void below. The watch triggers parachutes that slow their fall. Once on the ground they automatically pick themselves up and both hands move around looking for something, but I can't begin to imagine what it is exactly. They slide across the floor, open the door to the box and access one of the servers. Joseph pulls out a metal rod and inserts it into a USB port, making the screen light up with The Pentagon's logo.

'So that's where they are!' I scream internally.

And it's as if everything is now clicking into place. My hands must be trying to access the servers, with Frank's help on the other side, and I'm guessing that must mean that they're getting closer to finding me and once and for all this nightmare will be over.

Cameron and Joseph have finished setting up, I imagine them going back to the air vents to escape but they make a drastically different choice: the sewers. They change into scuba diving wetsuits, which allow them to swim and dive. The two enter the toilets, open the lid of the toilet bowl, and climb into the pipes. After a few minutes they notice that the water is moving very fast, they look back and see large brown objects coming towards them. The feces hit them like bullets sinking into their skin. The water flows more than before, spinning them in circles and turns a brown color which encapsulates them. The water speeds up and the two hands fall into the sewers. They are completely covered with feces. The current is very strong, and they are pushed violently and quickly. They move as best they can to the side, but the suit prevents them from sticking together. Cameron climbs on his partner and jumps off the suit in mid-air. He sticks to the wall and fires a mini-net that catches his friend and pulls him out of the water. Joseph manages to get out of the suit and sticks to the wall. Cameron frees him from the net.

The two of them have managed to cling to the walls and are walking through the sewers. They find a tunnel through which they climb. At the end of the tunnel there is a part where there is no water and they can move along the ground. Something is coming towards them fast.

They activate their infrared camera buzzer, illuminating the rats that flood the scene.

The hands jump and stick to the ceiling. There are lots and lots of rats. Small cannons come out of the clocks and start firing. They are laser guns. A few of the rats are dead and the rest are moving away. The hands see the trap door of the sewer. They open it, climb out and put it back the way it was, upon which I see a drone waiting for them.

But once again, I lose vision and I'm left in the dark, unable to help my creations any longer, without knowing where the drone will be taking them. But the worst part of it all, is that they have each other whilst I am totally and helplessly alone in my office, forced to scour away in the time that I have been given and work for those that threaten me. But in the end, I will truly unmask them and make them pay for what they did. That is if my hands do as I designed them to and rescue me before it's too late.

My attention is suddenly drawn to a black leather notebook that peaks behind the rest of the books that litter the almost bare bookshelf. I stand up and make my way towards it, and bring it to my desk as I sit down and open it to read it. I quickly flip the pages and land on what appears to be the last diary entry.

Monday 6th June
Dear Henry

If you read this, it means that something has gone terribly wrong. Today I will be testing the machine that we've been building. I will be the one testing it. Since all previous experiments on monkeys and mice have been successful, I'm sure that nothing will go wrong, but just in case I'm taking a few precautions. And that starts with writing this letter to you. My main fear is that the Quantum Machine will have different side effects for different species, and perhaps that will differ from primate and humans too, as it has with mice, who lost their mobility and died within minutes. The process will be recorded and you will have access to it, so that you can see firsthand what went wrong.

But I shouldn't have anything to worry about, everything will go well and today will be the greatest day of my life.

In the unfortunate event that I fail, Henry, you are the only one capable of continuing my work here. This is why I have recommended you as my successor. I hope you will take up this opportunity, and see it as an honor to continue my legacy.

Your esteemed professor,
Julian Forty

Ever since I saw Adam this morning, I knew that the man behind the curtain would be no other than my old university mentor, Julian Forty. Only a mind as brilliant as his would be capable of creating something as revolutionary as what they deem 'The Quantum Mind'.

It is only now that I really understand why Julian would spend so many hours locked inside his lab, working tirelessly through the night. He would never let anyone in, and I can only assume it was because he feared that others would find this miracle and take it off his hands.

He must have been preparing this for a long time, an idea that would have grown inside his mind for decades, made only possible with the funding of such an organization. He was always worried about the loss of knowledge, of experience, because of what it would mean to an individual. He feared that once we left this world, there would only be traces of us in books and memories of others, too scarce and intangible to do anything. We would be so rightly gone.

And perhaps, that is the same fear that I have. But there is a difference between Julian and I, between the Quantum Mind Project and my own. I would never hurt anyone to make ends meet, whereas they would, and have. I've been brought here against my will and have received nothing but weapons pointed at my body and threats being shouted to get me to cooperate. It's not the right way to do things.

I straighten in my seat; leaning forward, I log on to the computer with my own username and password. The first thing I want to do is watch the video of the experiment gone wrong. I quickly move through the files until I find the folder labelled 'experiment recordings'. Here, I find multiple video files, and I click on the most recent one.

As the video plays, I pay close attention to what is being shown. I can see Professor Forty as he prepares himself for the experiment whilst explaining in great detail the specifics of the operation at hand. The camera pans around the room in which military personnel from all divisions and people dressed in black crowd the room.

Out of all of them, one very elegant woman stands out, although I'm unsure as to why. I'd say she's over fifty, but my guesses could be off. Her face looks familiar, but I can't quite picture why. I zoom in and monitor each of the attendees' names as most of the military personnel wear a nametag, making a note of them on my notepad.

I also see that there are members of the FBI, the CIA and the White House, one could only guess what their intentions are. The mystery woman wears no badge (obviously, knowing my luck). I'll dig into the archives later to see if I can place her mysterious gaze to a name and calm my scrambling brain as it searches for answers, unable to find any.

A military officer takes the floor, and addresses the attendees with sophistication and an imposing tone.

"Dear members of the Court of Pi, as many of you know my name is General Jason Anderson, and I am in command of the Quantum Mind Project." A man, portraying sharp features begins, and from his presence I can only guess that he must be Adam Brown's superior. With a shiny bald scalp, a triangulated nose, pronounced eyebrows, deep in concentration, he continues.

"Today is a great day, Professor Julian will test the quantum machine on himself. Today will be a historic moment for all of mankind. If the result is successful, in a few months our plan will be the reality we have all been hoping for." He continues in a rough deep voice, which appears to dominate the room, as all members of the audience erupt into claps.

Every single person is grinning with joy and excitement, as they clap in awe. All but one: and that is none other than the mysterious woman, who keeps a serious and directed gaze.

The experiment begins shortly after. Julian sits in a special chair and puts a helmet on his head. There are no wires attached to the helmet. His index finger presses a button with a blue light similar to the one on the big quantum computer. He closes his eyes. A blue light just like the previous one illuminates his helmet and counts down the numbers from five to zero. When he dials zero, all the lights in the helmet go out …

Everyone stands, silently watching Julian in awe waiting for a response. But Julian does not wake up, he remains still and paralyzed in his chair. The attendees look at each other in confusion and wonder what is happening. A person wearing a white coat approaches Julian. He wears large round glasses and has tousled hair which covers his eyebrows slightly. I deduce that he must be a doctor.

The man looks at one of the monitors, shakes his head in dismay and bluntly says: "Julian has died in the experiment."

It's only been a few minutes. The mysterious woman comes up to Jason and scolds him in front of everyone else with no remorse, although I struggle to hear what it is exactly that she's saying to him.

Everyone starts to leave in a haste, piling one behind the other as they make their way towards the door, pushing each other out of the way. The recording stops just as the room is cleared, and Julian lays motionless on the chair.

Adam and the doctor from before re-enter the room. Adam whispers to him.

"Let's activate plan B. We can no longer proceed with our current plan. Take Julian to the depot. We'll keep him in case we can reverse the process later."

As far as I can tell I'm the ingenious Plan B they've decided to implement. But one thing that I know is that I shouldn't try the machine on myself. I think I know better than that.

Mice have something similar to humans that apes don't seem to have. But I'm not exactly what it is. This is where I have to start, and only by looking at Julian's progress will I truly be able to see where he started going wrong.

I have a long road ahead of me. I never thought of approaching the problem in this way, even though it's also a dilemma that has kept me up at night. For example, my friends, the hands, have some, but not all of their knowledge and information from the original brain. This was only possible because of the regeneration and extractions of the cells of the original brain. The other brain is entirely artificial and contains the information processed by the algorithms run and the models I created.

The Quantum Mind's approach however, focuses on moving the information stored in the human brain to a computer and later transfer it back for absorption. This last step depends on the remaining capacity of the recipient brain. But on a first glance I can see its initial risks: what will happen when you incorporate it? Will there be two different people controlling the same brain, or will only one prevail? Which one will that be?

My plan must be in phases. It has to be. Or else it won't work. The first three will be known by Adam whereas the others will only ever be known by myself: that is, until it is too late.

My plan is simple enough for the first three phases. Basically I have to carry out what my captives want me to do: read information transferred from the brain to the computer, move information without posing a risk for humans and to transfer information the other way; from the computer to the brain, whilst avoiding risks that might affect the receiver.

My secret plan on the other hand is not simple at all. It is a hunt for information that drives my mind crazy. I will: check who will have control of the brain, discover the objective of the Quantum mind and the people involved. That peculiar woman puzzles me most of all as I get a feeling at the back of my mind that she is somewhat familiar … I must find out who she is! I will also not only collect but destroy all the information surrounding this project.

And finally. The last phase and by far the most important one:

I must get out of here.

All of humanity depends on it.

Chapter 31

John – Remembering the past

At that moment the general receives a phone call, and as he answers it for several minutes, he keeps pacing around the room in what I can only assume is frustration.

"They're telling me that the truck they found is empty." He informs us when the caller had hung up, dropping the phone in annoyance. "There is no container, everything is gone, as are our chances of finding evidence at this point. They have cordoned off the area as per my request, and are now investigating the possibility that the contents of the lorry were transported by air from that point to some other place. But we'll have to be sure." General Williams informs us.

"Sarah, take a group of military personnel and someone from Zara's group and go to Canada! Now!" The general orders, in a haste, fumblingly pacing around and rubbing his head in frustration.

"Jenny, do you mind going with them as well? I need you and Michael there," I ask her. She nods in agreement.

"John, can you call Michael to pick up his equipment and meet us there right away?" asks Zara, already on her feet and ruffling to check if she had everything in her bag.

"Right away, Zara."

The Army prepares a helicopter and provides Jenny with clothing for the mission. Everyone is dressed in camouflage, in order to avoid suspicion.

Zara puts the pad in her bag, closes it briskly as she motions for me to follow her out in the opposite direction as the helicopter takes off with Jenny inside. As we're escorted out, I can't help but feel that we're missing something, but I just can't put my finger on it.

It's a couple of hours until Jenny, Michael and the military are up in Greenland as they scout the area on the Canadian border. Jenny has made sure to video call me, so I can see everything that they see and can be informed with the progress of the investigation. From what I've been told it is wintertime, which means that the area is sublimated under a thick blanket of snow bearing the cold temperatures of the environment. Fortunately, it hasn't snowed since they discovered the area. So, at least things aren't as bad as they could be.

The truck was found recently. Jenny told me that around the vehicle, there was an infinite number of military footprints, similar to the model as those found at the scene of Henry's abduction. I had Dilya run tests to clarify our findings, and our assumptions were correct. They were the same model of boots.

Jenny and Michael have been working closely together with the military hoping to find any leading clues to proceed with the kidnapping operation.

Despite me being absent from the location, I receive live feed to keep myself in the loop of things, and I'm glad that I can help out the team.

On the ground there are four large ski marks and in the middle of each of these, two look like wheels.

These are from objects similar to the skis that military transport helicopters carry. I bet this is a ten CH-47F Chinook, but I'll have to talk to Dilya to double check.

"They must have used it to load the prototype and take it away. I'm going to send the photos to the Pentagon so they can detect movement of such a helicopter via satellite. I don't think radar would be able to track it," says one of the military men, as his voice rebounds from my headphones.

After several hours on the ground, the military orders a truck to transport the vehicle back to the Pentagon. It is beginning to get dark, and they must return. The cold could become a dangerous setback. From their gloomy expressions and tired movements, I can see that they are exhausted. In a few hours they will return to the Pentagon, discuss the details, and then they'll return to New York by a military helicopter. They won't be comfortable, but at least they will move faster, and we can finally catch up as a reunited team to plan out our next steps.

This sucks. Ever since I came back from the office, I haven't been able to sleep. I've been sitting on the couch in my flat for hours watching TV without even being able to pay attention. My head hurts from the constant foreboding tension. I remember the cafeteria shooting scene. A brown hand which could possibly belong to Cameron. I think it's stupid, but could it possibly be his? Afterall, the footprints found belonged to him and the driver. But how can that be?

I pick up my phone and call Michael at once.

"Michael, sorry, did I catch you at a good time? Can you talk? I'm sure you're just playing with your stuffed animals, so it won't be that much of a distraction."

"Yes, just wait a minute, I'll put Winnie the Pooh to bed in a second," Michael replies sarcastically.

"Ha ha, you're such a joker. Let me ask you a question that's been on my mind. When we exhumed Cameron's body, did everything look normal to you? Did you notice if he might be missing fingers?" I say as I scramble for thoughts. It then hits me.

"Michael, Michael," I alert, "are you sure his hands were his? Did they have the same DNA?" I continue, as my brain rambles for answers.

"Come on, man, are you kidding me? Of course, all the fingers were there. Otherwise, I would have indicated it in the report." He answers jokingly.

"Okay, fine, maybe you're right, but I think I'm going to ask for a new exhumation. What about the DNA? You didn't check that right? I need you to verify the DNA. Let's make this interesting. If I find anything you've missed, you buy me dinner and drinks." I ask, as I wait for him to accept my proposal.

"Do what you want, man, but I think we're wasting our time," he says before quickly adding. "On second thought, I'll take the bet."

"Thank you, my dear, dear, friend. I'll let you go to sleep with your precious plush toys," I whisper soothingly, as I hang up the phone.

Hours go by and I can't sleep. I'm going to move this along. We need to get the body back to the lab as soon as possible. I want to make sure it's Cameron's body once and for all.

I pick up the phone and call my boss to tell her about the idea. Is it a hunch? Yes, probably. But maybe just maybe, I could finally be onto something. Because the hand that shot us in the van looked very similar to the photos Cameron's brother had of him. And it couldn't be a coincidence.

After telling Zara my theory she authorizes me to talk to Jessica. And I'm glad that for once, my boss doesn't think I've completely lost my mind.

"Hello, how's my favorite judge? How was your day?" I say to butter her up.

"Can you talk?" I continue, as my voice shakes with anticipation.

"John, it's good to hear from you. It's been an exhausting day. So, your call is just about the best thing. How's the case going? I hear it's been taken away from you," Jessica replies with a calm and soothing tone.

"Unofficially, no. We have a lot of support from other corporations and a new boss. I wanted to ask you a favor in exchange for a little dinner." I begin.

"I need you to reauthorize the removal of Cameron's body. Again. It's hard to explain, but I think I'm onto something. You're going to think I've completely lost my mind, but I think the hand that shot me from the moving van the other day was Cameron's. It's possible that we missed something, maybe Michael made a mistake when analyzing the evidence, or something, I don't know. It's important, please?" I say as I scrunch up my face, waiting for the inevitable 'no' for an answer.

"John, you have always been a person with a great sixth sense. It has never failed you until now, and if you ask me again, I'm sure that you're likely right about this. So, tomorrow, as soon as I get to the office, I'll authorize it. you have nothing to worry about, we'll get to the bottom of this. I promise," Jessica replies, and I can hardly contain my enthusiasm.

"Thank you, thank you, Jessica! You have no idea how much this means to me!" I reply excitedly, as I begin to jump up and down in excitement, throwing my arms up with joy.

"But as a favor I will be expecting a dinner in return. I do think the Spanish restaurant deserves a second visit. Don't you?" Jessica replies with a positive and encouraging tone, as I hear her laugh.

"Well, Jessica, consider it done." I reply. "It would be my greatest pleasure to have dinner with you again. I'm sure we'll have fewer surprises this time round." I laugh, and I can hear Jessica giggling too.

I continue to talk to Jessica on the phone for what seems like an eternity, as we get lost in telling each other stories about our lives; because after all we are very good friends. We both live alone and are whole-heartedly dedicated to our work, so I guess that's something that brings us together.

I tell her stories about the shelter and how I had to beat up other kids to defend my sister. How I had to protect my friends from those that threatened us on a daily basis, as they fed upon the weak and defenseless. I tell her how I had to fight to keep others from taking our food, our warm blankets, and the very few things that we had left of our life before: my sister's teddy bear and my red toy truck.

Life in the shelter forced me to grow up, as it took my childhood away from me, and presented nothing but the necessity to survive and get past it. These stories serve me as a reminder of the pain of the past, as it continues to haunt me even today. Telling them is my penance as I am reminded that I have not yet found my mother, and I am not even close to knowing wherever she may be.

I remember her well, even though it was a very long time ago, but if I close my eyes I can distinctly make out the outline of her face, her deep dark eyes and her subtle smile beaming with pride, although this was often hidden and barely shown. She had a very strong character, and for that I admired her. Ever since I was little, she always told me that I had to be a hard worker. She told me that without ambition I wouldn't get anywhere, that I would be stuck in the past longing to escape the grasps of doing nothing. She was always busy with her work, and would often leave for extended periods of times, until one day she simply never came back.

We often had guests coming round the house, and our mum would lock us in our rooms, while she talked to them, but that didn't stop us from sneaking around the house to beat our boredom. She never let us meet them properly but we wanted to put our curiosity to rest.

The only time we ever met one of my mother's guests was when a young woman was accompanied by her son. The two mothers would go off by themselves to talk, for which I can only assume were gossiping about their past lives as that was the only friend I assumed my mother had.

But that friendship didn't last long. One day I heard them arguing, shouting back and forth about something I was still too young to understand and now too old to even remember.

I know that I cried for days, begging my mum to invite the son back. Because after all of those evenings we spent with him, we had the best time hunting frogs around the swamp.

Chapter 32

John – New leads … Same results

At noon, Zara, Jenny, Dilya, Robert from the FBI, Willy from the Pentagon and I are in one of the meeting rooms, as we wait for further news of yesterday's hunch, crossing our fingers, hoping that I am getting somewhere with my assumptions.

In the center's forensic laboratory, Michael is analyzing the body of Cameron, and we have a full view of him during the entire time, as we divert our efforts elsewhere for the time being.

"Let's hope Michael finds something. In the meantime, let's tie up some strings. What have we got, Willy?" asks Zara, impatiently tapping the side of her pen on her notebook while she begins to take notes, as the meeting commences.

"The vehicle was reportedly carried by a ten CH-47F Chinook helicopter equipped for snow." He begins.

"I knew it!" I whisper to Jenny who is sitting cross-legged next to him, with her eyes peeled on Michael. My hypothesis shocked her this morning when I first told her. It was either because she could not believe how something like that would ever be possible, or because she couldn't believe that she hadn't beaten me to it. I think it's probably the latter.

"We discovered that it was stolen from one of our bases in Alaska." Willy continues.

"We are looking into whether it's perhaps linked to the theft of other military weapons. We are trying to see whether we can tie any of this back to Adam. What is also interesting to see is that during the past couple of months, we have had an unusually high number of resignations, so we are now seeing whether perhaps, it was because they were teaming up with Adam on whatever it is that he is up to." He continues.

"Alright, Willy, thank you," Zara replies. "Do we have any idea what Adam might have been up to this entire time, and why he struck now?"

"That's a great question, Zara, and I think that we are now discovering what Adam was really up to during his last days working for the Pentagon. We recently found a proposal from Adam about a secret project that he wanted to implement, called the Quantum Mind, which is something that was in talks on the down low for some time. Julian Forty, a world-renowned university professor specializing in neurosurgery, living on the outskirts of New York actually, was the one who Adam got the idea from and wanted to collaborate with. Apparently, it was an experiment to extract a person's knowledge and store it in a computer, but it was rejected by the R&D department because of the moral and ethical dangers it posed, if it were to ever fall into the wrong hands. And as you can imagine, Adam didn't take this very well …" Willy concludes, as he looks around the room to find nothing but faces deep in thought, as we are realizing that we've got something bigger to deal with.

And with this I don't even hesitate to think of our next steps.

"Dilya, find out everything about Julian Forty. I want to know everything about his career, his connections with Adam, anything that could help us find out just what type of person he is. I want to know all of it." I instruct, getting up from my seat and pacing up and down the room in distress.

There's a knock on the door, at which point we realize that Michael is no longer in the forensic lab but rather right in front of us.

His face unhinged.

And I for one can recognize his expression from a mile away. It's the expression he makes when he knows he's made a mistake, and from the sweat dripping down his face I know it's a big one.

"What's wrong, Michael? You don't look so good," asks Zara with a comforting tone in her soothing voice. She brings a hand up to his shoulder and walks him over to a chair.

"I … I … I …" Michael fumbles.

"I found something that I missed when I did the original autopsy on Cameron's body, it's nothing that we could have ever expected. I'm sorry, but I don't know how I could have missed something like this." He begins as his hands shake nervously, and he burrows his head deep within the palms of his hands.

"It's alright, we're here for you," I say. I crouch and kneel beside him, as he lifts his head to continue explaining what it is that he has discovered.

"I'm afraid that this sends our investigation into a whole new direction. Look, here, look at these X-rays," Michael says as he connects the monitor and shows us the images from the fingers to the elbow.

"See the wrist to hand junction? Well if you look closely you can see that there are small screws, like the ones used in operations to join bones together. But if you look further, and through the analysis I conducted, you can see that the hand doesn't contain any DNA." Michael continues.

"But how can that be?" Zara asks as she expresses a look of confusion.

"That's because it's not a real hand. It's a 3D printed hand!" Michael explains as he begins to put the pieces of this unsolvable puzzle together. "The material used is similar to that of a human bone, which is why I missed it the first time round." Michael concludes with an involuntary smile as a result of his discovery.

Unable to keep my excitement, I bolt up and down, screaming at the top of my lungs.

"I knew it! I knew it! Cameron is alive!" I spin towards Jenny, grasping her arms. "Didn't I say that? What a great idea it was to re-examine the body! Now we know why the hand we saw looked like Cameron's. It's because it was. Because he was driving the car. He's alive, from head to toe!" I exclaim with a childlike enthusiasm.

"I'm sorry to contradict you, John." Michael begins, as he pulls me out of this state of euphoria. "The body is Cameron's, but the hands are not. I've checked the DNA on all parts of the body. That body belonged to Cameron. The only thing that didn't belong to him was his hand, his right hand. That was the only thing 3D printed, the rest of his body is entirely his own," says Michael, as he struggles to understand the connection.

"Impossible. I saw him shoot at me from the van. Now I'm sure it was him. Cameron is alive, that body we found in the grave can't possibly be his." I argue back with a growing confusion.

"But it is, John. The only thing out of place is the fake 3D printed hand. But how could that be the one you saw shooting at you, if it wasn't attached to Cameron's body?" Michael replies. "Maybe it's another one of his tricks, to throw us off."

"We need to open more graves and check that the other victims are not missing anything. We're going to ask for warrants and DNA tests on their families," says Zara as she directs the team.

"We're going to split up geographically. Michael, you'll run the autopsies from here. We'll handle the permits and forensics. This way we'll work twice as efficient."

"You're not going to take care of anything," says a voice racketing off the walls, as a group of people enter hastily into the room.

The FBI agents assigned to the case have just arrived.

"From now on, you are all suspended, we are handling the case. Give us all the information you have," says one of the FBI, throwing his hands on the table.

"Well, it's not going to happen, because guess what? You're all under arrest," says Robert, who has been paying close attention. "Take them to the cells, we'll question them later," he growls as his eyebrows furrow deep in concentration.

One of the FBI agents makes a sudden movement and before we know it he moves his hand to his side pocket and pulls out a gun, pointing it straight at us. Out of the corner of my eye, I realize what is happening, and I lunge towards him, knocking him to the ground, as I punch him into a state of unconsciousness.

The rest of the FBI agents follow in action, getting ready to draw their own guns, but stop as soon as they turn around and see police officers crowding the room, with their guns held up against their skulls. They're outnumbered, and clearly surrender, with a pitiful look of disdain.

"Come on, guys, give us just one reason why we should give in. We're getting there, I can feel it, we're close. You can't just come over and get rid of everything we've uncovered so far," says Jenny, frustratingly darting her eyes back and forth across the room.

But she is met with nothing but disapproving glances and growling protests as the FBI agents shout in anger. And so that response, we do what we must and lock them into the cells for further questioning, as we keep an eye on them. Michael and Jenny will interrogate them later, whilst Willy and I will leave for Washington to witness one of the autopsies that is currently being undertaken. Meanwhile Zara and Robert will supervise the autopsies that are being done right here in New York. We must be cautious, because we never know who may be involved. With so much interest growing about the case, it's now more dangerous than ever to trust anyone. Because who knows who will be next to betray us and collaborate with the wrong side.

As I finish the morning's preparations, I make my way directly to Washington in the Pentagon helicopter that's been provided for me and Willy.

In that instant I receive a call. As my phone vibrates, I am shaken back to reality as thoughts of what could happen next evaporate into thin air.

"Tell me, Dilya, have you found anything?" I ask impatiently, silently wishing that we've uncovered something important.

"Yes, I've looked into everything I could find about Julian. It's really interesting. It turns out he was Henry's professor and mentor at the University of Medicine. What a strange coincidence, don't you think?" Dilya asks, as I hear her typing furiously through the phone.

"But here's where some of the pieces of the puzzle begin to fit together. Julian and Adam were close, really close. Especially over these past couple of months, they had been talking frequently, daily almost. But get this. Since the FBI gave me access to Julian's historical phone records, I went and did some digging myself. As it turns out they had been talking to each other for years, the first calls started more than a decade ago, even before The Quantum Mind Project was even a thing, if my research is correct." Dilya adds, and her inquisitive tone gets me thinking.

"So then why on earth had they been in contact for so long?" I ask.

"I have no idea, John, none of this makes sense." Dilya answers, and the call goes silent as we are too absorbed into the mystery that continues to puzzle us all.

And once again I'm trapped within my thoughts only to be stopped ever so suddenly by yet another phone call.

"Hello, Pris, how are you? It's been a long time," I say as I answer her call which forces me to hang up on Dilya.

"Hi, John, I'm fine. Do you have a few minutes to chat?" she asks.

"Sure, go ahead, What's up?" I reply in a tone of positivity, masking what really worries me.

"I've been informed that the police are exhuming the bodies of the murdered men for analysis. Is this true? Can you give me an exclusive? We also know that the FBI has taken you off the case. What can you tell me about all this?" she says in her typical news reporter voice, as she burdens me with hundreds of questions, for which as per usual I have no answers to.

Pris is lovely, but right now, she serves as nothing but the deep thoughts inside of me that I've been trying to push down all morning. But how is this possible? Who on earth told her?

"Pris, give me a few hours, I'll hold a press conference, but please keep it secret until then. I will give you the exclusive, I promise. But stop it. If this information reaches the killer's ears, it could ruin the whole investigation. And that is a risk we don't want to take; we are so close now.|"

"You know me, I'll keep this information quiet as long as I can. But if you don't call me in five hours, I'm sure my boss will make me share the news publicly."

"Thank you very much, you're a sweetheart," I say before I hang up.

I take a deep breath, raise my chin and square my shoulders.

Time to get to work …

Chapter 33

John – The attack

I arrive in Washington and find a quiet place to call the team. Jenny broadcasts me the live feed so that I am kept up-to-date, and can see the interrogations of the FBI agents, which are about to begin. The three of our captives are in different rooms, ready for our questioning. Jenny and Robert enter one of the rooms where Tom, the boss of the other two agents, is located. The camera picks up the image and I can hear everything that is being said.

Robert strides in and sits on the chair in front of Tom, laying a file just out of reach of the prisoner.

"Tom, I thought you'd be smarter than that. You didn't have a blemish on your record, and now look at you. What are you involved in? Why did you want to take the case? We know nobody ordered you to do it. It was your initiative to take it over. But why? Who's behind this? Who contacted you? Cooperate and you'll get a reduced sentence," says Robert, hoping to overwhelm Tom with his questions, as he appears to be staring him down whilst Jenny paces around the room for an extra dramatic effect. My team's plan seems to be working, when even through the camera I see a little twitch in Tom's eye.

But even if I'm miles away I can pick up Tom's hesitancy and I know he won't give up anything that easily.

"You know I won't say anything. I'll be out of here in no time. So don't waste your time. Make a wrong move, and your lives will be changed forever." Tom warns as he rocks back and forth in his chair. His calm composure irritates Jenny, who strides forward and slaps her hands on the table.

"You're out of your mind! You don't own the FBI! No one's coming to get you." She spits out but Tom doesn't even flinch under her hateful glare. In fact, a sly smile curves on his lips which sends a shiver down my spine.

Nevertheless Robert stares at Tom, maintaining fixed eye contact, while the other leans back on his chair, casually, a smile still plastered to his lips. A smile that troubles me for some reason and I reach into my pocket for my phone …

But I'm too late.

An ear splitting crash echoes out of the screen monitor, so loud that my hands immediately fly to cover my ears and I see my teammates do the same from inside the scene. Jenny screams and launches herself out of the way of a crumbling stone as it ricochets towards the center of the table, whilst Robert positions himself in front of the door, just as it gets blasted apart. A large hole in the wall opens up and further boulders plummet with unbelievable force towards them. From the limited view that I have over the broadcast, I can see the chaos unfold: Tom getting up, moving hastily around the room and catching Jenny and Robert unprepared for the blow that he delivers to their heads. Unable to do anything, I shout angrily at my screen, as I see my friend's unconscious body crumple to the floor. Their skulls hitting the floor hard and their bodies going numb. My hands holding the monitor become slack and I drop it, shaking with worry. I take a deep breath and pick it up to almost drop it again as I frown at the army Hummer pulling itself into the room. I can only gape at the screen as a couple of soldiers in helmets come out, their faces covered with gas masks. One signals Tom to get into the vehicle and the others burst into the two rooms and rescue the remaining agents. From the corner of my eye I see Tom grin at me as if staring directly through the camera. He takes out a gun and the next second the live feed goes black.

A buzz sounds from my pocket and I numbly pick up. It's Michael.

"John, bad news, the center has been attacked and the detainees have been taken away. They've cordoned off the area, which is now swarming with helicopters and new reporters trying to get to the bottom of the story. But we've lost track of our escapees." He informs me, as I drop my head in frustration.

"Jenny and Robert have been taken to the hospital, the medics got here as soon as they could but they're in a poor condition, because of the high CO_2 intoxication from the fire's flames. They're being taken to the hospital as we speak." Michael informs me.

I can't do anything but hold out hope that it's not too late for my friends.

Chapter 34

Henry – With every answer comes a question

I am tirelessly working in the lab; they have brought me all the material I have asked for. I have spent several days accessing the quantum computer and understanding how it works. In just a few hours I was able to learn the programming language that allows me to read the information from each neuron and pass it to the data repository.

I take a live mouse and put a small helmet on it to extract the information. The helmet dials the numbers from five to zero and the light goes out. The little creature stops moving and, sadly, dies. Within seconds I access the computer and see that the size of the stored data is larger than it was before the test. The rodent's knowledge has been transferred to the machine. Before dying, I checked that the information in each neuron had not been lost.

The issue that concerns me is the demise of the mouse. The transmission speed of the apes, the mice and Julian's was the same. I repeat the test with another mouse and monitor the behavior of its neurons and connections between them when the information is extracted.

I get another little mouse, as I caress the little creature in between my fingers. I feel nostalgic, as I surged with the memories of my childhood spent tirelessly in my bedroom's lab. I don't like experimenting with live animals, I used to do it before, but not anymore. The helmet covers the head again, it activates, and the numbers appear: five, four, three, two, one and zero. The experiment fails again, but I discover that the brain has collapsed. Exactly the same way as it occurs once a machine short circuits. I immediately think of electricity, of the movement of information inside. After several hours, I discover that the speed of transmission between neurons in the brains of mice and humans is faster than that of apes. This is the reason why the brain collapses during transmission. It is simply the result of the machine short circuiting. I find that the speed of extraction must be adjusted to the speed of transmission between neurons of each individual. Only then can the collapse be avoided.

Throughout the night I develop and test the synchronization programme. I get up and make an espresso, to keep myself awake and in control of my experiments. The machine at the end of the office dispenses high-quality coffees, and I never fail to utilize what I am giving. At the touch of a button I can select the type of coffee I want, which country the coffee beans come from and the exact type and amount of cane sugar that I would like to use. In just a few seconds the cup is full, and the gentle warming aroma fills me with relaxation and joy, as with every sip, I am overwhelmed with calmness. For a few minutes I think of Ann and my friends, the hands I long for. I like the color of the cup, bright red and poignant. I quietly pick up another mouse, put on the helmet and start the process. The numbers appear again, and it descends from five to zero in seconds. But this time, as the numbers disappear the animal continues to move. This is excellent news; we are making progress. In just a couple more tries, I'll be able to try it on myself.

I go to the computer and see that there is more data stored in a new file. I want to pass this information on to another recipient. I know that the file is binary code, the content is digital and can be read easily, but I don't want to spend my time on this. I relentlessly start working on the code that will allow me to move the records to another brain.

Several days pass and it is completed. Another mouse is ready with the helmet. I press the button, the number light is green and the numbers go up from zero to five. The copying of information to the other brain is complete.

They are both alive: the donor and the recipient. I approach the donor and place them both in a square enclosure with a part that is a labyrinth. It's funny, they both move in the same way. I'm going to put a piece of cheese inside the maze. The mouse that donated the information from its brain approaches the maze and finds the cheese. It picks it up, transports it and gives it to the recipient.

Interesting behavior, I never thought a mouse would give a piece of cheese to another mouse when it is its favorite food.

I comment to myself and note down my observations.

In the enclosure I put a plate with water and another piece of cheese in the middle without it getting wet. The donor enters the water, takes the cheese, transports it and gives it to the receiver again.

There is something intriguing about this. It seems that the recipient dominates the donor. Maybe it's a matter of intelligence. I log on to the computer and look at the size of the files.

The file extracted from the recipient is larger than the donor, perhaps that is the key as to why there is a power imbalance.

I select two other mice and extract the information from them. I check the size of the files and the largest one is still the one from the first receiver. I put the helmet on and import the information from both; now the receiver has the data from three brains.

I place a large piece of cheese on the plate with water. The donors approach the piece and move it to the recipient mouse, who begins to eat while the others stand still. Once the recipient has finished eating, the donors devour the rest of the cheese.

In other words, the most intelligent mouse dominates all the others. This is very, very interesting.

But it is also dangerous in the hands of these people. I'll have to hide this information to make sure they can never witness the true power of this experiment. No one will know about these experiments. Luckily, I hacked the lab cameras with images of me working on the computer, so we are all in the clear for now.

Now it is time for me to try it on myself.

I put on my helmet and press the button. My brain tingles and the numbers go from five to zero in a couple of minutes, as I feel slight zaps and vibrations surrounding my head.

The process is over. I get up and check the computer. The file is several terabytes long, so the process has taken longer than what I had expected.

Now I try a mouse, plug it in, extract the contents of its brain mass, and then put on my helmet, absorbing the mouse's knowledge. After a few seconds I can access the mouse's memories, its information. I look at it and make it move its front legs, its hind legs, I force it to run, to turn around, to walk. I am excited, I make the mouse walk. I dominate his mind and his movements. Now I inject a serum that ends the mouse's life. The mastery ends, but the memories and knowledge remain in my brain. I go back to the computer, I place some wires in my brain to visualize the internal assembly and the neuronal connections. I discover how to differentiate the information in the brain, both mine and that of the small mammal.

I spend hours researching how to capture the data again until I manage to modify the program and try it again. The memories and the mouse data are gone, the test has been successful. I access the computer again and irretrievably delete the file with my data, to cover up any traces of what my childlike curiosity has produced.

I am exhausted, tired of the endless experimentation and decide to call it a day.

I leave the room and go to the bedroom, still thinking about the experiment as endless possibilities of 'what if?' continue to taunt me.

Information can be transmitted. Other humans and animals can be dominated. If this becomes public, this criminal organization could take over the world in just a matter of seconds. Thinking about the possibility of diversifying this infinite power unsettled me. I have to come up with a plan to put an end to all this; I will tell them I have nothing yet, I think they can hold out for a few months. In the meantime, I will investigate how to digitally read the information, I am very interested in what was in Julian's brain.

Once in the room, I lie down and fall into a deep sleep, but before that can happen I see my hands again. And this time they come out from a hatch in the ceiling. And looking around the chaos that has somehow erupted I can vaguely make out the NY police symbol, and so I imagine they must be at the precinct.

The hands drop down to the floor and as a vehicle approaches quickly, they stick to the underside and disappear together with the vehicle.

As they leave the building with the vehicle, they go through a large hole in the wall leads to the street. In that instant catch a glimpse of Jenny and Robert lie senseless, as other officers now pile into the building, of which they can only assume that they will be hoping to revive them. There is a lot of smoke from the explosion. The last image we are able to see are the officers remove the bodies and leave them on the asphalt. The sound of ambulance and fire brigade sirens fill the void of silence as the Hummer speeds out of sight.

Meanwhile, the Hummer drives through the city until it reaches a dock where a military frigate is located. The frigate opens a hatch, and the vehicle drives inside. The military and FBI agents emerge from inside, as Cameron (which I am looking through his perspective), Driver and Joseph watch the scene from below the vehicle.

"Thank you very much for rescuing us, comrades; we were in a lot of trouble. We'll have to hide in the base from now on and disappear," says Tom.

"Yes, from now on you will be members of the base. You will follow the established plan and get back in touch with our people in the FBI. It looks like we'll have to put pressure on the doctor to finish the project quickly. We don't have much time. We know that the Pentagon is investigating everything related to the disappearances of personnel and weapons. It's a matter of days before they realize what we're up to. There's no doubt they'll be wanting to shut us down soon enough."

It is two o'clock in the morning. Driver's watches scan the military vessel which now holds the Hummer. The ship begins to move and leaves New York for the open sea. There are fifteen military personnel on board and the three members of the FBI.

"Cameron, Driver, come on deck, the three of us need to be together." Joseph instructs.

They are my obedient hands and go on up. They remain outside the wheelhouse, from where we will observe any maneuvers. The frigate sails for hours and the temperature drops to several degrees below zero. The ship sets course north, and thanks to my protective cold neoprene suits my hands can now withstand temperatures of minus eighty degrees below zero. The boat stops. Lights approach, the noise of several rotors is heard in the distance. After a few minutes, a huge helicopter lands.

"It's the ten CH-47F Chinook, get ready to go up!" Joseph exclaims.

The hands quickly slide down to the deck and attach themselves to the underside of the ship, as my new neoprene suit allows them to camouflage themselves by copying the color of the environment or any object around them. A door opens and down through it comes General Adam. Who else could it be.

"Tom, my dear friend, when we heard you were going to be interrogated we mounted the rescue operation and here you are. It's good to see you again," says Adam, shaking Tom's hand fiercely.

"We were so close. I think any minute more and they would have injected us with truth serum. The Pentagon and my FBI colleagues have no limits," Tom replies.

"The boss called me a few hours ago and ordered me to take you to the base. From there we will devise a plan of action to slow down the investigation. They are moving too fast." Another military officer adds.

During the conversation, the hands slipped inside the Chinook. Me and Driver have never been in such an aircraft before. As we enter, we see several armed military personnel; they are watching Adam and Tom from their seats and are oblivious to our presence thanks to the camouflage of the suits that make them semi-invisible.

"Come, hide here. This place is safe, I sense it," says Joseph.

I am sure based on my own experience that the neurons in Joseph's brain hold memories of the operations he took part in. Maybe he doesn't remember, but they act like a sixth sense. Driver is transfixed by a logo from inside the helicopter.

"What's the matter, Driver? Move, we're going to be found out."

Driver doesn't move, he is still, motionless. Joseph pushes him and hides him.

"Are you crazy? What's wrong with you?" says Joseph with an angry look on his watch.

"I'm sorry, I don't know what came over me. I recognized something, but I can't figure out where I've seen it before," he replies.

Adam and the others get into the ship, fasten their seat belts and the aircraft takes off without rising too high above the water so that the radars can't detect it. In a few hours they will be at the secret base. The secret base where they are keeping me. And I will be rescued once and for all.

Chapter 35

John – Stressful times

It's ten o'clock in the morning and we're holding yet another press conference to explain what has happened so far, and to bring the public up to speed with the rapidly changing course of events. As everyone is anxious to hear what has happened, I made sure to call Pris earlier and give her the exclusive, to give her an edge with some of the information that we're going to share today.

Zara approaches the lectern to speak, placing one foot in front of the other and laying her notes in front of her.

Looking directly at her, with their cameras flashing uncontrollably, are more than fifty journalists from different states whose only role today is to cover the story in as much detail as possible.

This conference does nothing but stress us out a hell of a lot more. Thank goodness my boss knows exactly what she's doing, because if it wasn't for her I don't think any of us would be able to address the hungry crowd of news reporters.

She approaches the microphone and clears her throat before starting her delivery.

"Good morning, everyone. I am Captain Zara, the commanding officer in charge of the Dream Killer case, as you may all already know from my previous introductions this past week." She begins, clearing her throat for clarity.

"We have called you here today to inform you of certain developments in the investigation, as we have had to repeat all of the autopsies. In doing so we've discovered something that has shifted the course of our investigation."

The room begins to murmur in surprise, as the lights of cameras beam around unlimitedly.

"What we have noticed is that our killer amputated every single victim's hand, and replaced it with an identical copy, for which, we think, would have been 3D printed." She explains as the confusion within the room grows, and whispers grow in volume.

"We believe that this would only have been possible by a sophisticated cauterization process to later bind the fake hand to the using special medical-surgical screws. This would only be possible should the murder be highly skilled in medicine, and the practice of surgery. At this moment in time the murderer has ninety-nine hands, which means that so far ninety nine people have died."

"That being said, with so many clues now appearing left and right, we are confident about our chances of finding him".

As Zara addresses the crowd, and the reporters take turns to ask questions, Pris, like usual, takes center stage, asking direct questions that brighten up the case. She's amazing. I don't know how she manages it, but just like the best journalists out there she knows exactly what to say and how to weave her way to the truth.

It's a skill she developed when she was young and alone in the shelter, with me. Whenever we were being apprehended by the older bullies. She would somehow manage to bribe them to leave us alone by threatening them that she would share some of their deepest secrets that she had uncovered from their sleep talks. Most often she would also bargain with them by sharing secret information she had uncovered, such as how to find the sweets that had just arrived for the cafeteria. She knows exactly where people's weaknesses lie, but most importantly she knows how to exploit them to her own advantage. If it wasn't for her having our backs, we would've been beaten up on more than one occasion. She was our guardian angel, our fighter, of some sorts. And I for one couldn't be more grateful to have had her in my life back then, and even now.

"We haven't had any new cases for several days; do you think he will commit another crime soon?" asks Pris inquisitively, as I notice her scrambling to jot every single detail down. Her green eyes focus on Zara, who forms a reply.

"We don't know, but we think the murders have stopped for now. We think that the hundredth may be the last one. The victims die, as you know, after being given pentobarbital, and as 100 doses were stolen from the hospital, the murderer only has one remaining. We have to act quickly if we want to save the last innocent life."

A journalist in the room raises his hand and asks poignantly, as microphones and cameras dart across the room.

"We have heard that the Pentagon is involved in the case, can you confirm that?"

"Yes, that is correct, the pentagon is involved. We don't know who we're dealing with, but there's a probability that they are former military recruits," replies Zara, with a confident tone.

The cameras continue to flash and more hands are raised in response. I sigh, ready for the next question but luckily Zara ignores the raised hands.

"Now, if you will excuse me, we must finish the press conference. We've got work to do" Zara finishes as she begins to make her way towards me to leave the room.

But before we are escorted out, a journalist stands up and asks:

"Captain, could you also tell us why an Army Hummer smashed the wall of the police station? We also know that three members of the FBI have been arrested."

"I'm sorry, I can't give any information on this at the moment since we are still investigating the event. Now, if you will excuse me, we have a lot of work to do." Zara concludes, as she joins my side, and we leave the press room.

How is it possible that they knew about the FBI? That we had three agents in custody? They know everything, but, of course, it's easy, everyone saw the attack in broad daylight and on television, because our building overlooks the street. But even then something's not right. Nothing makes any sense.

We drive to the hospital, my thoughts swirling in a whirlpool, and arrive in twenty minutes. We make our way to the specific hospital room, thanks to the nurse, and find Jenny awake and very eager.

"Hi, Zara. Hi, John, good to see you." She says in a hurry, as if she is only saying it because it is good manners. She clearly doesn't wait for an answer and sits up on the bed. "What's the latest news? Did you catch them?"

"Jenny, relax a bit, you still have twenty-four hours of observation left, be patient," I say with a calm voice but it doesn't work on her as she tries to get out of bed.

"Don't mess with me, John, I'm in a really bad mood. Talk to the doctor and get me discharged. I'm perfectly fine!" she replies with a tone of frustration as she sighs in discontent.

It's clear that Jenny is very, very angry.

She tries to get up but I stand in front of her and pull her back gently.

"John! Will you just…"

"Jenny, relax." says Zara, placing a reassuring hand on Jenny's shoulder to stop her from jumping back into action. "We are still investigating what happened. We haven't found the Hummer. It has disappeared. But yes, I'm afraid that they are ex-military officials, and they know how to do their job very well. They could come back."

I know Jenny so well that even with her fully determined face, I can tell that she is deeply worried.

"Come here." I say as I pull her into a hug. After multiple complaints and statements about her injuries getting worse, she complies and reaches in for the hug, whispering a simple ow.

"Jenny, just rest for a bit. The doctor has told us that you'll be discharged tomorrow, so in the meantime enjoy this delicious box of chocolates." I tell her, as I hand her the box, and a slight smile creeps on her cheek. She thanks me for it and offers me one which I definitely do not refuse.

After helping Jenny gobble her chocolates, we leave her to rest and go in to see Robert. He extensively runs us through all the details of what he knows. Before passing out from exhaustion, he pleads us to avoid talking to anyone from the FBI without him. We promise him that we will wait for him and stop all steps with the current FBI investigation.

Zara and I leave the hospital, and as we approach the car, we hear gunshots up ahead which blast and echo loudly through the vibrations of the street. We immediately drop to the ground and pull out our guns as we aimlessly try to point at the sources. A bullet passes over Zara's head and pierces the car door, warning us from moving. We realize that the bullet has come from a drone that is rapidly approaching.

We both aim our guns and fire, but our efforts go in vain, as the drone picks up speed and continues to dart straight towards us. We quickly get up from the ground and recover our positions, by running across the road and taking cover behind another car. The drone keeps firing towards us, with no remorse nor sign of slowing down its attack. The screams of people fill the air, as pedestrians run around aimlessly, creating a scene of uncontrollable chaos which envelops us within.

"Come, Zara, over here!" I exclaim, pushing my way through the crowd of fleeing bystanders.

We run directly into Park Avenue on the corner of 103rd Street, and scan our surroundings, keeping high alert of the drone that is still chasing after us. In our direct eyesight, we see an antique shop, located in the corner of the street, and decide to take our chances there as we take cover. Running towards it, we scramble through the door, and frantically yell at the clerk to hide. In the midst of this chaos, the drone has been able to follow us, and descends in order to scan the shop from the outside as it runs its program for several minutes. In between Zara's measured breaths, the glass in the door explodes and the drone enters brutally. The shop assistant is lying on the floor behind the counter, paralyzed and unwilling to move. As we take cover, the drone scans the room as it emits blue waves to recognize a standing figure of which it rapidly shoots at, before realizing its lifeless composure. The drone shifts upwards and continues to scan other parts of the shop. The cupboards, chairs, mirrors, armors, pots, guns and all the antiques.

The drone moves forward and again emits a blue light, aiming its ray towards a metal suit of armor, a knight holding a crossbow. The drone incorrectly perceives the armor as a human figure and the crossbow as the object it has to identify. It positions itself in front of the crossbow and takes a couple of images, as it appears to try to decipher its intentions, and in a few seconds one of its lights turns red. That I presume indicates that it is a weapon. The drone starts aimlessly shooting towards the armor as its bullets ricket off the surface. The arrow comes out of the crossbow at high speed and embeds itself in the device, shattering it and causing a short circuit which causes the drone to vibrate uncontrollably. The armor moves, picks up a sword that was part of the figure and hits it hard until it shatters it completely.

The armor walks a few meters towards a coffin.

"You can get out of here now, Zara, I've crushed the drone," I say.

Zara puts her hands on my helmet and takes it off.

My face and hair are drenched in sweat, with the stress of the situation and the discomfort of the disguise.

"Maybe from now on, instead of bulletproof vests we'll have to wear armor," I comment, laughing and eliciting a laugh from Zara as she pants heavily.

"I'm going to call for reinforcements and get us out of here," she says.

Before leaving the store, we make our way towards the shopkeeper, and turning him up, we can see that he is lifeless and was killed in action.

Within minutes, reinforcements and an ambulance arrive at the crime scene. Two Pentagon military personnel enter and take the drone for analysis.

"Mr Duffy, what happened? Can you give us any information? We know that a drone has fired in the middle of the street," a voice questions and brings me to life, as the cameras flash and blind me.

I look at the journalist: of course it's Pris.

"I can only say that we have the drone and we are going to analyze it in detail. We are lucky to be alive."

"Could there be any connection with the attack on the police station the other day?" asks another journalist, as she extends her microphone towards me.

"We will look into it, but it is too early to draw any conclusions. As soon as we know something, we'll hold a press conference. I'm sorry, but we have to leave. Thank you very much, we'd love to give you more information, but we can't, sorry," Zara replies, as she interludes into this impromptu interview.

All this is starting to worry me, the chaos, the uncertainty of all is now taking an ever-controlling toll. In my opinion we are close to something even more important than the Dream Killer. And these attacks are just a signal that we are getting closer to finding out the truth. There is now an interest stronger than ever in taking us down. Every member of the team is in danger, and I feel like it is my responsibility to protect them at all costs.

As we recollect ourselves from the chaos of today, we start once more what we set out to do today. Finding Julian. We get in the car, and we drive in silence, until we reach our final destination. As we get out of the car and make our way towards the front door, Zara decides to knock to see if anyone is home. But no one answers.

"There is no one," says a female voice, behind us.

A lady next door dressed in a dressing gown with curlers on her head looks at us strangely. She approaches us, and continues to talk.

"Are you family?"

"No, ma'am, we are police officers. Lieutenant John and Commissioner Zara."

"I am very glad to see you; I was very anxious and was thinking of calling you. It's been many months since Mr Forty has been here. If you ask me, it's not normal. It's normal for him to be away for a couple of weeks, but never for such an extended period. The last time I saw him, he was leaving with his military friend. I'll confess something to the both of you in full discretion: Mr Forty is very handsome, I have to say and many times he invited me to his house. We danced in the living room, we had a few drinks and, well, we had a lot of fun." She giggles at her own amusement.

Zara and I look at each other, deep in thought.

"Since you're here and you are policemen, I know where he keeps a copy of his keys. You go in and have a look, see if you can find out where he is."

The lady bends down and picks up a key from under the mat. It's a mat with a picture of a scale with the number pi. Some letters encircle the sun around a semicircle but are quite faded. I can hardly read the words: 'The Court of Pi'.

"Let's see what we can find. You, madam, stay in your house for your own safety. Do you understand?" I say, as I take the key from her. She nods and rushes away, down the road.

We take out the weapons and enter the house, careful to not make any sudden movements. What we observe is that everything is in order. We go upstairs and come to a room towards the end of the hall, which appears to be his study. The door is locked, but that doesn't stop me from trying. I love opening doors. Ever since I was in the shelter, I learned how to open them. I used to open all the locks I wanted. It was extremely useful, as it helped us to calm our stomachs by stealing some snacks to keep us well nourished. After a few minutes, we manage to get in. It's a typical scientist's office, full of gadgets and papers lying around in pure disorder. Zara keeps her gun pointed at the door, covering me as I look through the papers on the desk. As I rummage through the mess, I don't happen to see anything unusual. Looking around the room, I can see on the back wall that there is a bookcase with a lot of medical books.

A red one with the same symbol as the doormat catches my eye. Its title is The treasure of our minds. I walk over, pick it up, open it and start to read it. It is a scientific study on the search for an alternative to memory loss. In the introduction there are four names belonging to four renowned scientists. I'll take it with me, in the hope that Dilya will help me find these people, I'm sure they're involved in the Quantum Mind Project. I'll call for the team to come and analyze the house, and find anything that could prove helpful.

We leave the house and tell the neighbor that we haven't found anything strange, but that we will open an investigation to inspect the house in detail. Zara and I get into the car.

"John, shall we grab some burgers at our favorite coffee shop and chat? Stress makes me so hungry these days." Zara points to her belly.

"I thought you'd never ask. How about we don't talk about work?" I offer, as I tilt my head back in laughter.

"Done, let's talk about films." She agrees, giggling in efforts to release the accumulation of stress.

But we both know that until we reach the end of this mystery, none of us will be stress-free.

Chapter 36

Henry – Game On

"Come on, wake up! You've been asleep for over twenty hours! We need to see progress," an angry voice wakes me up from my peaceful dreams.

I awaken and see Adam, dressed in his uniform, frowning down at me.

"Twenty hours? That can't be right. I'll take a shower right now and meet you in the office in ten minutes. Next time, maybe don't let me sleep more than eight hours." I answer, getting up quickly and going into the shower, avoiding his disappointed gaze.

I go directly to the bathroom to get ready. As I turn on the shower, and lie beneath the dripping drops of water, I get a vision once more.

I see my hands inside a military helicopter, as it approaches a snow-capped mountain, before slowing down and moving steadily towards the rock. The helicopter is twenty, then ten, then two meters away and then finally it goes through, as if there was no real material impeding its way. As if it was simply virtual reality cloaking the famous entrance to the secret base. The helicopter lands in a kind of hangar created deep within the penetrated mountain. There are a multitude of helicopters, planes, tanks which flood the scene. The propellers stop and the helicopter halts its movement. The tailgate opens and the passengers get out. A short old man, with wrinkle covered face and a scar on the right side approaches the other men. He looks at them sternly and shakes their hands fiercely.

  My hands hide in between the seats and underneath the darkness to avoid being seen.

"Welcome to the base. From now on you will be full members and you will collaborate in investigations to detect sympathetic members and convince them to join us." The man says, having shaken everyone's hands. "You will monitor the movements of many of our associates and if you detect any anomalies you will report them immediately and we will take corrective action. Today we had to eliminate the owner of an antique shop. We were lucky that the police were passing by, it served as a diversion and now they consider it an attack, something to throw them off balance, I'm sure. The victim started to fall behind in payments to the organization and seemed to be having second thoughts, so the only way to minimize risks was to eliminate it. Our sentiment and expression analysis application started to generate alerts every time we connected with him. It was unfortunate that our drone was destroyed and didn't take out the cops in the process."

"Mr Jason, it's a pleasure to be here and to work for the organization. We have heard great things about you from when you were in charge of the CIA. They said you were impeccable with your decisions," says the man I recognize as Tom, looking very amazed as if he is talking to his hero.

"Making good decisions will prevent anyone from questioning you, because you will never change your mind and because you are never wrong. That was my motto, that's why I was and will be admired. The top of our organization follows these values: ambition, equality, power and determination. The weak are ruled, the strong are empowered and those who do not think like us are eliminated. In this way we will rule and destroy those who are not with us. We will return to living under order, discipline and control once more," Jason says, smirking with joy and content.

"People will be happy because we will give them well-being, stability and security. We will change the world by eliminating those that oppose us. We will not waste resources on prisons and jails. We are many in our organization." He continues. "Country states will be at our mercy and will ally with us."

The five of them leave the hangar, walking leisurely and leaving only the maintenance workers and the military personnel in charge of securing the tanks, planes and other weaponry.

Joseph, Driver and Cameron wait in the helicopter for the right moment to go. And I can only hope that they are coming to save me.

Adam and the two other soldiers accompanying him leave the room, slamming the door behind them.

After twenty minutes, I write the code on the computer for the file viewing programme. The hours go by and night falls. I hack into the cameras and look at the monitor. I manage to access the information extracted from Julian's brain. I visualize him from the beginning of his life, to now as he is more than sixty years old. Undoubtedly, seeing him is slower than having him in my brain, but I don't want to take any chances of having him infest my own. I know that, if I chop up the information, I could incorporate only parts of it into my brain, and that's what I'm interested in. If Frank had access to that information, he could easily sort through it. The images follow one after the other and I fast forward to see his time at university. Everything remains recorded, the thoughts in text, the images, the memories, the conversations, it's incredible.

"Man, you're not as smart as I thought you were." A voice laughs and I whirl around, glaring at the sudden visitors. "Did you think we weren't going to find out about the hacking of the cameras? You haven't slept for several hours and today you come in and spend the whole time in front of the computer. What a coincidence. You were looking at Julian's information, weren't you? Exciting, isn't it?"

Jason and Adam are right in front of me.

"I knew this guy would try to play us. He's very smart and he knows we're depending on him. I'll tell you what, you better hurry up, for your little friend, Ann's sake." Adam laughs bitterly and I clench my fists, glaring at him with a glare so hateful, it could've withered flowers.

Jason snickers, turns and leaves the room. Meanwhile Adam walks up to me menacingly, wrapping his hands around my throat.

"Tell me the truth, what have you discovered?" He snarls, tightening his grip in a way that knocks the air out of me. I can barely breathe, much less answer his question but I manage to choke out an answer.

"So far only the viewing of the files." I start to lose my breath as Adam hurts me even more, squeezing so hard that I'm sure to have bad bruises for days.

"We could have figured that out ourselves! That's not what we brought you here to do!" He snarls. "We want that information in our minds. We want to process it! The visualization is the easy part, it would only take a skilled engineer a few days."

Adam, like always, is in a very bad mood, raising his fist and driving it at high speed towards my face; he catches me off guard, but I manage to turn instinctively and luckily avoid the blow.

Something catches my attention but I fail to see what it is until suddenly, something crosses the room and hits Adam's surprised face. From behind, an open hand delivers a karate chop, knocking him down permanently.

Adam lies senseless on the floor.

"Cameron, Joseph, Driver," I say in disbelief and with glee, as I am overcome with emotion. "What are you doing here? It's good to see you. It's been a long time. How are you?" I ask when I see the hands, my heart racing with excitement and joy.

I grab the three of them and hug them tightly, as I bring them towards my chest. They have saved me from what would've given me a pretty good bruise.

Joseph recounts their journey, excitedly claiming that they used their special training to help them along the way. He gives me horrifying details of their times in the sewers and after mere seconds of stomaching all that I can I interrupt him, thanking them all for the rescue.

"No problem, boss. How are you doing?" asks Cameron, turning on a worried face on his watch.

"We brought you your glasses so you can communicate with Frank. We have a lot to tell you. The state bodies are working together to clear all this up. Your kidnapping has mobilized the FBI, the police and the Pentagon." Joseph reports in excitement.

"The other hands are following the agreed training," Driver says, leaning on my shoulder.

I put them on the table as I whisper quietly: "We need to move quickly. I'm going to need all your help. It'll be hard. Most likely impossible. But don't worry."

I stare at them with a determined face.

"Game on, boys, because I've got a plan."

Chapter 37

Henry – The flight

Adam still lies motionless on the ground, thanks to Cameron and Joseph having knocked him out cold. The three hands came at just the right moment.

I put on my helmet and perform a new transmission of my knowledge. Then I put the helmet on Adam and discover, with no surprise, that the amount of information in Adam's brain is considerably less than there is in mine. There is no risk of short-circuiting the brain, so I press the transfer button and the indicator goes from zero to five in a few minutes. The information passes into my neurons. I now dominate Adam.

"Guys, don't hit him when he gets up, his mind and his movements are controlled by me. What you see in front of you is a machine for transferring the knowledge of the human mind from one person to another or from several people to others. The dominant one is the one with the most information, but that doesn't mean he is the smartest."

I put on my glasses, delete the downloaded file with the information in my mind and establish communication with Frank.

"Hi, Frank, I need you to transfer everything from the quantum computer. Give me a few minutes and I'll send you the location and its network address, the admin users and their passwords. I've got it all. It has strong access controls, so you'll have to get around them first. Make sure to leave no trace behind. Send the encrypted information to the servers, and then access it from there. Set maximum security. If you see a risk, tell me and abort the operation at once. Once you have everything, delete it all. Let me know once you are done. I will try to destroy the quantum machine." I order Frank. I am filled with adrenaline and the force to keep going consumes my whole being.

The glasses give me flexibility, I feel confident now.

Adam opens his eyes, stands up and I set him to work. In just a matter of seconds he's pulling out just about every rock and roll move that has ever existed.

"This mind-control thing is so much fun, who knew I'd see this dork dancing?" I laugh.

The hands laugh too. I know they look up to me. I'm like a father to them and they know that time is ticking against me.

"Chief, we must leave as soon as possible," says Joseph sternly.

"Yes, but first I want to disable the system. Frank, have you been able to do anything?"

Frank indicates that all information has been sent to and permanently erased from the quantum computer; they will not be able to use any of it. In addition, Frank has formatted the disk drives, the memories and spread a virus that destroys certain hardware. The computer I was using before is now just a rectangle of metal, as all its secrets have been wiped clean.

Adam stops dancing and heads towards one of the doors. Cameron takes the lead and the rest of my hands slip into my dressing gown to take cover, as we follow the soldier.

Adam's mind control allows me to know all the security codes and open the doors. No one suspects anything when they see me with the general, and he speaks the same phrases and calls everyone by name as he used to.

In Adam's mind, I discover that the person called Jason has an office and that Adam(and therefore I) can also access it. I have to find Jason and see if I can work out anything. After several minutes of walking around the base we go into the room I was so desperately trying to find. It has a screen and a keyboard on the desk. I walk over and move the mouse. The monitor turns on and I type in the password, thanks to Adam's knowledge. I look at the image on the desktop, it's a picture of them both, Jason and Adam, with a prize at a costume party. I can see Adam, Julian, a man who looks like the man who wore Jason's name tag, and the woman who was in the room the day Julian died. There are three other people, a man and two women whose faces are obscured by their disguises. With my glasses I take a picture and send it to Frank for identification. I insert a flash drive to copy all the information stored in the computer but after I'm done, I leave everything as it was, with no trace of my presence. If this Jason guy enters the room anytime soon, we're in deep trouble.

Luckily, we're able to leave the office without being caught. After frantically running through the corridors, and going through incorrect doors, we arrive at the main hangar.

"Hi, guys, I wanted to show the doctor one of our fighter jets that we stole from the army. Leave us alone in the hangar, I'll take care of security," Adam orders the officials in charge.

"Frank, look up the aircraft model, and send the flight instructions to Driver so that he can get accustomed to the specifics of flying it. Make sure to implant the artificial intelligence flight pilot algorithm as well. We're going to need it,"

"Did you say flying a fighter? That's going to be crazy. What's a truck or a car got to do with a state-of-the-art aircraft? You've lost your mind," says Driver, although his tone betrays him, as I know that deep down he is bursting with excitement.

I smile at him briefly, then look forward at Adam in a way that makes it seem that I am following his orders.

We get on the plane and Adam stays outside watching. I scan Adam's memories to make sure he hasn't seen the hands. Indeed, he hasn't, and he won't remember anything that took place under my own mind's domain. I am like a ghost: in and out. Undetectable.

Driver starts pressing buttons and pulling levers. He lowers the window, as he experiments with his new toy.

"Have you learnt how to operate the plane?" I ask anxiously, as I know that we are running out of time.

"Yeah, I've got it down. Don't worry, you're going to love it, mate," replies Driver.

"Mate? Driver! Have you been learning slang?" I ask him but he ignores me.

I am very surprised. I find it funny that the hands learn the language of the street by themselves and use it openly and freely.

The plane's engine starts vibrating through and the aircraft heads for the hangar's runway. The military hears the noise and out of nowhere they flood back into the hanger to find Adam lying on the ground 'unconscious'.

The soldiers have climbed into the Plasma weapon and are about to fire when Driver presses the lever and the fighter leaves the hangar at high speed without giving them a chance to react.

"General, General, are you all right?" a soldier asks.

"I don't know what happened. Where am I?" Adam responds groggily, staring into space.

Meanwhile, the fighter fails to gain altitude and begins to descend and circle around, flying aimlessly with the effects of turbulence.

"Quickly, Driver, do something! Didn't you learn how to operate this plane?" I ask anxiously, holding tightly onto the side of my seat. I am not exaggerating when I say that I am holding on for dear life.

"Not exactly." He admits and I immediately rage.

"You said you had it under control!"

"If I had told you the truth, you wouldn't have let me start controlling the plane. But I had to fly it! The soldiers came at us in no time and I had to take rapid action. I only needed a few more minutes, I promise," Driver replies as he scrambles around, flipping buttons left and right.

The plane is still descending downwards, we have less than 2500 meters to cover until we hit the ground. At this speed we're bound to crash in less than ten seconds. Joseph jumps up and pulls Driver away from the controls. When we are about 50 meters from hitting rock bottom, Joseph quickly takes charge, wrapping himself around the stick and stabilizing the plane, lifting it upwards.

"I remember this!" exclaims Joseph, with pure joy in his voice. "I love this; I used to fly planes all the time. In fact, I had one myself, as well as a pilot's license back in my day. I wanted to be a fighter pilot, but I didn't pass the final test, I'm afraid."

This is the first time I have seen Joseph radiate such positivity and excitement.

"You could have said that before, couldn't you?" I shout back through the noise, smiling. "We were about to crash, and all you did was stand back and watch?"

"Shame on you! As Driver would say, we could've all gotten smoked!" Cameron screams.

"Well said!" Driver praises him. "We most definitely could've landed on the wrong side of the grass!"

I turn away, tired of their slang phrases and see the aircraft entering US airspace. After a few minutes, two fighter jets are positioned on either side of it.

"Identify yourself, you are in our airspace," says a voice over the radio.

"I am Henry Silverstone, the neurosurgeon who was kidnapped a few weeks ago. I have managed to escape. Please help me."

"We cannot verify that information now, set a course for the coordinates we are going to give you, it is a military runway where you will have to land."

I receive the coordinates over the radio, the two fighters are positioned behind me with their missiles ready for any suspicious movement. I know that if we follow their orders, nothing will happen to us. After a few minutes we spot the airstrip, I can see several anti-aircraft tanks on the runway and ambulances. We'll have to clean up all the plane's tracks when we land.

"Boys, get the first aid kit and be ready to wipe every fingerprint off the plane," I said.

"It's not necessary, we have a special liquid in our mini-packs. Let me check where there are traces. All I see are finger marks on the lever. And besides, we agreed not to walk around the plane, so we only have a small area to take in account," Cameron replies.

"You are developing your mental ability. That's very good, your hybrid brain is advancing rapidly."

I am very proud of my creations, and I am pleased with the progress they have been making in my absence.

Joseph takes charge on the controls of the F35-B aircraft with vertical take-off and landing capability. I contact the control tower for instructions on how to land. Joseph knows how to handle it, but it has to look like I'm the one handling the plane, so I arch myself towards the controls and fake my movements in response. The aircraft descends and lands gently on the runway. My hands quickly hide inside my jacket, and we get ready to leave the plane.

Some base vehicles approach and soldiers get out with guns pointed at the plane. We are given instructions over the radio to open the cockpit, and I press the controls and levers that are indicated to me. The glass opens and I climb down the ladder that unfolds from the plane, with my hands in the air.

"Welcome, Mr Silverstone, it is an honor to have you with us and to know that you are safe. I'm Colonel Ivan Perez and I'm in charge of the base. The Pentagon, the police and the FBI know you are with us."

"Please give me a phone. I have to call John Duffy and my girlfriend Ann, I think she's in danger." I explain, as my expression mirrors the worry I have for my girlfriend whom I believe to be in peril.

The colonel leaves me his mobile phone at once and I call Ann, luckily it's a number I remember. No one answers my call. I send her messages, but get no answer. I ask the Colonel to order John to call him on this number.

After a few seconds, the phone rings and the Colonel answers: "Yes, he's here with me, I'll pass it on to him now," replies Ivan.

He passes me the phone and I press it against my ear urgently.

"Hello, Henry, how are you?" asks John.

"John, I'll tell you later. I need you to find and protect Ann. She may be in danger."

I continue to monitor Adam mentally, but I don't know what might have happened when he discovered we were leaving.

"All right, Henry, don't worry, I'll take care of it personally. Give me her address. We'll arrange to get you to New York right away," John replies.

"Be very careful, they are terrorists and I have destroyed part of their plan."

"So you are in danger too." John observes.

"I suppose I am but it doesn't matter! Protect Ann!"

I speak anxiously and John notices the concern lurking in my tone. They have to act quickly.

"I will, don't worry." John promises.

But I don't think a promise will be enough.

Chapter 38

John – No time to waste

"What's the matter, John? You look upset," asks Jenny.

She is standing near the door, looking into the room, where I stand anxiously pacing after my call with Henry. Her eyes have a worried glow in them but I have no time to fill her in just now.

"Let's go, I'll explain on the way." I walk past Jenny and out the door. "Organize a group of at least ten armed agents to go all together. We must go to the flat of Ann, Henry's girlfriend."

I gather the rest of the team and run to the garage, while Jenny leads a group and picks up assault weapons, bulletproof vests and protective helmets from the armory. Several police vans are already prepared, when we arrive and they climb into the back of the vehicles, which speed off with sirens blaring. My heart is racing, I am extremely worried about Ann.

I dig through my pocket and grab my phone, inputting a number to dial.

"Willy, it's John. Can you take care of Henry's transfer? He has fled from his kidnappers."

"Hello, John; I'm coordinating everything to bring him to New York for questioning. We'll have him with us in a couple of hours."

"Thanks, Willy; we're going to get Ann. Henry is really worried about her. He's called her a number of times, but she's not answering."

The vans arrive at Ann's flat. The policemen are armed with special operations equipment. They go down the back gate and force open the front door of the 24-storey building. Ann lives on the twentieth floor. A police helicopter approaches the rooftop, soldiers descend and point assault rifles at possible exits as the officers climb the stairs and reach the door leading to the corridor. They open it and head directly to Ann's flat.

The house is open, I feel a shiver. Two officers enter, covering each other in the hallway. After some minutes, they signal for others to come and explore the premises. They move towards what appears to be Ann's bedroom and an agent falls to the floor, luckily he moves and finds shelter. There is someone inside. Zara reports over the radio what has happened.

Thanks to a device they can see that there are two people in the room. One is kneeling by Ann's side and the other is armed and pointing his gun towards the door. Two specialists enter the room and shoot the armed one, who dies instantly. He is dressed in military uniform, the other one has his hands in the air, is dressed as a field medic and has a syringe in his hand.

"Don't move and throw what you have in your hand!" shouts a member of the special forces.

He throws the syringe with his left hand and pulls out a gun with the intention of using it against my team. The officers react by shooting him in the forehead and kill him instantly.

I approach Ann, her pulse is slow. Whatever has been injected into her is having the desired effect. The security forces make sure there is no one else in the building and allow the ambulance medics access to the compound.

"We must get her to the hospital as soon as possible, she is in a very serious condition. She is losing her pulse and breathing heavily," says the doctor with a tint of gravity.

"We're coming with you," Zara tells them.

Jenny, Zara and I go with the doctors in the ambulance, knowing that they have to mobilize the security forces at the hospital and that they cannot take her to a military hospital. Zara organizes the security arrangements at the hospital. Jenny sits next to Ann. John dials the colonel's mobile phone.

"Sir, this is John Duffy. Can you put Henry on? Okay, thanks." John waits a couple moments and then Henry is on the line.

"Henry, we're taking Ann to a hospital. When we arrived, we found two people in Ann's bedroom and we had to shoot them down. One of them was a military doctor and he gave her something. I'm not going to lie to you, we've been told she's in serious condition and I don't know how much longer she has."

I can hear Henry suck in a shaky breath and a lump builds up in my throat.

"I'm sorry I failed you."

Chapter 39

Henry – A lethal injection

I clench my fist, feeling guilty for running away. I thought that by controlling Adam I would have time to protect Ann. A feeling of hatred comes over me, my priority is to go to Ann and be by her side. Everything else can wait for now. It's time to initiate Plan B. And that starts with Macarena. Another one of the hands that saved me from the base. She stayed behind to keep us updated on what they would be planning next. The hand with quite a chipper attitude, always eager to learn new things. Highly energized but also feisty at times. She was perfect for the job. Her intelligence along with her incredible skills were the main reason she was such a valuable asset.

"Macarena can you hear me?" I ask through the black glasses I'd put on.

"Si señor! Loud and clear!" she replies with her enthusiastic and charismatic personality that bleeds through even across countries.

"Perfect, glad to hear it, how are things going over there."

"Well I think you should see for yourself," she says and I focus on the scene she transmits to me.

It's like I'm physically back in Greenland, and I can see Jason gathering what I can only assume is the organization's committee to brief them. In a fit of rage, he has killed the military and security personnel in the hangar, as I see them lurking on the ground, bleeding over the floor.

"The situation is complex, gentlemen." He begins as he draws the crowd into one of the meeting rooms, after showing them the chaos that he had unleashed in a rage of fury. "The Quantum Mind Project has been sabotaged from within. We are investigating it. We believe Henry hacked our quantum computer and now it's just metal and plastic. All our progress has been completely erased. In retaliation, I have decided to act against him. We injected his partner with a serum that attacks her brain and will kill her within hours. This will serve as punishment. Henry is no longer of any use to us, he has done all the work he was brought in to do." Jason explains.

"He thought that destroying the machine would be enough. What he never could have imagined was that Quantum Mind had a twin. Everything that was done or programmed on one was replicated on the other quantum computer in parallel. How naive. He thought he was deleting his memory files, but we got those too. The only thing we didn't get was the transferred brain data reader. But that's easy enough to get and we'll be able to access that in a few days."

Jason looks at the committee members, who have virtually logged on.

"We think Henry did something to Adam."

The door opens, Jason turns and Adam enters.

"Dear councilors, I am sorry for what happened to me. I think Henry must have given me some kind of drug, I can't remember anything."

The council knows that Adam is a key person on the organization's organizational chart that they cannot do without: he is loyal, courageous, disciplined and has great vision and military field experience.

"Adam, I'm glad you're back with us, we've taken the first steps in going against Henry. I am informed that our men successfully delivered the serum that will kill the life of his girlfriend's, Ann, brain. In just three days' time his girlfriend will be dead, because there is no antidote. This is what we do. If anyone fails us, they pay for it. If anyone betrays us, they pay for it. If they don't complete their orders, they pay for it. Now, organize a team to read the data collected from the copy we made in the other quantum mind."

Adam reaches over and puts a hand on Jason' shoulder.

"As you wish."

Adam leaves the room and Macarena follows, screening everything he does.

"Lead me to the other quantum computer. Hurry, I want to see for myself that it's intact, I don't trust Henry." Adam orders two of his trusted soldiers.

They go through several corridors and down several floors in the lifts.

They arrive at a door, Adam places his hand and the machine reads his iris.

"Wait for me here, you don't have authorization."

Adam logs on and goes to the quantum computer, enters his username and password. He can see that Henry's memory files are there. He deletes them permanently. Everyone will think it was before the escape. That Henry deleted them. When in reality it was Adam that modified the access logs.

Well in reality, it would be me, Henry. I have no more time, it seems that Jason has finished the meeting and wants to meet immediately. I check that everything related to Henry has been deleted, that I have left no trace, and I force Adam to leave the room to meet with his superiors.

Through Adam, I received the worst of the news. Ann will die in the next few days. The effort to control Adam is at its peak, so I decide to disconnect from his mind and focus solely on how I can save Ann from the doors of death.

"That's enough for now, Macarena, keep me posted," I say and the connection dies.

It's three in the morning when I arrive at the hospital where they've transferred Ann and it's the same one we work in. John and Zara greet me, asking me how I'm doing, and give me the latest updates on Ann.

"Hi, John, I appreciate everything you are doing for me and Ann. I'll tell you all about what I've been through later, but first let me see Ann and run some tests on her. What I can tell you so far, is that we are dealing with a dangerous organization, with extensive military assets," I say, as I am unable to stop tears from running down my face.

"We understand, Henry, we'll be here waiting. This is my boss Zara, Willy from the Pentagon, Robert from the FBI, and my colleagues, Jenny and Michael. Dilya is the IT specialist and she's online if we need anything."

I enter the room where Ann is, she is unconscious and her heart rate is slowing down by the minute. I know I will lose her in a few days and I have to act quickly. I run all kinds of tests: brain scans, ultrasound tests, blood tests. I have the hospital at my disposal and everyone wants to help me: everyone from the director to the cleaning staff. Everyone loves me.

It is ten o'clock in the morning. I have summoned the investigation team to brief them on the case.

They are all gathered in the hospital's steering committee room.

"Thank you all for coming, I am going to tell you how Ann is doing and everything that has happened to me during these weeks. First of all, Ann is in a very serious condition, she was injected with a deadly serum for which there is no known antidote. It attacks the brain, it forces it to shut down completely and destroys it from within. It was manufactured in World War II by the Nazis. The formula must have been stolen from somewhere in the UK, Russia or even the US. I think I can imagine who is responsible. Honestly, I find myself unable to save Ann."

I keep silent for a few seconds, and I pour myself a glass of water, of which I empty it in seconds. My face conveys sadness, agony and pent-up rage.

"Secondly, I want to tell you about the place where I was kidnapped. I woke up in an army truck carrying a weapons prototype. I was forced into a ten CH-47F Chinook helicopter and put to sleep. The helicopter transported the experimental weapon to a military base in Greenland with fighters, helicopters, ships, submarines, tanks, missiles … They have a big army, thousands of men. They are inside mountains that are impossible to recognize."

"I was taken there because they are developing a project called the Quantum Mind; the idea was developed by my former university tutor, Julian Forty, a very good person who died during the experimentation phase. The project extracts information from the mind into a quantum computer and they want to transfer it to other minds and read it. I destroyed the computer, but there is a replica with all the information. Now they are able to extract all the information without the person dying. In a few weeks they will be able to read it and maybe transport it to another mind."

They all look at me with great attention. They had found out a lot of things, but now they are certain that a great organization and a great danger is looming over America. And worst of all, it could endanger the whole world.

Chapter 40

Henry – The rescue

I'm at home with very little time to spare. I want to save Ann. I told everyone it was impossible, but I'll try. I gather all the hands. They have been training for weeks, both physically and mentally. The largest group is the military, special forces and police; there are more than fifty of them, followed by the medical personnel with about fifteen more. Joseph coordinates the military, Cameron the police and special forces, Mayka the medics, and Driver leads the rest.

I know the hospital very well; for a few hours I explain my plan and how to proceed. Frank distributes the digital 3D plans of the compound. There can't be any dead hands after this. We will rescue whoever is captured later. We have to be quick and, as we know, the hospital is armored by the police, the military and the FBI. So above all, we have to be discrete. We can't be seen.

It's twelve o'clock at night. Driver has the transport ready. We'll be using a large black lorry, similar to those used for home delivery. I'm wearing my mask, today I'm going to be hAInds again. I need the hands of the special forces, the military, the police, the make-up artist and some people from the health sector.

We will all go in the truck, but only those selected will enter the hospital. We leave the estate at once and head for our destination. Minutes pass, but my concern is getting the better of me. Several hours have passed and Ann's brain will continue to move towards self-destruction, unless I can do something. But that something is still a mystery to me, as there is no antidote. Frank monitors her condition remotely and I can see her vitals brought to life through my mask. The situation doesn't look promising.

We have parked the truck several blocks away from the hospital, to avoid being noticed. We can approach the roofs of the buildings that are connected until we reach the hospital grounds. The hands climb up the wall; clinging on to the sides and making their way upwards. It's exciting to see how they climb to the top, there are more than sixty of them, so I am overwhelmed by the swarm of my creations. Eight are attached to my suit, allowing me to climb up the wall like a spider. I'm dressed differently today, I'm not wearing a trench coat. Because today I am Hainds, and I am wearing his suit. My suit is black, tight, flexible, I look like a ninja: stealthy and undetectable. After a few minutes we see our target, the security forces are protecting it, it's going to be very difficult to get in without being seen. Frank sends me the surveillance positions in the hospital. The access to the FBI computers allows him to obtain this data. One of the roofs, the one on the kitchen module, is unprotected. We throw down some cables that will allow us to move without being seen. One by one, the hands move to the other building, all except one, who will be in charge of collecting everything and taking it to the truck. Now we are where I wanted to be. I have to say that it was easier than I expected. Most of the blocks are connected to the kitchen block.

"Chief, the security plan has a problem, it's designed to protect the entrance, but once inside there is no surveillance except at the door to Ann's room," says Cameron.

This is great news, we really won't be seen. We go down the emergency staircase inside the building and come to the kitchen, which is open. In the evenings they serve meals to the on-call staff and certain patients, but now it is deserted. We enter the changing room and see the clothes worn by the delivery staff. I take off my mask and camouflage myself, pulling on a false disguise. Luckily, we have brought the make-up artist, who puts on a wig, a moustache and instantly transforms our secret weapon. My hands slip into one of the costumes, stacking one on top of the other and forming a perfect human figure, who now wears the wig and moustache. Cameron and Joseph stand in for the face, simulating the nose and mouth with their fingers and other hand parts. The make-up artist makes it look like a real face, putting on a wig, beard and spectacular make-up. I hadn't planned this, but it's a great idea, I'm sure Cameron came up with it.

"Well, boss, we're all set, let's get some wagons and deliver the food," says Cameron.

Ann's room is on the thirty-fourth floor. We pass doctors, nurses and other staff of the center before we finally reach the right area.

I pause. I hear voices. I turn.

I let out a relieved sigh.

In the corridor is John, Zara, Jenny and Michael. What a surprise, I thought they wouldn't be there. I smile, releasing that they really are nice people and remember guiltily about my plan and the worry it would cause them.

I shake my head and push the thought out of my mind. We walk up and pass them, grab some plates, wave to the policemen guarding the door and go into room 3466. Once inside, I take off my suit and put on my mask. I instruct the hands to come out of the costume and spread out in different parts of the room while I call Frank to prepare the getaway.

My plan flashes in my mind but there is no time to worry. I must get Ann away from here. I must take her somewhere unexpected, where no one will find her.

I must take her away but not as Henry Silerstone…as HAINDS.

Chapter 41

Henry – A good cause

"John, at last we meet again," I say in a deep commanding voice which unsettles him.

"Everything seems to be developing at an unexpected speed for me. I recommend that you be the ones to drop your weapons and order your men to stand down. Look above you," I say as I point upwards.

Jenny and the others look up at the ceiling and see guns pointed at them; all their heads are dotted with red dots from the lasers on each watch. They can't believe what they are seeing. I can be sure that they are now starting to tie up loose ends, as they realize why there were fingerprints all over the place. They must be thinking that HAInds is indeed a madman, a very clever madman who makes hands wield weapons, move, obey him and appear to be alive.

"Ann will not survive, but she will join the group. I will make her my last creation; as you know, I have one dose of pentobarbital left. She will not suffer, none of my friends suffered any form of torture, they all volunteered to continue living. They had gone through enough, as had their friends and families."

My distorted voice of hAInds produces a strong respect for the security personnel.

One of the officers moves his assault rifle towards me. One of the hands swings out, reaches for the weapon and engages the safety catch, four others rush towards him, grab him and hit him. The officer falls and loses consciousness.

"He'll be fine, he's just been knocked out though I advise you, don't try it again or the consequence will be far graver. Don't think of me as a murderer. You have bigger problems with that terrorist organization."

I look at Zara and John. The hands reach over and lift Ann up. From the hAInds' backpack they pull out a holster, and put it on her, adjusting it to fit her body.

"Drop your weapons, lie face down on the ground with your hands behind your head." I instruct.

All members of the surveillance team drop their weapons and stand on the floor as instructed. The hands pull ropes from their small assault packs and tie everyone up, in and out of the room.

"This is the army speaking, drop your weapons. You are surrounded, you have no way out," a voice echoes into the room and surprises me for a second.

A light from a spotlight enters the room; outside, a helicopter is using its loudspeaker, soldiers are aiming from one of the side gates.

"I guess the plan didn't work out as well as you'd hoped," says John bitterly, biting hard on his lip.

I approach John, take him by the chin and say:

"I like you and I mean you no harm. I recommend that you don't waste any more resources. My plan will go ahead anyway."

Five objects are fired from the roof, two break the glass and three hit the fuselage of the helicopter. They are five hands: Driver, Helix, Bruce, Ali and Vanessa. The last three hit the soldiers and quickly cut them down. Driver and Helix drop a gas bomb and numb the pilots by taking over the controls of the aircraft.

"I told you, John, my plan will work, it's for a good cause." I promise.

The hands open the windows and I throw Ann's body into the void, then I follow with all my assistants right behind me. In the darkness of the night a noise is heard, a plague of drones. Over two hundred drones streak across the sky and pick up everyone including Ann; several hands are attached to the holster strapped to her body and they fight back. Driver and Helix land the helicopter on the roof of the building, and are picked up by the remaining drones but are dropped seconds later as the special forces gain a look of surprise. They can't believe what they are seeing, they watch in amazement as Driver and Helix fly away and disappear into the night.

The two hands land in the block of flats where they parked the truck. The drones rise, scatter and move away. I take Ann in my arms, holding her tightly as I descend the emergency staircase at full speed, the hands reaching down the walls of the buildings. On the street, everyone climbs into the vehicle and I pull Ann in with me. Driver starts the car and we drive away watching as the hospital building gets smaller and smaller.

Chapter 42

John – An Interview

At the hospital, nurses and doctors loosen our bounds and get us out of the mess hAInds has put us all in. I get up, my back still sore from having been stuck on the floor and turn to everyone around me.

"All right everyone back to work. Michael, do a fingerprint sweep; I want you to identify everyone who just turned up in the room and in the hospital. We know the victims, it should be easier for us now. Jenny, stay with him, we're going to the office, we've got a lot to tie up. We'll be in touch." I order making my way across the pearly white hallway.

After hours of extensive research, coffee breaks and mental breakdowns we finally uncover the secret of what hAInds is doing. At last, after all those months of puzzlement and wonder we have discovered what his hands really are. They are alive. They can move, think, act. It's incredible and also…rather terrifying.

Dilya calls me regarding some further information she has uncovered about the victims and I make my way to her room where Jenny, Michael, Willy and Robert are waiting expectantly.

"Guys." Dilya reports as soon as she walks through the door. "I've noticed a common pattern in many of the victims. They were terminally ill with different pathologies, with a life expectancy of one to four months. Today, in addition, we received a box with ninety-nine letters, in which the victims sign their names to wish to live and inject themselves with pentobarbital. They claim that they are solely responsible for their own desires. In each we have found a memory card with a digital recording of them injecting the serum themselves. It appears that hAInds only supplied them with pentobarbital for self-administration. HAInds is not a murderer, he is the one supplying the serum, he could only be accused of stealing it."

I ponder this for a second then get back to business. "Let's send officers to the victims' homes and their families. I want to know how he contacted them.

Look at absolutely everything. Cross-check phones, emails, look at any photos they have with friends, anything that might give you clues. We are going to revisit the families of the first three murders starting with Anthony Parker."

Zara and I go to visit Anthony immediately, taking one of the cars from the parking lot and driving there as fast as possible. The journey is a tense one with neither of us speaking, mostly thinking of what Dilya has told us. When we arrive, we knock on the door where Anthony greets us and invites us to coffee and tea. I introduce him to Zara, whilst informing him of developments in the investigation, in particular concerning Cameron's right-hand man.

"Anthony, we have discovered a pattern in many of the victims. They were sick. It turns out that they all had one to four months to live. I was wondering if you have any boxes with photos of Cameron's last year of life," I ask.

Anthony opens a cupboard, takes out a cardboard box. He lifts the lid and shows some photographs of Cameron with friends on trips with him. There are a lot of them, over a hundred. We examine them carefully one by one. Suddenly I notice one that catches my eye: Cameron in a familiar coffee shop. It's from the hospital where Ann and Henry work. He appears happy with his fingers in a victory sign and a big smile on his face. Is it a coincidence or was he there for a reason?

To find out, I telephone Dilya.

"Dilya, check Ann's neurosurgery hospital for Cameron's records. As soon as you find anything, call us."

Zara and I finish looking at the photos and ask Anthony to leave them with us for the investigation and that they will be returned to him as soon as they have been scanned.

"John, let's go to the hospital. I'm going to call Jessica and get a search warrant," says Zara, already heading for the door.

Once at the center we meet with the director and ask him to authorize Dilya's access to the computers. We need to check the visitors' book. We show them the permission that Jessica has given us.

"John, you're not going to believe this. Cameron was a patient at the hospital. Guess whose?" says Dilya says to me on the phone.

"Henry's or Ann's?" I ask, running a hand through my hair.

"Henry's. It is curious, the payment transactions to the hospital do not appear in the bank's files, but they are present in the hospital's receipts," Dilya tells him.

"Zara, let's go to Henry and Ann's offices; it seems that Cameron was a patient of one of them." I tell her hurriedly. "We need to find Cameron's file."

We choose Henry's office as the place to look. If we find anything, it will be easier, as Ann is unconscious. We access the computer, but find nothing. The hospital director brings in the department secretary and instructs her to help with the investigation.

"Do you know this man, and have you seen him around? Anything you can remember would be helpful," asks Zara, holding up a photo of Cameron to the person in front of her.

"Of course I know him, he's Cameron, a patient of Henry's who had a malignant tumor in his brain. He and Henry became great friends as the visits became more frequent," says the secretary, whose name appears to be Amanda.

Amanda disappears and returns with a folder full of papers on which you can read 'Cameron Parker' written in felt-tip pen. With her right hand, she moves the dossier across the table towards the officers, who read it in detail and check the details of the diagnosis.

"John, something doesn't sit right with me. Dilya found the relationship of all the victims to the hospitals through the bank transactions, but, in Cameron's case, there's nothing there. The transactions are in the hospital's payment system, but the bank transactions have been erased. I don't understand, whoever did it didn't want it to be known that he was sick and that he was going to this center. Why so much interest in Cameron? What's behind this private investigator? What's so important? He wasn't one of the murdered victims, but why do his fingerprints keep coming up?" asks Zara.

"We should visit Henry and ask him. Come on, let's go, let's not waste any more time," I reply.

We both get into Zara's car and drive off in the direction of Henry's house. The hospital director says goodbye to us with a smile and, wishing us good luck, turns around and his smile transforms into an expression of anger and rage, which we don't see as we drive away.

Zara and I arrive at Henry's estate. We are impressed. Huge stone walls surround it. we knew that his intelligence had brought him great benefits, the building must have a very advanced security system.

A device comes out of the door and is directed towards the driver's window.

"Welcome, you may come in. Mr Sylverstone will receive you immediately," a voice echoes.

The gate opens and we drive through. The site contains many trees, flowers, a wide variety of vegetation, a lake with various birds, and is surrounded by grass. We enter the driveway and a short, chubby, human-shaped robot approaches and opens the car door for us. He gets into the car and parks it. Another butler-like android offers Zara some juices and with a robotic voice invites us inside. The house is a reconstructed Victorian palace. We enter the foyer, which is a combination of a classic and modern building. It has large windows with a wonderful view.

"Dear Zara and John, it's a pleasure to see you again. Can I get you anything?" asks Henry with a worried look on his face, appearing through one of the doors as he kisses Zara on the cheek and shakes John's hand.

"We have bad news about Ann. HAInds took her from the hospital. I'm sorry, we tried to prevent it, but he escaped. I preferred to tell you in person," says John.

"I know, I heard about it on the news. I've had the phone off so I could sleep. I've been pretty upset about Ann."

Henry's eyes water.

"We also wanted to see you about a patient of yours, Cameron Parker." Zara notices how affected Henry is.

"Cameron Parker, yes, I remember him very well, he was a patient who had a malignant tumor. I detected it, it was impossible to cure. He was a great person, he used to talk to me a lot about his brother Anthony. Yes, I remember him, although I didn't have much contact with him. We met on several occasions and then he disappeared. I didn't hear anything about him until today," says Henry.

Zara and I realize that there is something hidden in Henry's story. According to Amanda, Cameron's death had a great influence on him but he claims that he has not heard more of the detective until today. We look at each other, silently agreeing on something: one of them is lying, and they have to find out why.

"Thank you, Henry, we don't want to bother you anymore. We've got to get on with this whole mess. As soon as I have any news, I'll call you."

I shake his hand, and Zara kisses him on the cheek.

"Take care of yourself, Henry. We're going to have officers guarding your house in case anyone thinks of trying anything against you," says Zara.

"I thank you from the bottom of my heart, it will make me feel safer," says Henry escorting us out.

Zara and I leave the house; the robot brings the car to us and we jump inside ready to collapse. It's certainly been a couple of hard and risky days.

But there will certainly be a lot more to come.

Chapter 43

Henry – The truth

It is half past nine in the evening, all mobile phones and landlines start ringing at the same time and conversations are interrupted. It is time. Television broadcasts nation-wide come to a standstill and on all computers, tablets and other devices, an image of hAInds is initialized. The loud, distorted voice of the mask creates a dark atmosphere.

"Dear citizens of America, I would like to introduce myself to the entire nation and explain what has happened during the last few months. My name is hAInds, and with me are my dear friends, the hAInders, which I created with both artificial and natural intelligence. I have been portrayed in the news as a murderer, but the truth is that I have not killed any of the victims. They were all depressed and heartbroken because they were sick, with terminal pathologies. What tormented them most, apart from the pain of their illness, were their families and friends."

"The pain they felt was terrible both physically and mentally. The only thing I am guilty of is supplying them with the serum of sleep without return. I could have bought it, but I would have run the risk of being discovered."

People at home, in transport, on the street and the US president follow the images on their screens or the conversation on their phones. No one can escape my message.

"But I also want you to know that each of the ninety-nine victims have been given a second chance. They voluntarily agreed to continue their lives with me. As you can see, on my arm is one of these beings. His name is Cameron and he was a well-known private detective."

I show Cameron on the screen, who starts to walk on his thumbs, to perform acrobatic somersaults and goes on to say a few words:

"Good evening everyone, my name is Cameron and thanks to the boss I'm here today. He's a great guy, he gave me another life, a totally different life. Our goal is to be able to help people decide what they want to do with their future."

The camera shows all the other hands, moving, jumping and conveying a sense of joy. Some people are laughing and clapping. Others are simply silent. The screen shows me as hAInds again.

"Many of you may wonder how my hAInders live, move and talk. Each one has two brains; one is natural, created from stem cells and neurons that I extracted from each body, to generate a brain with an organ printer. The other is an integrated circuit with the power of a computer and custom-made software. In the latter I have incorporated machine learning, deep learning and other algorithms that allow them to be intelligent. All of them have relearned their lives through videos, photos and memories they had in the neurons that I removed with microsurgery."

"I want to send you a message of reassurance: I will only act one more time with one person to try to save her. She is a person who has been injected by a dangerous criminal organization with a deadly serum that will collapse her brain in less than forty-eight hours. Once I save her, the hands and I will be available to the world to fight crime and to aid justice. Fear not, for I am not a murderer."

The screen turns off and everything goes back to normal; people embrace each other. I've done my work. HAInds is not a psychopath or a murderer as the police, politicians and the press once believed. I have just begun creating trust among people to earn their support. But there is a long way to go now. This is only the beginning.

Chapter 44

Henry – The birth of the Quantum Mind

It's time for my daily check in with Macarena so that I can know what's going on back in Greenland, and I programmed it at the exact time after HAINDS made the reveal. I know for a fact that Jason, Adam and the other military officers have seen the message from hAInds. Everyone falls silent, Jason holds his chin with his fingers and tells everyone to sit quietly.

"We need to catch hAInds and bring him and his hands here. We could add a new army of hands to our mission, they seem to be obedient, and with all our manpower and weaponry we could accomplish our goals. But for that I've enlisted some very special help," says Jason. "Meet neurosurgeon Gustav Herman and Japanese computer engineer Fudo Nakamura."

Gustav is a German neurosurgeon who works in one of the organization's companies. He has a privileged brain located in a huge, stretched head covered in blond hair. Round black glasses cover his sea- green eyes and are supported by an extensive nose. His swollen lips contain multiple wounds created by what I can tell is his habit of pressing his sharp fangs on them. He does not hesitate to hit his collaborators as a result of his bad temper ,forged by what is described as a 'difficult childhood' in his records. It says that his parents fled after their country's defeat in World War II. Gustav and Jones are great childhood friends. Fudo Nakamura is a Japanese computer engineer, sushi lover and martial arts expert. From what I can see, he measures 1.50 cm and looks like he weighs more than 90 kg. He always has something in his mouth to calm his inexhaustible appetite. The color black is present in his daily life through his clothing and work material. His skill in managing computers began at the age of four when he accessed his father's computer and hacked into the systems, multiplying by ten the salary of his father, who lost his job but discovered a gold mine in his son and reported it to the organization that supported the expenses of his family.

Fudo hates chaos and works with the goal of restoring order and control over humanity, which he considers selfish, self-centered and doomed to failure.

"They are the best in their countries." Jason declares with a raised chin and confident smirk. "They have been members of the organization for many years and will help us in the Quantum Mind Project with the twin quantum computer. They'll start working on it immediately and update us tomorrow morning."

And with that Jason storms out of the room. I take that as my chance to switch off and try to get some sleep, even if it is for only a couple of hours. But I know sleep will be impossible as worry for Ann consumes me.

At the estate, I am injecting Ann with medicine, as she lies motionless on one of my operation tables. All the hainds observe with concern what is happening, darting their eyes back and forth between Ann and me, as I dash from one side of the room to the other, grabbing equipment. From the hainds' expressions, I know that they can feel my pain and suffering, and thanks to their analytical software they are able to sympathize with me. Time passes and the poison intertwines itself between Ann's neurons.

Time is running out.

I slam my fist against the table, shaking as tears start rolling down my face. I can't bear the thought of not being able to help her. I can't bear the thought or losing her…

Ann's right hand starts to move and her vital signs accelerate, her heart rate reaches a speed within the allowed limits. All hands scurry away as Ann opens her eyes.

"Where am I, what am I doing here? Henry, you're alive!" shouts Ann, hugging me and kissing my face, as the sun shines through the window's curtains.

"It's a long story, Ann," I say as I caress her face gently. "I bought you some clothes to make you comfortable at home, I hope they fit."

I show her several boxes and bags that I have bought online while trying to get Ann back. With medication, the process will be delayed for several days.

"Wait, I've already remembered. Two men grabbed me and I lost consciousness! What happened? Tell me! What am I doing here?"

"We'd better get you dressed. We can have breakfast and then take a walk around. What I have to tell you will take time."

One of my robots prepares us fried eggs with bacon, Ann's favorite dish. She likes them when they are cooked just right, at high speed and a hint of olive oil drizzled above. The freshly baked bread crunches and I dip it into the soft, yellow yolk.

I am watching Ann in her final days, before she will be lost to our world, and she will no longer be with me. I struggle to contain my grief and I pull a grave face for her.

When breakfast is over Ann comments on how well the robot cooks. Ann knows them all and enjoys talking to them, they are like people; if they had skin around them, she wouldn't be able to identify them as robots. They are perfect.

As we are done, we make our way out into huge garden as we take a leisurely stroll along the shore of the lake.

"Ann, what I'm about to tell you is hard to take in and it's going to be very hard for you to adjust to." I say calmly, hoping to break the ice.

I pause and I take both of Ann's hands. Her eyes well up with tears, as she is unable to control her emotion, even without knowing what's to come.

"When I escaped and landed at the base, I called you and you didn't answer; I then spoke to John to get them to come to your house;. I was scared out of my mind. The people who kidnapped me are part of an international criminal organization, they are heavily armed and apparently have plans to overthrow governments all around the world. They are very dangerous, they forced me to work for them by threatening to end both of our lives. I had to flee; I had no choice. But because I escaped, they decided to punish that which I love most dearly: you. They sent two people to your house and they injected you with a deadly serum. It will cause you to collapse shortly, I managed to delay it for about five days. There is a remote possibility of extending your life, but there is a great risk involved."

"Henry, do whatever you have in mind, I trust you completely and I know you will sacrifice everything to save me."

"Thank you, Ann, let me tell you something else. A few months ago, I was diagnosed with terminal cancer, and there is no cure. You are the person that knows me the best and so you can understand the pressure I'm on daily as I can't help saving others. But if I die, I will be unable to save any more lives. And that worries me greatly."

Ann hugs me, as she wraps her arms around me tightly and weeps bitterly. I stroke her hair gently and our foreheads meet, as our tears stream down our cheeks. We cry inconsolably as the pain of possible loss is heart-breaking.

Cameron, Joseph, Driver and Mayka watch the scene from a nearby tree branch. Minutes pass, and I bring my hands up to my cheeks and rub the tears away.

"Let me tell you my plan. When I received the news of my illness, I saw a friend of mine, someone who went through the same thing and whom I helped to reinvent himself. He had a life-threatening illness and now he is alive. He managed to overcome it. Today he is with me and with others who also survived in a way that will surprise you. Meet my good friend, Cameron."

I point to the ground and Ann sees a hand, which approaches her and she lets out a startled shout as Cameron speaks: "Hi Ann, I'm Cameron; it's a pleasure to meet you in person, I've met you many times. The boss can't stop talking about you, I can assure you that you are what he loves most in the world."

Ann looks at Cameron, then at me and faints suddenly.

"Boss, don't look at me. There were several options: die of fright, scream like crazy, run away, and this one. At least she's breathing."

"Quickly, get me something to revive her," I shout frantically.

Mayka comes over and holds a canister to Ann's nose. Ann starts to wake up and the first thing she sees is four hands looking at her and my face perched over her. She reaches for her glasses, takes them off and puts them back on as if thinking her eyes were deceiving her.

"This is the craziest thing I've ever seen. What have you done, Henry? Have you created hands that have a life of their own?" asks Ann puzzled in thought.

"You won't believe it, but yes, hands have a life of their own and two brains: one natural and one artificial. Meet Driver, Joseph and Mayka, who have been with me the longest. There are ninety-seven more at home." I start to explain.

"Ninety-seven more? Do you have one hundred hands in total? Henry, where did you get them?" asks Ann as she tries to process her internal shock.

"They were all people who were going to die. I talked to them and they wanted to continue their lives in this other way. But there is still something else I want to tell you, but don't be scared."

"More? All that's left is for you to tell me you're a serial killer, a sniper or the head of a smuggling gang." She laughs.

Ann is disoriented, she holds her left hand to her head, she can't believe her eyes.

"Well, I haven't murdered anyone, believe me, but I'm the one they nicknamed the Dream Killer , that's me. I'm hAInds. The victims wanted to die and continue living; I just gave them the serum, and they injected it. Believe me, they wanted to go on living and I have given them that continuity." Henry explains.

Ann stands up, looks at him and says: "We don't have much time left, can you do the same for us? I don't want you to go, I don't want to lose you."

She hugs me with all her strength and cries.

After the ordeal is over, she bends down and reaches for the hands, caresses them, holds Mayka and asks, looking at them: "What is your life like now, is it worth it, how do you feel about it?"

"Believe me, Miss Ann, it's worth it. Helping Henry and being with him is the best thing that has happened to me in a long time. He is a great person, a great professional and, above all, our best friend. We are back to being ourselves again and to recover memories and have feelings," Mayka replies, holding her hand and caressing Ann's face with great affection.

"We look forward to having you as part of our family," says Joseph.

Ann smiles as I take both her hands and hold them tightly, and we hold hands as we walk back inside for Ann to rest before I tell her the rest of the plan.

Chapter 45

Henry – The endgame approaches

Once I've checked Ann's vitals I let her rest and start getting to work on the plan. There's a long way to go, but for now I need to keep Jason in check. I look at my screen, eager to see what my enemies are up to.

Jason takes the floor once more and updates the committee on the progress.

"Gustav and Fudo have been working for hours on the project, interpreting Henry's advances in brain information transfer. Fudo has managed to develop the file-reading programme and agrees to read Professor Julian Forty's copy. They have seen a brain die and shut down. Fudo has traced the disk and discovered that someone has erased information, accessed the logs, but he cannot guess who did it, only the time it was done. He checked the log in and out and discovered that Adam was in the room at that time."

"Fudo did some good work. I'm convinced that Henry altered his mind; I've known Adam for years and he's incapable of betraying us. I suggest you extract the information from him again and see what happens," says Jason.

Adam's helmet is fitted. The indicator reads five. They press the button and the numbers decrease from five to zero. The information has been transmitted in three minutes. Fudo compares the files and sees that this file is slightly larger. It must be because it's only been a few days since the two extractions from the same mind.

They switch on the main monitor in the room to view the data from Adam's brain, the first thing they discover is the images of Adam accessing the computer and deleting the memory file catalogued as Henry_1.

"Henry tested himself and generated his and Adam's file, then somehow made his file disappear from both computers. Let's keep visualizing."

Fudo's file reading programme manages to initiate a sequence for each different action. Everyone keeps seeing memories. Until they discover other videos.

"Wait a minute, what I can see on the computer are multiple experiments on mice," says Fudo.

"I need to repeat those tests, get some mice." Gustav commands.

Gustav does different experiments extracting and importing the information into the mice, following the same steps recorded on the copy of the quantum computer. Stunned, they discover how one mind dominates the other. Meanwhile, the information in Adam's file is re-imported to leave his brain without Henry's manipulation. Adam wakes up, remembering nothing of the escape. He only remembers that something hit him and he fell to the ground.

"Jason, what am I doing here? Why are we in the twin quantum computer room, and who are these two people?" asks Adam.

"There's little time to explain, Adam, we must move fast. Henry controlled your brain." Adam sucked in a breath and Jason continued. "We know how he did it thanks to our experts Fudo and Gustav. Let them get on with their work, we've got the project where we want it. We can extract the information from the brain, read it, re-import it and, most importantly, master the other. The latter is a lucky thing that we will use to our advantage, I can think of a couple of immediate actions. Our scientists will discover this last part as we visualize the hospital cameras. We have some new little friends we need to bring back to base."

Jason and Adam leave the room and go to Adam's office, where they will watch the videos to see if they can find any information.

There's no time to lose. I can no longer control Adam. But I have to save Ann.

I shake her awake and explain my plan.

"We have several options, Ann; we'll explore them all and select the best one for both of us. When I was at the base, I worked on the Quantum Mind Project. They've invented a machine that extracts all the knowledge from one person in order to read it and incorporate it into another mind. I discovered that one of the minds dominates the other due to it having the most information. I experimented and managed to dominate a mouse and a military man on the base. I was able to escape. I lost control over that person because they recently discovered how to finish the quantum mind project without me. I destroyed the computer when I was there, but they had a hidden copy as backup where I think they have all the information to finish the project."

I explain as I stroke Ann's hair; she looks up at me and we start walking, talking about the possibilities. Ann has a lot to learn and we have little time left, a few days at most.

After several hours of walking, Ann has gotten to know the hands better and is getting attached to them. She thinks it's amazing to have a new life and memories thanks to the videos and the retrieval of information in their brains. The difference now is the quantum computer with which they will retrieve all the memory. Excitement invades her body, she recognizes that it is a step towards immortality which gives her a certain fear, but she must choose: stop or continue living and she does not want to throw everything into the abyss. I know that she loves, that she admires my work, and deep down she wants to help me. She knows I feels guilty for having escaped and does not want to see me torture myself. She knows me well, she will never let me express that feeling of guilt and that it causes her deep and intense suffering.

Cameron doesn't stop making jokes and playing with Driver, the two of them connect wonderfully. Ann has found a friend in Mayka, to help her through these tough times. Meanwhile, Joseph is on high alert, keeping an eye out for anything unexpected that might happen to them.

We enter the house and I introduce Ann to each of the hands one by one to the new tenants; I haven't had much time to get to know them, but I will. Ann enjoys the comic artist, the clown and the stylist who does her nails, make-up and hair. The estate is a microcosm full of life and good people. She thinks she is in 'very good hands' and laughs to herself at the double meaning of the phrase.

Joseph calls Cameron, Driver and Mayka; the four of them meet in the gym, completely oblivious of the fact that I can overhear everything.

"Guys, we have to be on our toes. Henry is going full steam ahead with his plan and I don't think he has time for anything. I'm worried, I have a feeling the organization will go after Henry. The military don't give up their targets, especially those who have discovered their secrets. They have let him loose for now, but they will wait for the dust to settle before they try again. If they can get some people to continue Henry's work, then they will kill him. I heard him say that there is a twin quantum machine and that it was a copy of everything that was run, stored or programmed on the main one."

"He destroyed the main one, but it's only a matter of time before they attack us. We will mount guards at the estate and always, always one of us will be with the two of them. We will be accompanied by the special forces hand group."

"I completely agree. Good thinking. The police have put surveillance on the door for us," Cameron replies.

"There are only two agents, that's not enough, they won't spare any resources until they finish him off. He knows too much, it's strange they haven't tried it already," says Joseph.

"You think it's not enough what they've done to poor Ann?" says Mayka bitterly.

"For these people that is insignificant. As I say, the risk they now have of being discovered is high. The police will question Henry to identify all those who collaborate with this criminal organization."

It was a day full of emotions and so much exhaustion. At a very early time, Ann goes to my bedroom and falls fast asleep.

I write her a note and leave it on a bedside table, next to a picture of her which I treasure dearly. I leave the bedroom, as I make my way down to the garage, to get inside into one of the cars. I am wearing the stealthy suit and the hAInds mask. Cameron and four special forces hands accompany me.

I arrive at John's flat and quietly open the door as I enter the living room. I see that he is sleeping in front of the television. I order my hands to place themselves on his ankles and wrists preventing him from getting up or moving. I walk over and I wake him up.

"Hi, John, how are you?" I speak and he bolts awake, struggling against my hands in a futile attempt of escape. "Don't try anything, I'm going to tell you something I've discovered. I want you to see me as a collaborator, not a criminal. The organization operates globally, has important partners and connections. It is financed by millions in contributions from its members. They are everywhere; you should start investigating the antique shop where the drone attacked you and the owner died. His death was not accidental; he was a collaborator of the organization."

"He started to get into debt and fell behind in payments. The moment a partner does not show solidity in his commitment, they liquidate him. I think they have experts who can continue Henry's work, they will soon have the whole project and they will start to know all the big secrets and, what is worse, dominate minds. Watch out, they can subdue anyone, starting with you."

"What's in it for you, what's the point of helping now? How do I know we can trust you?" asks John, squirming around to try to get a better view of me but my hands hold him tight.

"I have given one-hundred people a chance to get on with their lives; I think that is more than enough proof. I'm going to leave now, don't try to stop me. I am not your enemy; we have a big problem, and we must work together."

The light in the building goes out creating a sheet of darkness in which I can leave stealthily. Accompanied by the hands, I disappear from the flat, keeping a careful eye on the officer. John doesn't move, he doesn't want to try to stop me. I can see his opinion in his eyes. He thinks HAInds seems sincere, honest and can be of great help.

Once I drive back home and change out of my suit, Frank and I start working with the quantum computer. Frank ordered all the components and hired a private plane to bring them from China. All the data is transferred, he can now see all the information extracted from Adam's mind. The problem is that he has no time. I put on the helmet as I start transferring the information from my mind; now all the records are in the quantum mind, in the bug, as I call it. Tomorrow, I will use it on Ann and hope that it will do something to save her.

Chapter 46

Henry – Trying the Quantum Mind

"Hey, boss, there's someone else coming, I think you should see this." Macarena calls me, and I stop my progress and go visualize the scene. U.S. military Lockheed C-130 Hercules aircraft crosses the Labrador Sea. I realize Macarena must be hiding somewhere inside.

Inside are several high-ranking military personnel, including Air Force General Edward Smith, which my Artificial intelligence image recognition software detects. From Franks' data I learn that Edward Smith is one of the presidents of the USA's most trusted men. He supports short pearly- white hair and bright sky blue eyes and has a personality that stands out as his ability to dialogue is unprecedented and has been known to be an expert negotiator on key state issues. Collecting fancy watches and formula 1 cars are his greatest passion and therefore doesn't usually miss any of the races. He wears the Nautilus 5711/1A steel watch from the Patek Philippe brand, one of his favorites that he bought on one of his trips to Geneva. He is a very reserved person with a great sense of loyalty towards the people around him. In turn these people admire him for his ability to work, sense of order, respect for people and discipline. He has never spoken ill of anyone.

They are returning from supervising military maneuvers, carried out jointly with several allied countries. Inside, a gas invades the entire aircraft, causing all the crew to fall into a deep sleep except for the pilots, who are wearing special masks. The aircraft descends until radar cannot pick up its signal. For several hours it flies at sea level until it reaches the coast of Greenland, approaching the mountains and entering one of them. Adam watches the landing from the checkpoint, watching the rotating blades slowly halt as the engines stop. A team from the base enters the plane and carries General Edward Smith away on a stretcher.

He is ushered into the quantum mind room where Jason, Adam, Gustav, Gustav, Fudo and other personalities from the organization, who have arrived especially for the event, are waiting.

They connect the helmet to the general and press the transfer button. The numbers go from five to zero in a minute. Jason volunteers to have them check how much information he has, they put the helmet on him and extract it. Jason becomes dominant, he has more information than the general. They then transfer all the data to Jason.

Edward waves one hand, then the other, stands up, looks at everyone.

"Adam, Henry's kidnapping was a success. Now, thanks to our new guests, we can say that the project has completed phase one," says Edward.

Look at how Jason can control him, he can speak through Edward's voice and I can assume by bis evil smirk that he is accessing all his captive's memories, thoughts and secrets. This will be the key to our success.

"Quickly, let's get Edward on the plane and send him to the Pentagon to continue the plan." Jason is ecstatic about his command of the general.

All members of the room congratulate each other. The organizing committee will receive the pictures of the successful event.

Without wasting a minute, the general climbs into the plane and takes off from the base at full speed. They will now justify the delay due to adverse weather conditions. The plane, after several hours, comes back on radar, reassures the military command and continues on its course to land in Washington.

Jason receives a phone call. He knows who it is, a smile spreads across his wrinkled face. I order Macarena to connect to Jason's call line so that I can hear the whole conversation.

"Jason, it's me," a strong female voice says. "Good job. Now I see you made the right decisions. The target is close, keep it up and I will finally reward you as you deserve. Don't mess up."

"I'll stick to the roadmap and plan, don't worry," Jason replies confidently but his grin vanishes as the lady speaks, fear immediately masking his face.

"I hope so, no more delays and no more mistakes. I was very forgiving to you once before or have you forgotten about the incident with Professor Julian's essay?"

"It won't happen again," Jason replies.

"I know it won't. I'll make sure of it." She snarls and then without a hint of emotion she says sarcastically "Have a nice day."

The conversation ends and Jason exhales quietly with the feeling that he has pleased the entire Court of Pi, especially its leader.

And just when I thought things couldn't get any worse, Franks alerts me of an unusual movement outside the main gates. I stare anxiously out of the window as a black Hummer H2 vehicle pulls up and parks. Four armed men, hooded, dressed in black and wearing bulletproof vests, get out of the car. Stealthily, they approach one of the walls protecting the estate, climb over it and enter the garden. I frown at how easily they can move with the night vision goggles they have across their eyes. They can see clearly in the dark. The group approaches the house, throws a rope and climbs up to the roof. Stumbling, I lean further to the window, cursing at how professionally they enter one of the chimneys leading to one of the guest bedrooms. Their commando leads everyone with him, obviously knowing the house as if he had seen a blueprint of the estate beforehand.

I instruct one of the hands to follow them and they get a live feed for me. Two of the thugs carry thermal and motion-detection cameras, very useful for missions like these, when they need to be cautious and know when there are people around. They leave the room and enter the gym, where there are multiple small pieces of equipment but clearly they hadn't come all the way to go to the gym. They wander around the house finally stopping in one of the rooms upon spotting a silhouette lying on a bed. They enter with assault rifles pointed at the figure covered under the sheets, a long-haired woman with her back turned.

"It's not Henry. Must be a friend." The commando tells the others.

The four of them leave the room and explore the rooms and outbuildings one by one. A great silence fills the mansion. They go down the stairs and reach one of the basements of the house, where they find one of my offices, the one that is not secret. There is light, the door is ajar so they cannot see inside, there is a person in there; he is not moving, his head is resting on his arms, he must be asleep. With great caution, they enter and point their guns at my head, four aligned red dots are fixing on my forehead as their fingers press the trigger and four shots are heard. I was not expecting this, I close my eyes and prepare for the pain.

I open my eyes at the noise and see the four assailants falling to the ground.

"Henry, get down on the ground!" commands a voice from my left.

I immediately confirm that they have come to end my life and am glad to have my fellow hands with me. From one of the drawers, I take one of my masks, put it on and order Frank to turn off all the lights. Two of the assailants don't move, the other two start shooting in all directions. I pull up the tracking system of which the hands are connected to and discover that Joseph, Driver and Cameron are in the office.

"Relax, boss, we're just in time," Cameron says through the helmet without the visitors being able to hear him.

"Thanks, guys, I owe you one. Frank, activate the alarm status of the house and the estate, and tell the special forces to protect the room where Ann is. We'll take care of these." I order.

Joseph knocks down one of the two remaining officers. The one that is left discovers something moving with his night vision device and throws a metal ball at it. Something falls.

The terrorist stuffs the object into his backpack and escapes without stopping shooting. The hands chase him.

"Be careful, he can see in the dark, don't take any risks!" I tell the hands.

I put on one of the bulletproof jackets from one of my suits and run to Ann's room. A few minutes pass and I reach her. A first line of armed hands protects the hallway, a second is at the door, and a third surrounds the bed along the floor, walls and ceiling. Ann, sitting on the bed, knowing that something is very wrong. I enter the room with two machine guns in each hand.

"Are you all right, Ann? Don't worry, a criminal tried to kill me, but our boys saved me. I'll stay here to protect you while the hands chase the assailant and search the house. Here, take this gun just in case." I pass one of my guns to her and she gives it a worried look mixed with disgust.

"I've never used one in my life," replies Ann and she tries to hand it back to me but I push towards her and explain how to use it.

"You aim at what's in front of you and shoot as many times as you can, without stopping until one of us kills the other," I say with a smile.

I want to sit with her and reassure her that everything would be okay but there are things I must do. I press my mask and contact the central computer.

"Frank, check the cameras, tell me how many people have entered."

"Four: three have been shot on sight. We have ninety-nine hands located, but one is not showing any signs," says Frank.

"Who is missing?" I ask anxiously.

"Cameron, sir. I can't reach Cameron. His watch is off, he's not sending any signals. The last one was in the office." Frank transmits.

"Can you see where the one who fled is?"

"Yes, he's out of the house, he's running through the gardens, and he's getting close to one of the walls," says Frank.

"Quick, all special teams hands, go after him, I'll stay here with Ann. Joseph, coordinate them. I want him alive. The rest of you search the house for Cameron, he may have suffered a blow and lost consciousness."

The hands place their weapons on the top and run in a group, get out of the house, spot the terrorist, close the distance; they are less than two hundred meters away. The pursued climbs and jumps over the wall, the hands too; there are more than fifty of them, some of them shoot, but they don't reach him. You can tell he has experience, he knows how to move in this kind of situation.

There are less than a hundred meters left for my troops to capture him. At that moment, the hands stop.

"Retreat, hide, don't be seen!" I shout over the radio.

The hands turn and run away, jumping back over the fence.

An Apache helicopter appears on the scene, descends and the criminal jumps in and escapes.

Back at the house, they search for Cameron with no luck. I fear the worst, that he is dead somewhere. That he died during the chase or that he is lost due to some failure caused during the confrontation. I have no time to lose, I must continue. They've discovered me, it's only a matter of time before they show up again. Turning around and taking my mask off, I face Ann.

"Ann, we must stick to the plan. We don't have time, they will try again," I say with concern.

"Do what you have to do, you have my support in everything. Why don't you call John and have them protect you?" asks Ann, holding my hand.

"I can't, we'd be found out. Our hands and feet are tied. All we have to do is speed up our steps."

Henry's phone rings.

"Yes, hello?" asks Henry.

"Henry, it's Willy from the Pentagon, are you okay? We've detected an Apache helicopter outside your house. Don't move, we're sending in special forces to protect you, but you'll have to give us permission to stay on the compound. I think they are planning an attack on you. In a couple of minutes two Apaches will land on your estate, several anti-aircraft are on their way. Robert, John, Zara and their team will be there too."

"Thank you very much, Willy, can you land and protect me?" I reply, as I am overcome with joy and Willy promises that help is on the way. I grab my mask and speak to my own team.

"Frank, Joseph, continue with the state of emergency; nobody, nobody can leave the secret areas. Simulate the entrances to these as you know, fake bookcases, mirrors, screens and so on, as we have established when there are visitors. Hugo, I need you to come in, and I need you and your wife to do me a favor. Go in where you know, avoid the front door."

I have called my great friend Hugo. He and his wife know all about me, they know the hands and the secret of hAInds. "We are on our way, my dear friend," replies Hugo.

Hugo, my childhood friend, lives in one of the houses near the estate; I pay him for everything. Hugo has a payroll for services he provides to several of my companies.

The two houses are connected by a secret tunnel built a long time ago. It was the quickest way to see each other whenever we wanted to.

Hugo and his wife will be service people, they will mislead anyone who approaches or stays in the house.

"Is there anything else you want, sir?" asks a voice as he knocks on the door of the room.

I open the door and rush to hug the people on the other side.

"Hugo, Helen, what a pleasure to see you again, my friends. Thank you for coming."

Hugo is a tall, stocky person with a large frame and short, curly brown hair. He always wears a smile on his face and is a great listener and talker. With a mammoth sized imagination and a profound, unparalleled love of superhero comics, he always carries a few comic books with him and lets us read them, making sure that our hands are cleaned first. He rarely gets angry and never shouts. He has great strength and a curious hobby, he photographs birds and collects them into an album which already contains thousands of them. His nose is round like a meatloaf and covers his gold tooth which was his adoring grandfather's before he passed on.

Hugo's wife, Helen, is a kind, extremely nice and adorable woman. Always in a good mood, she works at the orphanage where she grew up and feels very lucky for it. All the children adore her and the social representatives too. Being the daughter of immigrants from Africa, Helen had a complicated childhood, especially when her parents died in a plane crash returning from their country and she had to be raised in an orphanage. She swore that she would dedicate herself to giving the love and affection to the children that she had longed for during the years. Helen's hair stands out with her well-cared dreadlocks being full of multiple colors. As she says, color is life, joy and humor. Her dresses do not go unnoticed. She designs them, weaves them and shows up wearing a different one every day.

A big smile spreads across my face. I go over and give Hugo a big hug. Ann comes up to him, too, and they embrace again. Hugo and Helen are both dressed in their service attire.

I explain the whole story and introduce them to each of the hands. They already knew Cameron, Joseph and Mayka, but when they see the house with all the others they laugh and tell me that they are like the story of 101 Dalmatians.

We look out of the windows and see two Apache helicopters landing in the garden. Military men with guns come down from them, approach the door and ring the doorbell. Hugo comes out to greet them and invites them to wait in a small room. I immediately enter the room and shake hands with them.

"Hi, Henry, we got here as fast as we could," says Willy. "My men are scouting for positions and will stand guard to protect you. We have already found a Hummer and my men are examining it. Honestly, I think they were about to enter your house and end your life. It a good thing we came. We'll protect you."

"Do what you have to do, just know that I thank you for it," I reply.

Meanwhile, John and his men investigate the car; fortunately, the hands have wiped the boot prints and their handprints from the surrounding area and the estate. They will not know that they gained access through the wall and entered the estate.

"There are no prints inside the car, whoever came here knows what they are doing." John tells Willy on the phone, and I overhear the conversation. "What I can see is that the helicopter landed here, it must have picked someone up from the car and left. Dilya tells me that the Hummer belongs to the air force barracks. An Apache helicopter is missing and six soldiers are unaccounted for. This is the organization's doing."

"I'm afraid they're everywhere."

Chapter 47

Henry – Evidence

It has been a very long time since my last update with Macarena and so I log onto the database and connect with her. She gives me short wave and then turns around to give me a view of our opponents.

Several kilometers away, at the well-known military installation Joint Base Andrews, is General Edward Smith, who personally directs the preparations for the flight that will take the US President to a G-7 meeting in Canada. Edward has been overseeing the travel logistics since he became an air force general as well as keeping up with his role as the protector of the president.

All equipment, objects, computers, food and belongings are on the plane together with the crew and their security guard.

Air Force One starts its engines and patiently awaits the arrival of the world's most powerful politician. The presidential motorcade approaches the plane; the president steps out of the car and climbs the stairs. Once inside, he greets crew members and security one by one.

"Welcome, Mr President. At your service. Everything is in perfect condition, and we are ready for take-off," says Edward.

"It's a privilege to have your protection, Edward. Thank you for your dedication."

"An honor, Mr President," replies Edward.

The president enters the oval office of the plane. The general follows suit alongside another military officer and takes the chair opposite to the president.

"Edward recount the details of the anti-aircraft security you wanted to tell me about," the president says, listening attentively.

Edward places a briefcase on the table, opens it and a gas numbs the president. The briefcase contains a keyboard; the assistant takes out the brain-reading helmet, puts it on, plugs it in and the numbers go from five to zero.

"Quick, compare it to the size of Jason's," Edward whispers to the soldier.

"Jason has more information," replies the military man.

Jason, who is residing at the base, puts on the helmet and the information is transferred. He now controls the two of them, both Edward and the president who wakes up. He approaches the soldier and says to him:

"Well done, soldier. The organization is very proud of you, you will go on to tackle great responsibilities and challenges after this. You have shown great commitment for which you will be rewarded."

The two military men leave the plane's office, their heads raised high; at this moment, the organization is in control of the president and the general. The quantum machine is in the hold of the plane, guarded by the terrorists. They placed it there and established the connection to the base in Greenland, to transmit the information to Jason. Jason is now the most powerful mind in the world.

The Apache helicopter that escaped from around my estate enters the military base in Greenland. Adam remains in the hangar waiting for the only survivor of the raiding party.

"I'm glad to have you with us, Sergeant Lopez. I've called a meeting of the committee so that you can tell us the details of the raid and what is so important that you had to tell us in person. Come with me."

Adam, Sergeant Lopez and other armed military personnel enter the tunnels of the base. The sergeant tightens his grip on the backpack he carried during the raid on my house.

They enter the meeting room, switch on the monitor and all thirteen members of the committee log on. Jason takes the floor.

"My dear colleagues today is a historic day. The President of the United States of America is being mind-controlled by me as is the General of the Air Force. We will achieve our great goal, and there will be no turning back. Only one thing remains. We must remove Henry from our path. Today we tried but failed in our mission to end Henry's life. With us is Sergeant Lopez, who will explain the details of the operation."

López approaches the monitor and stands at the head of the table.

"Today at twelve o'clock at night, a group of four special operations experts raided Henry's house with the aim of eliminating him. We took every precaution and entered his office, where he was sleeping with his head resting on his arms on the desk. His forehead was our perfect target, the four of us had him in range with our lasers. We were about to fire when we were attacked and two of us were shot down. The light went out though we kept firing, I visualized something moving and threw a metal ball at it."

"I took it and put it in my backpack. After they killed my partner, I got out as best I could. When I got to the garden I looked back and a very large group of hands were chasing me to stop me. After a thrilling chase I saw the helicopter and got in. I opened my backpack and found this."

Lopez reaches into the backpack, pulls out Cameron and shows him to everyone present. Macarena gasps softly and I swear under my breath.

"The hands shot at us and chased us. The hands live and protect Henry! I'm convinced that Henry is hAInds, the serial killer, the one who gave the message on television the other day," says López.

They all look at Cameron, they see that it is a hand with a large watch turned off. One of the soldiers brings an armored glass and they place it inside.

Jason and Adam walk over, open and touch it.

"Whatever it is, this hand is alive. Call Gustav and Fudo to examine it, wake it up and run a thousand tests. I want to know everything and see if we can reproduce it."

The scientists, accompanied by Adam and several soldiers, leave the room and go to the quantum computer room. They will not be able to access the mind, if it has one; the quantum machine is on Air Force One.

The chairman of the committee addresses everyone:

"Jason, set up a raid on Henry's estate. We need to take him, his lab and all his hands. It will be a full-blown assault, one insignificant man is not going to jeopardize this mission, destroy him!"

I whisper to Macarena for her to follow the scientists into the other room where the scientists are filling Cameron with wires and sensors. He has been put through scanners, x-rays, and blood tests.

"It's funny, the blood is A-positive and pumps at the same rate as a human. The clock is complex; if we opened it, it would die because it doesn't know the system. It has two brains. It is a marvel of science and technology. Henry is gifted," says the doctor.

Fudo connects a cable using one of Cameron's clock output ports. He checks with his computer that the circuits are working properly, but he cannot access the system. The software was created and encrypted by Henry. The artificial intelligence is safe from hacking.

"Can you wake him up?" asks Adam.

"He received a severe blow; the brain scan indicates that he is healthy; we will try to wake him up with electric shocks."

Gustav places several wires in the palm area. Straps hold the fingers to prevent it from escaping. The current is activated, and the fingers begin to move slowly, the watch lights up and the eyes open and look around. Cameron processes all the information stored in his memory and visualizes the moment when the object hits him. He closes his eyes on the clock but continues to monitor the scene through the micro cameras. He recognizes Adam, so he shuts down, preferring to gather information about what they are going to do with him.

"Henry, Cameron is alive. I've just received a location signal from one of our satellites. He's in Greenland, in the military base." Frank reports, obviously not realizing that I was connected to Macarena and could see Cameron very much alive myself.

"I can see that. Thank God he's alive, we'll have to rescue him, but he'll have to wait several days, I want to talk to him. Can you make contact?" I ask, feeling distressed by the news.

I put on the mask, and Frank makes the connection.

"Hello, Cameron, how are you feeling?"

"Chief, I was worried about you. Are you alright?" Cameron replies.

"Yes, we're all fine, you?"

"I've just woken up; I've been covered with cables but I think I'm at the base. Don't worry about me, I'll get out of this. You guys focus on the plan, and I'll see you in a few days."

"It's great to hear from you, Cameron; we'll come for you as soon as we can. Macarena's around if you get into trouble."

"I know, boss. I'll keep you posted on what happens around here, though I'm sure Macarena is already doing that. As soon as I can, I will escape, but first I must get to know everything there is to know about the organization and its plans."

"Okay, my friend, be very careful."

Frank cuts the communication, he knows that the base could detect it if they wanted to.

Adam grabs the doctor by the lapel and shouts at him: "Put more current into it! He has to wake up."

The doctor turns the power back on. Cameron makes movements as if he is having a breakdown.

I know he is messing with them, and I smile. He'll be alright after all.

"General, I have to stop, he may spasm. His vitals are dropping," the doctor says worried.

"All right, stop," orders Adam.

Cameron stretches and becomes totally paralyzed. He appears to be dead, except for the speed of his vital functions, which slows down on the monitor.

"I think we overdid it with the current; the hand went into spasm. Let's let it rest. In the meantime, I'll investigate it internally," says Fudo.

Fudo is left alone in the room; little by little he discovers the engineering of the watch through 3D ultrasound cameras. He discovers that it functions as a heart and lungs to oxygenate the blood. Perhaps on a larger scale, the technology could operate on men with a more powerful device.

The hand remains in the box without moving. Fudo unhooks it and takes it away for another test. Cameron takes the opportunity to switch on the thruster and hit him in the back of the head, knocking him out. From the watch he extracts a new suit designed and made by myself. This suit leaves no trace of fingerprints and with it Cameron will be able to move freely around the base without being seen. He escapes from the room and moves along the corridor ceilings and walls. Henry sees the scene through his contact lens, but Cameron wants to confirm that he is free, sending a coded and encrypted message to Frank: 'I'm free, I've escaped'.

The hand enters the committee's meeting room; no one is there, which allows him to walk around the room and check the switches. In a cupboard he discovers the video and TV monitor connections, turns on the screen and switches on the video. The committee discusses plans for the attack on Henry's house and the future of humanity. Cameron records it all and transmits it to Frank. Moments later he closes the cabinet, turns off the devices, puts all the objects back in the same position they were in and leaves the room.

"I'll wait around and see if I can figure something else out," says Macarena. "Connect to Cameron's watch. I'll call you if I get further updates."

"Thank you, Macarena, and nicely done." She waves and disconnects. I tell Frank to set up the link to Cameron once more and I see what he is up to.

At the end of the corridor there is a closed door, fingers are placed at the top touching the ceiling, Cameron waits for the opportunity to enter the room.

The door opens and two armed soldiers come running out, they must have realized that Cameron has escaped, knocking out the engineer. Cameron quickly enters the room and looks up at the ceiling in one of the corners. He switches on the suit's camouflage to observe the scene. It's a very large room with large monitors, computer screens that allow Cameron and I to see all the continents. General Adam and Jason have their backs turned, talking to other military officers. The screens focus on the hangar area, and I see soldiers entering in three Apache helicopters. I whisper to Cameron, and he focuses the sound receiving device on the conversation.

"As we discussed, I want no survivors; raze the entire estate, destroy the house and make sure Henry is dead before you return. We will not allow any failure," says Jason.

"Come on, get out now. We've been informed that the Pentagon has sent in troops. If the operation gets complicated, we'll send in stronger reinforcements," says Adam.

"Frank, get me Henry, quick, it's very urgent," Cameron orders. He is hidden nearby and has seen and heard everything.

"Tell me, Cameron, what's going on?"

"In a few minutes, three Apache helicopters will leave in order to destroy the estate. In a few hours they will be there. Don't waste a minute. I have discovered that Jason and Adam carry microphones and micro-cameras as a security measure to prevent any future mistakes. We need to tell Frank to access these devices!"

Cameron becomes silent, quietly, observing what is happening in the base's operations room.

"Thank you, Cameron, I'll start right away. Take care, we'll get to you as soon as we can." I exclaim.

I had captured some information through the cameras but not all, thanks to Cameron I will be able to establish a defensive action against this dangerous organization.

"No rush, boss, I'll probably go out for a bit of skiing and snow climbing," Cameron replies.

"Always in a good mood. We'll keep in touch. I'll call you when it's all over."

"Okay then, boss," he says before the transmission goes dead.

Chapter 48

Henry – Dominating the world

The plan is in progress, the pieces of this never ending puzzle are finally falling all into place. One by one, fitting snugly together as if supporting each other through every single thread inside of them. Just as I had predicted all those years ago. But I had never once known how truly possible it could be, even if I really hoped that it could be. But now all that stands in the way is Jason. His team. His plans. The Quantum Mind. I've known they've been planning something for a while. But I've never been truly able to discover what they wanted to get at. And that's why I have Macarena, patiently following them around and watching their every move. I have eyes and ears everywhere.

Washington hosts an urgent meeting of G20 countries proposed by the United States. Some pests have destroyed thirty per cent of the world's agricultural plantations in the last week. Australia is the only country that has not been affected by this catastrophe; it has closed its borders, flights and trade with other countries to protect itself. The plague is an airborne macrobacterium that spreads through the air, destroys crops and causes a deadly disease in humans. To date, one million people have died and more than three million have been infected. Governments are unable to stop it.

The G20 meeting is attended by the presidents of Argentina, Australia, Brazil, Canada, China, Germany, France, India, Indonesia, Italy, Japan, Mexico, Russia, Saudi Arabia, South Africa, South Korea, Turkey, the United Kingdom, the European Union and the United States.

The meeting is being held behind closed doors in one of the rooms of the White House, due to the US hosting the event. During the first hours, all attendees have presented their views and shared their data. The president takes the floor to begin the second session, in which solutions will be discussed.

"Dear members of the G20, I would like to present the solution proposed by my government. Faced with this grave situation, we believe that one of the strategies to be followed should be the implementation of a new world order, a new system, an egalitarian system based on the following point: the disappearance of money. The government will provide citizens with all the goods they need: perishable and imperishable, movable and immovable. All personal property will pass into the hands of the government within twenty years."

"Anyone who is against the egalitarian system will be confined to an egalitarian education school. If he or she does not change his or her mind after four months of rigorous training, he or she will be taken to the exclusion zone. All persons will be able to develop their talents, if they have any. The state will provide them with training and education. The world's population will only and exclusively work in those activities that give them pleasure. Countries have no place in our new egalitarian system."

"From now on we will simply be the Earth. This is my government's proposal and it will have to be implemented over the next few years. We will start right away and hopefully we will not cause major disruptions. We have drawn up the roadmap per country and per task to be developed."

Murmurs and eyebrows rise among those assembled. The President of Russia rises.

"This is stupid, the most moronic thing I have ever heard at a high-level meeting of such importance. You and the Americans are crazy!" he shouts.

The American president crouches down and puts on a gas mask, an invisible gas comes out of the microphones and puts the G20 guests to sleep one by one.

The gas disappears, and the president removes his mask. One of the walls opens and Jason, Adam, Gustav, Fudo and other military personnel appear.

"Come on, let's start extracting the information from each of their brains and then implant it in mine. I will be able to dominate all the governments and the organization will bring order to the world. You, my loyal collaborators, will benefit," says Jason.

One by one, they put on the extraction helmet and feed the information into the quantum computer they have brought to the White House. The process takes a couple of hours. They will now connect Jason and the information will be imported into his brain. Jason's ability is superior to any of the leaders, so he will be able to overpower them.

"Now I'm going to be the most powerful person in the world," Jason says as he puts on his helmet.

One by one, the helmet transmits the contents to Jason's brain. The process takes almost an hour. The military wakes up the presidents of the governments. Jason controls them, he can make several of them speak at the same time in different dialogues, in different languages. He knows all their lives, their secrets, betrayals.

"Presidents, the purpose of the meeting has been achieved, we will apply the egalitarian system throughout the world, all in favor raise your hand." Jason booms through the American President.

All raise their hands, controlled under Jason's power. He smiles, Project Quantum Mind is a success. He hugs Adam, his great friend and partner. Now they will return to the base, where they will control all the politicians without arousing suspicion.

The presidents are leaving the White House. Their planes will take them back home; once there, they will begin to impose the egalitarian system.

Adam and the others board a helicopter that will take them back to the base in Greenland.

The changeover to the new system is rapid, only some days have passed and the world is beginning to see the effects of the meeting of the presidents.

The plague has disappeared.

Prison inmates, drug addicts, people with mental problems, the homeless, the disabled and those who are a burden on the state have been eliminated. The press only reports positive news.

Money has disappeared from circulation.

During the first days there were big riots, but they have all been quelled. There is fear, a lot of fear in the streets, nobody dares to criticize the new system. The crowd is silent because, after all, they don't have to worry about money.

There are many people sympathetic to the new change, they have housing, food, electricity, water, telephone, no restrictions. The army and the police control domestic life. There are no robberies, no murders, people walk around without fear. Alcohol and drugs have been banned and all the companies that manufactured alcohol and drugs have been closed down. The fields dedicated to drug cultivation have been destroyed and the people who made a living from this business have disappeared.

There are no countries, all armies are directed from Rome, where the new regime of equality lives. A committee of the presidents of the former G20 countries rule the world, manipulated by Jason.

Terms such as race, sex, age, nationality, religion, caste, social class, occupation have been abolished.

The working day has been equalized, everyone works the same number of hours. Everyone has a built-in chip that captures all their data, geolocation, health information, hours worked and many other variables. The new world forces people to keep fit and take care of themselves, and the government sees this as a way of making people happier and reducing health costs.

Vacant jobs that people don't want are filled by robots or by individuals not in tune with the system who are managed through the figure of the dominator, a military man in charge of the organization that governs their minds. Each military officer can rule over a thousand people thanks to the Quantum Mind Programme.

I order Macarena to let me know of any further developments and hang up on the line. I am still going through with my plan; the plan to save myself, hoping that it will work. I need it to help the hands, Ann and most importantly the whole world from this Quantum Mind Project …

Chapter 49

Henry – The plan

My eyes squinting at the monitor, I see John, Zara, Willy and Robert approach the estate and identify themselves on the camera. The gate opens and the car in which they had come speeds off. I hear the knock echo around the house and look back at the front door, which opens as Hugo steps out to greet my guests.

"The master is waiting for you in the library, please come with me."

Hugo holds open the door and the visitors enter. Shutting down the security cameras and stepping out of the secret compartment hidden behind a bookshelf, I walk calmly out the door and pretend to look surprised to see John and his team. I approach them and shake their hands.

"Hello, my friends, thank you for coming, would you like to have a drink?"

"No. Thank you very much, we'd love to, but we don't have time," says Zara.

Her bright baby blue eyes stare unblinkingly at me. A small pucker forms between her brows. She cares about my safety. I turn to John, who gives me the same stare. They all care.

Suddenly I feel an incessant throb in my heart, which can only be described as guilt.

"Henry, you are in grave danger. I think they tried to break into your estate yesterday, but something at the last moment prevented them." Willy explains also giving me the same worried look and my heart throbs harder.

"We have installed two helicopters and other vehicles to protect you. Besides, the FBI and our team will be outside, so we wouldn't be surprised if they come with something more powerful now. They want to take you out as soon as possible," John says.

"Thank you," I say, meaning it entirely. "I wanted to know if you've heard from Ann."

I hate having to make them look like fools and going on wild chases but I have to keep Ann safe. I feel even worse when Robert gives me a pained look.

"Sorry, we don't have anything. In any case, as soon as we know anything, we'll let you know. Now, if you'll excuse us, we must go. I hope we can talk more quietly when this nightmare is over," he replies.

"Thank you again for all you are doing for me. I'll see you out."

I lead them towards the front door and escort them to their car. The four of them get in and leave the estate but remain close by. They will be outside providing logistical support and will be ready in case they have to go in to save me.

I go down into one of the secret cellars and gather all the hands, Ann is next to me.

"Friends," I begin and all the hands come closer. Ann clasps my hand gently in hers. "Tonight is going to be a particularly difficult night. I hope everything goes well. We will be divided into two teams, the medical team, and the combat team. All will receive instructions from the people in charge of each area."

All the hands look up expectantly.

"As you know, the organization tried to assassinate me the other day." All the hands went on the tips of their fingers, angrily. "They had no luck, but, much to my regret, they captured Cameron. I spoke to him today and he is safe. You know what he's like, he's in good spirits and he managed to escape."

The hands celebrate the news with shouts and shake each other as if they were people hugging each other.

"Today they will attack us; three Apache model helicopters are on their way. Frank has updated your memories so that you receive information on the model, speed, weak points and many other details. There are two helicopters outside and additional anti-aircraft forces are on their way. It's going to be tough and we may take casualties. Joseph is the commander-in-chief of the troops, you must listen to him in everything he tells you. Unfortunately, I can't lead you because I have to save myself."

That last sentence earns a gasp from the hands.

"I am dying, I have an incurable disease, but I think I have found a solution that will extend my life. We will be locked in the secret operating theatre, an enclosure that only a few of us knew about and that was designed and built for this day."

They all look at me and listen attentively, they have never seen me so worried.

"Margaret, Mayka, Jacob and the rest of the doctors, medical and cleaning staff will go into that room, lock us in and we won't come out until we finish our mission. It's going to be a hectic few hours. I hope we can all join in the defense of our home and our lives."

My finger turns, I extend my palm, and Joseph climbs on it.

"Joseph will be responsible for military and special forces. He will set the defense strategy; remember that you are targets for the Pentagon, FBI and police forces. They don't know you're on the side of the good guys."

"We will fight to the end, Henry," says Driver. "You gave us this life, we want you to keep looking after us, and we want to grow our family soon. We will not fail you, and if we have to die, we will die proud to fight for all of us. Proud to fight for you!"

"Henry, Henry, Henry, Henry, Henry!" All the hands chant.

Ann hugs me, she knows what all those miniature lives mean to me. I am their father, I brought them back to life, to their memories, to their personalities.

She comforts me; all of them do. I never expected to receive so much love. I know it's a very risky plan but I trust my team. I always will.

I take my hands one by one and hug them. Margaret, Mayka, Jacob and the rest of the medical team stand beside me and I walk with them, entering the operating theatre and closing the door.

As I order the hands around and remind them of my plan, a hundred concerns swarm in my mind. My biggest problem is Ann. I don't know how much time she has left, I have to act fast.

We stare at each other, then kiss and say goodbye to the rest of the hands.

"Guys, thanks for everything. Don't worry, I'm sure everything will be fine and I'll see you in a little while. You can start with the plan," I say.

The operating theatre has all kinds of equipment and gadgets. I had prepared everything beforehand with great efficiency, even Frank was converted into a small computer. In the center of the room are two large catalytic lights with built-in cameras, aspirators, anesthetic gas tubes, suspended monitors, two operating tables, an instrument table, LCD monitors with cameras for telemedicine, touch screen integration systems and control of surgical equipment. Additionally, I can see the hands through the other monitors installed all around the room.

Ann and I are instructed and placed on the operating tables, sheets covering our bodies. We are both given anesthesia for the pain, which Jacob injects into our right shoulder. I watch as he leads the team to perform all kinds of extractions of stem cells, healthy neurons, and blood. The team consists of about fifteen hands, which will now decide what the next step should be and how to proceed.

I have full confidence in them.

In the room I can see how Joseph gives instructions to his team and explains the strategy. All around the estate hands have installed microphones and cameras inside and outside the estate to provide surveillance. From the base in Greenland, Cameron records and transmits the conversations from the command post to Frank. This allows me to be informed of everything that happens.

One part of the group will remain in the house and the other outside ready to defend the attack. They visualize thousands of possibilities and defense alternatives, thanks to their artificial intelligence they can run simulations and evaluate probabilities of success or failure.

The night is approaching, the defense groups are hidden, prepared and armed.

A loud sound shatters the silence of the night, lights strike the darkness in our view of the outside landscape through the monitor. The hands, hidden in strategic positions, make out the shapes of three flying artefacts approaching through the starry sky.

"General, we've spotted three Apache helicopters approaching us," says a voice over the radio.

"Wait until they are on target and open fire," replies the commanding general.

Anti-aircraft vehicles lock on to the target, all three devices lock on to the screen.

"Target in range, General."

"Open fire," he replies.

Three missiles are aimed at the three killing machines, one hits the target and it explodes. The other two are intercepted before reaching their target.

The two Pentagon helicopters take off and chase the other two. One of the organization's helicopters manages to get behind them and starts firing, hitting one of the propellers. The Apache loses control and crashes to the ground. Fortunately, there are no casualties, the crew members parachute several kilometers away from the estate. Another explosion is heard: the other Pentagon helicopter has been destroyed.

There is concern among the personnel forming the shield of Henry's house; only the two anti-aircraft vehicles are left against those two metal devils, which are advancing at high speed. Through this commotion Frank manages to intercept the Pentagon's radio and I overhear their frantic conversations.

"General, we have anti-aircraft defenses in range." They radio Adam.

"Destroy them." The general orders.

Several projectiles cross the darkness, hitting the defenses and rendering them useless.

"Get the troops down and into the house, I want Henry's head brought to me." Jason orders.

"Hold on, General, they are firing on us. We must withdraw the attack until we spot the enemy."

One of the helicopters sees the other begin to spin around and descend until it hits the ground. An earth shattering BOOM! blasts through the monitor and white flashes light up the screen as a bomb goes off .

Drones.

"Drones! Damn Henry! He has hundreds of them!" Adam exclaims through the radio. "Shoot them down."

The helicopter's side doors open and the soldiers fire, deflecting some drones, but they are unable to shoot them down, as they are wearing bulletproof armor designed by the one and only hAInds.

The two hundred or so drones surround the device. Joseph, Driver and several hands from the special forces group jump out and position themselves on the plate without being seen. They activate the camouflage suit, get inside the ship and enter the cockpit. There are two pilots, and they are hit. Driver and Joseph take the controls of the helicopter and steer it towards the small flying objects. The others close the cockpit entrance door to prevent the organization's military from gaining access and taking over the helicopter again. Joseph fires; the bullets shatter the glass causing a hole, the hands activate their thrusters, go through the hole and fly a few meters until they reach the drones. The iron dragonfly crashes to the ground a few kilometers from the estate.

"Frank, inform me of the casualties." Joseph orders.

"None from our side," says Frank.

"Everyone back to their posts. They will try again. And this time they will be much more prepared."

Chapter 50

John – End of the line

Police officers witness the battle of lights and explosions. Gunfire slices through the noise of helicopters and the screech of engines. Overhead the fight is in full flow with helicopters crashing to the ground and buildings in flaming balls of fire. I notice how the helicopters maneuver through the sky overhead dodging blasts and opposing fire. I marvel at the mastery and technique behind the pilot. How his expert reactions and coordination result in such a display. I look down as a sudden buzzing fills the air around me and notice that my radio received a message from Willy.

"John, let's meet in the operations truck, I have to tell you something."

Within minutes, Zara, Robert and I are in the military truck with which the Pentagon ran the operation.

"It looks like we are close to discovering the identity of hAInds. We ordered one of our satellites to visualize the battle. Look at the images," says Willy, pointing to the monitor.

"As you can see on the screen, an army of over two hundred drones is coming out of one of the outbuildings of Henry's house. If we zoom in, we can see some familiar passengers, the intelligent hands, the hAInders that hAInds was referring to. They are all there. All of them. They are incredible. The way they move, act and think. Look at how agile and mobile they are. It's unbelievable, no one, no one could have dreamed of such a thing."

Willy opens his hands in disbelief but his eyes emit nothing more than absolute awe at what he saw.

"I have never seen anything like it in my life; they are an army of highly trained hands. On the tape you can see how it is a perfectly orchestrated plan, everyone knows what they have to do, there is a planned strategy."

Everyone looks at me but I turn away and grab my phone, urgently inputting a number.

"Dilya, give me Henry's background. I need to know everything about his life, what he studied, plus medicine, courses, money in the bank, property, anything you can find," says John.

"Do you suspect Henry?" asks Zara.

"Yes, he's my prime suspect, it's him, for sure. I also suspect Ann is in that house. As soon as I get the report, we'll have to ask the judge for an urgent search warrant," I reply.

For dozens of minutes, they visualize the film in detail. They have counted more than thirty hands on the drones in the images and note the details of them. They all have a watch, a mini backpack and a kind of propellant at the end of their bodies. They move at high speed and seem to communicate with each other. The phone rings, it's Dilya. I switch on the speaker so that everyone can hear the conversation .

"John, I'll tell you what I've found. Henry lost both his parents. His mother died in a car accident in California when they were on holiday when Henry was a young age. She was suspended from a branch and fell to her death. The boy described to the police all the details of the last image he had of his mother: blue eyes behind the fingers of open hands, showing blood on the palms. The hospital provided him with psychological help to overcome the trauma. Henry regained consciousness in the hospital after several days. His father survived, but lost both hands in the accident. The center kept them for years, and Henry collected them after graduating."

"The story is starting to make sense." Robert murmurs.

"He's a real all-rounder. By the age of twenty-three he already had advanced degrees in aeronautical engineering, medicine, computer science and mathematics. He is a billionaire; he has patents all over the world, especially in China, as well as multiple companies in many different sectors in several countries. We have accessed certain payments on his credit card and discovered that in the last year he has visited a doctor specializing in rare diseases, her name is Samantha Evans. She informed us that her disease was incurable and that she did not have many months to live, but when we wanted to go into details, she asked for a court order. After that, she kindly hung up on us."

"All the pieces fit together. Henry is hAInds. The picture we found everywhere was of the vision he had of his mother. It has to be!" I exclaim.

"Maybe he wants to extend his life by becoming a hand. I'm going to ask the judge for an urgent search warrant and we'll go in and get him." Zara reports.

"I'll call for reinforcements," says Willy.

Minutes later, military vehicles, vans of the special forces of the police and the FBI surround the estate. We know there will be an armed struggle, they will have to face hands and hAInds.

It is seven o'clock in the morning on a cloudless, sunny day. John has a megaphone in his hand.

"Henry, we know you're hAInds. We have a warrant to enter. You are surrounded. Don't try anything with your drones and smart hands. It won't work, turn yourself in."

The door of the house opens and a figure appears with his arms raised. It is Henry. He walks slowly out, crosses the driveway and heads for the front door of the estate.

"Don't shoot, don't shoot. Yes, that's right; I am hAInds. I freed the hands, so you won't find them. I gave life and the illusion of life back to people who had incurable diseases, that is no crime. Today I tried to save myself from an incurable disease, but I had no luck. I will not survive, that is why I have decided to turn myself in and tell absolutely everything about the criminal organization that kidnapped me, their plans and how they intend to dominate the world. All I ask is that they don't shoot, I am unarmed."

We see him approaching the entrance gate, he is less than 400 meters away, his pace is slow, he looks very tired. In the air we hear the roar of a plane. We all look up at the sky and see an F 35 approaching at ultrasonic speed, they open fire on him but Henry moves with startling speed and dodges them. He looks up and fires a device at the plane causing it to get knocked down and crash into the ground. Henry smiles and continues walking towards them.

"Please, my friends, I am not the bad guy here I promise you."

His voice is cut off by another plane which fires at him again Henry tries to take it out but before he can, a missile from the plane crashes straight into him. The explosion shatters his body, leaving no trace of him. The missile has reduced him to ashes. The fighter turns around and escapes into the blue sky at low altitude so as not to be detected by radar.

"Your secret's out, you arrogant brat. We have won. Victory is ours. Thank you, Henry, for your services!"

Jason shouts.

Adam hugs Jason.

"Now, there is no stopping our plan."

Adam appears overjoyed.

My men and I can't believe our eyes, Henry is dead. This time they didn't think twice.

The door of the house opens again and a female figure emerges from the house accompanied by Hugo and Helen. My team and I run towards her, it is Ann who is wheeled by the assistants to the place where the shell exploded. There is no trace of Henry's body, only ashes. Ann gets out of the wheelchair and hugs Helen, crying bitterly.

"He's dead, he's dead!" She sobs angrily. "He didn't deserve this. He was a very good man. He fought for people's lives, look at me, he managed to cure me in the end."

Zara hugs her and whispers that she is sorry about Henry, that it was inevitable and that a plane took his life. After a few minutes, Ann is more relaxed.

"Ann, I'm glad you're alive. How is that possible? Are you okay?" I ask.

"Yes, John, I'm alive. Henry found out how to clear my brain of the serum they gave me. It was a long labor, when I woke up he said he was going to talk to you, that he would explain everything to you, that he had committed no crime and that he was sure everything would be all right. He told me that he only had a few months to live and that he would die with a clear conscience for having saved so many lives. I am saddened by the way he has gone, but at least he did not suffer the pain that awaited him over these months, which gives me some peace of mind."

Those present turn at the sound of black SUVs entering the estate and approaching their location. Several soldiers get out of the car with guns pointed at them; among the officers is Edward Smith.

"You are all excluded from the case and detained. You are charged with obstructing a military and government investigation, as well as appropriating classified material and sharing it with other units. You will all be tried by a high court. You, madam, and your assistants are free to go. Oh, I forgot, condolences on the death of your fiancé," says Edward in a sharp, strong voice.

Zara, Robert, Willy and I are stunned, unable to believe what we have just heard. The army collects our weapons, we are forced into the cars and the vehicles drive us away from the scene.

Helen helps Ann with the wheelchair and is taken inside the house. The new officers and military personnel assigned to the case have a search warrant. They accompany them and begin a thorough examination of the house; they remove all vehicles and clear the area of objects left behind after the battle.

For hours they search the estate. Unfortunately, they don't find the hands or the drones; they don't find anything.

After several hours, an officer approaches Ann. He stops and takes off his cap looking down at her solemnly.

"Miss, we are leaving. We have everything we were looking for. Rest assured. I'm sorry to hear about your boyfriend's death."

"Thank you, I know you do your job. Don't worry about me, I'll lie down and rest. It's been a hard few days. As for Henry I'm sure that he's in a better place and body," she said smiling.

The officer nods and leaves her there smiling and staring at the horizon …

Chapter 51

John – Allies

Zara, Michael, Dilya, Jenny, the FBI agents, the military and those of us who were involved in the hAInds case, view the advancement of the equality system with great concern. Thirty people are in custody due to the case. We are all locked up in an army prison, we only have contact in the yard or during meals.

"This has gotten out of hand, there is no logic to it. The world has totally changed in a couple of weeks after our arrest," I say.

"I agree completely, John. It makes no sense what is going on. What we see on TV is a deprivation of freedoms and must be a massacre. Where are all these people they say no longer exist?" Zara exclaims.

Over the prison loudspeakers we are called to one of the rooms. The group enters and sits down. Guards force us out of the module. In front of us is a ten CH-47F Chinook helicopter. We are forced to get in, all of us are handcuffed and restrained so that we cannot escape.

The aircraft takes off. I think it's the same one that took Henry to the Greenland base. I quietly point it out to the rest of the team.

A few hours later, it enters the Greenland mountain, the occupants thought we would crash before we got through the deception but we didn't and as we land in the hangar, the doors open and we are forced to descend.

Adam approaches us.

"At last we have you in a safe and controlled place, you almost blew the operation. But don't worry, with a few months of training you'll see the good we're doing for the world. People are happy whether they want to be or not." Adam laughs.

"You're crazy," says Willy, glaring defiantly at him.

A sharp, hard blow hits Willy in the face and he falls to the ground. Robert and I duck.

"Willy, are you all right?" asks Robert.

"Yes, it's just that my pride is hurt. I'll deal with him another time," he whispers angrily.

With assault rifles pointed at us, the group of Zara and the others left the hangar where we saw some of the planes, helicopters and other weapons at their disposal.

"You can look around; this is just a small sample of what we have. Are you impressed? Wait till you see our operating theatre."

Adam smiles, his face beaming with enough happiness to last a month. He opens a door and enters the control room. Everyone looks at about a hundred people controlling all kinds of equipment and visualizing multiple cities and countries. Several screens show where all the G20 presidents are.

"Impressive, eh? We control the world from here."

We all turn around, at the top of the room we see Jason.

"Hello there, my dear colleagues. I just wanted to let you know that you are very lucky to still be alive, but I don't think it will be for long, unless the training we are going to provide you with is successful and you decide to join our organization," says Jason.

I look around the room trying to memorize everything. I gesture for Jenny to do the same. We both look absent-minded, but we are able to graphically retain what we see. At one point, I look at the door and see a hand gesturing to me with its thumbs up and disappearing. He gestures for me not to worry. It's Cameron, hAInd's hand, I can recognize him from the hAInds video.

"I need to go to the toilet." I demand with a long-suffering face.

"You two, go with him and make sure he doesn't try anything." Adam orders and two burly, well-built me shadow me.

I enter one of the toilets. In front of the door, a hand suddenly appears. It lights up the clock and texts me.

John, it's me Cameron. I was caught, but I managed to escape. What on earth are you doing here?

The clock display provides a digital keyboard for me to type on.

We were arrested at Henry's house, that is, hAInds'. He is hAInds.

You're wrong, he's not hAInds, Cameron texts back. I was caught a few days ago and escaped. I have sent word to hAInds, he will surely come, you must be patient. They can't find me. I will protect you, but they are very, very dangerous. Be very careful with Jason, he is the most powerful, he has in his brain all the information of the G20 presidents and he dominates them. He used the Quantum Mind Program, Cameron replies on his screen.

I know him, we have investigated the case, I write.

I must go, I'll talk to you later.

Cameron activates his suit's camouflage and disappears.

I open the door, wash and dry my hands while being watched.

"We can go, guys. Though you could've been more helpful someplace smaller." The two men glare at me but seriously, they can hardly fit past the door due to their massive size.

"We don't care, you moron. Be lucky we don't brainwash you. We have contributed to a better world, free of evil, greed, lust. Our new system will cleanse civilization of bad feelings. We have abolished money and banished the main problems to the people."

I yawn, definitely not on purpose and head out to the meeting room. I re-enter the room. Jason takes the floor.

"You will witness a new era, a new change. We are a powerful international organization, formed several centuries ago. We don't want power; we want order and happiness. What kind of world did we have? Drugs, corruption, alcohol, murder, robbery. This we have eliminated in two weeks, thanks to a detailed plan."

"The Quantum Mind Project, as you can see on the screen, is a success. Henry finished what his mentor started. I dominate the brains of the most powerful presidents in the world. People are beginning to love them and hate them, they will be the visible heads for a while, then they will no longer serve us, and they will pay for their greed and arrogance. We are cleaning the streets of toxic people, millions of individuals have disappeared. Do you know where and how? When we find such individuals, we arrest them and put them in containers and take them to a specific location on the planet."

"We have abandoned millions of undesirable beings, those who are a great drain on society. If they survive and accept the system, they will be integrated into the new society."

"In my village it's called dictatorship, depriving the individual of his freedom. You're crazy," Willy replies.

Jason walks up to him, stares at him and smiles.

"We'll see if the training will change your mind; it would be a pity if you weren't with us, you could lead part of the organization. We have very good reports on you. All of you. We want you to be part of our family."

"How do you control the presidents?" asks Zara.

"I can dominate anyone who has less information in their brain than I do. Now with everyone I've absorbed, I'm very powerful. I could do it with you too, which I don't rule out in the future. But honestly, I prefer the ones that give me power. Remember General Edward Smith? He opened the door for me to subdue the president, and the president to possess everyone else. The secret, as you know, is the quantum mind, we extract a copy of the information from the brain, we compare it with the size of our own, if it is smaller we import it. We can also visualize thoughts. What we didn't know was that we could dominate others."

"You are crazy. Sooner or later you will fall. This system is not reliable," says Robert.

"I wouldn't be so sure; look at the cameras. I think people are happier, the message we have given them is to work to help the system. Without work, the welfare system falls apart. A child, a teenager is happy because his parents support him. He doesn't have to worry about anything, only about studying and getting good grades. If you take that pressure off him and he does what he likes, he is happy. He knows he has to help out at home, with the housework. This system is the same," Jason replies.

"What about the people you kill? You are murderers," Michael replies.

"We don't kill, we give a second chance, but they must fight for it and redeem themselves. We help many of the terminally ill and inject them with the serum of eternal sleep. In a manner of speaking, we do them a favor."

Jason smiles and walks as well as talks. He is happy with his world, with his order.

"Now you will see my power, look at the big screen."

On the monitor all the presidents appear seated, doing nothing. The U.S. President stands up and starts to walk, everyone looks on without flinching, one by one, they start to walk as well. Jason, Adam and those present laugh and hug each other in joy. After a few seconds, they all sit down. It makes me extremely sad to see all this.

"You see? I control the world. It's easy."

We are not amused, we are worried, but we don't see any way out of this terrible situation.

Adam addresses us.

"We will now take you to your cells, where you can think. Tomorrow the training starts and we need you fresh."

All the prisoners are led to our cells; we have a dinner plate on a table, a bed and a toilet with a shower. We are provided with sleeping clothes, black overalls, a winter anorak, and boots.

At night, we are unable to sleep. I walk around the room under the watchful eye of a camera that watches me. I look at the device. If I want to escape, I'll have to think about how to fool the camera first. Tired, I lie back against the pillow.

"Hi, John, don't move. It's Cameron, your head's a bit heavy, but I can take it. I'm under the pillow. I've got a plan but you've got to trust me. Don't rat me out, I'm trying to help you. I know you're a good guy. Remember when we worked on a case together?"

"But how are you going to get me out of here? You're a hand!" I whisper.

"How do you think Henry got out? Three little hands helped him escape," says Cameron, sounding slightly offended.

"All right, what do I do?" I ask, as my brain starts to connect the missing pieces of the puzzle.

"When I open the gates, you talk to your people and we'll get the hell out of here. I've got weapons for you."

Cameron approaches the camera; a device comes out of his watch, which he inserts and emits a signal that shows that I am sleeping, breathing and moving every so often. He has inserted a film with random movements.

"Frank, can you tap into all the cameras in the cells now? As we escape, I'll tell you the physical IP addresses of all of them so you can manipulate the images. Open the doors when you can." Cameron comments to Frank.

"Done, Cameron, cameras hacked and the cell doors are open," replies Frank.

I put on my suit, my boots, and grab my anorak. I walk into Zara's living room and whisper to her:

"Get up, we're leaving. Put on all your clothes and take this."

Zara obeys and holds several assault rifles, bulletproof vests and protective helmets. One by one she releases the others. All of us are grouped together as if we were a commando. Willy asks permission to lead. We all agree.

"Wait a moment, I have to introduce you to our savior," I whisper, pointing to an empty wall.

Cameron deactivates the camouflage and activates a message on his watch.

"Hello, friends, don't shoot me, I'm going to help you."

Zara gasps and covers her mouth quickly as everyone else's eyes widen. But no one says anything. For a few minutes, Cameron explains the plan with his watch showing a hologram on the wall of the base plan. Together we decide on the best route to take and Cameron takes care of everything.

"Frank, disable the alarms on the sensors and cameras." Cameron orders.

"Done, I have disabled the data capture programme. No data, no alarms," says Frank.

"Report if you spot patrols and their geolocation."

"Received."

Frank sends an emoji of a hand and his thumbs up to Cameron's watch screen.

"We can go," says a message on the clock screen and we prepare for the challenge ahead.

Cameron activates his camouflage and becomes invisible, leading the group by moving along the ceiling and making subtle movements, which allow us to know where he is. Cameron inserts a tiny metal rod taken from his watch into each opening mechanism and Frank opens the door.

The entire team must pass through the main room, where there are only a couple of operators who watch over the presidents' sleep. If anything were to happen in the world, the alarms would go off and the room would be full of staff in no time. Zara and Robert move towards the exit door, motioning to the others to come closer, making no noise. Everyone is at the door, the operators' backs are turned. One of them stands up, stretches out his arms and sits back down in front of the screen.

Frank opens the exit door and we escape. The next corridor leads to the hangar. At the end, before entering, there are some cupboards where oxygen cylinders and other equipment are stored.

Cameron, a two-man patrol is on its way out of the hangar, Frank transmits.

Hide behind the cupboard. A patrol of two soldiers is coming. Cameron projects the message on the wall.

Everyone hides, the door opens and two people cross the wide corridor. As they pass by the wardrobe, Willy and Robert hit them, knocking them senseless to the floor.

Put on their sensors! Cameron reports.

Jennifer and Michael look for the sensors, they are on the wrists of their hands. They take them off and put them on.

Quick as a flash, Cameron approaches the door, Frank opens it instantly and he enters. Cameron camouflages himself again and eyes the perimeter, there are four men in different locations. He enters again and projects the hologram of what he had seen.

Organize a plan to knock them out! Cameron writes to the group. They can't set off the alarms. If they do, they'd close the hatches and we wouldn't be able to get away. Frank says the Chinook is ready to go and full of fuel.

The door opens again and the team splits up. Seconds later the soldiers drop to the ground and I turn to see Zara rubbing her hands. She quickly sets to work finding the sensors. We know we have only a few minutes before we are discovered. Zara finds a device, one I've never seen before and on the screen I can see a route to the north about three hours away.

Willy is an expert helicopter pilot, having flown helicopters on many missions and as we reach the Chinook, he races ahead to prepare it for flight. Once we are all inside we look around, trying to find something of use. Inside there is food, fuel and warm clothes, it looks as if our captors had been preparing for some kind of trip.

The rotor starts to beep, the command room alarms go off, the hatches start to close. The helicopter lifts off, turns and fires at the other ships, nullifying any pursuit and escapes from the hangar at high speed. They have not had time to react. All the alarms in the base are sounding. The escape has been a success and the group celebrates by shouting and hugging inside. I bump into a small cabinet on my way to fist pump Cameron and notice a radio, which is blasting with frustrated voices.

"Someone must have helped them escape! I bet it was the damn hand!" Jason shouts.

"We should have killed them. It was a bad idea to bring them here." It sounds as if Adam punched the table really hard and something snaps from the other end.

"You're right, but we've got the world under control, it's only a matter of time before we find them again … They have nowhere to hide," Jason replies.

"Yes. And next time I'll take care of them myself!" Adam growls and the line goes silent.

Willy is a good pilot, he flies several meters above the ground, avoiding all kinds of obstacles. After a few hours of flying, the landscape becomes monotonous, icy slopes surrounded by huge mountains. In the distance, the radar and sensors begin to show a multitude of motionless dots. The aircraft accelerates, Willy calls everyone into the cockpit. What they see is bleak: millions of bodies lying on the ice. They are all dressed in thin yellow overalls covered by a thick layer of ice and snow. It is a graveyard.

"Come on down, Willy, we need to take a closer look and check for survivors."

Once on the ground, we notice that all the bodies around us are frozen, the temperature is minus twenty degrees. No one could survive in these conditions for more than twenty minutes.

The group must go on. We know what happens to people who upset the egalitarian system. Zara lets out an angry grunt and I comfort her all I can. But until we figure out a way to eradicate the current government and go back to the old system, this grotesque way of punishment will continue to happen.

"I know where we can hide." Willy speaks, leading me out of my dark thoughts and back to reality. "It's a former secret military base set up about two hundred miles from here, on a lonely island. Only two of us know about it, and the other fellow died a few years ago. It was a project I personally led," Willy says with a smile that conveys the hope of staying alive.

I nod and he sets the aircraft on the right course as we all sit, silently hoping that we will be able to stop Jason and his goons before it's too late.

Chapter 52

Henry – Always Together

It had been several weeks since Hugo had given Ann the sedative. The brain had to recover all its functions and be cleansed of poison. That is what I told Hugo before I died. I asked him to look after Ann as if she were his own, gave him instructions as to what his hands should do, and left a letter for him to read to Ann.

"Good morning, Ann, how are you feeling?" asks Hugo.

"I'm fine, thank you, Hugo. How long have I been here?" She sits up and spins her head around in every direction.

"Two weeks," he replies and Ann flinches as she thinks about all the lost minutes and days.

Hugo however, mistakes her flinch for something else. "You need to eat something. The serum has kept your vitals stable, but you've lost quite a fair bit of weight. I've made you some toast, juice and an omelet."

"Thank you, I appreciate it."

Ann satisfies her hunger with the food prepared by Hugo's wife Helen and thanks them both for all they have done for her.

"Henry gave me a letter to read to you in case something happened to him," says Hugo.

"Please read it, Hugo, I can't wait to hear from him."

Dear Ann:

If Hugo reads this letter to you, it means that I couldn't save myself and something went wrong. At least I have saved you. I give you all my property, except for a part that I have decided to share with my best friend Hugo and his wife. I understand that you don't want to live in this house and you want to continue with your life in your flat. I think it will be a bit bigger now; I have bought the building, for many reasons that you will discover.

I hope you will continue to prove your worth by healing patients. You know that you can use the quantum mind to retrieve the copy of my brain's knowledge and information from the computer. You are the ideal person to continue my work. I have full confidence in you and I am sure you will succeed. I love you very much.

Henry

Hugo is teary-eyed.

Ann hugs Helen and cries for minutes but Ann is too shocked to shed tears.

"Ann, we'll take you back to your flat. I think it will be best for you and your recovery," says Hugo.

"I agree," she says, snapping out of her daze. "The longer I stay here, the more I will remember Henry, and I must avoid going into a depression."

"We'll take you as soon as you're ready."

Ann takes a last walk around the house, picks up some of Henry's photos and objects and makes her way to the showers. The water refreshes her and she treasures the way the water drips down her face, the perfect excuse to deny the tears that roll down her cheeks. Henry was her world and now he was gone.

Gone.

She shakes her head and steps out of the shower to get dressed into a pair of jeans and a black shirt.

"I'm ready," she says to Hugo and he leads her to the car.

After an hour, Ann enters her building and goes upstairs to her flat. She sits down on the couch and switches on the television, hoping for a distraction, which she definitely receives. Every channel showcases the same news: A new system. She can't believe her eyes, a new system has been implemented in the world. Hastily, she turns on the laptop and reads how everything has changed, the rules, the new regime. Everything has changed …

She gets up and goes to her chest of drawers.

This has gotten out of hand. Order must be restored.

Ann sits in front of the mirror, turns her head to one side and puts her hands on her head to carefully remove her hair. She is wearing a wig of her own natural hair, which Henry had custom made for her.

A small scar encircles her head. She stands up, places the wig on a bust and opens a chest.

"My friends, you can come out now," says Ann.

All the hands except Cameron come out of the boot and shake hands to celebrate that they have survived.

"The operation to transplant my natural brain into your head was a success, don't you think, Ann? Now I'll have to get used to this sexy, wonderful body and put on more than twenty kilos. Let's start with chocolates, chocolates, ice cream, hamburgers and fast food." Ann exclaims loudly.

"Henry!" says a voice coming from the watch on a new hand. This hand is young with bright yellow nail polish and a small ring, which had been a present from Henry. Ann's hand. "If you so much as put an ounce in my body, I'll strangle you."

"Just kidding, darling, I'll look after your figure as if it were a treasure. This jewel must last. The bad thing is that I have to get used to living in a woman's body," says Ann/Henry, twirling a strand of the wig hair.

"And I'm living on one hand!" Ann says furiously ...

"Don't complain, I've given you the functionality of being able to get out of the body and make your own life whenever you want."

"Best of all, we're back together and your plan has worked out perfectly," she says. "What shall I call you now, Henry or Ann?"

"Ann, what a joker you are. Just because my brain is in your body doesn't allow you to call me Ann."

"I know, Henry, I love you very much, darling, and I thank you for saving me, even if I have to live in the form of a hand from now on."

"Everything went wonderfully well." Henry smiles and lays down his hand, allowing Ann to climb on. "The only thing I didn't like was not telling Hugo and his wife the whole truth. We'll do that in a few weeks, they'll understand. Now let's go find Cameron and dismantle the egalitarian system so that everything goes back to the way it was."

The hands cheer and high five each other causing a massive round of applause as they celebrate the victory of their boss, their friend and their father.

Epilogue

Ann is preparing breakfast, still getting used to being a hand while Henry takes a shower. It's a different life, she's happy. She wouldn't be in this world if it weren't for her boyfriend.

"Honey, how are you feeling!" Henry shouts from the shower.

"I'm doing great, trying out this new body and these two brains you've given me. You were great, you managed to integrate all my thoughts and memories. What amazes me most is the ability to feel. How did you do it? I can have feelings, I still love you, I perceive sensations of joy, fear, pain, compassion. You didn't create that with any algorithm," says Ann as she picks up a cup and starts to make coffee.

"I have no idea, I think it's the implanted neurons that cause the feelings. When I created Cameron, it was one of the issues I was most concerned about. But a few weeks ago we did the hardest thing yet: transplanting a brain from one body to another, and it works. In addition, I used quantum mind technology to pass all the information from your brain to your hand. In a way it was lucky to be kidnapped by The Court of Pi. I feel very happy and proud. The bad thing was that we couldn't save yours, it was impossible. There was no cure, just as there was no cure for my body. I was lucky it was blown up by a fighter missile."

"I know, Henry, but at least I have a new life." Ann tells him.

"Yes, you'll let me know how you feel, what you perceive and how well you integrate with the others. I saw that you did this morning with the group and that the clown made you laugh out loud."

"Henry, how did you come up with your transplant?"

"It's a long story. When I was told I had an incurable disease, I broke down, but Cameron gave me the courage to carry on. My first thought was to become a hand, but I had to trust someone and I don't think any doctor would be able to do that ethically. I thought of you, but your feelings of love for me were so strong that they could jeopardize the operation. So I started to select people who were going to die and talk to them to give them another life."

"Frank would track down the candidates, we would visit them and talk to them about the plan. Cameron would turn up and chat to them, he's a wonderful guy. They all wanted to go on living, we talked about how, after a while, we would introduce ourselves to the families and explain what had happened. At first I didn't want to have so many hands, but the desire to keep people alive got the better of me. I think when we rescue Cameron, hAInds will be back in action. The idea, as I told you, was to have the hands turn me into a hand or to transplant my brain into a person who had a terminal illness in that organ. That's why I have some from the health sector."

"The whole plan suddenly changed when you were injected with the serum. Your body was perfect, mine couldn't be used. I've been secretly researching brain transplantation in humans for years, I tried it on mice and it worked. The tricky part is handling it and reattaching it to the other organs in the other body." Henry explains.

"That's exciting, keep going with the story."

Ann has moved to the bathroom to continue the conversation.

"When Jacob Byrne, the transplant doctor, told me he wanted to join the team, I was overjoyed. He would carry my whole plan to be a hand. In parallel we spent a lot of time talking about the idea of brain transplants between people and we started to do them successfully in mice. He gave me the idea of trying it with you; he said it was risky but the best option, we could both continue to help the world by healing people. I didn't hesitate and trusted him. He is a very serious and professional hand."

Henry picks up the shaving cream and starts applying it to his new face.

"You wouldn't think of shaving my pretty face, would you!" Anna shouts.

Henry notices and quickly takes it off, grabs a bottle and applies an anti-wrinkle cream.

"Much better. Now, what a fright you've given me; excuse the scream, but I'm going to have to tie you up with your new body." Henry puts on a mechanical hand that he controls with his mind, whilst Ann climbs on his shoulder and caresses him.

"As I was telling you, everything changed with the serum. On the day of the operation, Jacob led the team in a masterful way, it's all recorded. There were several very critical tasks where we almost died. The first was separating the brains, the second was transporting them, and the third was the implant. The hands, having the hybrid brain, do everything very quickly, they create and evaluate different scenarios immediately and can achieve microsecond movements. All of its capacity was essential for the grey mass not to die. I'll show you the video of the operation, Jacob told me, it's spectacular. The most dangerous thing is that at one moment there could be two Anns acting at the same time. One in the hand and the other in my body. To avoid risks, I left you sedated and there was only one Ann, the one who died in Henry's body."

Henry gets dressed and goes into the kitchen to eat the breakfast Ann has prepared.

"I've made you breakfast, honey, but don't get used to it," Ann says.

"I'm sorry I can't prepare it for you, it's a disadvantage that you don't have to feed yourself," he says, smiling.

"I see it more as an advantage, you don't get fat, you don't waste time and you don't need it," replies Ann with a smile on her watch.

"You're right, it's a big advantage."

"Henry, you have a call. I'm putting you on speakerphone," says Frank.

"Boss, how are you? I've missed you," a familiar voice says, and Henry is overjoyed.

"Cameron, I'm so glad! Are you all, right?"

"I'm just peachy!" Cameron replies and Henry laugh. "How are you doing? Good to hear from you."

"We're fine, everything went just as I thought it would. There were some last-minute changes that I'll tell you about. My body was destroyed by an organizational shell in the attack, but I got a very nice one, from a very attractive woman you know very well; I'll tell you about it."

"And Ann, how is she?"

"I'm wonderful." A shriek is heard from the other line. Cameron is clearly surprised to hear her speaking. "Dr Frankenstein has made me one of you."

"Are you a hand?" asks Cameron.

"Yes!" replies Ann with a smile on her watch.

"What good news! You'll love it once you get the hang of it. We can do amazing things!" Now he was clearly bragging, listing off things he could do that Henry couldn't. He stopped halfway, probably realizing that Ann couldn't care less. "I'm so glad you're both safe."

"Where are you? At the base?" asks Henry.

"No, we're heading to another location by air; I'll pass you the coordinates. We've escaped," Cameron replies.

"We have?"

"It's a long story," Cameron replies. "Very long actually. Very exciting but extremely long. Long-story-short, I have some new friends with me; they are old acquaintances of yours who I helped escape from the base. Remember John, Zara, and the rest of their team? Well, we're all on our way by helicopter to safety."

"Take care of yourselves. Send the coordinates when you can and we'll come and help you," replies Henry.

"All right, man. I'm glad you guys are okay."

Communication is cut off. Hours later, Frank receives the coordinates of the secret base on the island. Henry gathers all the hands. For a few minutes he explains the details of the call and sets up the preparations for the mission. They all leave the building and head for the estate in the van driven by Driver.

They enter the estate through a secret tunnel built long ago. They approach one of the hidden outbuildings. It resembles a large hangar, where an ultra-modern, multifunctional hand-shaped aircraft awaits them.

Driver takes the controls, starts the engines and flies away from the country at high altitude. The other hands comment with surprise and delight to Henry how wonderful and incredible it looks.

The countdown is on. In a few endless hours they will meet Cameron again.

"Henry, I have news about the woman in the photo of the event you sent me from Jason's office. You're not gonna believe it boss; but …"

Frank stops speaking. Henry turns to him one of his eyebrows raised and his hands on his hips.

"Yeah, what is it?" he says impatiently.

But his heart skips multiple beats and his heart rate races faster than the aircraft that they travel on. He waits and motions for Frank to continue, feeling prepared for the revelation but nothing could prepare him for the truth.

"Her name is Margaret Duffy."